KT-363-994

LOUISE PHILLIPS
LAST KISS

HACHETTE
BOOKS
IRELAND

First published in 2014 by Hachette Books Ireland
First published in paperback in 2015 by Hachette Books Ireland

Copyright © Louise Phillips 2014

The right of Louise Phillips to be identified as the Author of the Work
has been asserted by her in accordance with the Copyright, Designs
and Patents Act 1988.

All rights reserved. No part of this publication may be reproduced, stored in
a retrieval system, or transmitted, in any form or by any means without the
prior written permission of the publisher, nor be otherwise circulated in any
form of binding or cover other than that in which it is published and without
a similar condition being imposed on the subsequent purchaser.

All characters and places in this publication, other than those clearly in the
public domain, are fictitious. All events and incidents are the product of the
author's imagination. Any resemblance to real life or real persons, living or
dead, is entirely coincidental.

A CIP catalogue record for this title is available from the British Library

ISBN 978 1444 789 386

Typeset in Bembo Book ST Standard by Bookends Publishing Services, Dublin
Printed and bound by Clays Ltd, St Ives plc

Hachette Books Ireland policy is to use papers that are natural, renewable
and recyclable products and made from wood grown in sustainable forests.
The logging and manufacturing processes are expected to conform to the
environmental regulations of the country of origin.

Hachette Books Ireland
8 Castlecourt Centre
Castleknock
Dublin 15, Ireland

A division of Hachette UK Ltd
338 Euston Road, London NW1 3BH
www.hachette.ie

PRAISE FOR LAST KISS

'Louise Phillips is exactly the kind of writer that lovers of detective fiction will enjoy no matter where they live, and is an equal to James Patterson, Sara Paretsky, Patricia Cornwell or any other authors of cracking good police procedurals'
San Francisco Book Review

'Unusual and unsettling'
Irish Times

'A dark and terrifying psychological thriller that grips you from the start and doesn't let you go until the very last line'
Virginia Gilbert

'My God, what a book. I just couldn't put it down … Fantastic'
Lynsey Dolan, Sunshine Radio

'[*Last Kiss*] is among the best crime writing in the world – a top notch thriller'
Mike Philpott, BBC Radio Ulster

'Chilling and original … it has an ending that you just can't see coming'
Eurocrime

'Fast-paced, dark and intriguing – and well worth reading'
Novelicious

'[*Last Kiss*] was dark, it was deep, it was scary, it chilled me to the bone. It was brilliant!'

8000372131

'The tension was so well described that I felt myself wanting to shout
"Look behind you!"'
Bleach House Library

'I was holding my breath … superb!'
Siren FM

'Thanks to Phillips for restoring my faith in the
psychological thriller, and in some style!'
Raven Crime Reads

'A page-turning, gut-wrenching thriller which will undoubtedly earn
Phillips further accolades and hordes of new fans'
Lisa Reads Books

'A well-crafted book that takes you on a thrilling journey,
full of twists and turns'
Celeste Loves Books

Red Ribbons, the bestselling debut novel by Dublin-born crime author
Louise Phillips, was nominated for the Ireland AM Crime Fiction Book
of the Year award at the BGE Irish Book Awards in 2012. Louise won
the award in 2013 for her second novel *The Doll's House*; *Last Kiss* was
shortlisted in 2014.

In addition to her novels, Louise's work has been published as part
of various anthologies and literary journals. She has won the Jonathan
Swift Award, was a winner in the Irish Writers' Centre Lonely Voice
platform, and her writing has been shortlisted for prizes such as the
Molly Keane Memorial Award and Bridport UK.

Last Kiss is her third novel.

Also by Louise Phillips
Red Ribbons
The Doll's House

For Caitríona and Carrig

Northamptonshire Libraries & Information Services NC	
Askews & Holts	

PROLOGUE: 1982

The young girl walked towards the forest dressed in an oversized grey coat and black wellington boots that belonged to her father. Her head was bent beneath a raised collar and her long black hair shrouded her strained face. To a stranger, Ellen could have been taken for someone older than her fifteen years, hunched over like an aged soul.

As she reached the outskirts of the woodland, the ground underfoot became slimy, laden with fallen twigs and leaves. Early light sprinkled between the overhead branches, but she didn't look up, not once. When the first droplet slid down her inner thigh, it touched her kneecap with the gentleness of a moth. She had felt the back pains a few hours earlier, and even though they had eased, she knew it was her time.

Amid the creaking and rustling of the trees, she heard something move in the undergrowth. For a brief moment she stood still, a cold chill spreading through her body as another bead of the amniotic fluid reached her swollen ankle. She swallowed hard, looking all around her, knowing she needed to find somewhere safe, and that the life she had hidden inside her for so long would soon have to leave. Placing a hand beneath her coat, she held the underside of her engorged belly. A sharp breeze from the valley tossed her hair rebelliously in the wind, as if it was the only part of her still free to choose.

She had left the house when all inside were sleeping, sneaking around, no longer feeling she was part of it. The village, too, looked strange with its empty streets, and the moon still visible, hanging low in the early-morning sky. When she passed her old school, she imagined the sound of young voices in the yard, and felt utterly alone.

Now deeper into the forest, again she heard something move behind her, but when she turned, she saw nothing. A surge of amniotic fluid flooded between her legs, drenching her undergarments, the veil of liquid glistening in the flickering sunlight, before it soaked into the earth.

A sharp pain, like an iron rod, shot through her. She held her belly, more fearful than she had ever been. She wanted to cry out, but stopped herself. With her wet garments stuck to her skin, she continued walking once the pain had passed, faster than before, like a scared animal scurrying further into the dark.

The next contraction grabbed her insides like a twisted fist, shooting through her lower abdomen, before ramming her spine with the might of an iron bar. She placed both arms around her swollen belly, her stomach heaving, her dry retches fighting hard against the nothingness inside. For months she had barely eaten, needing to keep her secret safe, but now she knew that the child inside, briefly quiet, would not remain so for long.

It was with her back to a fallen tree trunk that she laboured alone for hours, before the pain became so strong that the urge to push defied everything else. Her screams came back at her through the forest walls, long piercing wails, until finally she heard the cries of another. She stared at the baby girl lying between her legs, covered with blood and mucus, relieved that that part at least was over.

Placing the baby in the large grey coat, she cut the cord with the carving knife she had taken from the house, then wiped the tiny face, clearing the mucus from its nostrils.

After delivering the child, she felt so cold, her eyelids barely able to stay open as the blood leaving her body formed a black circle around her. Ellen didn't know she would die that day, nobody knew, but when she closed her eyes for the last time, she could still hear the baby crying, a shrill sound, calling for a mother unable to answer, almost as if she knew that part of her had been taken.

If there had been an inquest into her death, it would have found she died because of irreversible shock, brought on by haemorrhage and exposure during childbirth. The woman who burned her body didn't care about that, taking the baby into her arms as if it were her own. It was a miracle the child survived. Questions would be asked, but none that she couldn't answer. Everyone knew Ellen was never quite right, soft in the head, a creature more to be pitied than scorned. Her disappearance, like her life, would soon be forgotten.

Walking back towards the village, she kissed the baby's forehead. The child wailed, scrunching its face like a piece of shrivelled rotten fruit, a primal instinct kicking in, telling it that something wasn't right.

The woman thought about killing the infant then, but decided against it. Instead, she held her hand tight over the baby's face while she smiled down at it. When she finally released her grip, the infant spluttered, then wailed even louder than before.

'Now,' the woman said to the child, 'I've given you something to cry about.'

PART 1

PART 1

I

2014

I HAVE REASONS for doing what I do. You may not know them yet, because I haven't told you, but that doesn't mean they don't exist. It's too early for judgement calls, far too early for that.

I'm considered attractive. I was described by an ex-lover as having an elegant face. Like everyone else, I have minor aesthetic flaws, which I'm keenly aware of. They are rarely commented upon; usually only the good bits are. I'm thirty-two. Not too young and not too old – but for what? I kill people. I could dress it up, say all kinds of stuff about it, but for now, all you need to know is that I do.

I stabbed a man recently, slit his throat and left him dead in a hotel bedroom. I tied his body up with ropes. If I told you I positioned him picture perfect, you wouldn't understand what I mean, but soon you will.

My online tag name is Cassie4Casanova. The first time I used it was nine years ago in Paris. I was twenty-three then. I thought I knew things about the world. I guess we're all guilty of that kind of stupidity. The man I was with had a darker side, but his badness was far easier to manage than the rest. That last afternoon, I met him at the Hôtel du Maurier. I took a photograph of myself beforehand. I was standing at a bookstore window. I gave the glass a sideways glance, checking out my appearance. It was a clear reflection. I could see the shine at the end of my nose. I thought it made the image more realistic. I often do that sideways-glance thing. Sometimes my face looks questioning; other times the glance is accompanied by a smirk. That day, I seemed bemused. The reason is unimportant.

In the photograph you can see the reflection of the flowers from the florist opposite, and a partial window display of Les Belles Boulangerie Pâtisserie. They both added a nice balance. I was wearing a cream raincoat. The collar was up, as if I had walked out of a *Dick Tracy* comic strip. I can see all of this as if it happened yesterday. I remember slowing the exposure on the camera lens to catch the movement of people walking by, each of them unaware of my thoughts. I take a lot of photographs, self-portraits. The camera is the eye. See how the picture is building up?

Less than an hour after I left the bookstore window, I stood outside the hotel. It was on a narrow street, set between the Latin Quarter and Saint-Germain-des-Prés. The small wrought-iron balconies were charming, with their fleur-de-lis design, the red and pink geraniums plummeting through the bars. Inside, the hotel was very different. It had more grandeur, with greater sex appeal.

On the top floor, the glimmer of an overhead chandelier shone down the gold and ruby hallway that led me to him. After I'd tapped on the door, I heard his footsteps. Opening the door, he looked angry. He liked to drink mid-afternoon. But that day, his eyes seemed sharper than normal, piercing, the whites of them almost dazzling. He had wickedness on his mind.

All he wore was a pair of faded jeans, and I could see the tightening of his chest muscles, the curled blond hair on his chest, his tanned feet. He was quite extraordinary in his way, that dangerous mix of fulfilment and disaster, beauty and ugliness so close they almost sparkled. 'You're late, slut,' were his first endearing words, as he held the door ajar, waiting for me to go inside. I walked past him. I heard the click, click, click of my red stilettos, his favourite, on the shiny marble floor as he locked the door.

Even with my back to him I knew his eyes were on me, taking without touching. It wasn't long before he yanked my hair, kissing me feverishly, as if his life depended on it. My lipstick smeared his face and mine, like a stamp of ownership. I usually wear Carmine, a purplish red.

I saw the champagne cooling on a side table. He popped the cork, then handed me a glass. I swallowed fast. The bubbles felt cold, the tiny droplets teasing my face, mixing with the smudged lipstick.

I had a role to play. I looked chastised, the way he sometimes liked it. I was still standing in my raincoat as he talked about one of his favourite artists, Degas, and all his many masks. I balanced on my red high heels, him pretending a lack of interest, engrossed in his own clever conversation. I reached out, opened the top button of his jeans.

'My little whore.' He smiled.

I'm not a whore. If men pay, they believe they own more than your sexual favours, they think they own YOU. It's not money I seek. It's not that simple.

I removed my coat, slipping out of my dress. His right hand yanked my hair again. 'I want you,' he whispered, his tongue swirling in my ear as he pulled off my underwear. I caught a glimpse of myself in the mirror, and thought of the woman in the bookstore window. My nakedness changed me, but like Degas, I still wore my mask, one embroiled with lies and deceit. He groped me, as if I was some fiendish plaything, and again I stared at my reflection, seeing a stranger looking back.

He often took me from behind. I played my role with well-rehearsed modesty, pleading with him to stop. Afterwards he asked if I despised him. He was gentle then, crying big boyish tears, which I relished.

It was only in the tears that he was of any consequence. The killing didn't come easy – endings are like beginnings: they change things. I DO CARE.

I've told you about this man because I need you to know something else about me. I will put myself in danger for what I want. Killing Pierre was risky. Others knew of my connection to him. But the truth isn't always simple. It has its own concealments, and I have plenty of those.

CHRISTCHURCH, DUBLIN

KATE PEARSON TAPPED her fingers on the steering wheel, lost in thought, the sight and sound of the windscreen wipers swishing back and forth her only distraction. It was one of those damp mornings in the city when the relentless rain caused everything to look grey and dirty. She wore a small silver locket around her neck. In it were photographs of her late mother, and her son, six-year-old Charlie. Without thinking, she reached up to stroke it between her index finger and thumb.

Ahead of her, Christchurch Cathedral stood witness over the lanes of bumper-to-bumper traffic. She had already planned her day: she would review last month's case files. Other psychologists at Ocean House teased her about having obsessive-compulsive disorder, but she knew the more times she examined something, the more she usually saw. It was her tried and tested method, and had stood her well, the forensic examination, raising fresh questions, leading to a greater understanding of a client and their mental well-being.

When her mobile phone rang, she cursed herself for leaving it in her handbag rather than putting it in the hands-free set. She rummaged through the bag, with an eye on the stationary traffic in case it decided to move. The caller hung up as she grabbed the phone, but she recognised the number: the Special Detective Unit at Harcourt Street. Pulling the car into a side street, she pressed speed dial, and within moments she was talking to Mark Lynch, a detective who delivered information with equal efficiency and brevity. 'Mark, I assume this isn't a social call.' She took a pen and notebook out of her bag. 'What do we have?'

'Murdered male, Rick Shevlin, married, mid-forties. He worked as an art dealer in the city.'

'How was he killed?'

'Multiple stab wounds – frenzied attack. The body was discovered by Housekeeping this morning.'

'Housekeeping?'

'He booked into the Earlbrook Hotel last night. According to his wife, he had a late meeting in town, but I can fill you in when you get here.'

His last comment sounded at worst like an order and at best an irritant. 'I'm sure I don't need to remind you, Mark, that I work *with* you, not *for* you. But it's not far. I can take a short detour.' She emphasised 'short'.

'Appreciated.'

Duly clipped, she thought. A male-dominated environment presented its challenges, but she was up to them, and at the back of Lynch's minor power struggle, a man had lost his life.

Twenty minutes later, she was in the car park at the Earlbrook. If Mark Lynch was there, the technical squad would be in situ and, most probably, Ian Morrison, the state pathologist. Seeing the crime scene first hand was crucial, an opportunity she couldn't afford to miss.

It had been two years since she had begun profiling killers for the Irish police. The first case had brought her into contact with Detective Inspector O'Connor, the investigation of the murdered schoolgirl, Caroline Devine. The last time she and O'Connor had crossed paths was six months earlier, during the canal-murder inquiry, prior to his suspension. She had heard he was due back within weeks, but that didn't necessarily mean he would pick up where he had left off – covering up evidence wasn't something easily brushed aside. She had felt guilty about not being in touch, especially as she had played her own part in him coming clean, but she'd had her reasons for keeping her distance, complicated ones.

On entering the lobby of the Earlbrook Hotel, the first thing that struck her was its opulence. Large crystal chandeliers hung from beautifully carved ceilings and Romanesque archways. Two stone pillars led the eye directly towards the marbled staircase where a uniformed officer was stationed either side at the top. Management wouldn't be happy with police activity interfering with daily procedure, but a dead man took precedence, especially a murdered one.

After one of the techies had helped her into a white body

suit, Kate braced herself, then walked into Room 122. Despite the police activity in the room, as at any other crime scene, time was somehow standing still. Every contact leaves a trace: a statement drummed into every police officer during training. In the preservation of the crime scene, they were all attempting to stop time, gathering information that would hopefully lead them to the killer.

The bulky, bullish frame of Ian Morrison stood on the opposite side of the four-poster bed to the lanky Mark Lynch. Between them on the blood-stained white sheets lay the naked corpse. Not for the first time Kate thought there was little dignity in death. Neither man turned to acknowledge her, giving her the opportunity to take in as much about the scene as she could before she was briefed.

The murdered man lay face up with his feet at the top of the bed, his right ankle tied to the brass bedpost with what looked like a one-inch double-knotted rope. The left leg was bent at the knee, set at a perfect ninety-degree angle to the one opposite. Lynch had been correct when he described the attack as frenzied. Even without Morrison's autopsy report the body was a mess. The victim's throat had been slit, a hideous gaping wound with blood coagulating down his neck. The multiple stab wounds formed gorges of congealed blood across his chest. There was so much blood on the bed it looked weighted down by it. Slash wounds to the face, legs and arms were too numerous to quantify. The victim's eyes were wide open, his head turned in the direction of the two windows opposite, as if they had seen Hell in all its anguish.

She moved closer to Morrison and Lynch, remaining fixated

on the dead man's eyes. What had they seen before death? She swallowed hard, working to maintain her composure. She imagined the killer in the room – what were his or her last movements? Had guilt, ecstasy or both run through their mind during the attack? Had they felt fear? How well had they known the victim? What role had Shevlin played in his own demise?

As she stared at the dead man, another image was forming in her mind, that of a crucifixion. The room, suddenly, felt clammy. She could smell the Luminol kit that the techies were using on the blood spatters, and in her mind, it was as if everything was overlapping, different images criss-crossing with endless possibilities.

It was the tying of the ankle that had first made her think of a crucifixion, but if it had been a crucifixion, the ankles would have been tied together; the left leg had been left free. The positioning of the arms was important too, both bent at the elbow joints, each hand under the body at the midpoint of the back.

'Are the hands tied behind his back?' she asked Morrison, keeping her voice even.

'Yes. The same as the ankle, a double overhand knot.'

'It's certainly frenzied,' she said, moving even closer, her eyes studying the wounds on the dead man's torso.

'We always seem to get the cut-and-slash ones, don't we, Kate?' Lynch smiled.

The smile didn't impress her. At first, she had warmed to Mark Lynch, liking his efficiency and attention to detail, but during the last investigation she had noted a darker side to the young detective. It had slipped out while he was interviewing a vagrant, and once she had witnessed it, she had felt that something not so sweet teetered below the surface. She let his last remark go unanswered.

'The body has been purposely positioned,' she continued. 'It's more than the use of ropes. The killer has something to say.'

Ian Morrison leaned over to examine the victim's fingernails, but Lynch's interest was spiked by her last comment. 'Which is what?' he asked.

'At first I thought of a crucifixion, but then ...' She paused, as if contemplating the value of her next point.

'Go on.'

'Look at the positioning. It's very specific.' She tilted her head to the side, again staring into the dead man's face. 'Mark, do you know anything about Tarot cards?'

'I'm not into fortune-telling, if that's what you mean.'

'The body ...' once more, she hesitated '... is laid out like the Hangman card from a Tarot deck.'

'Meaning?'

'It's one of the higher Arcana cards. I profiled a case in the UK a few years back. The killer believed the cards had powers. He thought they were guiding him. The Hangman,' she continued, 'depicts a man hanging upside-down by one foot, usually suspended from a wooden beam or a tree. The gallows he's suspended from forms a tau cross, while the position of the legs,' she pointed to the body, 'forms a fylfot cross. You can see how one leg is bent under the other with the hands tied behind the back.'

'So what does it tell us?' A slight impatience had entered the detective's voice.

Morrison looked up, his interest, too, aroused.

'It's associated with a god called Odin from Norse mythology,' she replied. 'Odin hung from a world-tree, an Yggdrasil, for nine days. He wanted to obtain wisdom and retrieve the runes, or words, from the Well of Wyrd.'

'The Well of what?' Lynch raised his eyebrows.

'Wyrd,' she repeated. 'It was regarded as the source of mystery and knowledge. The moment Odin glimpsed the runes, he died, but the knowledge was so strong that he immediately regained life.'

'I don't think there's much chance of that happening here,' interjected Morrison, in his deadpan style.

'No, I agree,' Kate said, matter-of-fact. 'What are your observations, Ian?'

'Our guy was tied up after death. Although the ropes are secured tightly, the blood vessels haven't reacted as I would have expected them to if they had been active.'

'Go on.' Lynch looked down at the body as if it had taken on a whole new meaning.

'Blood vessels leak, imparting a blue-black colour to the tissues. There's no sign of that here.' Morrison pointed to the area around the ankle, before moving further down the body. 'There are whip marks on the buttocks, but judging by the skin, they were probably made prior to death.'

'If the ropes were applied after death, Ian,' Kate stood back from the bed, 'then the scene was stage-managed by the killer.'

'That's not my area of expertise. I'll know more later on, but for now, all three of us can see the obvious. His throat has been cut. If it turns out to be the cause of death, the most likely scenario is exsanguination, with the external jugular vein and carotid artery severed.'

'And the other possibilities?' Lynch asked, pushing the pathologist while he still had him in his sights.

'It's possible he choked to death on his blood or an embolism occurred, air entering the jugular vein.'

'Was the same knife used throughout?' Kate, like Lynch, was keen to get as many answers as possible.

Morrison let out a deep breath, as if it helped him to concentrate. 'It's impossible to say, but we're talking about a large blade, capable of deep penetration.'

'How large?' Lynch wasn't letting go.

'Too soon to tell exact dimensions, but I'll give you what I can once I've done a full examination.'

'And the trajectory of the wounds?'

Morrison gazed at the detective, contemplating, Kate thought, whether or not he should reveal any more at this point. Finally he said, 'The puncture wounds are relatively straight, possibly coming from above with the victim lying down.'

'Any idea of time of death?' Kate quizzed.

'At least seven hours.' Morrison pointed to the victim's face. 'The corneas, the clear covering over the pupils, are cloudy and opaque. If the eyes were closed, this could take up to twenty-four hours. The process speeds up when the eyes are open.'

'Placing the time of death at around two a.m.,' Lynch said.

Kate again looked at the victim's eyes. 'What are those dark marks around the pupils?'

Morrison appeared pleased with her question, replying with enthusiasm: 'It's called tache noir, one of the most important post-mortem changes in the eye. If the eyes are open after death, the area of the sclera exposed to the air dries out, which results in a yellowish, then brownish-blackish band, which is what we have here. This level of discoloration will appear around the seven-hour mark.'

Kate walked over to the windows, which looked out onto the hotel car park, then turned to face both men. 'Ian, were the eyes forced open?'

'I can't be sure. As soon as death occurs, the muscles in the eye stop functioning. He could have died with his eyes open or they could have been opened afterwards.'

'What about DNA?' Lynch looked up from his notebook.

'It would be tricky. Even if we could pull a sample, it's unlikely we'd get enough to produce an adequate profile.'

'Anything else?' Lynch asked.

'Yes, the concentration of potassium within the vitreous humour—'

'The what?' Lynch sounded irritated again.

'If you didn't keep interrupting me, Detective, I might be able tell you.' It was Morrison's turn to be irked. Kate smiled to herself.

'It's the thick jelly-like substance that fills your eyeballs. It increases slowly after death, but is already clearly visible here. Understandably, the body temperature has dropped too, from the normal temperature of 98.6 degrees Fahrenheit. The body loses heat at a rate of 1.5 degrees per hour, but in a heat-assisted room like this one, it loses it a lot slower, yet our man's has dropped over four degrees.'

'I see,' Lynch replied.

'You'll have to wait for the full autopsy report if you want any more than that from me. The only other obvious detail is a series of older tears in the skin, especially on the upper thighs and arms.'

'And the cause?' Kate asked.

'They could be self-inflicted, but again, I'll know more once I've had a chance to examine the body in detail.'

Kate turned to Lynch. 'Were the room lights on or off?'

'Off. Why?'

'The curtains are open. I assume they were that way when you arrived.'

'Correct.'

'There's plenty of lighting in the car park outside. It would have lit up the room if the drapes were pulled. The buildings opposite are at a lower level, so the killer may have felt they couldn't be seen.'

'What are you getting at, Kate?'

'Perhaps he or she used the exterior light to prepare the victim, and there's something else.' Both men looked at her. 'The lack of blood spatters and pooling beyond the vicinity of the bed is odd. It doesn't look as if our victim put up much of a fight. Ian, did you find any notable signs of a struggle on the body?'

'No obvious ones. I'll be running full pathology tests for possible drug intake prior to death. We'll pull fluid from the eyes too. It's the last fluid in the body to peak. If the victim was drinking prior to death, the vitreous alcohol level will tell us if our dead friend was on his way up or on his way down.' Morrison pointed to the eyes again. 'We can also look to the vitreous for any signs of Fentanyl or 6-Mam, both derivatives of heroin, as we won't find these or their metabolites in the blood samples.'

'What about cocaine?' Lynch pointed to the corpse. 'As well as increasing aggression, it's used as a sexual stimulant. Our friend here hired an escort before he snuffed it.'

'Thank you for your scientific observations, Detective.' Morrison didn't sound appreciative. 'That will all come out in the toxicology reports.' He turned to Kate. 'If the victim was compromised prior to death, in other words, if he was drugged with any form of sedative substance, and wasn't physically able to defend himself, it would explain the localisation of the blood spatters. It would certainly have made him more susceptible to having his throat slit. After that,' the pathologist looked cheerfully from Kate to Lynch, 'he was a dead man one way or another.'

I use the Rider-Waite Tarot cards, not because they are popular. They chose me. Some people think the cards are evil, but fear drives their ignorance. The same kind of stupidity that is capable of terrible things – unsavoury behaviour from closed minds combined with a dash of terror.

Part of knowing the Tarot is the understanding of numbers. We all have a birth number. For most, it's a single digit, 1 to 9. It's easy to work it out. All you have to do is write down the date you were born. Let me help you – the ninth day of the eleventh month in the year 1990. Add the numbers together until you reduce them to a single digit: 9 + 11 + 1 + 9 + 9 + 0. This gives you 39. Then add 3 to 9 and you get 12. Break it down again, 1 + 2, and you have 3.

There are exceptions to the single-digit rule: in numerology the master numbers, 11 and 22, require special attention. They are for those who are endowed with extra gifts, and are usually found in people who have had a challenging upbringing – the inference being a dark one. Perhaps you don't believe your life can be preordained from birth, that pure evil exists, or that people are born with it. I have experienced evil at first hand. You learn to sink or swim. One man's evil is another man's pleasure. I was born on the eighth day of October 1982. That makes me the number 11, the number of the Master Teacher. The words 'intuitive', 'prisoner', 'mystical' and 'alternative consciousness' are all part of it, but there is so much more.

I'm not egotistical, or over-fond of the term 'Master Teacher'. I prefer 'illuminator' or 'messenger' – but maybe I'm splitting hairs. The numbers are what they are.

I have a *new* man in my life. His card has yet to be chosen, but the Lovers would be the icing on the cake. He called a few moments ago: he needs to see me *desperately*, he said. I won't deny I took pleasure from this, his voice barely above a whisper, as if the little wife was close by. He wants us to go back to the hotel.

I sensed his excitement when I agreed to meet him – his voice becoming confident, saying how he knew the room was important to me, his words full of sexual suggestion. I encouraged him, manipulating, teasing, relishing. He lapped it up like a sex-starved dog. The control game is beginning, and he thinks he might be in charge.

The Wheel of Fortune is one of my sought-after cards of the Tarot – spin the wheel and take a chance. Do nothing, be afraid, and all could be lost. Maybe that will be his card. I need to move to the next level. I won't make the same mistake as I did with Rick, although I take pleasure in knowing that I was the one who introduced him to the cutting. Even seeing the blade became a turn-on for poor Ricky. Like me, he enjoyed the initial surge, the sight of his own blood, and knowing he could do it added to the joyous, electrifying appeal. His delight was obvious, and he thought he had me exactly where he wanted me, but concealment is one of my better-learned art forms.

After the night of the party, everything changed. Rick sealed his fate, and four weeks later, it was goodbye, Rick. I can recount the evening frame by frame, hour by hour and moment by moment. Everyone wore masks. It was the usual private affair – invited guests only, making the participants feel special, elusive and selective. The location was out of town, top secret, isolated, a large country house that belonged to someone born into money. It had been done up especially for the party. There were private rooms for those who preferred coupling, but Rick wasn't looking for that: his ego demanded more.

When we arrived, the beam of his headlights shone across the wide pebbled drive. I wore a gold dress, low cut at the front and back, with earrings that dangled and glistened like fairy lights. My hair was up, a long fringe hanging sideways across my face. I remember seeing my reflection in the tiny passenger mirror and thinking I looked like someone else. I can still see the eagerness in his eyes, even after he had put on his masquerade mask. I knew the party was supposed to get him up close and personal with people who mattered, but I hadn't known I was part of the prize. I hadn't seen that coming, his desire to share me with others, as if I was his favourite pig at a fair.

The party started with the anticipation of sex, everyone waiting for the first participants to get down to it, as if it was a dance floor, not a sex-play area. It wasn't long before bodies were sprawled and entwined across half a dozen double beds rammed together, making it impossible to tell which leg was connected to which body in the mass nakedness. I have no doubt Rick visualised the fun he would have – a highly charged turn-on. I should have known there was another reason he looked so satisfied. I was the sacrificial offering to be slaughtered. I don't like being downgraded and objectified. I don't have issues with sharing, but I have issues with choice.

I should have trusted my instincts. When we arrived and he opened the car door, I had thought about not moving – a flicker of foresight told me not to go inside. I wavered – BIG MISTAKE. Danger, like evil, is subjective, and as the lights and sounds of the party spilled onto the drive, it was as if they were calling me for a dance. I heard my feet crunch on the gravel and, as my body moved, it seemed to belong to someone else.

I soon realised I was the target for Rick's collective goonies. He had led me down a long, dark corridor into the private room, on the pretext of being alone, and my stupidity slapped me across the face. I wasn't the only trophy female there, but I hadn't come prepared for a forced gang-bang: if I'd known, I would have taken a knife with me, slit their throats and cut off their excuses for manhood, used on me to prove their worth.

The pendulum swung the other way on the night I killed him. I was fully conscious of the knife in my bag. Part of me wondered why no one else knew it was there. The recollections come in waves – watching him open the door to that tart, imagining what was going to happen next, the pendulum in my head swinging back and forth, knowing that calmness would come in time.

After the whore had left the hotel room, I turned the key in the door. At first he seemed surprised, then pleased, thinking I had come back for second helpings, his ego getting in the way again. He knew nothing about me, not really, so when I produced the Special K, he thought he would experience a high, swallowing his drink down fast. I like to think he knew what was happening in the end – lessons are for learning.

I waited: everything would happen in good time. Once his body weakened, I would have my best chance. I let him see the blade before I used it. Perhaps he thought I was playing another game, but I soon got his attention.

Slash, the first cut across his throat – blood gulping from his neck.

Slash, the second cut deeper than the first, his back arching in spasms, spurting more blood. I kept counting while he clenched his throat, stabbing him hard. His body folded, recoiled. The final blows of the knife took the last of my anger.

The bed, even in the dark, was red with blood. I felt the rush, even though the blood was not my own, and waited like a common thief. I stole his last breath in my kiss. In retrospect, it was all inevitable, but I felt weary when it was done.

The aftermath was far more fun – tying him up like a piece of meat, his eyes beautifully hellish, staring out onto the lights of the car park, the same way I had looked out on the light of the party shining on the drive, calling for a dance.

The Hangman card could have gone either way. I know that now. It is the interpretation of the card that is the key. I will spin the wheel of fortune for my *new* lover. I will rein him in. There will be no mistakes this time, not now that I am so close. His need is evolving, and he is on the brink of wondering why he sees his boring wife as his partner, not me. He hasn't said as much, but I can sense these things. It's determining my next move, which I assure you will be interesting.

Men can be fickle but are deliciously capable of being manipulated. They each have a notion of the perfect woman, which is often difficult for them to articulate, but it is there. Of late, he has become closer to my way of thinking. I can see it in the way he talks about her, almost as if she is slipping from his consciousness. It might be tricky, although he recognises his need to turn his back on the banal, boring life she shares with him. Part of the beauty is that she is unaware of the magnitude involved. She has her suspicions, but they are not important. If anything, they lean in my favour. Ultimately she will retreat, crawling back under the safe, mediocre stone where she belongs. I will put her there. Nothing surer – just watch me.

THE EARLBROOK HOTEL

KATE WATCHED IAN Morrison as he carried out his final examination on Rick Shevlin's body before its removal from the hotel room. Bit by bit the rest of the evidence would follow, the scene consigned to memory, and whatever crime-scene evidence, photographic or otherwise, the police had managed to collect. She had taken her own images, which she would examine later, but right then, the issue of the dead man having been immobilised or substantially weakened was playing on her mind. It tied in with another theory, one she wasn't yet willing to share.

A hotel room offered secrecy, she thought, a place to meet someone you might not want others to know about. If the victim had been rendered considerably less hostile, the killer would have been in charge from that point onwards, if not before.

Kate flinched when Mark Lynch patted her arm, his hand lingering longer than necessary.

'Is everything okay?' he asked.

'Yes, I'm fine.' She hadn't expected his touch. Maybe she had forgotten what it was like to be touched by a man. She and Declan were barely on speaking terms, she procrastinating about their official separation for weeks. *Bury your head in the sand, Kate, like you always do.* Damn him, she thought. Concentrate. She stepped forward and away from Lynch. Thankfully, he took the hint.

Staring at the corpse, she thought again about the positioning and application of the ropes – those at the victim's ankle and the ties behind his back. If Morrison was correct, and the ropes were applied after death, there was some kind of payback in the ritual for the killer. Was it dominance, a fetish or a means of re-enactment? Whatever the reason, it reinforced something. The man's nakedness and the whip marks implied a level of sexual activity, but there was more to this, she was sure.

'Mark,' she called.

If he was irritated by her summons, he didn't show it. This investigation, she thought, was putting the detective on a positive high.

'You said Rick was an art dealer. What else do we know about him?' she asked, lowering her voice as he got closer. 'Had he any priors?'

'His record is clean.'

'No sexual history on the PULSE database?'

'Nothing on file, but as I said earlier, he used an escort service – at least the once.'

'How do you know?'

'His mobile-phone records – we traced the last few calls. The second last was to an escort company called Connections. I've already spoken to the madam.'

'You're sure the escort arrived?'

'Yeah – the guy on Reception spotted her around eleven, shortly after the booking was made, but she left well before midnight. Rick then rang his wife at twelve fifteen. Probably a guilt call.'

'And the guy on Reception, did he see her go to Rick Shevlin's room?'

'No, he didn't, but the timing fits. I have the escort waiting at Harcourt Street. It's always good to get the information while it's fresh.'

'I'll join you if that's okay.' Whatever plans she'd had for the rest of the day would have to be put on hold.

'No problem.'

'Did you find anything else like this on PULSE?' She took a couple of steps closer to the bed.

'Nothing with this MO.'

Her mind began working overtime. If Rick Shevlin had engaged an escort, and then phoned his wife, who had been the next visitor to his room? A jealous lover or someone else? She leaned in closer to the victim's face. 'What's that on his lips?'

Morrison took a few moments to consider. 'It could be lipstick.'

'A deep purplish shade of red if it is,' she replied, as if thinking aloud.

'It could belong to the escort,' Lynch added.

'Or the killer,' she replied. 'If Rick was drugged before death, and considerably weakened, we can't discard the possibility …' she hesitated '… that a woman did this. The physical balance of power would have been on the side of the killer, even if they had been physically smaller.'

'A woman?' Lynch also leaned in closer. 'We'll take a swab and send it to the lab.'

'What then?' Kate asked.

'If we're lucky, we'll get enough to produce a good DNA profile. If not, it'll be a long path ahead.'

'How so?'

'For a start, there isn't a lipstick database. Assuming we can get a full breakdown of the lipstick's properties, it will mean contacting the manufacturers individually. We can email them the results of the sample, but if we do find a match, there's no guarantee it's not a worldwide product.'

'A wide net?' She raised her eyebrows.

'We'll start with the probability that as the crime happened in Ireland the lipstick was bought here too. Although it's unlikely it will be matched to a particular batch number, you never know. Either way, if we find the killer, we'll be looking for a match.'

He directed his next question to Morrison. 'I assume you'll be doing the full works?' He glanced down at the victim's genitals as the body bag was zipped up.

Morrison frowned, as if the detective's last remark was the only surprising thing about his morning's work. 'You assume right, Detective, and I'm sure your superiors will be proud of your investigative know-how.' A broad, sarcastic smile was etched across the pathologist's face.

Lynch didn't rise to the bait. 'We're all here to catch the bad guys – or girls, for that matter.'

Kate gestured to the en-suite. 'Have the techies found anything in there?'

'Find anything, guys?' Lynch bellowed.

The techie nearest the door turned. 'It's looking very clean.'

'Surprising,' Kate muttered, but Lynch heard her.

'What's surprising about it?'

'The blood is localised, but there's too much here for the killer to be able to leave the place completely clean. If they washed up here, they were extremely thorough, or else they could have used another room in the hotel. How many are there?'

'Thirty in this wing – they start at 100 and go up to 130. They're all cleared at this point. It will take a while to check them individually.'

'Start with the rooms closest. I can't see this killer walking along the landing covered with blood. There is another possibility, though.'

'Which is?'

'He or she brought their own equipment for cleaning.' Kate walked over to the bathroom. 'Guys, any residue down the plughole?'

Again the techie nearest the door answered: 'No. It was the first place we checked.'

'And nothing at all in the sink?'

'Nothing.'

She turned back to Lynch. 'There may be nothing on the PULSE database, but this killer has acted before, done something very similar.'

'What makes you so sure?'

'The scene is too organised and controlled. The killer came prepared. They knew every step they wanted to take and, most likely, everything they did, they did for a very good reason. Nobody reaches this level of violence overnight. If there's nothing on PULSE, there'll be something on Europol or Interpol, but you might have to go back a long way.'

'How long?'

'Ten years, possibly more. There will be a trail, nothing surer. It's simply a question of finding it.'

HARCOURT STREET POLICE STATION, SPECIAL DETECTIVE UNIT

KATE USED HER own car to drive to Harcourt Street police station, keen to have some time alone. It was partly why she liked to go out running whenever she got the chance, getting away from the multitude of voices and opinions. The killer, she thought, carried a large calling card – ropes, a sizeable knife, possibly enough drugs to sedate the victim – and had most probably planned everything about the attack, including the clean-up operation afterwards. When it came to planning a murder, men and women were very similar, but the taking of another person's life was less likely to be random when it came to a female killer. A lot would depend on whether Rick Shevlin was sedated or not, and whether the lipstick on the victim's lips had belonged to the escort.

Pushing through the double doors into the Special Detective Unit, she practically bumped into Lynch. 'Perfect timing,' he said. 'I'm about to chat to the hooker, Annabel Weston.'

'I meant to ask you, Mark, about the hotel security cameras. You never mentioned them.'

'Out of order.'

'What?'

'I know. The chief super wasn't impressed either.'

She followed him along the corridor to Interview Room 4C, where a uniformed female officer stood to one side.

'Shall we?' he asked.

Kate nodded. 'Her name is Annabel?'

He paused. 'I doubt it's her real name. In that line of business, it's less about the truth and more about getting laid.'

There was no denying his smarmy inflection. Mark Lynch was letting his rank as SIO, senior investigating officer, go to his head, she thought. 'Remember you said you'd check her brand of lipstick?'

'And I will. I'm not a rookie.'

'I didn't say you were.'

This interview was going to be interesting. If she had to, she would rein in the detective's fervour. As if he was reading her mind, he practically bounced into the room. 'Annabel, good of you to wait for us.'

The escort stood up immediately. Kate could tell she was nervous, but she soon regained her composure. Even though she was dressed in black leather and knee-high platform boots, like a dominatrix, she didn't look tacky. As soon as she spoke, Kate noted her upper-class Southside accent. Her clothes were part of her working image, but not necessarily part of her.

'I didn't really have a choice,' she said.

He smiled at her, then said, 'This is Dr Kate Pearson, Annabel. She's a psychologist.'

Kate reached out to shake the girl's hand, noting how young she looked, and how expertly her makeup had been applied. With her raven black hair, she wouldn't have looked out of place in a fashion magazine, but she wasn't in the mood for shaking hands: she kept her arms firmly folded in front of her, like a form of protection.

'I've met her kind before,' she said, looking at Kate. 'They want to mess with your head.'

'Very well,' Lynch replied, unconcerned. 'Let's talk about Rick Shevlin, the dead man in Room 122.'

'He was alive when I left him.' She practically spat the words. 'Look, I don't know anything. I didn't even know the guy's name. But now you say it, he did look like a Rick. It rhymes with prick.'

Lynch was standing too close to Annabel for Kate's liking. It might have been an interview room, but it was as if he wanted to invade her personal space. 'Let's all sit down, shall we?' she ventured.

'Absolutely.' Lynch waved Annabel to a seat, then pressed the record button for the interview, and took care of the opening preliminaries: time, date and the names of those present.

'Let's start, Annabel, with you arriving at the hotel room. Was there anything different or strange about Rick Shevlin?'

'No. It was the same as any other job.'

'Your first thought?'

'Getting the guy to come off as fast as possible.'

'Was he obliging?' Lynch began walking in a circle around her. It seemed to Kate, and probably to Annabel, that he was physically inspecting her. 'Did he want to do anything kinky?'

'They usually have a wish list. The pervs pay better.' She attempted a laugh.

False bravery, thought Kate.

'So Rick was a perv, was he? What was his speciality?' Lynch seemed to be enjoying himself.

Annabel didn't answer immediately. Eventually she said, 'For the most part, he wanted the usual stuff: sucking his prick, licking, teasing, but he liked having the upper hand as well, dishing out his fair share of pain, slapping me about, a bit of rough stuff, you know what I mean.'

'Do you like the violent pervs?' He leaned over, as if to intimidate her.

'Detective, take it easy,' Kate said, with a look that said, 'Back off.'

He took a couple of steps away.

'I seem particularly attractive to pervs.' Annabel perked up slightly. 'I'm told they like me.'

'What's your secret?' Lynch still looked as if he was relishing the conversation.

'They like the way I dress. You don't think I wear this gear for comfort, do you?'

He turned to face her. 'What are your special tricks?'

'Do you fancy some, Detective? Looking to do a few turns on the side?'

Kate could see his irritability bubbling under the surface. He hadn't taken kindly to Annabel's last remark.

'Listen, you,' his voice was filled with venom, 'a man has been murdered, and you happen to have been the last person we know to have seen him alive. Don't waste your time with any sideshows for me. I'm not interested.'

'And I don't have time for this shit.' She folded her arms again. 'As I told you, I don't know anything.'

'You managed to get very close to Rick Shevlin,' he retorted.

She stared at him. 'I have rules, you know. He wanted me to do stuff, but I wasn't having any of it.'

Kate hoped a less intimidating approach would get more answers. 'And what are your rules, Annabel? What did he want you to do?'

'No kissing. I don't do anal. No fingers or anything other than his prick goes inside. If it does, it costs a lot extra.' Then, looking directly at Kate, sensing an ally, she stood up. 'Listen, as I keep saying, I don't know anything. I need to get back.'

'You'll go when I say so.' Lynch's tone was controlled but harsh. 'Dr Pearson asked you what the punter, Rick Shevlin, wanted. Now be a good girl and answer. I don't need to remind you that you've broken the law so let's try to be civil to one another.'

'I wasn't the only one in the hotel room. Rick was there too. Remember, he booked me.'

'But he didn't do anything illegal, did he? And now he happens to be dead.' Lynch wasn't going to let her off easily.

'Looking to be fucked isn't illegal, but me fucking him is. That's sick.'

'I don't make the rules, Annabel. Now, who owned the whip, you or him?'

'Me.'

'Do you have it here?'

'No. I only bring it if I'm asked.' Then, in a flirtatious tone, 'Are you specially requesting it, Detective?'

Again, Lynch didn't bite, but it was obvious to Kate that the girl used her flirtation as a false shield.

'We'll need the whip when we finish here. I'll get a female officer to accompany you. I don't want you disappearing on us.'

Kate looked directly at Annabel. 'The victim had whip marks on his buttocks. Did he ask you to whip him?'

'As I said, he liked to inflict pain, so it surprised me when he wanted to be punished too – it was as if he couldn't make up his mind.'

'Outside of the rough stuff and the whipping,' Kate continued, 'did he look for anything else?'

Again Annabel stalled.

Kate took another approach. 'Had you agreed terms before you arrived?'

'Yeah, but it didn't stop him looking for more.'

'So tell me, Annabel, what did he want you to do?'

'He was into the hard stuff, cutting and the like. He said he liked the sight of blood, really got going when he saw it. I don't do cutting. I told him that.'

'What happened then?' Kate kept her tone soft.

'I distracted him. He slapped me about for a bit – he even got hold of the whip at one point – but when I started stripping, he let me take over. Then there was more of the usual stuff: pulling at my clothes, biting me – my tits were killing me after. Look, I've bruises everywhere, the wanker.' She pulled up a sleeve to show a bruised arm. 'When he got into the swing of things, it meant I could get out of there faster.'

'What then?' Lynch asked.

'After he came off, I told him to have a shower. I said the wet would add to the turn-on when he came back. The egotistical bastard actually thought I was enjoying myself. When he went to the bathroom, I checked under the bed and the pillows. That's where they usually hide the knives.'

'Find any?' Lynch leaned in closer again.

'No, but it didn't stop him wanting it. He said he would pay me a hundred euros extra if I did the cutting on him. He brought out a shaver blade – desperate to see blood, he was, but I wasn't having any of it.' She shuddered.

Kate looked at Lynch and wondered briefly if Annabel's distaste gave him pleasure.

'Well, Annabel,' he whispered in her ear, 'Rick's got plenty of blood on him now – not that it's capable of giving him a hard-on.'

He was enjoying the power struggle, Kate noted. The more vulnerable the girl became, the more pleasure he got out of it. If Annabel defied him, he came across the heavy, putting her where it suited him best: inferior to him.

It surprised her when Annabel went to the victim's defence: 'The guy wasn't the worst – I mean, he didn't deserve to die.'

'So when his time was up with you, what happened then?' Kate kept her tone measured.

Annabel lowered her voice. 'Like most of them, he wanted rid of me as fast as he could, as if I reminded him of shit.' Then her tone sharpened: 'Nothing new there.'

'Had he booked you before?' Kate pressed her.

'It was the first time.'

'What about ropes?' Kate continued. 'Did Rick Shevlin have any, or did you bring any with you?'

'No, there was nothing like that.'

Kate smiled then, hoping to put her at ease. 'What's your real name, Annabel?'

'Victoria.'

'Meaning "to conquer" or "conqueror".' Kate's response was gentle.

'I don't like them using it – the punters, that is.'

'I can understand that.' She gave the girl a reassuring look.

Lynch interjected, 'You're wearing a very distinctive pink lipstick. Do you ever wear red?'

'Sure.'

'We'll be confiscating your lipsticks along with the whip.'

'What? All of them?'

'It's a murder investigation.' He smiled.

If he heard Annabel mutter, 'Wanker,' he chose to ignore it. Stopping the recording and closing the interview, he said to her, 'Wait here until I send in your escort.'

When they stepped outside, he asked Kate, 'What do you think of her?'

'I think she's telling us the truth. Rick Shevlin wasn't a novice in this area. He behaved like someone who'd hired escorts before. If the toxicology tests tell us sedation was used, drugs and poisons aren't unusual where a female killer is concerned.'

'Why's that?'

'Sometimes because it's less messy?' She shrugged her shoulders.

'Are you serious?' He didn't attempt to hide his surprise.

'I said sometimes, but not always. Also, some women prefer not to be around when their victim dies, but, obviously, neither is part of the MO here. Most likely if we find sedatives in his system, it will be because the killer wanted him weakened, and they may also have wanted him conscious when the wounds were inflicted. Assuming Rick Shevlin doesn't swing both ways, I doubt a man tied his naked body up like that.' She could tell he had reservations about it being a female killer, but she continued, 'I would press the madam on whether or not Rick had hired any of her other girls. Maybe someone else was happy to give him what he wanted, and sought revenge. Either way, we now know the reasons for the smaller incisions on the victim's body. If someone else was prepared to experiment in the cutting department, they could have been emotionally closer to Rick Shevlin than Annabel – I mean Victoria.'

'Emotionally?' Lynch sounded sceptical.

'Contrary to common belief, there's a whole host of reasons why men use escorts, and I'm not talking dinner guests. The physical violence here, the whipping, but especially the desire for cutting, to see blood, tells us a lot about him.'

'That he was a perv?'

'There was certainly a control and power element to his preferences, but the real answers are not always obvious. If someone had got close to Rick Shevlin emotionally, we might have the first key.'

'I'm listening.'

'When Victoria left, Rick obviously had another visitor. He, or she, may have been watching him. There are too many prearranged elements for this attack to have been random. Rick was chosen, but right now, we don't know why. The sooner we have the answer to that, the better.'

'We've checked out the wife's alibi and it's rock solid. She was at home with the children and Rick's mother when Rick was done in.'

'As I said, Mark, the killer didn't arrive at this juncture overnight. When you start digging, take into account all the elements you've seen, and don't necessarily restrict your search to murder. Often, there are signposts early in an offender's cycle. We need to build up a picture, and right now all we have are fragments of something a whole lot bigger.'

I

AS I MENTIONED, the new man in my life is married. He hangs on my every word, utterly attentive, but then again, they all are when their needs are aroused.

He could be the one. Love can be transient, and my survival is on the line. This is life or death for me. If I choose unwisely, I'll pay a high price.

When he was younger, he used to paint, abstract mainly, oils on large canvas. He says he was angry back then. Later, when the anger of youth faded, he became disillusioned, doubting his craft. I've seen it before, creativity limited by fear, or by living with those who fail to understand you. I know his wife. She has a role in all this. He says, when he looks at the art work he did back then, that it's as if it belongs to someone else. I detect a note of regret behind his words and that intrigues me too.

I have a weakness for men with an appreciation of artistic endeavours. You see, there is always a hook that goes beyond physical appeal. Part of it is his manner, solid without being forceful, projecting a form of knowingness, almost as if he had lived on the earth before. I am drawn to that increasingly, surprised by it, not having noticed it before now. With fresh desire, there is often obsession and fear. The last time he kissed me, I bit him hard on the lips. They bled, and I tasted him. Afterwards, when he had come inside me, he slept like a baby. The afterwards is a test too. Sometimes they act entitled, or the adoration changes and you are like leftover food on a plate, discarded and unattractive. The very thing they wanted to devour becomes despicable. There was a time when I allowed this type of rejection to hurt me. Now I don't give them that satisfaction. It is best to learn this early on. Life is too short to waste your time on dogs.

But my new man is lovely. When he woke, he kissed my forehead, checking that I was okay. We made love again, and after he fell back to sleep, I took one of my photographs. Not of him, of course. I only do self-portraits.

I locked the bathroom door behind me. My skin was still slightly flushed from having been with him. After showering, I put on my sleeveless black dress. It was simple and modest, but tight and shapely. I closed the clasp of my pearl necklace and stood back. The large mirror above the wash-basin took up most of the wall, with two smaller side panels. I posed with my camera facing one of the panels: the larger reflection held my profile, and a small panel captured the back of my head.

The bathroom, with its small blue and white tiles, reminded me of a water fountain I'd once seen in a travel book, the white ceramic basin simple in comparison. It is important to get the balance right, the intricate mingled with the plain, the light with the dark.

The reason I like that photograph is the knowingness in my eye. I pressed the camera button like a marksman taking a shot. I had a knife in my bag too. Does that surprise you? You can't be too careful.

There is another detail about the photograph that I like: as I held the camera to my left eye, I pointed the tip of the blade below my right in absolute alignment to the centre of the pupil. It gave a perfect focal point.

When I left the bathroom, my new man was sitting up, the bedclothes covering his lower body. He didn't ask what had delayed me, not wanting to waste time on trivia. I wondered – Does he already know there is something strange about me?

'Did you have a nice sleep?' I asked.

'Yes, but I woke alone. It's a big bed. Why don't you come back in?'

I pointed to my fully clothed body.

'Don't mind that – I'll enjoy undressing you.'

I smiled. 'What if I told you I had a knife in my bag? Should I bring that into the bed too?'

He looked startled. 'Do you feel the need for protection?' he asked, his voice calm. I liked that too.

'I feel safe around you,' I said, more to flatter him than

anything else. I still haven't fully worked him out. Some people are more complicated than others.

'You know,' he said, 'part of me likes a sense of fear.'

There was no denying his arousal, and as he pulled me to him, I kicked off my shoes. He unzipped my dress, which fell to the floor.

'Leave the pearl necklace on,' he said. 'I like it.'

Desire is important: with it, normal rules no longer apply. I mentioned taking risks: when safeguards are abandoned, we are at our most primal. All relationships carry a note of warning that ultimately things will change, especially if others choose to meddle. I make a point of carefully studying my lovers' lives, especially those nearest and dearest to them.

MERVIN ROAD, RATHMINES

KATE CHECKED THE wall clock in her study for the umpteenth time: 11.55 a.m. The morning incident-room briefing was due to finish at midday. It was day two of the investigation and she knew a lot would ride on Morrison's autopsy report. They had already received preliminary results for the substance found on the victim's lips. Further tests would be done, but it was lipstick and, despite Annabel's extensive number of shades, none of them looked a likely match.

Having made the decision to work from home, primarily so she wouldn't be disturbed, Kate began flicking through her morning's notes. Mark Lynch might still have reservations about the killer being female, but the more she thought about it, the more the evidence pointed in that direction. Standing up from the desk, she began recording her notes into the phone.

'Hands tied behind victim's back, right ankle tied to bedpost, with a double-knotted rope, left leg bent at the knee, placed under the right leg at a ninety-degree angle. Head positioned at the bottom of the bed, eyes open, looking towards the windows. Extensive puncture and slash wounds to the body, indicative of a frenzied attack. Details of autopsy report to confirm exact cause of death, the existence of toxins in the bloodstream, and whether toxins were primarily sedative in nature. Potential sequence: sedation, slitting of throat, attack while victim immobilised or deceased. Initial pathology examination indicating ropes were applied after death. Require final confirmation as to whether puncture, slash wounds and whip marks were also post-mortem. Other areas of note: analysis of lipstick for its properties and DNA. Potential DNA profile from lips, under eyelids and other areas of contact.'

Kate thought about what she had said the previous day to Mark Lynch, that poisoning or drugging a victim was associated with women. She was well aware that things had moved on significantly over the last decades, primarily with women's changing social roles. Internationally, the methods of killing now included guns and knives, and had in some cases become more phallic, less associated with a woman's role as a nurturer. For male and female murderers, killing was a way of creating an illusion of control, but if the killer was female, the control might also derive from a history of abuse, a form of triumph over the past.

She pressed the record button again. 'The nakedness of the victim, exposure of genitals and the tying up of the body, before or after death, is likely to have been engineered by the killer, possibly creating an element of reward, and an act of post-death humiliation.'

It wasn't easy thinking about a woman as the killer. Statistically, even within changing societal norms, it was a rarity. The overriding influence was to nurture rather than to destroy. Kate had met many damaged people over the course of her career, and she had often wondered how different her life would have been if she had walked in the steps of some. Was she capable of killing, given the right set of circumstances? If they were looking for a female attacker, there was no doubt in her mind that something extreme had led the killer to this point, and it was unlikely that the trail of destruction would be restricted to the murderer alone. Others had played their role. Kate picked up an old photograph of her late mother. She was no more than twelve years old in the studio image, dressed up in her finery for the occasion. Her mother had been undeniably subservient to her father, and from the nervous expression on her young face, the subservience had started long before she had met him. It's a strange thing, Kate thought, putting the photograph down, how you think you know someone, yet when you lose them you start to see things you'd never noticed before. When she looked back on what she had witnessed of her mother's life, it seemed many of her mother's decisions were based on the conviction that she had never been good enough. It had probably been instilled in her long before that studio photograph had been taken.

Kate also wondered if that was partly why she pushed herself so hard, constantly wanting to overachieve. A work colleague had offered her advice once, saying it's important to be clear about your journey in life; otherwise, you're less likely to achieve your goals. There were times she questioned the nature versus nurture aspect of her upbringing, how much of her personality was genetic or learned. Lately, outside of work, and her love for her son, Charlie, the rest of her life seemed less clear. Whatever belief she may have had about her life being focused, especially when she and Declan were together, was long gone. Best to concentrate on getting through each day, she told herself – an aspiration, rather than a set path, that the answers would come to some of the many questions.

She opened the bottom drawer of her desk and brought out an old Tarot deck. It was a cheap copy, but it would suffice for her purposes. She pressed the record button for the third time. 'The Tarot card deck is made up of seventy-eight cards, of which fifty-six are over four suits, pentacles, wands, cups and swords. The Hangman card is one of the twenty-one Higher Arcana cards, along with the Fool at zero, completing the overall total of seventy-eight. Each card has its own individual meaning, and the interpretation of the card is influenced by those surrounding it in the spread. The spread is chosen by the Querent – the person seeking the reading.' Kate paused, thinking about her last words, then began again. 'Note. If the killer is the Querent, is the card part of a spread, and if so, how many cards are in it? What position does the Hangman hold? Are all the cards from the higher deck? The true meaning of the card may depend on other cards.'

She sat down at the desk, clicking the record button again. 'The likelihood of the killer having a history of violence is high, based on the level and organisation of the crime. A three-card spread could represent their past, present and future. Is the Hangman the middle card?' Stopping the recording, she fanned the deck in her hands, knowing the number of potential options was vast, dependent on size of spread and cards previously chosen. If the killing wasn't a one-off crime, had the cards been used before, and if so, where and when? What were the potential causes of or influences on gaps in time? Desire, stress, some form of payback or revenge? This case had never looked straightforward, but the more Kate thought about it, the bigger the haystack became.

She looked up at the clock again: 12.15 p.m. Mark Lynch would call at any moment. Pressing the record button for the last time, she put her final notes on the tape: 'Sexual and ritualistic influences of crime scene v. emotional dynamics. Several sexual inferences surround this case. Questions: Was sexual motivation the principal trigger? What other elements are at play? What is the emotional map inside the killer's head? Note: cause and effect require further exploration.

'The victim used the services of an escort, and was specific in his requirements, demonstrating a desire to dominate, to administer pain and draw blood, hers or his, a sexual fetish challenging the balance of control. Victim was also prepared to relinquish power, to become the punished – role-switching, opening up the possibility of victim having previously explored sexuality in groups, especially where role play is dependent on multiple partners.'

Turning off the recorder, she stared at the images on the laptop, considering the orchestration of the murder scene and the old adage that actions speak louder than words. Was it possible that whoever had killed Rick Shevlin had known he was alone, and had watched the prostitute leave? There had been no signs of forced entry. If the victim had known the killer, how close were they? What means did the killer use to gain access? Ian Morrison hadn't mentioned any needle points during his preliminaries. If a form of sedation had been used, it was taken orally, either under duress or with victim compliance. Was there a level of trust – a previous relationship?

The more she flicked through the images, the less sure she was of what she was looking for. Having segregated the photographs across categories, she examined close-up, distant and wide-angle shots of the room. Remembering what Morrison had said about the entry level of the knife attack, she re-examined the penetration points on the body. None of it was giving her anything new. She knew the method of killing was important, but so too was how the murderer had dealt with the body after death. There were no signs of panic or struggle. The whole process had taken time to orchestrate and follow through on – time the killer was prepared to invest. They had been careful in covering their tracks, coupled with the attention to detail, and the positioning of Rick Shevlin's body. How long had the killer remained in the room afterwards? Anger had played a part – no doubt about that. No one uses a knife in such a frenzied manner without a highly charged impetus. If the Hangman card was a signature, it had any number of meanings, but indecision, often associated with the card, wasn't one of them.

Flicking through the images again, she thought about being in the hotel room the previous morning. The sights and smells were still with her. She began noting as many sensory details as she could remember in the case file, imagining the killing happening during the hours of darkness. Then, the sights, sounds and smells would have been different from when she had stood in the room. Kate had leaned over the body in the way the killer might have done when giving the victim his last kiss. She might even have stood in the same spot. The connection, speculative though it was, made her feel as though she was grasping the threads of a spider's web long after the spider had left. Lost in thought, she jumped when her phone rang, but picked it up immediately. 'Mark, what do you have?'

'Morrison is still keeping his options open on cause of death, but he's confirmed substantial traces of toxins in the blood. Samples have been sent for analysis to get an exact breakdown. As suspected, the victim was tied up after death, the whip marks were made prior, and the slash and puncture wounds were definitely post-mortem.'

'Did he mention finding any needle points on the body?'

'No, why do you ask?'

'If Rick Shevlin was given drugs to knock him out, or reduce his defences, they must have been taken orally, opening up the possibility that he swallowed them willingly, and the existence of a previous relationship with the killer.'

'That would fit with the lack of forced entry.'

'And the killer being a woman.'

'You're still convinced we're looking for a female?'

'Yes, I am.'

'Well, Kate, Rick Shevlin may have been married, but he certainly wasn't monogamous. We have enough ex-girlfriends to keep us busy for a while.'

'Anything else come out of this morning's meeting?'

'It looks like the non-functioning of the CCTV cameras wasn't the only laidback thing about the hotel's security arrangements.'

'How so?'

'They operated on a key rather than a card system, keys attached to chunky gold rings with the room numbers engraved on them.'

'I guess it fits with the hotel's step-back-in-time image. Anything more on Rick Shevlin?'

'He moved in pretty elite circles, dealing in paintings, modern art for the most part, abstract.'

'Makes sense. Art dealers usually choose a specific form or period that works best for them.'

'That may be true, but Rick wasn't averse to the odd dabble in other types of deals.'

'What do you mean?'

'Apart from his small, profitable art gallery, rumour has it that it wasn't his main money spinner. Although the margins he took on the sale prices were high, compared to other galleries, every now and then he would make a big hit at auction.'

'I'm guessing it wasn't because he had a knack for spotting a bargain.'

'No. He liked to call in the help of a few stooges to rig things.'

'He put plants at the auction rooms to inflate prices?'

'Yeah, but it didn't end there. He had a long list of regular clients, but one of his ex-girlfriends told me he also sourced paintings for people on the lookout for something irregular.'

'Stolen?' Kate didn't attempt to hide her shock.

'Not stolen but, according to the ex-girlfriend, he gave the nod to fake work being original.'

'Wouldn't that have been noticed at the auction, or later?'

'He had his private sales too.'

'Can you prove any of this?'

'Not yet, but allegiances will start crumbling now that he's a dead Rick Shevlin.'

'That tells us a lot about him. It takes a certain type of person to extort large sums of money from people. His reputation would have given him credibility, but if he was prepared to commit serious fraud, it denotes a particular moral base.'

'Maybe the killer wanted to teach him a lesson for his greed.'

'I don't think money is a likely motive here, or if it is, it's only part of it.'

'Hold on a second, Kate. I have another call coming in.'

Kate's attention went back to the images on the laptop. She noted the various pieces of art work in the hotel room, most likely mass-produced copies. Was there anything of importance to the killer? She knew she was clutching at straws with a copy of a Monet. She recognised it as *Women in the Garden*, a scaled-down version of the original. When Monet had painted it, the canvas was so large he had had to work on the upper half with the lower section positioned in a dug-out trench, maintaining a single point of view. It was as she was thinking about the painting that her eye was drawn to another image, which showed the victim reflected in a side mirror of the dressing table. It framed him perfectly, the scale reduced because of the distance, but the image was set within the parameters of the frame, almost as if it was picture perfect.

'Kate, are you still there?'

'The dressing table in the hotel room, Mark. Was it moved?'

'How did you know? It was pulled out slightly from the wall on one side. I thought it might have been shifted as part of a struggle. One of the techies noticed the indents on the carpet from the more permanent position.'

'It wasn't moved because of a struggle, Mark. The killer adjusted the angle.'

'Meaning?'

'If I'm right, because she wanted to frame Rick Shevlin's reflection in the glass.'

'How can you be sure?'

'A photograph I took yesterday. From memory, I was standing at the windows … If the killer purposely formed a trajectory between the victim and the window, perfectly angling Rick Shevlin's dead body in the dressing-table mirror, she wanted to layer the scene, multiply and reproduce her deed.'

'I'm not getting you.'

'She isn't only creating a replica of the Hangman card. She's creating an image within an image.'

'Any idea as to why?'

'No – at least, not yet. I'll need you to double check the angle for me, to be completely sure, but this case is complicated. Our killer is extremely clever. Right now she is any number of steps ahead of us, and if I'm correct, unravelling this case won't be easy.'

PART 2

PART 2

SANDRA

I STARE AT my strained image in the bathroom mirror: I look like I've aged a hundred years. I pull the skin on my cheeks upwards, wondering about a facelift. *Who are you kidding?* I can't stop thinking about last night with Edgar. How I felt I was sleeping with a stranger.

It's already a quarter to eight, and the girls will be here soon. They'll sense something isn't right — they always do. Karen is like the proverbial bull in a china shop, shooting off at the mouth before her brain tells her otherwise. Lori is the opposite, quiet, nervous, but with the listening skills of an electronic device. But it's Alice I fear most. She can read me like a book. It's been the same since we were children. I bite my lip, pulling at my earlobe, the way I always do when I'm nervous.

I'd better put another bottle of white wine in the fridge, just in case – Sauvignon Blanc or Pinot Grigio? It's good to offer variety. *What's wrong with you? Your life is falling apart and all you can concentrate on is the stupid wine.*

I tell myself I have no real reason to doubt Edgar. Maybe it's all in my head. Sometimes I over-think things. Edgar says so all the time.

There's enough food in the fridge to feed the United Nations. Thank God for online shopping. I stare at the contents, wondering how to make space for the wine. I could take out last night's chicken or something else. I grab a carton of eggs and jump back as they crash to the floor. I push the wine bottle into the gap, slamming the door, before kneeling down to clear up the eggs. I need to settle my nerves. If I don't pull myself together, the girls will know for sure that something is wrong. But maybe if I talk about it, it won't seem so bad. It isn't only Edgar, though: it's all the other stuff I can't explain. I tug at my ear again, feeling it heat up some more.

Last night, I tossed and turned in the bed as if I had a fever. I had been thinking about Edgar being grumpy and evasive, wondering if that, too, was a tell-tale sign. I remembered a conversation I'd had with Karen – when she was having that affair with the Italian guy. She said it was easier to be grumpy when she got home: it was the best way to hide how ecstatic she felt inside. Anger took the smile off her face, keeping her husband's suspicions at bay. You wouldn't think Karen was the affair type, especially as she includes married men. I don't know how she carries it off. I couldn't. Perhaps it's like one side of her life is denying the other. It's ten years since we became roommates. We were in our twenties then, long before either of us got hitched. *But now that you might be the wife whose husband is having an affair, are you quite so forgiving? Didn't think so!*

I pour a glass of wine and empty it in one go. 'Take it easy,' I mutter. 'You don't have any proof – not yet.' There's that voice again: *Trust your instincts, Sandra. He's being too careful, giving nothing away.* I check myself again in the hall mirror. My ear looks as red as a hot poker. I fiddle with my hair, pulling it over my ear. Jesus, I look awful. The girls are sure to guess, especially Alice – she's practically psychic. *Do you know what you look like, Sandra? A withered plant that's been severed at its stem.*

Edgar was cool this morning, especially when I asked him why he was doing so many late hours. He said he hadn't realised he was, and asked me if I felt he was ignoring me, sounding so sincere. I could have asked him then, come straight out with it. *Are you having an affair?* I didn't. He offered to come home early this evening, said the two of us could have a romantic evening together, that he would do the cooking. Had he remembered the girls were coming over? Was that why he was so eager to offer, knowing I would refuse? He told me how beautiful I was, that he didn't tell me often enough, that, like most men, he was a fool when it came to such things. I muttered, 'Liar,' under my breath, and he must have sensed my mood, because instead of kissing me goodbye on the lips, he kissed me on the cheek, then hugged me. It wasn't a sensual hold, more like misguided comfort. He said something about me enjoying a productive day in the studio. Thank God he hasn't been inside. He'd know I haven't done any work in weeks. What else did he say? My mind is such a muddle.

Damn it, what's keeping the girls? Karen is always early. I think about Alice again, how her silences often say more than her words. A while back, I'd wondered about her and Edgar, if there was something going on between them. I had put it down to jealousy on my part, her being so damn attractive. Maybe I should have cancelled tonight, but if I had, it would have brought on a tsunami of questions. The interrogation would have begun with gusto. Phone calls back and forth, probably talking to each other behind my back. They've done that before.

My right hand shakes as I refill my glass. I've no intention of having a second drink so soon. Best to wait until at least one of them arrives, and even then I need to take it slow.

It's ten past eight, but it's still bright out. Maybe I should set up a table in the garden. Wear dark sunglasses to hide my eyes. *You're being ridiculous.*

The sound of the doorbell is almost a relief. No more time to think. I know it's Karen even before I reach the door – her familiar ring, two short blasts, then a final long one.

'Isn't the weather bliss?' she says. 'Are the others here yet?'

'No, you're the first. Come in. You look great.'

'Thanks. You look awful. What's up?' She plonks her replica Louis Vuitton bag under the hall table, the one she told us about the last time we had a girlie get-together. She got it as a bargain on a package holiday to Portugal. Nobody mentioned it being a cheap copy. Some people might think we're an odd bunch, the way we pretend nothing has changed since our twenties. It's partly why our relationship survives. We ignore material differences, avoid mentioning that some of us are far better off financially than others, and even though we don't always agree,

I guess, over the years, we've managed to be there for each other in our own wacky way.

'Nothing's up. I'm tired, that's all,' I say.

'I have the cure.' She holds up a pink carrier bag with two bottles. 'Thirsty work, this talking business.'

I laugh. *Keep up the show*. The bell rings again. This time there's two of them, Alice and Lori. Alice stands closest to the door, her blue eyes and blonde hair perfect as always. Lori is like a demure dark pixie, her ebony hair tied tight behind her. They look like chalk and cheese.

'Come in.' I plaster a smile across my face. 'Karen's already here.'

'Have you been drinking? Your chest is blotchy, and you look awful.' Alice skips past me with Lori in tow.

'Just the one.'

'I already told her she looks dreadful,' Karen says, coming out from the kitchen with four empty wine glasses. She holds them upside-down between her fingers. I can hear them clink against one another, and for an instant I remember seeing broken glass on the floor earlier but I can't recall why.

'Be careful,' I say. 'I think there might be some glass on the floor.'

'Where?' asks Lori. 'I'll clear it up.'

'I'm not sure. My head is all over the place today.'

'Don't worry about it,' says Alice, sounding confident and in charge. 'It's not like we're going to kick off our heels out here in the hall.'

'No, probably not,' I say, but inside my head, I hear that voice again, *Get it together*. 'What would you all like to drink? I've three bottles of wine cooling in the fridge.'

'I'm sticking to red,' says Lori. 'White gives me heartburn.'

'I thought that was only Chardonnay,' pipes Karen, as she places the four glasses on the coffee table in the lounge.

'She's moved on,' says Alice, 'dismissing all the world's wines unless they're blood red. Isn't that right, Lori?'

'Stop it.' Then, more tentatively, Lori says, 'You do have red, don't you, Sandra? It's okay if you don't.'

'Of course I do. Edgar always has a good supply.'

'Good old Edgar.' Alice slips in a mocking dig.

'Give it a rest, Alice,' says Karen. 'You're just jealous you don't have a husband like Edgar.' Her tone is more teasing than critical.

'Having a husband is overrated. I keep telling you that. You fall in love, get married, fall out of love, get married again or have an affair. It's a vicious circle, reliving the same old Greek tragedy.' She looks coyly at Karen. 'Most people lumber their way through life without knowing why they do things.' Then, remembering Lori's recent separation, she adds, 'I don't mean you, Lori.'

'I know.'

'He didn't deserve you,' Karen pipes in again.

'As Alice says,' musters Lori, 'having a husband is overrated.'

'Good,' replies Alice. 'I'd hate us to fall out before we have the wine.'

I had managed to put out a display of canapés, olives and a large cheeseboard with grapes in the kitchen. I ask Karen to give me a hand carrying things through. She likes being busy, and is happy to oblige. She is standing beside me when I look down at the cheeseboard and see the large carving knife. Why did I put it there? It's not suitable for cheese. Then I remember the eggs dropping from the fridge – did I take out the knife after that?

'What the matter?' she asks. 'You look like you've seen a ghost.'

'I could have sworn …'

'What?'

'Nothing. Will you get the cheese knives from the utility?'

'Sure.' But as she opens the door of the utility, she calls, 'Have you moved them, Sandra? I don't see them in the usual place.'

'I don't think so.' I follow her inside.

'They have to be in here somewhere,' she says.

'They must be.' My hands are shaking. I want to say: They're not the only things I've noticed being moved.

'There they are,' she roars, pointing to the counter where I usually store the extra spices. 'You shouldn't leave them out like that,' she scolds. 'They'll get dusty, and you'll have to keep rinsing them before you use them.'

'Yes, stupid of me. Give them here and I'll clean them.'

It's not long before we're all chatting in the lounge. The conversation is free-flowing, just as it is every time we meet, even back in the day when we shared a dingy flat in the centre of town. I have candles lighting the room, half a dozen at the fireplace. The house is warm with the under-floor heating on, now the evenings are getting chillier. Lori kicks off her shoes, moving her feet backwards and forwards on the travertine tiles.

'I love the heat coming from the floor,' she says.

'It's only a floor, Lori. Don't get too excited,' Alice barks.

'Why do you always need to criticise?' Karen hits back.

'I'm not. I'm simply making an observation.'

'Whatever,' Karen retorts. Then, standing up to pour another glass of wine, she asks me, 'Where's Edgar this evening?'

'I'm not sure.' I never asked him where he'd be.

'That's strange.' She settles on the couch.

'Maybe he's having an affair,' suggests Lori, the wine going straight to her head.

'He probably can't help himself,' sniggers Karen, 'with all us promiscuous women around.'

This is your moment, I say to myself. What's stopping you? He could be with the other woman now.

'You're very quiet, Sandra.' Alice gives me one of her looks. 'For Heaven's sake, stop biting that bloody lip of yours.'

I don't reply. I can't make out her face in the candlelight. I feel the others, too, are sensing something is wrong. I swallow a generous mouthful of Sauvignon Blanc, waiting a few more seconds. *The longer you wait, the harder it will be to retreat. Think of something else to say, fool them, or tell them.*

'Am I?' I reply, but they're not buying it.

'Sandra?' I hear the note in Alice's voice that tells me she won't let it go.

'What's wrong?' Lori moves forward on the couch. So does Karen.

Say it – go on. I take another sip of my wine. 'Edgar is having an affair.'

It's Lori's turn to swallow more wine.

'How can you be so sure?' Alice's words are delivered in slow motion.

'I can't be completely sure,' I reply, 'not really.'

'Jesus Christ,' says Karen. 'Do you know who he's shagging?'

I can't look at any of them. Maybe if I stop talking about it, it will all go away, become some sick joke. Their brief silence will be followed by a tidal wave. There is no going back now. I notice my glass is tilted. Some wine spills onto my lap, trickling down my leg. 'I think she's been here, the other woman, in this house – moving things.'

OCEAN HOUSE, THE QUAYS

IT WAS THREE weeks to the day since the discovery of Rick Shevlin's body in the Earlbrook Hotel, and it had seemed that the investigation had stalled, until now. Kate contemplated the phone call from Mark Lynch. He had told her more than the latest development in the case. He had told her that DI O'Connor would be back on duty, active in the investigation, from the following day. She knew she'd sat on the fence for long enough. She hadn't contacted him, which would make things awkward, but she was relieved he was back on board. Lynch was confident, but he didn't have O'Connor's experience. All she had to do was phone O'Connor – simple. So, what was stopping her? She'd grown emotionally close to him during the last investigation –

too close. Making contact might open the can of worms she had tried to keep shut. But still, she rang his number.

He answered immediately. 'Hello, stranger,' he said.

She noticed a cold edge to his words. 'It's been a while, all right. I hear you're back tomorrow.'

Silence.

'Will you be working on the Shevlin investigation?' She already knew he would be, although Lynch would remain as the senior officer. Still, there was nothing like asking a direct question to get an answer.

'I will. It's an interesting case.'

His words were still guarded, but at least they were on safe ground. She hesitated, then said, 'Maybe it would be a good idea to talk through the broad outlines. I could meet you after the ten o'clock briefing at Harcourt Street in the morning.'

'It's probably best if you call here. Tomorrow will be manic. I'll text you the address, but don't expect a palace.' He paused. 'Let's say in an hour.'

'Listen, O'Connor, I'm sorry I haven't been in touch.'

'Don't worry about it.' His words still sounded clipped.

Hanging up, she regretted agreeing to meet him at his place, but her guilt about not being in touch gave him the upper hand. When her phone bleeped with his text, she jumped. There was no going back now, not without making things worse.

∞

The address in Reginald Street wasn't far from Ocean House, located on the far side of the quays, deep in the heart of the Liberties, an area of Dublin dating back to the seventeenth century.

She had never thought about where O'Connor lived, but there was something almost desolate about the house when she reached it. The front door was painted a dark, depressing shade of green, and although all three windows to the front of the artisan dwelling had curtains, each was different. This was Flatland, she thought, a small house, subdivided into apartments the size of dog kennels. She heard him bounding down the staircase well before he opened the door.

'Step into my humble abode.' He was still distinctly cool.

She followed him to his flat on the first floor at the back of the house. It was small, but compact, and brighter than she'd expected, a sash window giving an attractive view of the city. 'Nice and cosy.' She smiled.

'I don't need much.'

She took in the contents of the room. A narrow kitchen, a small wooden table, two chairs, a sofa facing a portable flat-screen TV, and a walled unit with newspapers scattered across the top. There were two other doors, which she assumed led to a bathroom and a bedroom.

'Great view,' she commented, as he put on the kettle.

'I'd charge people to visit, but I doubt the landlord would like me turning his place into a tourist attraction.'

'I guess not.' She smiled again. She needed to talk about the case, but first she had to deal with unfinished business. 'I meant what I said – that I was sorry for not being in touch. I know I was the one who encouraged you to come clean, before the suspension.'

'I came clean, as you call it, because it was the right thing to do, not because of anyone else.'

'I know that, but still.'

He slammed the cups on the table. 'It's been six months, Kate. A phone call wouldn't have taken a lot.'

'That works both ways.'

'You're right there, but then again, you're always right.'

He didn't sound in a forgiving mood, she thought, as he placed a stainless-steel teapot, a carton of milk and a bowl of sugar on the table. Best to move the conversation to safer ground.

'You know the initial autopsy report confirmed Rick Shevlin was administered sedatives prior to his death, enough to knock out a horse. They would have rendered him defenceless within minutes.'

'So I heard from my enthusiastic replacement. I also heard that you believe the killer is female, and the connection to the Tarot cards is some kind of signature.'

'Our killer likes to play with mirrors, duplicating the crime scene, and the image of the Hangman card.' She took the card out of her bag and handed it to O'Connor.

'It's the number twelve. Is that of any consequence?'

'It could be. Some of this is in my report, which no doubt you'll get to see tomorrow. The card represents acceptance, renunciation and the forming of a new point of view, although a clear interpretation can only be made when it's seen with the other cards in the spread.'

'How many cards are in a spread?'

'Minimum of three, but it could be more.'

He looked at the card again. 'And we're not talking about a novice here?'

'Unlikely. And she is getting more out of the scene than the killing itself. The level of attack suggests heightened anger, determination and detachment.'

'Not a pleasant cocktail, Kate.'

'No, it isn't.'

'You sound like this case is getting under your skin.'

His tone was mellowing. Maybe this wouldn't be as difficult as she'd initially thought. 'There must have been an enormous level of hurt and emotional damage to drive someone to this, especially a woman.'

'Are you still seeing the good in the bad guys?'

'Some people are more mad than bad.'

'Maybe so, but pardon me for feeling more sympathy for the corpse than the killer.' He stood up from the table and went to the window. 'Christ, I'm looking forward to getting back to work.'

'How do you feel about working under Mark Lynch?'

'Probably as happy as he feels about working with me.'

'Will he look on you as a threat, do you think?'

'The force is full of egos, Kate. Now, tell me more about this killer.'

'Whoever she is, she's particular. The way she sets the scene is almost as if she is creating a piece of artwork. It tells us she takes pride in what she does. She has an ego. All of this is important to her. She is precise in her goal and her disposition of it, but the attack and the aftermath must be viewed as two separate components. There was a stressor of some kind, but she has an ability to detach. Once she'd slit the victim's throat, and released her rage, there was no remorse shown. Most likely she enjoyed the aftermath. Rick Shevlin was no longer a person to her. He became part of the image she desired.'

'Not someone you'd want to get friendly with, then?'

'As I said in my report, with that level of detachment, whoever did this is capable of giving the illusion that they live a normal life, meaning they will be able to integrate socially. We're looking at someone with intelligence in the higher percentile, ninety-five per cent or more, who has the presence of mind to calculate, to prepare, to keep her head level and be emotionally controlled when required. She is patient in completing her tasks, no matter how long that takes. As I said to Mark at the start of all this, the killer won't be easy to find.' She paused.

'And he's got nothing from any of the ex-girlfriends either?' His response sounded like a judgement.

'No, but now we have a new development. He thinks he's found another victim, an old case.'

'When did you hear that?'

'About an hour ago, before I phoned you.'

'Go on.'

'The case is outside the jurisdiction.'

'Where?'

'Paris, nine years ago.'

I

I'M SURE I have her rattled now, the little wife. She's like his face of respectability, his security, a form of adult comfort blanket. Deep down he, too, is insecure. That is why most men like to have their cake and eat it – sexual satisfaction aligned with emotional stability, but not always with the same person or at the same time.

I enjoy the feeling that we share something she doesn't know about. It's more intimate – being a secret. She doesn't bring excitement into his life any more, not the way I do. I've learned over time to be a good receptor, knowing exactly what I want. I don't meander.

I made another self-portrait today. I hadn't planned to, but

I found myself in a small grocery shop close to their house and caught sight of my reflection in one of those round security mirrors at the top of the store, the kind that obscures your shape, taking in as much floor space as possible. There was a man beside me reading the ingredients on a cereal box. I usually take my images in black-and-white. Colour is a distraction. The eye, the human eye, sees the world predominately in black-and-white, with endless grey scales. You think when you take a photograph you're capturing everything, but you're not. Parts go missing. With the human eye, our mind fills in the gaps. I like that the camera cuts to a kind of truth, the obscurities you create when you look in the mirror exposed. Yet no camera has the capabilities of the human brain: each has its own imperfections and deceptions.

In the self-portrait, I look small in the space, the image bringing me to an old memory, a photograph taken on a trip to Dublin, another reflection in a shop window. It was in O'Connell Street. I was seventeen. When I studied the image afterwards, I was surprised because I looked happy – my cheeks glowing, my pupils alert, my lips stretching to the point of a smile. The more I stared at the photograph, the more I saw. You see, I hadn't realised a part of me was smiling. The camera can do that: it can tell you things you didn't know.

Last night, I stood on their front lawn looking at the house, my shape caught in shadow. Everything was quiet and utterly still. There were no lights coming from the windows. I imagined her upstairs, perhaps peering out into the dark at nothing in particular. I visualised the troubled look on her face, part of her already knowing of my presence, and I could almost taste her fear.

They have a pretty house with a stone fountain tucked away at the end of their back garden. I laughed out loud when I looked at the two figurines, a little boy and girl — I named them the stone children. He has already spoken about her being infertile. He didn't want to talk about it at first, but then the floodgates opened. I had to fake empathy, having no interest in his whimpering. It intrigued me, though, her putting a permanent reminder of what she cannot have so close. I decided to play a little game with the fountain. I placed pebbles from the drive in the bottom of the stone basin. When I did, the water ricocheted with tiny spatters into the bowl. I enjoy making subtle changes to a place I visit. It's like leaving a mark. She might wonder about the pebbles, do a double take and ponder on the unexplained.

When she's nervous, she tends to get flustered, fiddling with things. She can't help it. Depending on what she wears, she can display that pretty-girl-next-door appearance, the kind of woman many men end up marrying. The attractiveness appeals to them sexually, while conjuring up goodness and potential home-making, prize maternal qualities for their offspring — sow your seed, reproduce yourself. I don't want children. One of me in the world is enough.

I don't doubt that men find her attractive and, on occasions, some may have allowed their imaginations to take flight, visualising a little fun, but they would never cross the line, not with her. She's not the type. Women see much more than men when it comes to the fairer sex. Men can be foolish in that department.

I've been playing other games with her too — moving things around the house, putting objects in places they don't belong. A few days ago I dropped an empty water bottle on their smooth lawn and placed flower petals near the front door, petals that couldn't have come from their garden.

She might have dismissed the water bottle as something left by a passer-by. It might have caused her to complain about people being sloppy and uncaring, but the petals, I would imagine, perplexed her. The inexplicable will cause anxiety. I don't want to frighten her too much – at least, not yet. For now, it's a bit like stepping into another person's life with the ability to make alterations along the way.

I have my own woman in the shadows, waiting for her time to pounce. She warns me not to get too confident and relishes my mistakes. She would have got a nice kick out of the failed Rick affair. At times I call my hunched shadow 'the witch'. She reared me, but she wasn't my mother. My real mother died in childbirth, aged fifteen. For a long time, I thought my life had taken hers. It isn't easy, believing your first breaths in this world killed another – especially when she was the person who gave you your life. It sets you up for being different. I discovered later that most of what I had been told was a lie. It wasn't me who killed her. She'd died because of abandonment, and because the woman in the shadows wanted it to be that way.

I never knew my mother, but part of me believed that she would be pleased if I killed the witch. I had thought the witch's death would end her control. I was wrong. It gave her cruelty greater power. I still remember her laughing in my face, telling me about burning my mother's body, calling her a whore, saying she was desperate for it, like some wild boar. I'm not looking for your sympathy. I understand the pleasures of the witch, and I know now she will never leave me. She will always be close by – my darkest shadow.

There are some things I have in common with my new lover's wife, one being that I cannot conceive either. Once I had a notion of having a child. I tried to visualise what they would look like. Would they have my hair, eye colouring, my high forehead? I suppose my lover's wife asked those questions too, but that is where our similarities end. I cannot comprehend her life, and she cannot envisage mine. I'm the one having sex with her husband, the one allowing him to do the things he wants to do, things she cannot contemplate. She is alien to me, and soon she will be alien to him.

The important thing about those who live ordinary lives is that they rarely think outside the box. They feel safe, and in their safety, they are most at risk. Would you warn her if you could? Or would you wait around to see what other games I have in store? Fear is a powerful thing, you must agree. Fear is like the eye of the camera: it obscures things. You will need to remember that point. It might prove to be important later.

REGINALD STREET, THE LIBERTIES

ALTHOUGH O'CONNOR WASN'T due back in work until the following day, his mind slotted into investigator mode when Kate mentioned the Parisian killing. 'This case, nine years ago,' his voice was animated, 'what are the similarities to Rick Shevlin's killing?'

'We have another male victim, Pierre Laurent, this time in his mid-twenties. He had a link to the art world – a student specialising in fine art. The body was also found in a hotel room. Again there were knife injuries, but that's not all.'

'Don't tell me he was laid out the same way as Shevlin?'

'The body was positioned differently. According to Mark Lynch, he was wearing a hooded robe.'

'So?' O'Connor seemed sceptical.

'The Parisian police initially thought the killing had religious inferences, the victim being dressed as a monk, but they also considered an association with the Tarot, the Hermit card in particular. It didn't lead them anywhere, but it was that link to the Tarot, and the belief on the part of the French police, albeit tentative, that the killer was female that has sparked Mark's interest about a connection between that case and the current murder.'

'Lynch did well, although not without your help. What else did he tell you about the Parisian investigation?'

'There was a candlelit lantern on a side table beside the victim's body. It didn't belong to the hotel, so it's likely the killer placed it there, especially if they were replicating the card.'

'And its meaning?'

'It's interpreted as a time of introspection, an inner search or reflection. If this is the same killer, it creates a pattern. We could have two cards within an overall spread. The difficulty is less about interpreting the individual cards, and more about working out what the overall spread looks like. The murder of Pierre Laurent happened nine years ago. That's a long time for a killer to be inactive. But the use of the cards may be her way of telling us she's on some kind of journey.'

'What do you mean?'

'The Tarot is seen as reflective of a life path. Everything is viewed within the context of your past, how it forms the person you are in the present, and moving on from there, the current mind-set and future of the Querent—'

'The Querent?' He sounded slightly baffled.

'The person who seeks the reading from the cards. The current mind-set is what the Querent believes will happen next versus what the cards predict, which can be contradictory.'

'I don't get you.'

'Do you have a deck of cards?'

'Yeah, somewhere.' He pulled open one of the doors in the walled unit, behind which were books, CDs, DVDs and other bits. It didn't take him long to find the cards.

Kate took the deck as he sat down, shuffling them. 'Let's say we're looking at a six-card spread and, believe me, there are many variations.' She tidied the cards neatly together. 'I've been thinking about a Celtic-cross spread.'

'Why?'

'It's a modification that arose over continental Europe, which would fit for most jurisdictions.' She placed a five of diamonds face up on the table. 'The A card,' she pointed to the five of diamonds, 'represents you – it's at the centre.' She placed the queen of spades over the first card, forming a cross. 'This card, the crossing or issue card, represents the crux of the issue.'

'How come you know so much about the Tarot?'

'As I told Mark Lynch, I studied them for an investigation in the UK.'

'I don't know about this.'

'Stick with me for a few minutes.' She positioned a third card to the far left of the other two, the three of hearts. 'This is the limitation card, the potential snag in your plans. It can represent your past, a challenging mother injecting defeatist thoughts …' her mind slipped back to her own mother, and how her lack of self-belief may have been formed because of her grandmother's harshness '… but, like the others, it's open to different interpretations.' Placing another card top centre, she continued, 'The crowning or conscious card represents what you can control, and the unconscious card, which I'm placing at the bottom centre, is the killer's unconscious or subconscious awareness. It's the part of them they're mindful of, an inner voice or layer that they recognise it would be foolish to ignore.' The final card she positioned to the far right of the first card. 'This card represents what is likely to occur in the future. It is not the final outcome, simply the next step on the journey.'

'How is this of any use to us?'

'If our killer is dealing with an issue, something deep set, possibly influenced by limitations from their past, they are acutely aware of the things they can control and, coupled with that, they have a perceived outcome in their mind. Everything stems from what went before. It's the same with all human behaviour. The past forms the present and, carrying on from there, an individual's future. If our killer is on a journey, and a concrete link to the Parisian case can be made, whatever happened in Paris nine years ago happened for a specific reason. It is also possible that the image created at each of the crime scenes is telling us something about the killer's current mind-set.'

'Which can change over time?'

'Precisely. The depiction of the Hermit card could be the killer's way of saying they were ready to retreat, adopting the life of the card through introspection and solitude.'

'Kate, you said the Hangman reflected acceptance or the forming of a new point of view.'

'Yes.'

'Then Rick Shevlin's murder could be the end of the road for our killer. They could be accepting their fate.'

'Or they could be moving on, looking in a completely different direction.'

'I don't know …' He stood up, almost agitated. 'The way I see it, the big issue is not whether or not these crime scenes are messages from the killer, but the fact that we could be dealing with a murderer who has operated undetected for a long time and isn't geographically contained.'

'O'Connor, I'll be honest with you. I have my reservations about Mark handling this case. He can be over-zealous to say the least.'

'Letting the power go to his head, is he?'

'Something like that.'

'Well, from tomorrow morning, whether he likes it or not, he'll be stuck with me.'

Kate noted the bitterness in his words. There wasn't a whole lot more to add, and it was only when she walked towards the door to leave that she noticed the photograph to the side of the flat-screen TV. It was of a teenage boy. His resemblance to O'Connor was undeniable. Without thinking, she picked it up. 'Who's this?'

Taking it from her, he placed it on the unit in the exact same spot. 'He's my son. His name is Adam.'

'A good, strong name.' She knew to tread carefully.

'It's my name too.'

She waited.

'I suppose you're wondering why I've never mentioned him.'

'You don't owe me an explanation.'

'Don't I?'

'You must have had your reasons for not saying anything.'

He gestured for her to sit down again, then sat opposite, putting the cards spread out on the table back into their pack.

'His mother and I separated a number of years ago. It was before I joined the force. We were very young. *I* was very young.' He placed his hands, palms down, on the table, his fingers spreadeagled. 'I could say a lot of things, Kate, but none of them would matter, except that I was stupid and selfish.'

'Do you ever speak to him, your son?'

'I made contact with him after I was placed on suspension.' He leaned back in the chair, this time pushing his fingers through his hair, as if he was trying to think clearly. For the first time, Kate noticed how tired he looked.

'He didn't want to know me. I thought time would help, but I'm afraid I screwed up big-time. I wasn't there when he needed me.' He kicked the leg of the table nearest to him. 'I fucked up.'

Kate thought about Charlie, how things had become difficult now it was obvious she and Declan would never get back together. Even at six years of age, Charlie carried his own baggage – *Why is Daddy not living with us any more? Does he not love us?* No amount of explanations could help him understand the *why* behind the three of them not being together.

'We all mess up, Adam. Is it okay if I call you that?'

'It's my name.'

'How come you stopped using it?'

'I couldn't bear to hear it. Every time someone said it, it was a reminder …' He looked at the photograph and away from her.

'I understand.'

'Do you, Kate? Because I sure as hell don't.'

'What about his mother? Do you two talk?'

'She is solid. She always was. She isn't the kind to hold a grudge, but she's told me not to expect miracles.'

Kate placed her right hand on his arm, not knowing what to say next. Looking at him, she wasn't sure if she saw anger, hate or confusion. Again, she waited. If she had learned anything over the years of counselling it was the importance of being a listener.

'I'm fond of you, Kate. You know that?'

She took her hand away. 'Yes, I do.'

'Us working together again, it could bring its own problems – depending on how we want to take it from here.'

'And how do you want to take it?' Part of her realised she was asking him to take the lead.

'I've already laid my cards on the table.' He placed one hand over the deck.

'I don't rush into things,' she said, 'with Charlie to consider.'

He smiled, but it wasn't the kind of smile that filled her with warmth. 'I guess that's where we differ, Kate. You're the patient one, considering all aspects before taking a chance.'

'There's nothing wrong with that.'

'No, there isn't, but at some point we all have to take a risk for what we want.'

Was he waiting for her to make the next move? She wanted to touch him, to show how she felt. Instead, she said, 'Can you give me more time?'

He reached out and stroked her cheek. The roughness of his

skin felt good. 'I guess some things in life are worth waiting for.'

She wanted to kiss him, more than she had ever wanted to before. It would be the easiest thing in the world to feel her lips on his. If she made the next move, he would take over, and the real reason, outside the investigation, for her being there would be reduced to two people wanting each other.

SANDRA

I REGURGITATE LAST night's conversation with the girls. They had all fussed when I said about Edgar being unfaithful, and how someone had been moving things around the house – everyone, except Alice.

Karen wanted to know if we were still doing it. She took my lack of response as a bad sign, as did Lori. I could tell from their faces that they knew the truth, even though they kept rabbiting on. Alice said I had no real proof, I could have imagined it all. I hated the way I instantly went to defend myself, like I had to pass a test with her. With her, at times, I feel I'm being examined under a microscope, needing to prove myself. I told her I didn't need proof, but even in her silence, she had the upper hand.

Karen poured me another glass of wine. Lori got tissues from the bathroom. I sat with a towel on my lap, fidgeting, nervous, ready to tell them everything.

I told them how Edgar had been retreating, pulling back from me. My voice had that desperate shrill tone, especially when I mentioned things being moved around the house, and how I was writing things down, small incidentals at first, like that time I thought I saw a woman's shadow in the garden, or the objects being moved from one place to another. Alice raised her eyebrows, and there was no denying her cynicism. The others gave me reassuring smiles, as if they wanted to believe me but weren't quite buying it. I shifted the emphasis to Edgar. It was safer ground. I explained how I had noted all the extra hours he had spent at work, the events he'd told me he needed to attend, with invitations for one.

Karen and Lori were like sponges, soaking it all up, but Alice wasn't letting go: Edgar was an international jewellery designer, with any number of rich and elite clients who wanted to meet him now his commercial range had taken off. I stopped listening after a while. I knew what they were thinking. That I had been unwell of late. Edgar had called it a bout of depression and said I was getting things mixed up because of the medication. All I needed was time out to recharge. No one called it a breakdown – but that's what they were all thinking. Lori said she understood about Edgar. Karen said all men were bastards. Alice looked wary.

When I told them about him visiting strange sites on the internet, Karen thought he was using it to see porn. It wasn't that, or not exactly. All three took notice when I explained about the internet dating site, and how the laptop in the study had been acting up, the one Edgar used when he was working from home. How I was working on it one afternoon when the whole thing crashed. I thought we'd lost everything so I phoned the girl we'd met at our school reunion, Marjorie, the computer geek. She talked me through rebooting it in safe mode, and afterwards suggested doing a few more background checks and defragmenting the hard drive. Alice got tetchy then, telling me to get to the bloody point, but I kept going.

I explained that it wasn't long before Marjorie suggested clearing the cookies. I didn't want to clear them all in one go. I thought there might be something important there, something Edgar might need. Instead I trawled through the links line by line, working out which ones were okay to delete. That was when I saw the first site link, and then, like a message you don't want to read, it repeated itself over and over, as the words Cassie4Casanova kept reappearing on the screen.

I

ALONG WITH THE eye of the camera, I'm keen on another eye: the inner eye of self. I like Rudyard Kipling's poem about the road through the woods, the one that is no longer there. The road is hidden by time past, weather and rain, with trees planted over it. But it still exists, underneath, where only the keeper sees it, and if you listen hard, you can hear the horse's hoofs, and the swish of a female rider's skirt on the old lost road. That hidden road is part of me.

I want you to imagine something. I want you to imagine that you see children playing in the park, pre-school children. There are swings and slides and climbing frames. The playground is colourful, and the sky is clear and blue. You can feel the heat of the sun on your face. There are parents too, huddled in groups. Can you see them all now? Perhaps you hear laughter or the sound of the swings swishing back and forth. I see something else. I hear other things. I see the children as if they are asleep. Their eyes are closed. They might be dreaming. The sky is turning dark, and I'm in the shadows. As I stare at the swings, their ropes fray, the seats break. When I turn to look at the slides, children's bodies lie in a heap at the bottom, on top of one another, like bags of grain. The climbing frame surrounding the playground locks everyone in. The image of the inner eye is disturbing, don't you think? It distorts things. It makes good things bad and bad things good. I've learned to do both. I've had to. My life is often in the shadows, but it constantly seeks escape to the light.

I remember an afternoon a long time ago. It had been raining. One moment the sky was clear, and then, without warning, it was thunderous, loud, dark and threatening, as if the heavens were angry. Things began to change, like the children in the playground. I found myself standing in a place I had no memory of. I looked for the familiar, something to make sense of the new. I realised slowly that, no matter how hard I tried, I wouldn't be able to find my way back to where I was before.

I wasn't alone and, like the road in the woods, the one that can't be seen, the person lurking in the shadows was hidden to me. But they were watching, following me, counting each breath I took. The woman in the shadows comes to me at moments of anxiety. Her presence is like an all-consuming claw, pulling me to her.

I didn't know what to do. If I stayed still, she would trap me, but if I ran, I might become more lost. Again, I had the feeling that what was happening was happening to someone else, that I was detached, broken. I began humming, loud and clear, trying to convince myself that I hadn't vanished, that I was still alive. I willed the clouds to clear, and the road home to reappear. Even when I heard louder noises coming from behind, leaves swishing, twigs snapping, I kept a steady pace until the rain came, fast and furious. I ran to the rhythm of Nature's wrath until finally the landscape altered again and small things became familiar.

When I looked back, all I could see was a dark mass, towering high. For a split second, I wondered if I'd imagined it all, until I saw her, the hunched shadowy figure, like an old bear. There have been times recently when I've wondered if I've become that dark shadow. Has she become part of me? I follow people too, meddling in their lives. And now my new lover has become the most promising of them all, and one way or another, we will play out our merry dance together.

HARCOURT STREET STATION, SPECIAL DETECTIVE UNIT

MATCHING THE CURRENT investigation to a similar murder across Europe had initially felt to Mark Lynch like trawling through an entire telephone directory armed with only part of a contact name. Certainly, the concentration on a female killer, the type of weapon used and the hotel-room location had reduced the odds considerably, but although he was still dubious about the Tarot connection, it had been the linchpin for the shift in focus to the Parisian killing.

With that cold case unfolding, another commonality was obvious. Both Rick Shevlin and Pierre Laurent had been killed in capital cities, and the hotel rooms were distinctly opulent. If there were other unsolved cases, narrowing the remit mightn't be enough due to the population density of capital cities. It was only when he had finished talking to Kate earlier that morning that news of another potential international connection came in. This time it was nothing to do with her analysis but, rather, something Rick Shevlin's wife had omitted when she was first interviewed. She had been slow to tell the family liaison officer, Claire Boyd, about it, but with three weeks of trust under her belt, Anita Shevlin finally confided her suspicion that she thought she was being stalked prior to her husband's death. Initially, she told herself she was being ridiculous, underestimating the relevance. The potential stalking added a new dimension: it led him to another case on the Europol database, of a murdered Italian businessman, this time in Rome. Again, it was a hotel-room location, but the wife of the victim, who was present during the attack, had survived, and she, too, suspected she was being stalked. Nothing was carved in stone at this point, but coming three weeks after practically nothing in the investigation, Lynch wasn't going to stall in contacting Alfredo Masciarelli of the Polizia di Stato in Rome. Thankfully, Masciarelli spoke excellent English, cutting down potential language barriers. Having talked through the Dublin and Paris murder investigations, Lynch asked, 'Can we rely on your full co-operation?'

'But of course. However, the senior investigating officer on the case you mention retired a year ago. His name is Andrea Giordano. He is a man with an insatiable memory. You can certainly view the full police report, but Andrea was an old style of investigator, and his nose was usually extremely close to whatever case he was involved with. It would be good if you spoke with him, but I will need to track him down. In the meantime, we can run through the standard procedures and I will forward whatever we have here.'

Before Lynch could respond, Masciarelli had disconnected. Round one to the Italian, he thought. The next call he made was to Chief Superintendent Gary Egan. The daily briefings were one thing, but Lynch liked the personal, direct approach, rather than sharing key information in a crowded room.

'It's still early days, Mark, but if these cases are solidly connected, we have a major international investigation on our hands.'

'I realise that, Boss, and I plan to talk to Andrea Giordano sooner rather than later.'

'Steady on. You can't be everywhere at the one time. You do know O'Connor is due back tomorrow?'

'Of course.' The detective's imminent return didn't fill Lynch with joy, but he held back, not wanting the chief super to think he was threatened by it.

'Listen, O'Connor has a lot of experience in this area, especially from his involvement a few years back in that European paedophile ring. He's a good, solid man to have in your corner.'

He wondered if Egan had sensed his reluctance. 'I realise that. He's a bit raw, though, having been out for months.'

'That might be a good thing, Mark. A fresh pair of eyes.'

He wasn't keen on the chief superintendent's request for O'Connor to follow through on the Europol cases, but if O'Connor went to either Rome or Paris, he would do so under Lynch's command. A wry smile came to his face as he wondered how his ex-boss would take instructions from him. O'Connor knew better than most not to challenge the line of authority, a roadmap within the Irish police force that only the ignorant or the plain stupid openly questioned. The next phone call he made was to Kate. Egan had pissed him off, and he would feed him information on a controlled basis from now on. Kate picked up his call on the second ring.

'Kate, we may have another connection.'

'Where and when?'

He got up from his desk, walking around the room with the handset close to his ear, his shoulders lowered as if sharing a secret.

'I contacted the Rome police earlier today. We have a similar MO, hotel-room location, the victim stabbed repeatedly, only whoever carried out the attack set fire to the hotel room. The victim was partially burned. His wife, although in a bad condition, survived. A hotel orderly spotted the smoke coming from under the door and raised the alarm soon after the attack.'

'Apart from the stabbing, and the hotel-room location, what makes you so sure they're connected? The burning doesn't seem to fit.'

'Circumstances may have dictated a change of approach, Kate, but it was something Anita Shevlin mentioned this morning.'

'What?'

'She believed she was being stalked prior to her husband's death, then afterwards put it down to an overactive imagination. The wife who survived the attack in Rome had the same concerns.'

'When did it happen?'

'In 2006.'

'The year after Pierre Laurent's murder?'

'Yes.'

She contemplated the short time span. 'Have you received the images from Paris yet?'

He didn't want to tell her they'd come a few hours earlier. 'Yes, they've only just arrived.'

'I can be there in half an hour. I'll need to see them. Anything of interest strike you?'

'Not yet – nothing we don't already know.'

'You may be right, but the visuals always tell their own story.'

He didn't need a lecture from Kate on observational skills. 'You know where we are whenever you care to visit.' His tone was deliberately businesslike.

He knew he had to keep a cool head, especially if he intended to remain the golden boy in this investigation. Thinking about O'Connor and Kate, he figured it wouldn't be long before the two of them started getting cosy. Any fool could see how O'Connor felt about the woman. A police officer with an inclination to let his personal life get in the way wasn't an ideal choice for Lynch in the investigation. And there was no denying that everyone in the Harcourt Street unit now knew about the guy's son, and how he'd fucked up his personal life for years. Gossip and innuendo were as important to cops as they were to everyone else, perhaps more so. The more you knew about someone, the more you could turn it to your advantage. He would keep O'Connor under control. If the chief super wanted O'Connor to go to Paris and other jurisdictions, he was placing him in a prime position to shine, and that didn't settle easily on

Lynch's shoulders. This investigation was a media goldmine: professional victim stabbed in a hotel room, possible bondage issues, the use of an escort, and now the international element. There was enough spin to make any decent tabloid drool.

Swinging around on his desk chair, he pulled the images from Paris up on his PC. The journalists were hovering, looking to get their piece of the action. It wouldn't take much for a minor leak to multiply and take wings, ending up on the front pages. Gary Egan wouldn't be happy about that. You're only ever as good as your last case, and O'Connor's reputation had already been damaged. If the chief super thought his involvement was drawing heat rather than averting it, that might be enough for him to assign the previously suspended detective to some boring desk duties.

Lynch knew the police force had plenty of weak links, those you could depend on to do your dirty work. Police officers who liked to court the press were common knowledge within the rank and file – 'lamps', shining their lights for all the wrong reasons. All Lynch needed to do was inadvertently mention to one that a recently suspended detective was being given a primary role in an international investigation. Fire in some previous alcohol-dependency issues, and they would run to their buddies in the media, salivating at the thought of being *a reliable police source*, yet again.

There were trustworthy journalists too, those who usually got the official low-down on high-profile cases, feeders for what the police wanted the public to hear. Some were held in high regard by the chief super. No, they weren't the ones to run to with a spin like this. Like the lamps, they had to be of a particular type, the kind used to getting their information from the same desperate, attention-seeking, loud-mouthed eejits – officers they could depend on to give them the dirt. He could see the headlines now, tabloids screaming about the effects of cutbacks, the lack of high-calibre personnel available to tackle major crime, the police policing the police, one rule for them and another for Joe Public. Oh, yes, the chief super and O'Connor would soon feel the pressure once the media started spouting about an independent inquiry. There would be talk about rash judgements, and all kinds of crap. It was par for the course, but still the heat would be felt, and quickly. The chief and O'Connor would have only themselves to blame. He was doing the right thing, even if others lacked his foresight.

Before ringing Freddie Walsh, a lamp with a bigger mouth than Dolly Parton's chest, he zoomed in again on the images on his PC. If he had missed something important about the photographs, it would undoubtedly give Kate the upper hand, and that wasn't a pill he was prepared to swallow. Kate had her uses, and he would manage them to his advantage. She wasn't one to look for attention or constant praise, but then again, she didn't have to deal with the crap he had to. Not everyone had his drive and ambition, and he would use that to his advantage too.

SANDRA

WAKING UP ON the sofa-bed in the studio, I have no idea
how long I have been asleep. Even though I haven't painted
for weeks, I still look on the studio as somewhere to clear my
thoughts. Edgar described it as my place to be alone. I have my
own key to lock it from the inside. He made a big deal about it
being the only one. He made such a big deal about all of it.

I begin shuffling things around, laying out brushes, thinking
about which colours I want to add to the palette. I have plenty
of ideas about what I want to paint, but nothing stays for long.
It's been that way of late. I get excited about a concept, and then
it fades. Next thing, I'm back walking around the studio like a
demented person.

I'm usually less nervous when I'm painting, or thinking about painting. I remind myself that painting isn't about jumping straight in. You can't create something the way you can bake a cake. There are no recipes. It's more complicated than that. *Edgar giving you this studio was a waste of time – all you're doing is making excuses.*

Mixing the colours on my palette, I use the five bases I've used for ever – cadmium light yellow, red, ultramarine blue, burnt umber and white flake, but soon they blur into one another, and I realise I'm crying. I wipe my eyes, but my hands are shaking. I put the palette down. I feel a chill inside. I think again about Edgar organising the studio as a surprise gift. The girls had known about it. They had been in on his little secret. It had bothered me that they'd known and I hadn't.

I curl up on the sofa-bed, doing that thing I used to do as a child when I was nervous, rocking myself back and forth. Somehow an emotional crevice has grown between me and Edgar. If anyone had asked me a few months ago about Edgar being unfaithful, I would have laughed at them, dismissed it as ridiculous. What's changed? *Maybe you're the one who has changed. Have you ever thought about that?*

I can't sit still. I walk over to the two long studio windows looking onto the garden. Again, I think about finding things in the wrong places, how I had blamed Edgar at first. He'd looked at me as if I was mad. Then, talking to the girls yesterday, they hadn't believed me either. Alice was the only one who said I might have imagined it, but the other two were thinking it.

The one place where nothing had been touched was the studio. I'm the only one who knows where I keep the key.

Could he be the one moving things around, and denying it? If he's lying about being unfaithful, he could be lying about that too – but why?

After finding the petals, I stopped taking the medication. Then he started leaving the tablets with a glass of water beside my bed. He must have been checking whether or not I was taking them. I didn't tell the girls about that, or that I've been crunching the tablets and flushing them down the toilet. The petals had been a warning that I needed to pull myself together.

Leaving the studio, I lock the door behind me, then hide the key. I listen for any movement other than my own, but I hear nothing. I look into the small study where his computer is, and I'm relieved it's switched off. I remember turning it off last night after the girls had left, but this morning it was on again. I asked Edgar about it, and he said he didn't remember.

It was Lori who asked me if I'd checked out the Cassie4Casanova link. I had, but all I managed was an error code. Alice wanted to know if I'd erased the link. I hadn't. 'Let's all look,' she had said, as if we were on some stupid adventure. It didn't take long to crank up the computer, all four of us huddled in the study, wine glasses forgotten.

I was certain the link would be there. I never thought of it being wiped, but there wasn't a trace, not a single reference to Cassie4Casanova. They all went through the motions, making suggestions as to how to restore it, but the longer it went on, the more convinced I became that none of them believed me. He has wiped it, I wanted to say, he has deleted the evidence, but I knew I was on shaky ground. The same way I knew they would all speak to one another about me afterwards.

I walk into the study, half expecting the computer to switch itself on without me touching it. My ear is on fire again, as another panic strikes me – what if one of them talks to Edgar? Would they? *Alice would*.

I pick up the phone on the desk. She answers on the first ring. 'Hello,' I say calmly, and surprise myself.

'What's up?' she asks.

'I want to make sure you don't say anything to Edgar about my suspicions.'

'Why would I do that?' Her words sound like a test.

'I don't know, but you need to promise me.'

'For Christ's sake, Sandra.'

I can hear her annoyance. 'Just promise me,' I repeat.

'I bloody promise.'

'Fine.' Before I can think of anything else to say, I hear the phone go dead. I tell myself we go back a long way – she wouldn't betray me.

HARCOURT STREET STATION, SPECIAL DETECTIVE UNIT

RIGHT ON CUE, half an hour after his last conversation with Kate, she arrived. Mark Lynch had already given his instructions to detectives Martin Lennon and Paul Fitzsimons to re-interview all of Rick Shevlin's ex-girlfriends, including any paid escorts. The fresh information from Anita Shevlin didn't only put a new spin on the international wing of the investigation: it meant all females connected to Shevlin had to be asked about a potential stalker. The staff at the hotel would be his next target. With the number of statements taken, more information should be forthcoming. If necessary, he'd get the chief super to agree to extra resources.

Having dismissed both detectives, he took a final look at the Parisian images before he gave the okay for Kate to come in. He had a nagging feeling he had missed something. The creepy monk outfit worn by the dead Pierre Laurent, coupled with the candlelit lantern, certainly added a freakish element to the scene, making it more like an image of a wake than a crime scene.

Unlike Shevlin's, this victim's eyes were closed, and although the visual Lynch focused on looked like a corpse at peace, underneath the dark monk's habit there was a bloodied mess, puncture and slash wounds everywhere except for the face. *Why not the face?* The victim had been handsome – even in death Lynch could see that. He flicked to a later image from the morgue. He'd had a good physique too, quite the artist's model, he thought. He would have to talk to Morrison. It would be a nice twist if the state pathologist found a similarity of pattern in each of the attacks, even if the ultimate cause of death differed. He already knew in Pierre Laurent's case that it had been asphyxiation. The police report mentioned a couple of ex-lovers confirming that he had liked physical punishment during sex, including being brought to the edge with a rope around his neck. Had it not been for the knife attack, it might have been dismissed as a sexual act gone awry, one of the participating parties going a step too far. The police had also found friction burns on the victim's wrists and ankles, consistent with bondage, only this time they had occurred prior to death. Pierre Laurent might have been little more than a lowly art student, but if it was the same killer, he had attracted their interest, just as Rick Shevlin had. What else, other than the obvious, had the two men had in common?

He couldn't delay talking to Kate any longer, but he was still staring at the screen as she walked in.

∞

'You wanted to see the images from Paris, Kate. Here they are.' He barely turned towards her.

'First tell me why you're so engrossed.'

'There's something about them,' he pointed to the screen, 'that's bothering me.'

'I'm listening.' She sat on the chair opposite, folding her legs, causing her skirt to rise above her knees. As he turned to face her, she caught him eyeing her legs, and pulled the lower part of her trench coat over them.

'Feeling the cold, are we?' he asked.

'A slight chill.' She hoped he would take the hint. 'You were saying about the images …'

'The victim was younger than Rick Shevlin. He was also laid out differently, and with a different cause of death. The slash and puncture wounds to the body, unlike Shevlin's, were concealed, and if there was any lipstick residue on the lips, either it was missed or it had deteriorated due to the delay in finding the body. Having said that, there is plenty to link the two deaths – a capital city, the murder taking place in a hotel room, the frenzied knife attack, a suspected female killer, a tentative art association, an inclination for kinky sex and, of course, the potential Tarot card connection, which led us to tie them together via the Europol database in the first place.'

'And the level of detail,' she added. 'Don't forget that. You were about to tell me what irked you.'

'Although the images are different, I can't shake the notion there's something else about the two scenes that unites them.'

'Like the images are telling you more than you actually see.'

'Yeah.'

'I felt the same way, Mark, about the photographs from the Earlbrook Hotel.' She pulled her chair in closer, flicking through the images on the screen, including those from the morgue. She finally ended up where she'd begun, on the wide shot from the hotel bedroom. Knowing what she was looking for this time made it easier. 'The scenes from the Earlbrook Hotel look savage in comparison. These images take on the appearance of something serene, and again, a practical replica of a Tarot card. The killer is re-creating the images to the point of obsession. Even though they depict different scenes, they have a visual hallmark.'

'Do you mean like an artistic style?'

'Exactly, but there's more than that. Remember how Rick Shevlin's image was re-created in the dressing-table mirror?'

He nodded.

'Look at this,' she pointed to the screen, 'the image with the opened bathroom door.' There was no denying Pierre Laurent's clear reflection: it perfectly framed the corpse, and again, as if it was part of a Tarot-card image.

'Look at the room,' she continued. 'It's small. There isn't a lot of floor space.'

'Meaning the options for creating the image would be limited.'

'And only one likely spot from which the image we're looking at could have been taken.'

'At the window again. Are you saying the killer is taking photographs?'

'Perhaps, but even if she isn't, she's setting up the potential shot. The position of the body looks like it was determined by the position of the mirror and the potential viewing point.'

'You do realise how big this could be?' he asked, almost rhetorically.

'Tell me why the Paris police believed the killer was female.'

'Similar reasons as in the Rick Shevlin case, although no lipstick was found.' His words were coming out fast and furious. 'The victim had engaged in sexual activity before death. He had been tied up, this time, presumably, willingly. A witness statement said they heard a woman's voice coming from the hotel room that evening, and the killer, despite inflicting severe wounds to the victim, never touched his face. The investigating team believed the killing had all the hallmarks of a crime of passion.'

If I could read his mind, she thought, Lynch is thinking this thing could be even bigger than his wildest dreams. She didn't have a problem with his ambition: it was his absolute hunger for success that troubled her – the greater the prize, the more lethal the fall.

He was pacing around the room now, becoming more energised. 'Kate, there is no roadmap for something like this. We need to move fast and efficiently.' Then, standing close to her, as she had seen him do with the escort, he asked, 'How high is the risk of the killer acting again soon?'

'That's impossible to say. The time span is nine years between the Shevlin and Laurent murders, and we're still in the dark as to more possible victims. I'm still not sure about that other case you mentioned, the one in Rome. The burning is putting me off, unless …'

'Unless what?'

'Unless she was re-creating the Tower card – it depicts a burning tower, but the wife being present deviates from her pattern of the victims being alone. If the case is connected, the stalking element is worrying. It illustrates a desire to get close to people in the victim's life.'

'And her motivation?'

'Probably to infiltrate and control.'

'Okay, Kate, if you can't tell me when, do you think she has already moved on to another victim?'

'Very probably – her level of motivation is high. Assuming, for now, the case in Rome is connected, it means the gap between killings can be short. If she has turned her attention elsewhere, the potential victim, and those closest to him, are certainly in danger.'

EDGAR

LORI'S PHONE CALL came as Edgar was driving to work. He'd known the girls had visited a couple of nights before. Since then, Sandra's mood had deteriorated further. He also knew he needed to keep Lori sweet: he didn't want any unnecessary complications.

'Hi, Lori, is everything okay?' he asked, keeping his tone upbeat.

'I've been holding off phoning you, but I need to warn you about something.'

'Warn me about what?'

'Sandra is suspicious.'

'Why, what did she say?'

'She's keeping notes on you.'

'Notes?' He didn't disguise his surprise. 'Hold on a second.'

He pulled the car into a side street. Once parked, he rolled down the driver's window to get some air. 'Lori, tell me exactly what happened.'

'When we called to the house earlier in the week, she told us. She's writing everything down.'

'What do you mean writing it down? What is she writing down?' He immediately regretted his anxious tone. He had to tread carefully, and her silence wasn't a good sign. 'Lori, I'm sorry for snapping. Just tell me.'

'She says she's writing down things about YOU.'

'Where? In a diary? A notebook?'

'I don't know.'

'And you didn't ask?'

'I didn't want to push her. You understand, don't you?'

'Lori, I need you to find out exactly what she knows. She trusts you.'

'I'll try, but …'

'But what?'

'She has no idea what's happening. She is completely off base.'

'Are you positive?'

'Absolutely – she's digging, but she hasn't found anything concrete. Maybe you should pay her more attention, make sure you keep her from finding out anything of value. You'll need to do more to distract her.'

'I've every intention of keeping her in the dark.'

'I know that.'

'Lori, I'll need your help. You're one of the few people she'll talk to. Call to her tomorrow. Go on your own. Tell her you're there to give her moral support.'

'I'd planned to make a visit either way.'

'Lori?'

'What?'

'Don't be tempted to say anything to her.'

'You're not threatening me, are you?'

'We both know what's at stake here. We can't leave anything to chance.' He turned the keys in the ignition, ready to drive away. 'You'll need to find out what she's writing in that notebook or diary, and where she's keeping it. Knowing Sandra, she's sure to be holding something back.'

Driving out of the side street, he remembered the darkened house from the night before. He had avoided his wife – he'd been too tired for an interrogation. When he had crept into the bedroom, the empty bed had surprised him. It was only when he went downstairs that he saw the light on at the back of the house, coming from under the studio door. Was that where she was writing things down? If she had a notebook, or a diary, knowing Sandra, she wouldn't keep it anywhere as obvious.

Maybe it was best to leave it with Lori. He didn't like being dependent on her, but there wasn't a lot else he could do. Still, if anyone could find out what was going on inside Sandra's head, it would be her. He had come to realise she wasn't the shrinking violet he'd once thought she was.

MERVIN ROAD, RATHMINES

KATE HAD BEEN awake since four that morning. Finding it impossible to go back to sleep, she took advantage of her temporary insomnia, and the peace of Charlie being out for the count, to once again review her file notes on the Shevlin case. It was now three hours later, and in many ways she still had more questions than answers. The two international investigations had broadened the frame of reference – they were all still male victims, all viciously stabbed, and with connections to the Tarot – but the focus of the killer now had a wider scope, including those close to the victims, or any future victim.

She was relieved that O'Connor was back on duty. It would take her a while to get used to thinking of him as Adam. When her mobile rang, she answered it, even though it was Declan, whom she had been avoiding for days.

'It's seven a.m.'

'Kate, you know why I'm calling.'

'I have the papers, but work has been mental.'

'Nothing ever changes with you, does it?' His words were full of cynicism.

Maybe he was right, she thought, but she was damned if she was going to let him take the moral high ground. 'I wasn't the one looking for some personal space, was I?' She had spoken louder than she'd intended.

'You shut me out, Kate, not the other way around.'

'That's your excuse, is it, for having an affair?' She turned to make sure Charlie's bedroom door was still closed.

'It's not about excuses.'

'Isn't it, Declan? Explain it to me, then. I'm all ears.'

'It didn't happen the way you're saying it. You and I drifted apart, that's all.'

'You said it was my fault, that I shut you out.'

'I didn't say that.'

'You did. You said it. What about Charlie, then? Were you thinking about him when you were off having your extra-marital affair?'

'Don't bring Charlie into this.'

'You're not the one listening to him ask for his daddy every morning.'

'That's below the belt, Kate, and you know it.'

'Maybe it is, but unlike you, I'm not the one wanting to railroad this separation.'

'Kate, I'm not having this argument again. Sign the papers and get the two of us out of this misery.'

'Mum.' She turned. Charlie was rubbing his eyes in his Batman pyjamas. 'I heard you shouting.'

'Declan, I have to go. We can talk later.'

Picking up Charlie, she asked, 'Are you okay, honey?'

'Was that Dad? Why did you hang up? I wanted to talk to him.'

'You can talk to him later.'

'I wanted to talk to him now.' A large pout on his face.

'Let's get breakfast first. Then you can call Dad back.'

'Do you promise?'

'I promise.'

Over breakfast, Kate thought about what Declan had said. She had shut him out, driven him away. She couldn't wash her hands of responsibility. It was an easy route to fire blame at him. She hadn't wanted it to come to this – mud-slinging and bitterness. She had tried to keep a brave face for Charlie's sake, bottling it all up, not talking to anyone, exactly the opposite of what she would have advised clients.

It was impossible to deny the emotional upheaval she felt towards Declan, and this new woman in his life, but at least he had been honest with her. She hadn't mentioned anything to him about Adam, or her feelings for him, which made her a coward, happy for her ex-husband to take all of the dirt.

∞

As agreed, she allowed Charlie to phone Declan after breakfast, but by the time she had dropped him at school, and was on her way to work, Kate already felt as if she had put in a full day, emotionally and every other way. She should have been pleased to get the phone call from Adam, but she wasn't in a particularly talkative mood.

'It looks like I'm off to Paris in a couple of days.'

'Mark told me that might happen.'

'What's the story with your follow-up report?'

Business as usual, she thought. 'I'll be working on it this morning.'

'Anything to add to what we've already discussed?'

'For what it's worth, I think our killer fantasises about her actions long before she carries them out.'

'That's never good. Anything more?'

If nothing else, she thought, this was taking her mind off Declan and Charlie. 'I've looked at the file notes again, taking in the possible international connections, and there is something about the level of pride she's applying to the images being created, both in the Dublin and Paris murders. The intricacy of detail, including shape, form and proportion, the framing of the crime scene, all require a level of intelligence and a form of creative genius.'

'Creative genius – Kate, that's a bit of a leap.'

'I don't think so, and remember, she also has the ability to keep a cool head. When most killers would be long gone, our killer stays.'

'Sounds like a fanatical nutcase to me.'

'She's fanatical, all right, and someone with an underlying mental disorder. I keep wondering, how controlled is she and what are her pressure points? Something caused our killer to snap, to take action against her victims. It tells us that, despite her ability to be in control, she can flip, becoming the very opposite. Two sides to her personality ...' Kate hesitated '... which probably explains her ability to seduce her victims into trusting her.'

'They wouldn't be the first males to believe something a woman said when she meant the very opposite.'

'We'd be foolish to underestimate her, and as for creative genius, only time will tell.'

'You said mental disorder, Kate. Are we talking psychotic, psychopathic?'

'I don't know – at least, not yet. Many people with mental difficulties are highly intelligent. There are psychopathic inferences here, possibly even sociopathic.'

'What's the difference?'

'There's an extended school of thought on the difference between the two, but one obvious difference is that a psychopath lacks empathy ...'

'Sounds like half of the people I know.'

'Statistically, about one per cent of the population have profound psychopathic tendencies; not quite half, admittedly, but it's high. Sociopaths on the other hand can demonstrate the ability to empathise. They can feel regret, their actions can affect them emotionally, which is why they're sometimes considered more volatile and less predictable.'

'Meaning, Kate, it's harder to work out their next move?'

'Absolutely – and we're only at the beginning. There's history here, lots of it. What the crime-scene images are illustrating is simply the end result.'

'Sociopaths can demonstrate empathy? What makes you think our killer has empathy?'

'If it's the same killer, she left Pierre Laurent's face completely unmarked.'

'So?'

'She couldn't bring herself to damage it. Something stopped her. For whatever reason, it was out of bounds. Our killer cares, all right. She cares enough to ensure she leaves the scene exactly as she wants it to be. It's her anger that demonstrates her hurt.'

'A *femme fatale*.'

'Your words, not mine.' He hadn't mentioned their conversation of the previous day. She reminded herself that she had asked him to give her more time. 'But there's something else.'

'There usually is with you, Kate.'

His voice sounds so upbeat, she thought. Maybe work does make the man. 'It's about her level of detachment. Our killer needs to be of a particular mind-set to do what she does. Think of it as a bit like the way a surgeon operates.'

'I'd hardly put a clinical operation to save someone's life on the same level as chopping a guy up, then playing creative with the props.'

'You're right, but surgeons have to detach at some level to do their job. They need to focus on the task in hand to bring it to a successful conclusion, and they do so in a clinical manner. There is no place for emotion and doubt when a surgeon is operating. In many ways our killer is the same. The planning of the killing is on one level. The act of killing is then charged with emotion, but the aftermath is clinical, her mind switching from one mode to the next.'

'You have to love the versatility of the female mind,' he jested, again sounding far more energised than he had the day before.

'It's not a laughing matter.' She heard the tetchiness in her voice.

'No, it's not, but it could be tricky down the line.'

'What do you mean?'

'A jury, despite their best intentions, tend to be biased, unwilling to believe a woman is capable of such things. I've been through enough cases to know how easily murder can become manslaughter, and a killer can walk.'

'If this murder is linked conclusively to the European cases, I doubt self-defence or mental or physical abuse will sway anyone. Multiple killings rarely happen without premeditation.'

'Maybe so. All I'm saying is that it can prove to be divisive when dealing with the fairer sex.'

'Listen, I've got to go. I'm nearly at Ocean House.'

'Before you hang up, there's a couple of things you should know.'

'What?'

'Mark's applied pressure to extend the size of the investigative team. He wants you at the midday incident-room briefing.'

'And what if I've other plans?'

'Kate, you know what the force is like. The case dictates everything. If you can't make it, say so, but the chief super is expecting you.'

'I'll be there.'

'Is your passport up to date?'

'Why?'

'He's also talking about you going to Paris.'

'For Christ's sake …'

'Don't shoot me, I'm only the messenger.'

'Well, tell Chief Superintendent Gary Egan and Mark Lynch I have a job and a life outside the force.'

'They'll be delighted to hear it.'

I

I WAS EIGHT years old when I first considered killing someone. Some years later, I confided this to a friend. She thought I was lying.

The desire to kill isn't as strange as you might think. Circumstances may vary, but what matters is that, once you've reached that point, you're aware of how easy it is. For me, it started with a need to rid the earth of a specific someone. I viewed my prospective victim, contemplating their death without one iota of guilt, and in some ways without anger. It wasn't a cold feeling. Nor was it primed with passion. If anything, it was completely calm.

I had reached a decision, considered the means — it was that simple. In the end, I didn't do it. Why? It wasn't the right time. I was still a child, and it had logistical difficulties I wasn't in a position to overcome. My eight-year-old self wouldn't have been able to get away with it. If she had been, I have no doubt she would have done it. People underestimate the power of children, perceiving their vulnerability as weakness. Never miscalculate the rat trapped in a corner, irrespective of age or experience. And, like the rat, we're all born with the survival instinct. Children are no different from their adult selves in that regard and, at times, more resolute.

Do you remember the road, the one in the woods that people can no longer see? That road remains steadfast in my mind. It is with me when I close my eyes to sleep and I see the myriad of evil faces. Do you believe in ghosts? I do.

I met my first ghost back when I first thought about killing someone. Her face was kind, almost as if she knew me better than I knew myself. It was the middle of the night, and there was a cold wind wailing outside, yet when I awoke, I was covered with sweat. I saw her then, looking bright within the dark. I should have been frightened, but I wasn't.

She was kneeling beside my bed, resting her head on the end, as if she was waiting for me to wake up. We were similar in age. She smiled, touched my cheek, her warm hand trailing down my arm. When she spoke, it wasn't in a language I understood. It sounded like the tongue of the ancients, all-knowing. Settling back to sleep, I felt safe. It was within this oasis of calm that the first stabbing pain shot through me, first in my chest, then further down my body. Opening my eyes, I saw her. This time her face and arms were covered with blood, and when I screamed, she backed away. Later, I could find no signs of her. The pain was gone and so, too, was the blood. But she had been real.

The next time I saw her, she told me she knew I wanted to kill someone, but that I should wait, endure longer. Evil defines you. If it pushes you hard enough, you'll break or, like me, find ways to survive it. When I lived with the hunched shadow of the witch, she extracted pleasure from my vulnerability, took joy from my hurt. If you've never reached that point, the one asking you if you want to die, or kill to survive, you can never understand me or my desire to take another person's life.

Until now, the only woman I have ever killed was the witch, but I need to rid my new lover of his pathetic security blanket. I've become more convinced than ever that he is the one. I can't allow her stand in my way. She is at breaking point. Little by little, she is falling apart, and when she least suspects it, I will destroy her.

SANDRA

IT WAS AFTER Edgar had left for work that I saw the shadow again. One moment it was there, the next it was gone. I felt such a strong sense of foreboding that my relief, once the shadow disappeared, was quickly followed by fear: if the stranger was no longer in the garden, they could be inside the house. I felt like a prisoner inside my own home.

Last night, I slept in the studio again. I didn't want Edgar reaching for me in the bed, whispering in my ear, willing me to wake up and have duty sex with him. We haven't made love in such a long time, but I couldn't take the risk that his old habits would return. It was Karen who told me sexual desire towards your partner rises rather than falls when you're having an affair. The libido is sparked by extra-marital activity, and you imagine you're having sex with your lover rather than your partner.

Lori phoned earlier, but I brushed her off. I needed to get out of the house, even though I was forced to agree to meet her later on. I decided to drive to Edgar's showrooms in town, as if I was some kind of secret-service agent. I waited for more than an hour before I saw him leave: I had made the decision to follow him. If I was wrong about Edgar lying to me, so be it, but if I was right, it was better to know the truth than be kept in the dark.

Considering everything, I don't know why I was so shocked when I saw him drive to that other house. Maybe I hadn't expected to discover something so quickly, but when he turned the key in the front door, I still couldn't quite believe it. He had walked up to the house with such familiarity, turning the key as if he was arriving home. How long has he been seeing this woman?

It took me a while to realise I was shivering in the car. I pulled my collar up around my neck for some warmth, and it was then I heard the voice inside my head saying, *You're in denial*.

I drove past the house, cursing myself for not being better prepared. I hadn't made a detailed plan. I had simply wanted to get to the bottom of things, but presented with reality, I needed to think about my next move.

I parked at the end of the street, keeping my eyes on the house. Ideas, notions, ridiculous explanations formed repeatedly in my mind, but one thought kept coming back: I needed to find out everything I could about this woman. Was she a stranger or someone I already knew? Were Edgar and her in this together, planning and scheming against me?

The house was no more than an hour's drive from the centre of Dublin, and I had visited Greystones, a busy seaside town, many times as a child. Alice and I had often gone there by bus. It felt weird being there again, and there wasn't anything particularly unusual about the house. It didn't look very different from any of the others on the street, except for one thing: I felt I had seen it before.

I've tried to tell myself there were plenty of logical reasons for Edgar being there. It could be a business meeting, the house belonging to a new client, or an old friend, a relative I hadn't met. It was seeing him turn the key that contradicted all of it, and with that came an attack of questions. What if he had another wife? What if we'd been living a lie for years? What if I was the other woman?

Fear was driving me, and it was fear that kept me there, waiting until he left the house, taking note of the time on a scrap of paper in the car. He had stayed there for at least an hour. When I saw him leave, I should have gone straight up and confronted him, asked him why he was there. *So what stopped you?* I DON'T BLOODY KNOW. *You're putting off the truth. More fear, Sandra, more bloody fear.*

I followed him back to work, thinking he might make another stop along the way, which would help me build up a picture, but he didn't. It was then I decided to phone him. His secretary put me straight through. He sounded in great form. He told me how he'd known I was in the studio last night, and hoped it had been productive. He wanted to tell me how much he loved me, that

I meant the world to him. It was all I could do to stop myself blurting it all out. He even suggested going away for a while – a holiday would do us both the world of good, he said. I let him think I was going along with it, but when he started talking about counselling, I pulled back. He said someone at work had mentioned that writing things down was often very helpful. He wondered if I'd ever considered that. *Had he found my diary?* Why was he talking about writing things down? Did he know I was keeping notes? I panicked, and could tell my voice sounded less assured. Could he have read my words? Had he found the old tea chest in the attic? It was his house too. It was possible, but he couldn't have stumbled upon it. His fear of heights would have kept him away from the attic. He hates that ladder. Maybe Alice told him. Was that it? I ended the conversation as quickly as I could, but driving home, I couldn't get the idea that Alice had betrayed me out of my mind. *The only person you can trust is yourself. Everyone else is a potential enemy.*

I needed to check the attic. I practically stormed into the house, rushing up the stairs, not even thinking about locking the front door behind me. The most important thing on my mind was to find my diary and, if necessary, another hiding place. I climbed the attic ladder and crawled into the tiny ceiling space. It was the perfect place to keep something away from his prying eyes. Then the questions came back, only this time there were more of them. How would I know if he had found it? Would I know if the diary had been moved? Even in the dark I could see it on top of the old tea chest. I pulled myself in further, curling up into a ball, the way I used to do when I was younger. I turned the pages one at a time until I reached my last entry. I felt relief. Everything was as I had left it. Maybe things were okay after all.

It was only on closing the diary that I noticed the gold ribbon page marker had been moved further than my last entry. Sweat rose on my neck, and my right hand trembled as my fingers reached for it. Opening the page, which should have been blank, I read the words in bold black letters: *YOU'RE A FOOL.*

I stared at the page. There was something familiar about the writing. That's when I heard someone moving downstairs. I thought about calling Edgar's name, but what if the person downstairs wasn't him? What if it was the stranger who had broken in, the person lurking in the shadows? How would I protect myself? And, once again, I felt cornered.

EDGAR

ARRIVING BACK AT the showrooms, Edgar was no longer sure how he felt about anything. Everything had changed. He knew he had made choices, which he had to live with, but now he was at the point of achieving his lifetime goals – professional success, financial security, respect and admiration for his designs – and his personal life was unravelling. To the outside world, everything looked perfect: career on a high, a wonderful home and a beautiful, talented wife. Despite the lack of children, he would have been considered lucky.

He thought about Lori too. The more time that passed, the more he realised he had made the wrong choice in hooking up with her. She was far from the timid flower that Sandra had described and he was now uncomfortable with the relationship. From the moment the whole thing had begun, he had known he was risking everything but continued to walk a dangerous path. She seemed to have gained a sense of power. He might have to talk to Alice, but what would he tell her? Certainly not the truth – that was something he couldn't tell anyone, not Lori, not Alice and certainly not Sandra.

Everyone makes mistakes, he told himself. It had all happened without planning. A few weeks ago, if anyone had said this could happen, he would have seen it as a sick joke. Now the joke was on him, and he knew he'd made one of the worst decisions of his life. Retreating without huge complications was no longer an option. He needed to keep everything from Sandra. There was no telling what she would do if she knew the truth. Her writing details down proved one thing, though: that she knew something wasn't right.

When his secretary told him his next client had arrived, he wasn't sure if he could continue pretending any more. Asking her to give him a few more minutes, he cupped his face in his hands, closing his eyes, as he thought about Alice, Lori and Sandra, and the history he had clocked up with each of them. Now his wife was like a stranger. He felt guilt, knowing he had played his part in the wreckage, but it wasn't entirely his fault, not by a long shot.

He could still recall the moment he had first seen her, really seen her, and how utterly beautiful and enchanting she was. He had been captivated. They had drunk plenty of wine, but she was the one doing most of the seducing, although there was no denying his attraction. From that first split second, he had fantasised about being inside her, feeling horny at the curves of her body, watching her legs below the hemline of her skirt, stretched out in the passenger seat, like one delightfully long temptation. Driving her home that night, he had visualised the two of them naked many times.

She told him to turn down a side road he hadn't travelled before. At first he didn't know where she was taking him, but he didn't ask. He simply drove until she told him to stop.

It was late, and the street was deserted. She smiled at him, a knowing smile, then got out of the car. He remembered watching her walk around to the driver's side, the headlights lighting her as she passed the bonnet, a ghost-like creature. At first he thought she was going to walk away without explanation. She had that kind of intrigue about her. She wasn't like any other woman he had ever met. Instead, she opened the driver's door, asking, 'What are you waiting for?' He hesitated. 'There's no need to worry,' she said. 'We won't be disturbed here.'

All his earlier fantasies became a reality, as she took him by the hand into the house in Greystones. He could still hear the click, click of her stilettos on the pathway as she led him to the back door, taking a key from under a garden pot. Once inside, he kissed her hard on the lips, her face, down to her neck and, opening the top button of her blouse, her breasts. His excitement rose. She felt his groin, undoing his zip. He was surprised at her forwardness, but liked it. Removing her blouse and bra, she shivered, and he held her. She let out a tiny cry, then brought him upstairs. She lay on the bed. Running his hand up her inner thigh, he felt her shiver again, and he had wondered if she wanted him to stop. He pulled away, then saw the satisfied look on her face and let his hand go further, realising she wasn't wearing any underwear below her skirt. She spread her legs, as he rolled her skirt up. She closed her eyes when he entered her, letting out the tiniest of groans. It didn't take him long. He was far too fast the first time. Afterwards, she stroked his head, like he was a little boy. He had wanted to give her pleasure too, but she told him it didn't matter once he was pleased. It was such a strange word to use, 'pleased'.

Yes, *she* was the one who had seduced *him*, rather than the other way around. There were two sides to everything, Sandra often said, and she was right. Had Sandra driven him away?

Instructing his secretary to send the client through, he knew that if he could turn back the clock, he would do things very differently.

SANDRA

ALONE IN THE darkness of the attic, I realised the person walking around the house was doing so with a sense of familiarity, almost as if my home belonged to them. Every sound I heard seemed magnified, but the footsteps were moving at speed. They were light, and I was positive they weren't a man's. Pulling back from the attic door, I tried to get a better view of below, going further into the dark, as a scared child might. When I heard the footsteps in the kitchen, I knew that, whoever it was, they were getting closer, and they would soon see the attic ladder. I thought too late about pulling it up, hearing their feet mount the stairs.

It was her lower half I saw first, wearing tiny black ankle boots and grey leggings. They could have belonged to anyone. It was only when I caught sight of her short black hair that I realised it was Lori, and let out an enormous sigh of relief, allowing my breathing to slow down. It took me a while to call her name, almost as if I was trying to gain some elusive upper hand. The reprieve of fear was quickly followed by another rush of questions. How had she got in? And why hadn't she called out? When she put her foot on the attic ladder, I told her to stay there, that I was coming down. If she was taken aback by my aggressive tone, her face didn't show it. I was nervous. I felt uncomfortable with my back to her. When I reached the bottom, she asked me, coyly, what I had been doing. I didn't answer, remembering the words in my diary: YOU'RE A FOOL. Had Lori taken me for a fool? Had Alice, Edgar, the whole lot of them?

'How did you get in?' I finally asked her.

'You left the front door open.' She looked at me as if I'd asked her the daftest question in the world, but she used a caring tone, like a parent who had caught their child doing something stupid. I kept hearing that voice in my head, saying, *Don't trust her*.

'Why didn't you call out when you came inside? I didn't know who you were.'

When she gave me a hug, I pulled back from her.

'I didn't want to startle you,' she said. 'I know how engrossed you get in your work, but when I saw the front door open, I thought …'

'You thought what?' I bit hard on my lip.

'Nothing – I didn't mean to startle you.'

'You were supposed to call later.' I could hear the increased tension in my voice. I realised I was trying to compose myself, to appear normal, even though I sensed something wasn't right. It wasn't just the words I had read in the diary, it was the way she kept staring at me. She seemed different, but I couldn't put my finger on exactly why. While she yammered on, I began thinking about who had written the note. Someone had gained access to my diary. I thought again about Lori walking around downstairs. Had she been looking for something? You don't trust her, do you? Before we went downstairs, standing behind her, I thought, one decent push, and she would topple.

'I'm sorry I gave you a fright,' she said, as if answering my doubts.

The image of pushing her down the stairs frightened me. She hadn't done anything wrong. I was the one who had left the front door open. It was when we were in the kitchen that she mentioned Alice, and how she had been bothered by the way she'd behaved a couple of nights back. 'It could be nothing,' she said, in an offhand way, 'but it's been playing on my mind. I didn't want to alarm you. I know how sensitive you are right now.'

'Sensitive?' I repeated, like a parrot.

'When you mentioned Edgar using a dating agency, I felt Alice was purposely holding something back.'

'What?'

'I wasn't sure if you knew.'

'Knew what?'

'She's used a dating agency, and for all I know, she still does.'

I sensed she was gauging my reaction. Did she think Alice was the other woman? Cassie4Casanova?

'I know we all go back a long way, Sandra, but I've never

really trusted Alice, not completely. I've always had the sense that she was holding something back, being far too guarded.'

I saw the words in my diary again – *YOU'RE A FOOL*. Had Alice written them?

'I think you need to be careful, Sandra.'

'Of who?'

'Alice, of course.'

'I don't understand.' As I listened to her, I noticed her demeanour, how self-assured she was, as if she had a sense of power, of control.

'Have you never thought,' she asked, a tinge of dramatic desperation in her voice, 'that Alice could be the other woman?'

INCIDENT ROOM, HARCOURT STREET STATION, SPECIAL DETECTIVE UNIT

KATE HAD BEEN to many incident-room briefings, and today, awaiting the arrival of the main players in the crammed room at Harcourt Street's Special Detective Unit, the assembled crowd wasn't dissimilar to those she had previously experienced, forging an atmosphere of tension, adrenalin and commitment.

Having finished her interim report that morning, she still had reservations about many aspects of the case. She thought about Charlie again, overhearing her conversation with Declan. It was as if the child had his own inbuilt radar, sensing when something was wrong. After talking to his dad, he hadn't wanted to go to school, delaying getting ready, unable to find his homework copy, unwilling to put his lunch box in his schoolbag or get dressed or tie his shoelaces. And once more, she thought, simply getting him safely to school had felt like achieving a minor miracle. Now, standing among the police officers in the room, keeping herself to herself, she considered the prospect of going to Paris.

Going away for a couple of days was certainly a possibility. Her workload at Ocean House could be managed. She hadn't been away from Charlie for so long; maybe a break was exactly what they needed. She would have to have Declan on board, but as far as Charlie was concerned, he would probably agree. It might mean him rejigging things at work, but he was the other parent, after all. Undoubtedly he would bring up the signing of the separation papers again, but what the hell was she waiting for? Everyone, including herself, knew it was over between them.

She checked her watch. The meeting was running ten minutes late, but a shuffling among the waiting crowd told her the top brass were on the way, and within seconds, Chief Superintendent Egan brushed past her with a face like stone. Mark Lynch couldn't have looked more delighted with himself, nodding to all and sundry as if they had been waiting for him and him alone. Adam O'Connor was the last to enter the room, and the only one to stop in front of her.

'Hi, Kate, good to see you.' He gave her a cheeky wink.

'You know me, anything to help the force.' She smiled. She had known him for more than two years, but somehow the recent shift to calling him Adam still felt odd.

He touched her arm. 'Are you okay?'

'Yes, fine.'

'Good.'

As his hand slid away, and she watched him walk towards the top table, she told herself to stop acting like a silly schoolgirl.

Gary Egan was the first to speak. 'Detective Lynch will start with an overview of the current investigation, specifically for those of you who have only just come on board. Mark, you have the floor.'

'Thanks, Boss.' Mark looked at the assembled group and cleared his throat. 'Up until this point, we've been dealing with the murder investigation of Rick Shevlin, a mid-forties male, husband and father, and well-known art dealer in the city. The deceased, as some of you know, was found in one of the bedrooms at the Earlbrook Hotel with multiple stab wounds. He was naked, tied to the bed with ropes at two points, hands and one ankle, and had been positioned in a very specific manner, which will become apparent once we review all the visuals. Prior to his death, he had used the services of an escort.' He gestured to one of the uniformed officers to start the slides. The lights were lowered and the first slide appeared. 'This is a wide shot of the crime scene. You can see the positioning, as well as the multiple slash and puncture wounds. The deepest sliced wound was to the throat, severing the external jugular vein and the carotid artery. It was the ultimate cause of death. We believe the weapon used was a knife similar in size to a large carving knife.'

Not for the first time since she'd met up with Mark Lynch again, Kate noted that he had certainly come out of his shell. She watched Adam too. His face was giving nothing away. Anyone else in his position might have been thinking that he should have been the one doing the update for the group, the man in charge. She knew, though, that he was also a man who could hide his thoughts well, an attribute that had stood to him in the force, but had been partly responsible for messing up his personal life.

The next slide was a close-up of the victim's face, his eyes staring out towards the hotel car park. 'Our killer wasn't satisfied with simply killing the victim,' Lynch went on. They had very specific ideas as to how they wanted the crime scene to appear. The victim's eyes were open, the hands and ankle tied with double overhand knots. We believe the likelihood of the victim knowing the killer is high. The fluid samples taken from the eye and the blood test have eliminated the consumption of either cocaine or heroin, but prior to death, Rick Shevlin had swallowed ketamine, more commonly known as Special K. Some of the potential effects would have been the onset of hallucinations, loss of consciousness and co-ordination and, in certain cases, aggression. There is nothing to indicate any violent behaviour on the part of the victim, but the lack of co-ordination and consciousness certainly reduced his ability to defend himself.'

Lynch paused, twisting his neck as if it was stiff, while everyone in the room kept their attention on the overhead screen. 'Slide number three may look somewhat ambiguous, but the dressing table,' he pointed to the slide, 'was repositioned, and you can clearly see the victim reflected in the glass. As with the attack and the tying up of the body, this was done by the killer,' he looked out to the gathering, 'one of the reasons being to form a replica of the Hangman card from the Tarot deck.' He smiled. 'The creation of the crime scene gave the killer some kind of payback.' He flicked back to the earlier slide. 'One last note on the eyes. The corneas are cloudy and opaque, escalated because the eyes were left open. It is believed a drop in temperature added to the progression. Roughly translated, our killer opened the window while they were getting through the task in hand.

'Forensically, we have very little right now. The hotel room was like the aftermath of a clinical operation. Our killer came prepared. The clean-up, unfortunately for us, was impeccable. Again, as many of you know, we did a full overview of the hotel's other rooms, sending in two separate tech teams, and have come up with nothing conclusive. All hotel staff are going to be re-interviewed, as are the victim's ex-girlfriends or known female associates. A recent development in the investigation has been Anita Shevlin's belief that, prior to her husband's death, she was stalked. I'll get back to that later. For now, I'll continue with the slides for all new personnel on board.' Pointing to the overhead slide, he continued, 'There was a lot of blood found at the scene, but none belonged to our killer. Examination of the victim's organs revealed some female tissue, which was matched to the escort, who is not a suspect at this time. Other forensic details include lipstick residue found on the victim's lips. We've got a full list of its properties, but not enough to produce a DNA profile. We do know that it's an internationally produced brand. The shade is known as Carmine, and it has been available throughout Europe, including Ireland, for many years. We certainly believe it could be part of the killer's signature.'

Flicking a number of slides forward to close-up shots of the slash and puncture wounds, he continued, 'As I said, the weapon used was large, and the trajectory of the wounds indicates our victim was weakened and attacked from above. Before I go through any more of the slides, we are now of the strong belief that this killing isn't isolated, and has potential connections with earlier crimes in Rome and Paris. We'll be working directly with our counterparts in both jurisdictions over the next twenty-four to forty-eight hours to expedite any fresh information there.' He loosened his tie, opening the top button of his shirt. 'We know from his wife that Rick Shevlin stayed in town because of a late dinner meeting. We cannot find any reference to a meeting scheduled through his office. Either it was personal, or Mr Shevlin didn't want others to know about it. Despite extensive examination of CCTV footage, we've been unable to pinpoint the victim's movements earlier in the evening. He had his phone off from around seven p.m., turning it back on to book the escort, and then around midnight to phone his wife from the hotel. Our victim wasn't squeaky clean. There is evidence to suggest he was involved with a number of shady dealings, but whether they influenced events or not, we simply do not know. His credit cards have no record of him paying for dinner, but then again, they don't record him paying for the escort either.'

'Thank you, Mark.' Gary Egan took over. 'This is going to be a multi-faceted investigation and it will stretch our resources to the limit. There is nothing new there, guys, but I'm hopeful that, with more manpower, we'll get closer to our killer. Detective O'Connor will be handling the Europol links, going directly to both locations. Dr Pearson, whom many of you know,' he pointed to Kate at the back of the room, 'will continue working with us on the profiling and behavioural analysis of the killer. Dr Pearson, have you anything to add before we move on?'

'My report will be finalised once I get an update from Detective Lynch on the Europol developments.'

'Good. But I'd like you to give us an overview at this point, specifically on the signature of the killer and the framing of the crime scene. I believe Mark has the next slides ready for you to talk us through.'

Bravo for communication, thought Kate, making her way from the back of the room to the top table. 'Thank you, Chief Superintendent.'

Lynch loaded a double slide, one depicting Rick Shevlin in the framed mirror at the Earlbrook Hotel, the other from the Parisian location. 'If you look closely, you can see the victim, Rick Shevlin, reflected within the wooden frame of the mirror in the room.' Then she pointed to the image of Pierre Laurent. 'Again, the victim is reflected in a mirror, this time the one in the bathroom. The reflection of both dead men is not accidental, and neither are many aspects of these crimes. We can make a number of inferences from this. The killer is careful, analytical, highly intelligent and specific. She – and there's sufficient evidence to believe we're dealing with a female killer – is capable of enormous anger, is more than willing to inflict pain, including torture, and does not suffer extensive remorse for her actions. It is not surprising that we're dealing with multiple crime scenes as this level of violence and intent is progressive.'

'By progressive,' asked Gary Egan, 'you mean there is the possibility of escalation in behaviour?'

'Yes. It's possible that her behaviour could become even more severe, and if the investigation from Rome can be conclusively linked,' she looked directly at Lynch for the first time, 'our killer may not be restricted to one victim at a time.'

'I see.' Gary Egan leaned back in the chair. 'Continue, please, Dr Pearson.'

'Thank you.' She looked away from the slide to the officers in the room. 'The killer's mind can also shift with relative ease from a concentrated and frenzied physical attack to detachment, when she can manipulate the crime scene to a minuteness of detail and creative imagery. In many ways the aftermath of the killing is as important to her as the killing itself.' She looked back at the double slide. 'Each of these images is similar to depictions of cards from the Higher Arcana deck of the Tarot – the Hangman in the case of Rick Shevlin and the Hermit in the case of Pierre Laurent. One of the questions I'm pursuing at the moment is who these images or messages are targeting. Are they for the killer herself, or are there other possibilities?'

'And what is your current theory on that, Dr Pearson?' Gary Egan sat forward now.

'The potential options are the victim, someone connected with them, the killer, or someone else entirely. I don't believe they're aimed at the victim.'

'Why not?'

'For a start, Chief Superintendent, the victims are dead. How the scenes are depicted isn't going to say a lot to either of them.'

'I see. Continue, Dr Pearson.'

'I think these re-creations are pointers or markers in an overall scheme or map in the killer's mind, which ties in with the Tarot-card connection and a potential card spread.'

'Let me be clear, Dr Pearson.' Gary Egan appeared perplexed.

'Are you absolutely sure the killer is re-creating these Tarot images because of some kind of card spread or map?'

'Not one hundred per cent, but it's a strong possibility.'

'And who is deciding on this spread?'

'Whoever is holding the deck.' She gazed at him blankly.

'Dr Pearson, I'd like you to stay back after we finish here.' Egan turned to the bookman, Sean O'Keefe, who, Kate knew, under the Irish police system managed the case file, or book as it was known. 'Sean, once Mark has gone through the final logistics of the current state of play, vis-à-vis ongoing allocation of duties, I want a full analysis of the Shevlin book. I need to review everything we have. This thing looks like it's going to be moving fast, and I'll be damned if we're not up to speed on it.'

SANDRA

IT'S DARK BY the time I drive back to the house in Greystones. I take the diary with me. I haven't a choice, now that I know someone has meddled with it. On the way, I call Edgar on the mobile. I don't want him to be suspicious so I tell him I'm going to visit Karen for a couple of hours, hoping it will buy me time.

On reaching the house, I phone her. 'Karen, it's Sandra.'

'Are you okay?' she asks. 'You sound frazzled.'

'Do I?' I try to control my breathing. Keep calm.

'Lori phoned earlier. She said you were upset.'

'What else did she say?'

'Not much.'

'Look, don't mind Lori.'

'Don't worry, I don't.' She lets out a laugh.

'I need you to cover for me.'

She doesn't respond, at least not immediately. Her silence feels like a judgement. Finally she says, 'What do you want me to do?'

'I need time on my own, time away from Edgar.'

Again a couple of seconds pass before she says, 'Do you still think he's having an affair?' Her question feels loaded.

'Look, I don't want you worrying, which is why I'm asking you to cover for me. I've told Edgar I'll be with you. If he calls, stall him – tell him I've gone to the bathroom or something. If necessary, ring me and I'll take it from there.'

'Where are you now?'

'That doesn't matter. I told you, don't worry. I just need space.'

For a while, I stay in the car, staring at the house. It looks empty. I know that the longer I wait, the more I risk someone coming back. I feel cold. I think about driving around the block, giving the car engine time to heat up again. I can't shift the chill, even though my ears are burning and my hands are sweaty and shaking. I think about why I came here. Did I want to see this mystery woman? What if she's with Edgar? I've given them the perfect opportunity to meet. They could be sitting in a bar now, laughing at me. If the house is empty, this is my best chance. How hard would it be to break in? *For once in your life take a chance – you know you want to.*

I step out of the car. Everything is happening in slow motion. I don't have a plan for getting inside, but somehow I know I will. I think again about the mystery woman coming back, finding me there, and for a moment I hesitate.

Before going into the garden, I glance up and down the

street. And, as if I've done it a million times, I walk to the back
of the house, turning the handle on the door. It's locked. Then
I notice two large ceramic pots planted with lavender and mint.
The smell is intoxicating. I lift the first pot, the smaller of the
two, and worms wiggle underneath. I lift the second, the one
with the lavender, and find a key. It all feels too easy.

As I turn the key in the lock, my heart is pounding, like an
internal warning system. *If you do this, there will be no going back.* I
don't know what I'm most afraid of, being caught, or the feeling
that, for some unknown reason, I might be doing exactly what
others want me to do.

Inside the house, I feel like a stronger person, having crossed
the line. I've broken in. I've done something completely out
of character. It's almost like a kind of freedom. I tell myself to
remain calm, but walking through the house, the deeper I go,
the more the fear is coming back.

I open the door onto the hallway from the kitchen, and when
it creaks, I have the strangest feeling that I'm being watched.
Standing in the hallway, my fear intensifies. There is a narrow
table with claw legs, and overhead, a small glass chandelier.
For a moment, I think about it crashing down, breaking the
dead silence. Looking at the staircase, I wonder if the house
has an alarm system. I hadn't heard any bells going off, but that
doesn't mean it isn't protected. Sometimes the alarm bells go off
elsewhere, at a security station. At any moment the place could
be surrounded, and I would be caught, like a common criminal,
having broken into someone else's home.

I think about getting out of there fast, visualising myself
running towards the back door, firing the key into the shrubs,

not having time to replace it under the garden pot, getting into the car and driving somewhere else, perhaps to Alice's house, confronting her with Lori's suspicions. If she isn't at home, it could be proof that she's with Edgar. I'm so fixated that I'm surprised to find myself on the bottom step of the staircase, as if it's challenging me, urging me to go further into *her* domain. Taking another step, I hear a whine, a cat wailing as if in pain. It's coming from outside, but it unsettles me. I realise I'm experiencing *déjà vu*, a feeling of something familiar, before I understand why. It's the smell.

HARCOURT STREET STATION, SPECIAL DETECTIVE UNIT

AS KATE MADE her way to Chief Superintendent Gary Egan's office, she figured that, if he wanted to talk to her directly after the incident-room briefing, the prospect of her visiting the international crime scenes had increased, and she would be carrying the white flag to Declan.

'Thanks for waiting, Dr Pearson.' Egan was practically bursting up the hallway, Adam and Lynch in tow. Once inside the office, it was Egan who spoke first. 'It looks, Dr Pearson, as if the link to the cold case from Rome, in 2006, has got stronger. Apart from extensive wounds to the face and body, the cause of death was also similar to Shevlin's, exsanguination

– and, like Shevlin and Laurent, the victim had a chequered sexual history.'

'By chequered, Chief Superintendent, you mean what exactly?'

'Michele Pinzini had numerous affairs, used prostitutes regularly, and a whole lot more, if you get my drift.'

'I see.' Kate could tell Egan was uncomfortable, so she didn't push the point, knowing she would get more out of the others later.

'The crime scene had other variables too.' Egan turned to Lynch. 'Why don't you fill Dr Pearson in?'

'Certainly, Boss.' He smiled at his superior, then turned to her. 'As I've mentioned to you already, this time the crime scene wasn't confined to one victim. The fire could have killed both the victim and his wife. Even with the hotel maid raising the alarm, the room was ablaze by the time the emergency services arrived. As the chief super has already noted, despite the fire we do know the actual cause of death, something that would have been difficult to determine if the blaze had advanced any further. The wife was found unconscious. She had suffered smoke inhalation. It was she who filled the police in on the victim's sexual history. She was pregnant at the time. Her unborn child also survived.'

'What else did she tell them?'

'That she suspected her husband was deeply involved with another woman before the murder, but this time, it was different from the others.'

'Because of the suspected stalking?'

'And because her husband's moods had grown darker, a lot

darker. Before the killing, she was concerned about his well-being as well as her own.'

'Why didn't she report the stalking beforehand?'

'She had mentioned it to a few close friends but, like Anita Shevlin, she couldn't put her finger on anything concrete.'

'Have you the images from the crime scene?' She was directing her questions at Lynch.

'It's another cold case, and unfortunately Italian paperwork moves even slower than our own. We should have it by the time you and Detective Inspector O'Connor arrive there.'

So it's happening, she thought. 'I'm going somewhere, am I?' she said, emphasising her surprise.

Egan gave Lynch a disgruntled look. He hadn't liked his reference to the speed of Irish paperwork, or that he had told Kate she was going on the international trip.

'Sorry to spring this on you, Dr Pearson,' Egan was keen to take back the reins, 'but we don't have any time to waste. I meant what I said at the briefing. It's imperative we move fast. We're a number of steps behind, with multiple crime scenes and case files to deal with. It is both fortunate and unfortunate that the two cases are outside our jurisdiction, and more unfortunate that we're dealing with stale leads.' He turned to Adam, who was leaning against the side wall, keeping quiet. 'I'm depending on you, Detective, to work closely with Dr Pearson, and bring us back something tangible.'

'Was any form of message left at the scene?' Kate directed her question at all three men.

'No, other than the fire being a potential Tarot card connection,' Lynch replied.

'Was Michele Pinzini drugged?'

'We know the victim and his wife had been out dining. They'd had an argument. According to the original investigation, Pinzini was very drunk. The autopsy report confirmed high levels of alcohol in his system. His wife also said he'd been drinking heavily.'

'Had he drunk enough to lapse into unconsciousness?'

Again Lynch answered: 'Possibly – but outside that, the police found traces of sedatives in his bloodstream and his wife's. The wife's statement said, one moment they were arguing, the next she was coughing her guts up in the room with the emergency services around her, and her husband was dead beside her.'

'The victim's age and profession?'

Gary Egan answered this time. 'He was in his forties, a photographer, and a very successful one. He did a lot of work for fashion magazines.'

'A photographer,' she repeated, contemplating how that would fit with everything they had so far.

Egan stood up. 'Dr Pearson, we can make all the travel arrangements at this end, but you'll need to confirm your availability for tomorrow.'

'Which destination are we going to first?'

'We've provisionally booked yourself and Detective Inspector O'Connor on a six a.m. flight tomorrow from Dublin to Charles de Gaulle airport, and then onto Rome the following day. That will give the Italian end of the operation time to pull out any case details we need. I appreciate this is short notice, but there's not a lot we can do about it.'

'I understand. Give me an hour.' It was her turn to stand up.

'I'm looking forward to reading your report, Dr Pearson.' Egan leaned forward to shake her hand, content in the knowledge that both her interim report and confirmation of travel plans were almost securely in the bag. 'O'Connor, will you walk Dr Pearson out?'

Adam held the door open for her, still the old-fashioned kind of guy, she thought. With Egan's door firmly closed behind them, she said, 'You kept very quiet in there.'

'There's no point in saying anything unless you've something to say.'

'I guess not.' She suspected there was more to it than that. 'I'll have to make a phone call. Is there somewhere I can go – somewhere private?'

'Sure.'

She was glad he didn't ask why. She wasn't looking forward to her conversation with Declan, but there was no way around it now.

SANDRA

THE FAMILIAR SMELL hits me, like a slap in the face, in the same way that the memory of Edgar turning the key in the front door of this house keeps coming back to me. The aroma of a man's cologne conjures up so much. He has taken me for an idiot. All I feel is anger, against him and her. The voice inside my head is telling me to forget about any alarm systems, or fear of being caught, and find out everything I can.

I wait a few seconds before moving, the silence of the house a form of security. There are no police cars with bright lights arriving outside. No one knows I'm here. Looking up the stairs, I'm conscious that I may not have a lot of time, but then another thought strikes me, causing the panic to rise again. I have no idea what I'm looking for.

I take another step upwards, telling myself to remain calm. Speed could mean missing something, but the higher I go, I realise I'm moving deeper into the belly of the house, and further away from any potential escape. What if she comes back? What if I don't hear her? What if, in my effort to find information, I become so engrossed in what I'm doing that she suddenly appears, standing behind me? Without understanding why, I have a vision of her laughing at me.

Downstairs, her touches had been everywhere, the lavish furnishings, the claw-legged hall table, the ornate chandelier. I turn around, looking behind me. The door to the living room is open, and I can see the gold-framed mirror hanging over the fireplace, two tan couches at either side. I think of her sitting in one of them, perhaps her and Edgar, raising wine glasses, joking with each other about me.

I continue up the stairs, and despite the silence of the house, and my weight pressing on each step, I'm not making any noise, as if I'm invisible. The only thing I hear is my heart thumping.

The first two bedrooms are small, furnished lightly with little more than a single bed. The last room, the one at the back, is the largest, a double, spanning the width of the house. I know it's her room from the moment I walk inside. There is a black silk dressing gown lying across the bed, and on the bedside locker, a pearl necklace. I pick it up, allowing the beads to slip through my fingers, before holding them to my neck, as if I'm pretending to be her. I feel the coolness of the pearls against my skin, then look up and see my shadow on the wall, large and looming. I don't close the clasp, but drop the beads back onto the locker.

I feel as though I'm choking, even though the necklace is no longer on my neck.

Feeling panicked again, I search for something that will tell me who she is – a photograph, a letter with her name on it, a driver's licence, anything. Did I miss something downstairs? Now that I know what I'm looking for, it should be easier to find it. But there are no photographs of her anywhere in the room, or any letters with her name on them. Maybe she doesn't live here all the time. Maybe it's a place she and Edgar come to be together. I turn around, checking I closed the bedroom door behind me. I grab a chair from the corner, placing it under the door handle at an angle. If anyone tries to come in, it will be a warning and give me more time. I cross to the bedroom window, I lift the lower sash. It would be a jump, but there are shrubs I could aim for. I rub my forehead, thinking about confronting her, calling her a bitch. *Stop wasting time.*

The air coming from outside is cold, now that it's late evening. I walk over to the dark cedar wardrobe. It's large and overbearing. There is a keyhole on both doors, but one has a brass key with a small red tassel. Turning it, I hear the click, and the two doors open wide. There are male and female clothes. Perhaps she's married. Or the men's clothes belong to Edgar. I rummage through them like a mad woman, checking the labels on the men's jackets and the size of the shirt collars. They are the same size Edgar wears. Could it be a coincidence? I remind myself that he has a key to this house and my stomach heaves.

Looking inside every pocket, I hope I might stumble on the final proof, but then I hear a noise coming from outside. I stop in my tracks, but it's only the breeze causing the trees to creak. I keep searching, knowing that at any moment she, the other woman, could appear, accuse me of breaking in, ask what I'm doing in her house, and how dare I go through his and her things, as if I'm the intruder. *But you are, Sandra.* I sense that I have more to fear from her than I can possibly know. She is the one in charge. I'm the one in the dark.

It's in one of the inside pockets of a man's overcoat that I find the rolled-up piece of paper. There is no denying Edgar's handwriting, even though it takes me a while to concentrate on the words: the name and address of a hotel in town. I've never stayed there, but I've had drinks in the bar. It's opulent, not my kind of place. I turn the piece of paper over, and on the reverse, there are three digits. A room number? I lean against the wall near the window, breathing in the cool air. My mind goes into overdrive, putting all the bits of information together. I followed Edgar here, and I know he has a house key. When he arrived, he stayed for nearly an hour, as if it was his home, not that of a stranger. His clothes are hanging in the wardrobe, or at least clothes that fit him, and then there's the smell of his cologne, and his handwriting on the piece of paper. How much more proof do I need that he is living a second life?

You hear all the time of people living secret lives. People who have multiple love affairs, false identities, an innocent woman not knowing she is living with a fraud, even a killer. It's all possible.

I look down at the note again, at Edgar's handwriting. He must have put it in the pocket. I double-check the size label on the coat: 38L. 'His size,' I say out loud, as if to drive the point home. I lean in, pulling one of the lapels towards me, knowing his habit of applying extra cologne once he's dressed. There's no denying the aroma. It's his. *You've been living a lie.*

Putting the note inside my coat pocket, I scan the room again. There has to be something else. I begin pulling out the drawers in the bedside locker, beside her bed, with the black silk dressing gown staring up at me. The bottom drawer is either stuck or locked. I need to prise it open. I pull the chair away from the door, run down the stairs into the kitchen and grab a sharp knife from the cutlery drawer.

In the bedroom, I don't bother putting the chair back under the handle. At first, there isn't a budge on the drawer. I'm holding the knife tight and my hand is shaking, but somehow, I manage to make a narrow slit. I wedge my fingers into the gap, but I can't get a proper hold. I'm sweating beneath my coat, so I take it off, letting it fall to the floor. Pulling the drawer handle with as much force as I can, I turn the knife in my hand, wedging the handle inside the narrow gap, twisting the blade and tearing my skin. *Careful, Sandra, don't mess up now.* I push the knife in further, knowing the gap is widening. When the drawer opens, the blade jerks upwards, clipping my hand. I see blood. It drips onto my coat. I press my right hand over the wound to stop the flow, but it seeps between my fingers.

I can't stop now. I shuffle items in the drawer from side to side, trying to work out what's important and what isn't. The drawer is full of shiny things, a metal letter opener, a cigarette lighter, a silver lipstick case, a pincushion with small steel pins, and a miniature pill box. At the back of the drawer I see something unexpected. It's another key, one with a large chunky key ring, with the number from the piece of paper. I think about taking it. If she notices it's missing, she will know someone has been in her house. Can I take the risk?

I pull my blood-stained coat off the floor, pushing the key into the pocket. I look back at the silk dressing gown. She must have worn that against her skin. Edgar touched her in it, sweeping the contours of her body as his excitement rose. I think about the two of them together, gleeful with their little secret, and feel utterly betrayed. In my rush to get out, I trip on the staircase.

It's only when I'm safely in the car that I begin to write all of it down in my diary – her address, what I found inside the house, the details of the hotel key. I become so occupied in what I'm doing that, for a few minutes, I don't look up.

Maybe that's why I miss her, the woman passing the car. By the time I spot her, she has her back to me. Could that be her? Should I confront her? I'm sure she's walking towards the house. When she's far enough away, I turn the key in the ignition. The engine starts first time. I reverse slowly, then do a sharp U-turn, looking in the rear-view mirror as I pull away. A part of me is willing her to turn so I can see her face. She doesn't. She keeps on walking, and the further I drive away, the more obscure she becomes, getting smaller and smaller all the time. I'm shaking again. I grip the steering wheel tighter. What if she already knows I've been there? What if she's one step ahead of me? What if she was watching me all along and is smiling to herself, curious about what I've been up to, and how much more it will take for me to crack?

I

IT'S MY TURN now. The scales need balancing. The judgement call is now mine. Remember the eye? Think about the hunter and the hunted. First they eye their prey, and then they stalk. Soon they chase and, finally, they will devour. My new man doesn't realise how much I'm drawing him in. I care little for his pretty wife, with her pretty past, and her not so pretty future. Consider yourself one of the lucky ones. Be grateful it's her and not you I have in my sights.

There has been another shift. Something is changing in the power game, and it is in my favour. I'm instinctual about such things, recognising the subtle variations in pattern.

Did I tell you I was born outside wedlock? Perhaps that's why

I care so little for the marital status. A stupid safety net designed to protect people from themselves and their vices. Rules bring structure and reliability. There is comfort in that for some. Not for me. Social normality and I don't see eye to eye. I've been on the fringes from an early age. I am suspicious of normality. Like the perfect picture, it has many unanswered questions. The guy going to work every day to do the same job, the woman desperately striving to better herself, people walking the same walk to identical houses, or sitting in their cars going one way and back the same. What's the question? Why the hell are they doing it?

They'll give you lots of reasons — ambition, routine, familiarity and all those well-worn clichés. My theory is simple: it's their fear and their need to be part of something safe that holds them back from doing what they really desire. I've never been part of something safe, so I don't worry about that. There is no safety net for me. I'll leave that to the people who like to conform.

When I think of my mother, I wonder if, maybe, she was like me. I've only ever heard her story in fragments, told by others, whispers from behind closed doors. I cannot be sure how much is true, but I've built up a picture over time. I see her as an outcast, living outside the pack. I hear she was considered odd, not socially acceptable. She didn't fit the mould. I've also heard she wasn't right in the head — 'a strange girl' was how some referred to her. I have my suspicions as to why she might have been that way. I grew up in the same house. I felt like an outcast too. Society doesn't look kindly on the fallen. When I see the road in the woods, I wonder if, one day, it will lead me to her.

You might never understand why I kill, or seek the affection of would-be strangers. The witch said she saved me from certain death. She took pleasure in the telling, hoping I might feel guilt and be grateful to her. Make no mistake. She did none of it to bestow love. You and me, we're more alike than you might think. I need love as you do, but my options are limited.

Unlike you, I don't have all the answers. The only person I judge is me. Look on me as the reverse side of your life, the life you might have led if things had been different. When you think of being loved as a child, I would like you to replace that memory with hate. The hunched woman in the shadows, the one who raised me, made me more fearful than any of you can imagine. Witnessing evil first hand, like love, will shape you. Your understanding will be based on it, including your concept of right and wrong.

The scales are in my favour now, and neither the little wife nor anyone else will stand in my way.

SANDRA

DRIVING HOME, I'M forced to slow down to let an oncoming car pass on a narrow stretch of back road. I'm still breathing heavily. I'm a criminal now. I've broken into another person's house, invaded their privacy. I screech to a stop as a stray fox crosses my path, but soon I'm picking up speed again.

It is only as I park the car outside our house that my breathing begins to settle. A lot of the journey home is a blur, but I still remember that woman passing my car. She must have seen me. Did she know I'd been inside her house? Would she phone the police?

I visualise them calling to my door, asking me where I was this evening, telling me there had been a break-in and they had reason to believe I was involved. Edgar would be shocked, and then I would blurt it all out. I would tell him it was his fault, and hers, that I was beside myself with fear and doubt, and that I had never done anything like this before. They are usually lenient on a first offence, especially if you admit to it from the beginning, and that's when I imagine myself walking into the local police station, saying I have to confess a crime. I know right there and then that I'm not going to do that, and I'm not going to tell Edgar either. Maybe I should go to the hotel and ask if that room is vacant, if I could have a look at it. *Pull yourself together. You're not the first woman to discover her husband is having an affair. What difference would it make if you see the room?* 'I don't know,' I say out loud. Then I remember that the woman didn't turn. She mightn't have seen me. With a bit of luck she wouldn't notice anything awry.

I ring Edgar on his mobile. It goes straight to voicemail. I wonder about phoning Karen then, but what would I say? I could tell her about someone writing things in my diary, that there is only one person who could have done it: the person who is moving things around the house. The same woman I watched with her back to me. If she'd been inside my home and written that note, she had read everything in my diary. She would know about my suspicions. Would she have told Edgar? Why wasn't she showing her hand? Maybe she enjoys playing games. Maybe Edgar told her I'd been unwell. She would know I was vulnerable.

I feel my heart racing again, and I know why. It's because something else is forming in my mind, and the more I think about it, the more I realise it's the only thing that makes any sense. This woman isn't just having an affair with Edgar: she has me in her sights too. Again, my hands shake. If he told her I'd had a nervous breakdown, she would think me easy pickings.

I can't stay sitting in the car, but what if the house isn't safe? I think about going to the police again, but they might think I'm mad. I can't take that chance. No, there has to be another way. But what if it's all true? What if, the next time she breaks in, she does more than move things around?

I could stay with Lori for a while, but I remember how odd she was earlier, and I'm not sure about Alice either: *Think, Sandra, has Alice given you any real reason to doubt her, other than her off-handedness and Lori's accusations?* I can't risk it. Nor can I go to Karen's, her husband would be bound to tell Edgar.

It takes me a while to work things out, but finally I ring Edgar's mobile again. When it goes to voicemail, I leave a message. I tell him I'm going away for a couple of days. That I've been thinking about things and, considering everything, it'll do us both the world of good to have a break, and that he isn't to worry. I can't afford for him to come after me.

I pack enough clothes to keep me going for a couple of nights, checking that I have my passport and credit cards. I have no intention of using the cards to do anything other than withdraw money from cash machines. I can take out enough to pay the hotel bill, and use the passport as identification. Our cards are on a joint account, and I can't take the risk that the credit-card company would share the information with Edgar. I check I have my mobile and diary. The last thing I put in my overnight bag is a kitchen knife. I have no intention of using it, but I feel better having it with me.

Driving away from the house, I realise I've put no thought into which hotel I will stay in – certainly not the one on the note. Part of what I said to Edgar in the phone message is true. Time alone is exactly what I need: time to work out who this woman is, and what she really wants.

I ring each of the girls. Edgar is bound to phone them. I need to make sure they're all saying the same thing. Afterwards, I think again about Alice being distant, Lori acting strange, and Karen's gushiness during the last call, almost as if she, too, has something to hide. For the first time since this whole sorry mess began, I ask myself the question I should have asked from the beginning. How much of this is my own fault? Hadn't Edgar only wanted what any other heterosexual male would want? Hadn't I been the one to deny him?

I could cope with an affair. But there is more to this. I know it as sure as I know she's been watching my every move. She wants more from Edgar than sex. She wants my life.

DUBLIN AIRPORT

KATE REACHED DUBLIN airport with less than an hour to the flight take-off time. There was no way she could avoid it being tight, her plans having to be put in place so quickly. It hadn't been as bad as she had feared talking to Declan, the two of them resigned to the inevitable, and in a strange way, that morning, she felt as if she was starting afresh, a new beginning of sorts.

Charlie had been delighted with the unexpected change of arrangements, and his obvious relief at seeing his parents getting on together, instead of the usual strained conversations he witnessed, caused her another pang of guilt.

When she finally got through to the departure lounge, Adam

was leaning with his back to the windows at gate twenty-six. Spotting her, he unfolded his arms and waved.

'They didn't arrest you, then?' were his first words.

'Not quite, although if looks could kill for cutting it close to the wire, I'd be on Death Row by now.'

'We still have another five minutes before boarding. We can grab a coffee over there.' He pointed to the coffee dock opposite.

She looked at the queue already forming at the boarding gate.

'Never mind that,' he said. 'We've been allocated seats.' Then he glanced at her small suitcase. 'And we're travelling light. I hate bloody queues.'

She was glad of the coffee, knowing they would talk about the investigation on the flight, welcoming a few minutes to settle and gather her thoughts.

'No problem getting Charlie minded, then?' he asked.

'I think he was happy to get rid of me.' For the first time in ages, she really smiled.

'I know that feeling.' His response was somewhat downbeat.

'Sorry, I didn't mean to …'

He put up a hand to stop her. 'It's okay. You don't have to walk on eggshells with me.'

'I know that.' She blew on her coffee. 'How are things between you and your son?'

He shrugged his shoulders. 'So-so.'

'What does that mean?'

'It beats the hell out of shit, that's what it means.' He turned to the departure gate – the crowd at their gate was dispersing. 'Come on,' he said. 'We'd better go.'

After a final check of the passports, they walked in silence through the tunnel to the aircraft door. Their next conversation would be about work, safer ground for both of them.

∞

The flight to Charles de Gaulle airport was under-booked, so there were only the two of them in a row for three. Kate took the seat at the window, and Adam the one beside her. She sensed he was still tetchy after their brief conversation about his son. He surprised her when, during the safety demonstration, he said, 'I envy you, Kate, the relationship you have with Charlie.'

'He's still very young,' she replied. 'There's plenty of time for him to turn into a rebellious teenager.' She hoped a light-hearted approach would ease things. She wasn't used to him being so open. Maybe his months off had changed him.

'I see myself in him, you know, when I was that age, especially the anger.'

'What were you angry about?'

'Everything.'

'It's all part of growing up, I guess.'

'Were you angry as a teenager, Kate?'

'I think girls and boys differ at that age.'

'You're not answering me.'

She thought back to her childhood as an only child, the fractured relationship between her father and mother: he had believed he was all-knowing, and her mother had done nothing to contradict him. She had spent so long coming to terms with the strained relationship between herself and her father that, in many ways, she had ignored the one she had with her mother.

'I guess you could say I was angry, at least for a time.'

'What changed things?'

'I don't know. One day I was looking at my parents and I realised they were as vulnerable as me. It was a kind of freedom, but scary at the same time.'

'So what happens if a child doesn't have one of their parents around?'

She knew he was asking about his son. 'Whether or not you're physically around when a child is growing up,' she hoped she sounded caring, 'a father and a mother are always part of a child's world. It's not simply the genetic make-up, but what you represent, especially in our society, when so much emphasis is still placed on a particular family model.'

'A somewhat out-of-date model.'

'Yes, but to the child it's still how the perfect family is presented.'

She thought about both of them failing in that regard and how, not so long ago, she wouldn't have believed she'd ever have this conversation with him. 'Declan and I are about to be officially separated – we will be as soon as the papers are filed.'

'I figured it was happening, all right.'

'My parents stayed together because it was expected of them. That wasn't an ideal situation either.'

'No, you're right there.'

She turned away, looking out of the window, the plane above the clouds now, the stark brightness in contrast to their mood.

'What matters most,' her voice low, 'is that a child feels loved.' She thought about her mother again. Despite everything, she had never doubted her mother's love, and somewhere under her father's anger, there had been love too. 'If a child feels loved, they have a better chance than most.'

'Did you feel loved?'

'I guess I was one of the lucky ones, even though I didn't always know it.' She turned back to him. He hadn't taken his eyes off her. 'Give your son time,' she said. 'Another thing we all need.'

'I owe him that at least.'

Surprising herself, she placed her hand on top of his, unsure how he would react, relieved when he squeezed it back. 'You don't need to worry about me, Kate. I'm made of strong stuff.'

'I know you are.'

Then he pulled his hand away. 'I guess it's time we got to work and earned some of the taxpayers' money. It won't be long before we're arriving at Charles de Gaulle.'

'You're right.' She was sorry their hands had parted. 'Where do you want to start?'

'Pull out that report of yours, the one you faxed to Lynch and Egan this morning.'

'I have a copy for you.'

'I thought you would.'

They read the report in unison. Although Kate had been over it half a dozen times that morning, she couldn't shake the notion that there was still a large piece of the jigsaw that she should have put together, and hadn't.

Interim Report on the Murder of Rick Shevlin

Compiled by: Dr Kate Pearson

Crime Scene Characteristics

- Primary crime scene
- Married male – mid-forties
- Worked as an art dealer – successful
- No known criminal record
- Location: Earlbrook Hotel, Dublin; hotel room offering privacy and secrecy
- Cause of death: exsanguination – throat severed
- Frenzied attack: multiple slash and puncture wounds to the body, slash wounds to face, whip marks to buttocks
- Puncture wounds relatively straight, trajectory from above with victim lying on bed
- Weapon used: equal in size to a large carving knife, capable of maximum damage, gaping wounds and deep penetration
- Blood localised to bed area and immediate vicinity
- Victim sedated prior to attack – use of Special K to immobilise him, administered orally
- Victim found naked and face up, his right ankle tied to brass bedpost at top of bed with a one-inch double-knotted rope. Left leg bent at the knee, at a ninety-degree angle; both arms bent at the elbow joints, placed under the body at the mid-point and tied together with rope identical to that used at the ankle
- Emotionally charged attack
- No sign of victim putting up defence – on entry of attacker into hotel room, or during the actual assault

- Re-creation of the Hangman card from the Tarot deck
- Estimated time of death: between 1 a.m. and 3 a.m.
- Minimal forensic evidence found at crime scene – female tissue in male genitals matched to escort, see 'Sexual and Ritualistic Influences of Crime Scene v. Emotional Dynamics' below. Lipstick residue: properties identified to major brand, but insufficient to create a DNA profile. All blood deposits found were matched to the victim
- Crime scene cleaned down by killer or someone else
- No forced entry
- Dressing table in hotel room moved; see earlier notes on framing of killing
- Hotel-room curtains pulled back allowing light from car park. For commonality and diversities between Dublin and Paris killings, see analysis below
- Depiction of both the Hangman card and the Hermit card at both scenes re-created in finite detail and reproduced through mirrors
- Other factors: victim advised his wife he had a late business dinner in town, making it necessary for him to stay at the Earlbrook overnight – no business meeting recorded at victim's office

Crime Inferences
- Crime scene: organised
- Use of sedatives rendering the victim immobile – broadening the physical characteristic of the attacker to include a female or someone physically weaker than victim

- Degree of planning: high
- Hotel room, offering killer privacy and time to carry out killing and creation of crime scene undisturbed
- Lack of forced entry – either the attacker had a key, or the victim allowed the killer in willingly
- Possibility of attacker being known to the victim based on no obvious struggle: medium-high Alternative: attacker perceived as harmless – for example, a member of hotel staff
- Attack savage, frenzied and fast
- Aftermath, scene re-creation – calm and prolonged
- Killer has murdered before
- Tarot cards: the Hangman (Rick Shevlin), the Hermit (Pierre Laurent), each a card of the Higher Arcana – possible card spread. Q: Is the killer the Querent or the Reader of the spread?
- Emotionally charged attack points to sole killer
- Effectiveness and efficiency of murder –
  (a) gaining access without forced entry
  (b) immobilising victim
  (c) severity of attack
  (d) creation of final crime scene with minimal forensic traces
  – indicates individual with planning, high motivation, calmness of execution, ability to detach and clear focus on task in hand; high intelligence, 95–100 percentile
- Creativity –
  (a) an understanding of shape and form
  (b) attention to detail

    (c) ability to visually re-create

- Minimum of two victims across two jurisdictions; explore work and recreational aspects of travelling between jurisdictions
- Time span between victims indicates potential stressors prior to killings
- Killer is on a progressive path
- Killer is capable of repeat and heightening attack
- Murders offer some form of payback – possibly revenge, emotional loss, failed relationship, desire for dominance, fetish desire and/or means of re-enactment
- Tarot card re-creations – message/signature/context still unknown
- Italian murder, if positively connected, opens up possibility of multiple victims per attack
- Drive – emotionally based and obsessional

Sexual and Ritualistic Influences of Crime Scene v. Emotional Dynamics

- Sexual fetishes illustrated at Dublin crime scene
- Paris victim known to have masochistic tendencies
- Dublin victim possibly at early stage of S&M – willing to give and receive pain
- Dublin victim: explore prior involvement in group sexual activity
- Self-harming/desire for sight of blood by Dublin victim possibly developed by previous sexual partner/relationship
- Dublin victim known to have had extra-marital affairs, including use of escorts

- Sexual involvement with both victims demonstrates an ability on the killer's part to adapt sexual behaviour based on the needs of their partner – see note re sexual grooming

Commonality and Diversities between Dublin and Paris killings

- Each a frenzied attack with the use of a large knife
- Diversity in age of victims – mid-twenties v. mid-forties
- Link to art in both cases – art dealer v. art student
- Successful financial businessman v. student
- Location of both murders: hotel rooms
- Depictions of Tarot cards: Dublin victim, naked, body positioned and tied like the Hangman card on hotel bed; Paris victim, wearing monk's habit, like the Hermit card, lantern by body, found on floor of hotel room, 2005. Rome victim 2006: awaiting further details
- Slash and puncture wounds found on both victims
- Cause of death: Dublin murder, exsanguination; Paris murder, asphyxiation
- Slash markings on face of Dublin victim v. untouched face on Paris victim
- Lipstick residue found on lips of Rick Shevlin v. no record of same at Paris killing
- Time span 2014 v. 2005/2006

Conclusions

- Killer: female
- Known to victims; possible previous relationships
- Psychopathic/sociopathic inferences

- Ability to detach, possible childhood or early trauma (see below)
- Interval between murders: indicative of emotional stressors prior to attack
- Killer: creative; will have link with visual art world – photography, sculpture, painting and or design
- Age: thirty–forty
- Attractive
- Ability to deceive and gain trust
- Capable of social integration
- A planner and a dreamer – will fantasise about murders in advance
- Manipulative/charming
- Capable of delusional thinking and distortion of information
- Seeks emotional fulfilment
- Attention-seeker
- Dangerous and volatile when provoked
- Uses sexual attraction to meet victims/partners
- Has the ability to compartmentalise killings
- Early trauma – damage during development of relationship between the id, the ego and the super-ego
- Ability to adjust to preferred sexual fetish – prior sexual grooming
- Will operate solely, or within a small group
- Lacks trust
- High level of hatred
- Emotionally damaged
- Violent attacks possible pleasure/release for the killer

- Creation of crime scene: reflective of visual awareness
- Takes pride in the end result
- Level of intelligence: HIGH
- Ability to avoid detection: HIGH
- Victims are chosen, and are potentially groomed
- Calmness of killer during aftermath of attack v. frenzied assault – further analysis required
- Risk of repeat killing: HIGH
- Time frame: subject to stressor/stressors
- Identification of stressor: unknown

I

THERE ARE TIMES when I feel lonely. People who keep secrets are often that way. Like others, I like to be held, to be kissed, and there are elements of previous love affairs from which I have taken pleasure.

Sex is different from kissing. My new lover is a good kisser. He says he loves my lips. I like the way he runs his long fingers through my hair, cupping the back of my head when he kisses me, before lowering his hands to my breasts, his fingertips warm to the touch, caressing each nipple, soft and teasing, and pleased when they become hard. Clawing at his skin with my nails, I can tell he enjoys the pain, feeling his arousal. Lately, he has started to cover my mouth with his hand when he is pushing in hard, my legs spread apart, as he shadows me like some beast. Afterwards, like the others, he tells me how much he needs me.

The last time we had sex, we didn't speak, not a word. We sat side by side in the car as he drove home. Once inside the house, he opened the top button of my skirt, then tugged the zip down. The skirt fell to the floor. I stepped back, kicking it to the side, and stripped in front of him like a burlesque performer. He looked on, obviously pleased. His kisses were more violent then, biting hard. 'Slow down,' I murmured, not wanting it to end too soon. He liked my suggestion of the ropes. I knew he would.

He tied my hands one at a time to each of the bedposts, nice and tight. Opening my legs, he tied the ankles too, kissing my inner thighs. I pretended an effort to escape, and felt the ropes tear into my skin, the pain wolfing me, him wanting me more than ever. His pathetic wife would never let him do anything like this. She can't or won't give him the sense of power he desires. I understand power: you need to be deprived of it to grasp its full appeal.

The tightened ropes, like his hands, felt rough to the touch, and when his fingernails cut my skin, I longed for him to use the knife, even the smallest tear. He enjoyed mixing my pain with his pleasure. Afterwards, I mentioned the blade. He didn't respond, but when he came inside me again, I arched my back, then turned to look at the gleam of the knife, and we both knew what would happen next.

'Are you ready now?' he asked, as if I had delayed the cutting, although he was the one who had needed convincing.

He made tiny slits on my thighs, the blood staining the bed, like some virginal bride's. At first, the sight of blood made his face contort, but then his desire swelled. The last few moments are always vital, and as a well-trained seductress, I knew how to perform, every movement, touch, expertly delivered. Despite being in control, I called out for 'help', knowing it would increase his want. He slapped me across the face, before covering my mouth again, his grip hard and desperate, as his body pushed in further and I no longer existed as a person. I felt myself disappear, but I could hear my laughter. He liked the sound, groaning like some wild boar, consumed with his own pleasure. I made sure his enjoyment was long and satisfying, timing my response to his thrust, teasing him at just the right moments. Then his release, stretched, prolonged, and fraught with yearning. Afterwards he was like a limp flower, wasted and fulfilled.

When he untied me, I was tempted to cut him unexpectedly, to see if he would flinch. I decided against it, asking him to lick my wounds, the way a lapdog would lick the wounds of a master. It was only then that I saw the shadow of the witch, fleeting from one side of the room to the other. She had seen the two of us together, and I despised the pleasure it gave her.

'Are you okay?' he asked, and I sensed his need to be assured.

'Yes, sleep now, my lovely.'

He closed his eyes as I lay silent, still looking around the room, hoping the witch would leave me in peace. I couldn't see her any more, but I know she likes to hide, waiting for her time to pounce.

The witch told me never to take pleasure from sex, that the

pain was my punishment for being a bad girl. What I know about badness, I learned from her. Like my mother, I became the object of another's desire. I haven't told you very much about my mother, but I do imagine myself as her babe in arms – Hush, little baby, please don't cry.

SANDRA

CHECKING INTO THE hotel room last night had been easier than I'd thought. I had an unsettled night, and each time I awoke, I felt the very same, as if a madwoman had taken over my mind.

With morning light flooding the room, I can't stay in bed any longer. I get up, walk over to the dressing table and pick up the leather-bound booklet on the top. Opening it, I read about the hotel's history, what number I need to call for laundry or to make a hairdressing appointment. I check the breakfast, lunch and dinner times, as if I'm a regular guest staying there for a couple of days' relaxation. That's what I said to the girl at Reception, that I was staying for two nights, maybe a little longer.

I slam the leather-bound booklet shut and go into the bathroom to brush my teeth before showering. The power of the water is strong, the warmth on my body a relief, a distraction from thoughts of Edgar and everything else. When I step out of the shower, the towel feels soft against my skin. I wrap it tight around me and brush my hair, untangling the knots with long, sweeping movements. Outside I can hear the clatter of bins, the hum of voices, cars driving past on the main road. Lifting the stray hairs from the bathroom basin, I chuck them into the bin, then wash my hands again, focusing on the water gurgling down the plughole. I hear other sounds too, the creaking of floorboards, like someone's footsteps. I look up, thinking the sounds are coming from above, but they're not: they're coming from the other side of the bathroom door. *Did I lock it?*

I bite my lip. If someone is out there, they know I'm here. They would have heard the shower. What if it's her? I hear more sounds from outside the bathroom window. I try to block them out, then hear a loud bang. *Was it a door closing?* It could have been from down the landing. I can't stay locked in a bathroom. I think about calling out. *Where's your mobile?* I already know it's in the other room. There's that sound again, the sound of someone walking around a room, but this time it is coming from above.

I unlock the bathroom door, turning the handle slowly, pulling the door back a couple of inches and peering into the room. I can't see anyone. I tell myself I'm being stupid. I pick up my mobile phone from the bedside table. I remember putting it on top of my diary last night, but the diary isn't there. Did I put it somewhere else? No, I wouldn't have. I look under the pillows, on the floor by the bed. I check my bag, and my overnight case, rummaging through each of the sections, knowing all the time I won't find it. I pull back the bedcovers. Still nothing. I retrace my steps, going over to the dressing table, picking up the leather-bound hotel booklet, as if it might give me a clue. I scan the room, looking at the bed again, the bedside locker, the dressing table, the chair tucked underneath.

I hear someone walking down the landing. I lean against the door, straining to hear more. Their footsteps are slow. I think they're going to knock or, even worse, open the door, but they keep on walking. I breathe a sigh of relief, and press my back against the wall, and it's then I see the diary. It's on the window seat. I don't remember leaving it there. I check the door is locked before walking over to it. There's something about the way the diary is positioned that bothers me. Then I realise it's not the positioning: it's because the clasp isn't locked. It's flipped open.

Picking it up, I sit on the window seat. I'm still wrapped in a towel, and my wet hair drips. I open the diary at my last entry. The one in which I wrote every detail I could remember about her house, including the key. It's exactly as I had written it, but when I reach the end, instead of closing the diary, I turn the page, wanting to see a blank sheet. It's the same handwriting, those large bold letters: *BE AFRAID*.

My hands shake again and I drop the diary. She must have been in the room. Perhaps she followed me last night. For all I know, she could have watched me while I slept, or maybe she came in while I was in the shower. I'm going to be sick – I run to the toilet and throw up until there is nothing left inside me, then curl up, like a scared animal, against the bathroom wall, scrunching my knees to my chest, knowing I'm not safe there any more.

Maybe in the studio I'd be safe. Edgar doesn't have a key. I try to remember if anything had been moved in there. I need to be sure. If she copied Edgar's keys, she wouldn't have been able to copy the studio key. I have the only one. I don't need to go to Reception. I paid them last night in advance. I can ring once I'm home; tell them I won't need the room for a second night. That something unexpected has come up. Or I could say nothing. I don't need to give them a reason. I don't need to explain myself to strangers.

In the studio I'll be able to figure it all out. I need to be somewhere she can't get to me. She could follow me once I'm outside, but I have to take that chance. I'm running out of choices.

Going down in the lift, I panic every time the door opens, scared that each woman stepping in might be her. I tell myself to get a grip, that maybe I'm imagining all this. These things don't happen to normal people. You don't wake up one morning and realise your life is in danger. Do you? But someone wrote that note, and they've told me to be afraid.

Once I reach the underground car park, the sound of moving cars, making screeching sounds, feels loud and threatening. I bite my lip again, and taste blood. I know I have to get to the car. I can see it from here. It's no more than ten metres away. A man passes with a child in his arms, a girl. She has curly blonde hair. She looks about four. I think all this as I'm walking to the car, the sight of a stranger and his child giving me courage. Once inside it, I lock the doors, making sure the back seat is empty.

Exiting the underground car park, the daylight beams into my eyes, blinding me. I indicate to turn right, waiting for a break in the traffic. I'm driving too fast, but I don't care. There are cars parked on either side, making the road narrow. A woman pushes out a baby in a buggy. I screech to a stop. The buggy is so close that I scream, then break out in a sweat. My ears are on fire. I roll down the window to say sorry, but she's roaring at me, telling me I'm an idiot. It's useless. I put my foot back on the accelerator. There are tears in my eyes. I can't go on like this. I can't do this on my own. I need to tell someone, someone who'll believe me.

FLIGHT FROM DUBLIN TO
CHARLES DE GAULLE AIRPORT

KATE WAITED WHILE Adam flicked back and forth through the contents of the report. She knew he would have questions.

'What makes you think she's between thirty and forty?'

'Shevlin was in his mid-forties, the victim in Paris was twenty-three, but that was nine years ago. It makes sense. I doubt Rick would go for someone older.

'Why not?'

'Men, particularly older men in their forties, fifties and sixties, are in the main attracted to younger women. Some say it is part of the evolutionary process. Older men can still reproduce, and the chances of conception are significantly higher with a younger model.'

'That's a bit harsh.'

'Simply saying it as it is, but Pierre Laurent sets the marker.'

'Because?'

'He was younger than the other two. Pierre may have been attracted to someone older, although I'd wager not much older. It's partly why I came to the age profile. If she was significantly older than Pierre, she wouldn't have been attractive to either Rick Shevlin or Michele Pinzini, assuming we make a conclusive connection to the latter. Remember, Rick also used the services of an escort, and Annabel was barely twenty. It's indicative of his preferences. None of this is absolute, you understand, merely a calculated analysis based on the facts.'

'Is there anything else about Pierre rocking your boat?'

'Apart from his age, he wasn't professionally successful or flush with money. Alongside the other variants in my report, he does stand out. Depending on what we discover in Paris, he could be particularly important.'

'Go on.'

'I doubt he's the first victim. His killing has all the hallmarks of having been carried out by someone who had killed before, but there's a chance he might have been the first serious adult relationship our killer experienced. After that, her choice of victim looks like it changed in age and profile.'

'Why do you think that was?'

'I have a theory, but it's no more than that.'

'Tell me anyhow.'

'Perhaps, despite Pierre's status, he was no longer needy

enough for her. Rich, successful men, those with partners, even children, are perceived to have it all, but many are still looking for more, and in some ways, because of their drive, are needier than most.'

'But in your report you said the killings are emotionally based, and obsessional.'

'They are, but the needier the victims, the more dependent they are on her. It's a game of balance and control. She seeks them out, men ripe for manipulation and control.'

'What's id, ego and super-ego?'

'Freudian theory.'

'Which is what?'

'The id is the unorganised part of the personality, which contains our basic instinctual drives and is present from birth. As humans, if we were to depend on the id alone, we wouldn't be able to operate as social animals. If you're hungry, for example, walk into a room and see someone else eating, you simply take their food. The ego is the one in the centre. It seeks to please the id, but in a way that will be beneficial in the long term, rather than bring grief in the short term. It acts as a mediator between the id and the super-ego.'

'Kate, I'm still lost.'

'Let's say you need to urinate.'

He looked at the queue for the toilet cubicle. 'I wish you hadn't mentioned that.'

'If you were relying on the id, you would urinate here, just as a baby would wet their nappy, responding to the desires and needs of id. But you're not a baby. You have learned through your super-ego that socially you should urinate in a bathroom.

The super-ego knows this, but the id still wants to urinate. The ego acts as a mediator between the two. It tells the id to wait. Are you with me so far?'

'I think so, but my id is getting impatient. I'll be back in a few minutes.' He stood up to take his place in the toilet queue.

While he was gone, Kate turned to look out of the window again, the blue sky bright above the clouds. Her mind drifted to past holidays with Declan and Charlie. An unexpected pang of sadness hit her hard. Perhaps it was a good thing, going away for a couple of days, leaving the normal structures and routines of life. Her mother used to say everything happened for a reason – a constant willingness on her part to accept certain things without question. Kate saw things differently: she invariably wanted to know *why*, and there wasn't always an easy answer. She was relieved to see Adam return to his seat beside her.

'You were talking about Mr Freud.'

'Glad you're still interested!'

'I'm like a sponge, Kate. I love learning new stuff.'

She laughed, but continued, 'I guess you could say the super-ego reflects the internalisation of cultural rules, mainly taught by parents, the father, according to Freud, but it also takes on the influence of non-parental figures, educators, teachers, people we see as role models.'

'All good so far.'

'Anyhow, things have moved on since Freud's theory of division. The id, the ego and the super-ego are still relevant today, but the model has been updated and revised, incorporating other elements, such as neurobiology, early attachment and environmental data.'

'You're getting a bit technical for me. How is this relevant to our killer?'

'Within neurobiology, we know the brain develops at a massive rate from babyhood to fully developed maturity at the age of twenty-five, and certain stages are identified. We have the development of our use of language, helping our role as social animals, and also the progression of the frontal lobes, providing higher functions, giving us the ability to plan, to hold off being impulsive, and, interestingly, the area of the brain known as the temporal gyrus.'

'What does that do?'

'It stores autobiographical memory. Negative interference, severe trauma in childhood, can adversely affect how the mind develops. If a child experiences trauma at an early point, the temporal gyrus doesn't develop as it should, and the child will have difficulty establishing a coherent sense of self.'

'They get fucked up.'

'Not a term I would use but yes, and if the damage occurs very early on, it can be devastating. I don't suppose you've heard of Tronick's Still Face experiment?'

'No, but I've a feeling you're going to tell me about it.'

'It illustrates how young babies are extremely responsive to emotions and reactions, and the social interactions they get from the world. During the experiment, a mother sits down face to face with her baby, who is about twelve months old. She plays with the baby, who is safely strapped in a high chair, engaging with her, giving positive facial and other physical expressions when the child smiles, points to objects in the room, and also makes signs and sounds to greet her, with the baby giving greetings back. What's happening is that parent and child are working together to co-ordinate their emotions and intentions. The positive feedback and interaction is what the baby is used to. Dr Tronick gets the mother to turn away from the baby, and when she turns back, she keeps her face perfectly still, showing no emotion. The baby girl quickly picks up on this, then uses all of her abilities to get the mother's attention back, smiling and pointing, because she's used to the mother looking where she points to, and reacting positively when she smiles. The baby also makes oral sounds, putting both hands up, but still the mother doesn't react. The baby then fires herself back in the high chair, scrunching her face, visibly upset, almost asking, "What's happening?" Very quickly, she lets out the screechy high-pitched sound we're all familiar with babies making, and keeps on doing it to the point of utter distress. The whole thing happens over a couple of minutes, but even in that time, you can see how the lack of response from the parent causes the baby great anxiety.'

'It sounds cruel to me.'

'Maybe, but what happens next is vital. The baby is feeling the stress of the situation, waving her arms about, her head completely turned away from the mother, and at this point, she loses control of her posture. The little girl has essentially turned away from the world as she knows it.'

'Jesus.'

'The mother comforts the baby, and soon everything is back to normal.'

'That's a pretty shitty experiment.'

'But it tells us that babies will adapt their behaviour and emotional development according to attachment and their environment. From a child's emotional development, what you have is the good, the bad and the ugly. The good is positive reinforcement from and interaction with a parent or parental figure, the normal stuff most parents do with their children. The bad is what the baby in the experiment receives, but that infant soon overcomes it when the mother adjusts her behaviour back to the norm. The ugly is when you don't give the child any chance to get back to the good, and they become permanently stuck in the ugly situation. The damage is done, and the only means of helping an individual move on is prolonged psychological assistance.'

'And you think, Kate, this is what happened to our killer?'

'The level of violence, destruction and emotional damage evident in the killing of Rick Shevlin and Pierre Laurent is acute. Behaviour like that is always gradual. It is the end result of many years of dysfunctional, negative and damaging elements, primarily childhood-trauma-based. If our killer was in her mid-twenties when she met Pierre Laurent, she would have become, in neurobiology terms, a developed adult – damaged, but developed. We have potential indicators as to how she has moved on since. What we don't have is the before, the baby to child, and the child to adult. Therein are the answers to the *why*.'

'In the meantime, we have a killer capable of killing again.'

'Yes, and despite her suffering in early development, including probably sexual abuse, and possibly physical and mental abuse, she is utterly dangerous. She is capable of carrying out extreme acts of violence, up to and including death, especially if someone doesn't behave as she wants them to, or attempts to stand in her way.'

I

TODAY THE SHADOW is different. Today the shadow belongs to me. It had felt like an age since I took a self-portrait. They are part of my identity now. Concrete proof that I exist, that I'm real. There are times I doubt it, which is partly why I grab life with such force, no time for trivia or small-minded people.

I find looking through the lens puts things in perspective. People are very trusting of photographers. They don't mind if you stop in the middle of a busy street, or look up to the sky, or sit in hotels, or outside cafés, hiding behind your camera lens. It was in a park that I took the image. Trees remind me of my start in life. I find the woods seductive. It was lucky the sun was shining. If it hadn't been, I wouldn't have seen the gleam of the silver drawer handle discarded on the grass, left in the park like unwanted litter. You need the eye to recognise how something small can be central to a perfect picture.

In the centre of the handle, there was an exquisite mirror. It was tiny, but it caught the sunlight, splintering the beams into a display of colour. Picking it up, I polished it clean. I knew straight away what I was going to do with it. I could see the photograph before it happened. I laid the handle on the grass facing upwards. When I leaned over, I saw my miniature self reflected in the mirror, a tiny person. I had my back to the sun, with my shadow looming like a giant, the miniature me caught inside the handle.

I am good with details. My memory is better than most, mainly because I'm prepared to face up to things, including the dark and ugly parts of life. Some people don't believe babies can remember things. I don't agree. I recall the first time the witch stuck the nappy pin into me, stabbing it into my upper leg. I imagine my young leg was nice and fat. I remember the sharp pain, and my wail. If I looked shocked, she would have liked that. She took joy from my pain, my reactions, part of her pleasure. Sometimes I was my own worst enemy, deciding not to show my weakness, withstanding the suffering with barely a grimace. The more I did that, the more she persevered. I soon switched tactics, screaming like a lunatic, giving her all the satisfaction she needed.

There are some parts I don't recall, but those I've lost are re-created in my mind's eye. The imagination is a powerful tool, often better than memory. While imagining, you can slow things down, look around and see who else is watching. When I imagine the witch plucking me from my mother's arms, before burning her, I see him there too. He is standing back, lurking. I was the witch's gift to him. A replacement for the girl left burning in the woods.

The witch said she followed my mother alone, that he had no part in it. He would have wanted her to think that way. I was groomed for his sexual satisfaction, so I knew him better than she did.

In the Grimms' tale of Hansel and Gretel, the witch helps the boy put meat on his bones, nourishing him to be devoured. That's how I see my early life, like the caged Hansel, being fed for someone else's needs. Some say the stepmother and the witch in the fairy-tale were one and the same, but in both roles she was evil, first in the abandonment, convincing her husband to leave the children in the forest, and second, in her cannibalistic desire to eat the boy.

In my case, he took me before the witch thought I was ready. He smelt the release of pubescent blood. She didn't like that, blaming me for encouraging him. She called me a slut, like my mother, too attractive for my own good, kicking me out of the bloodied bed.

The witch could change like the weather, and, like the pain she inflicted, I became suspicious of her kindness, the side of her that drew you in with false flattery. Once she had you hooked, she ripped you apart. A sick game, mocking my stupidity for thinking that somewhere among the horror, she occasionally cared.

HÔTEL SAINT CHRISTOPHE, PARIS

ONCE THEY LANDED at Charles de Gaulle airport, Kate rang Charlie and was relieved to hear him happy at the other end of the phone. A part of her felt guilty about being away, not because of the work but because she knew she had other reasons for being there.

Walking towards the taxi rank at the airport, they discussed Ian Morrison's opinion on the depth, trajectory and intensity of the wounds found on the bodies of Rick Shevlin and Pierre Laurent.

'I can understand his difficulty connecting the two, Kate, especially basing his comparisons on visual images.'

'But at least he said there was a strong possibility of the same type of knife being used.'

'It's building up a picture, I guess, and not a pretty one.'

Soon they were speeding away from the airport, through the suburbs and industrial areas on the outskirts of Paris. Kate had been to the city a number of times, but it was Adam's first visit. The drive into the centre would take them at least half an hour. Initially, she was happy to keep her silence, watching the Parisian world race by, but finally she said, 'I can't believe you haven't been to Paris before.'

'I doubt I'll get much of a chance to turn into a tourist.'

'You have a packed agenda for us, and I'm assuming it doesn't include sightseeing.'

'You assume right, Kate. We'll be meeting Inspector Girardot at the Hôtel du Maurier, where Pierre Laurent's body was found –' he looked at his phone '– in less than an hour, then on to Police Headquarters for a review of the case files. After that, we'll call at the art college where Pierre was a student. There's a teacher who knew him well. That should be interesting. Sometimes people give information more freely with the passing of time. They don't feel as threatened.'

'Just as well we had something to eat on the plane.'

'Oh, we'll eat, all right. I've made a reservation for dinner this evening at a restaurant close to our hotel.'

'For a man who hasn't been here before, you're certainly organised. Look,' she said, 'we're getting closer to the centre.' She pointed up a narrow street with a glimpse of the Seine at the top, and a florist on the corner.

'It certainly looks good, I'll give you that.'

'It's magical. There are plenty of reasons why Parisians are proud of their city.' Once again she stared out of the window, taking in the sights as they flew past. 'We're in the centre of the

Latin Quarter now.' She sounded like an excited child. 'It won't be long until we can see Notre Dame.' It was the first time he had seen or heard her so enthusiastic about her surroundings. He liked it. It reminded him of his younger self, the guy who hadn't fucked things up. 'There it is now,' she said. 'Isn't it lovely? Wait until you go inside – the atmosphere is like nowhere else on earth.'

'So, what's it like?' His curiosity was spiked.

'It's quite dark at first, but there is an amazing stillness despite the throngs of moving tourists. There's a sense of peace, with hints of light everywhere. You can see thousands of small candles flickering, each one lit by someone saying a prayer. The stained-glass windows let in light too. They have the deepest shades of blues and reds you can imagine. Each one tells a different story.' She turned to him. 'I'm afraid I'm not doing a great job of explaining it.'

'You're doing okay.'

'They still have mass there, you know. And there are glass confessionals too. I thought it was the strangest thing the first time I was here, being able to look inside a confessional and see the priest and the sinner talking to one another. Of course, you can't hear what they're saying, but it still felt odd compared to Ireland, where people sit in coffin-like boxes telling a barely visible priest their sins.'

'The last time I was at confession, I was probably wearing knee-length trousers.' He laughed.

∞

The taxi turned away from the Seine and darted down some narrow streets that Kate didn't recognise. It pulled up outside the Hôtel Saint Christophe, and Kate got out. She waited on the footpath while Adam paid the driver. The air felt cooler and crisper than it did in Dublin. Under any other circumstances, she mused, the two of them could have a great time exploring the city, but there was little chance of that, with all the work ahead and the flight to Rome booked for the following day. Still, she couldn't resist smiling when he carried both their bags up the steps and through the hotel's double doors. Somewhere in the back of her mind, she was pretending they were simply two people on holiday in one of the most romantic cities in the world.

'Once we sign in,' he said, 'I can book another taxi for us. How long do you need in your room?'

So much for the most romantic city in the world, she thought. 'Give me ten minutes to freshen up, and I'll meet you back here at Reception.'

'Wrap up warm, Kate. There's a chill in the air.'

In the hotel room, she took a quick shower and felt better for it. Her hair was still wet, so she tied it into a long side plait, then put on jeans, comfy Ugg boots and a warm top. She had a feeling that at some point they'd be walking around this city and it was best to be prepared.

When they disembarked from the next taxi, the Hôtel du Maurier looked far grander than the modest, but convenient, Hôtel Saint Christophe.

'Another opulent affair,' she said, as they went into the lobby for their first appointment. The interior was impressive too.

'I like your hair that way,' Adam remarked.

'What?'

'Put in a plait like that. It's cute. It makes you look younger.'

She wasn't sure if he was teasing or serious. 'I told you,' she said in jest, 'older men prefer the younger model.'

'Steady on there. I'm in my mid-thirties. As a man, my choices are still wide open. I can look one way, age wise, or the other.' He grinned.

She liked his sense of humour, and that he could get away with saying things others couldn't, but before she could answer him, she caught a glimpse of herself in one of the hotel mirrors. She looked about twelve.

'This must be Inspector Girardot now.' He pointed to a man coming through the front door.

'How do you know?'

'I'm a detective, aren't I?'

'Very funny.'

The tall, elegant, dark-haired man, dressed impeccably in a tailored suit and an open trench coat, made his way towards them. He looked older than Adam, and with a sophistication that an Irishman could never adopt.

'Monsieur O'Connor, I'm very pleased to meet you.'

'Likewise, Inspector Girardot. May I introduce you to Dr Kate Pearson?'

'*Docteur.*' He bowed his head briefly. 'Shall we get on with it?' His tone was friendly but efficient.

They went in silence in the lift to the second floor. It seemed Inspector Girardot was a man of few words.

'This way,' directed the French detective, as the lift doors opened, and they followed him down an exquisite corridor with ornate architrave, glistening chandeliers and beautiful tapestries on either side.

'Are all the floors the same?' Kate asked.

'No, no.' He stopped. 'The second floor is the most luxurious within the hotel. It has all the private suites.'

'And presumably extremely expensive.' Adam glanced around him.

'That, Monsieur O'Connor, is very much dependent on your budget, but the price would be out of reach for the average Parisian.'

'Did Pierre come from a wealthy family?' Kate asked.

'No, not particularly.'

'Any record of who paid for the room?' Adam quizzed, as they neared their destination, Room 133.

'I understand it was paid for in cash. Pierre Laurent used his real name, but gave a false address.'

'Any theories as to why he did that?'

The inspector shrugged his shoulders. 'It is possible he didn't wish to give the address of his student quarters. An art student with lots of cash might have been considered suspicious.'

'Was he involved in anything suspect or shady?' Adam was pushing Girardot, doing what he did best: police work.

'Not that we could ascertain.' Girardot stopped outside a room. Before turning the key, he said, 'It is unoccupied at present. You will find it very similar to how it was nine years ago. The Hôtel du Maurier had a complete revamp for the millennium, investing in good furnishings. The rooms have barely been altered since.'

Kate felt as though they were stepping back in time with the room's marbled floor, wooden parquet insert, Napoleonic furniture, ornate gold table lamps, paintings, the austere blood-red drapes, and the twenty-armed chandelier in the centre of the high decorative ceiling. While the two policemen talked, she walked around the suite, taking in as much as she could. It was only when Girardot opened the door to a smaller room off the main area, speaking about where the body had been found, that she turned her concentration back to them.

All three of them stood in what Girardot described as a dressing area, with one window, a panelled wall of mahogany wardrobes, a lady's chair and a chaise longue, both in mahogany and upholstered in red silk with a large fleur-de-lis design. The door opposite the one they had walked through led to the en-suite bathroom. Kate stood in the viewing point, with the small window behind her. 'The victim was laid out here.' Girardot pointed to a rug on the floor, but Kate had already visualised Pierre Laurent's body there, seeing the rug reflected in the framed bathroom mirror. 'It was over here that the lantern was placed, directly beside the body. I understand from the detectives who investigated the original case, the young man looked almost as if he was asleep.'

A frame within a frame, Kate was saying over and over in her mind. This was all about form, position and proportion. 'It was from here she created her perfect picture,' she said, her voice barely above a whisper.

'I don't understand.' Inspector Girardot looked confused.

Kate continued, 'The killer moved the body to the position on the rug because she wanted to frame it that way in the mirror.' Then she pointed to the window behind her. 'I'm standing in a frame, don't you see? A frame within a frame. It's where the killer stood to ensure she got the perfect re-creation of the card.'

Both men stared at her, and almost as if she was thinking aloud, she began taking small, steady steps around the room. 'Our killer sees the world in pictures, one frame at a time.'

'Why?' Adam asked.

'I'm not sure yet, but the reflection, the mirrored glass, the framing …' She trailed off.

'What about them?'

'We could be looking at this the wrong way.'

'I don't get you, Kate.'

'She's doing more than re-creating the card within the framing. She's also controlling and containing the image, almost as if she needs to perfect a different visual slant on the world, an alternative reality.'

Inspector Girardot seemed content to stand back in silence.

'You said you didn't think Pierre was the first victim, Kate.'

'He was strategic in the progression, certainly, but if my analysis is correct, and we're dealing with the aftermath of sustained early trauma, there will have been a primary event, where she first stepped over the line.'

'When?'

'We could be talking early adolescence. If she's the planner I think she is, she would have been careful the first time. She wouldn't have wanted to get caught, looking on that killing as a possible means of freedom.'

'Are you talking about another male victim, Kate?'

'I'm thinking parental figure, or figures, some early primary influencer.'

'Maybe the art college will tell us more about Pierre and why she picked him.'

Inspector Girardot coughed. 'Everyone at the college was interviewed during the original investigation.'

'With all due respect, Inspector Girardot,' Adam was quick to reply, 'we will want to talk to anyone who was around at the time of Laurent's murder.'

Kate took a couple of steps back from the two men, then entered the bathroom, with a view of the main suite and the dressing area to her left. She knew why the killer had created the scene in the smaller area, but why such opulence for the room, similar to where Rick Shevlin had been killed? It meant something to her. The killer may be affluent now, Kate thought, but there was every chance her beginnings were much more humble.

'Is there anything else you want to see in here, Kate?' Adam asked.

'No, I've seen enough.' Then she asked Girardot, 'When Pierre booked the room, did he request a specific number?'

'I'm not sure. We have the files ready for you to inspect, but why do you ask?'

'It makes sense that she would have chosen it. The room number is important.'

'Why?' Adam asked.

'The second two digits, 33. It's another master number.'

'What are you getting at?'

'At the Earlbrook Hotel, Rick Shevlin was murdered in Room 122, the second and third digit another master number.'

'What does it mean?'

'I don't know yet, but it means something to our killer.'

PONT DES ARTS,
RIVER SEINE, PARIS

INSPECTOR GIRARDOT HAD set up the meetings for Kate and Adam at the Beaux-Arts de Paris. They were expected there at two p.m., initially to talk with the director of the Institute, Julien Chéry, and then Jacques Guéguen, the head of fine arts, under whom Pierre Laurent had studied.

Having spent the remainder of the morning going through the case files with Girardot, Kate and Adam were left with less than an hour to grab lunch before their scheduled meeting with Chéry. The day was still chilly, but bright, and they decided to walk to the college instead of taking a taxi. Kate was familiar with the route, and it reminded her of her previous visits. The aroma of strong coffee from the various cafés opposite the Seine was tempting, but they opted for a couple of hot panini and takeaway coffees from a street stall as they walked down a flight of stone steps to the river below. There, the chill wasn't quite so bitter, protected by the riverbank walls.

Sitting on a public bench, it felt strange to Kate to be in Paris with Adam. All of her previous associations with the city had been personal and pleasurable, not work-related. It was hard to avoid slipping into recreational mode, but eating her lunch, she was content to sit in silence and take in the surroundings. It was Adam who spoke first, bringing the conversation back to work and their sole purpose for being there.

'Kate, earlier on I got the impression that more things have slotted into place for you.'

'It's good to visit the crime scene, but you're right. I feel I'm getting a deeper grasp of our killer – her motivation, and the level of anger and hurt involved.'

'Hurt?'

'There's no doubt she has been hurt and damaged emotionally. Her actions are fuelled by and infused with hate. The fact that she used a similar level of attack on both Pierre Laurent and Rick Shevlin opens up other possibilities too.'

'Like what?'

'You asked me about earlier victims. I think her hatred and anger belong elsewhere, a previous influencer in her life. Pierre and Rick might have disappointed her – they may have let her down emotionally. The same would apply to Michele, provided we connect the case – but the killing is a culmination of loathing, built up over a protracted period. The murders give her temporary relief, but the hate isn't going anywhere.'

'A pity there wasn't anything new in the case files,' he said, leaning back on the bench, having finished his lunch. He folded his arms tightly to keep in the warmth.

'No, but we still have the college.'

'Girardot was insistent they'd exhausted all angles.'

'Maybe so, but every victim has had some connection with the arts. And the way the killer creates the crime scene, and the visual consequences of the details within it, also point in the direction of the art world.'

'This Tarot-card business and the master numbers, it adds an extra layer of weirdness to the whole thing, don't you think?'

'They're important to the killer, but I'd be careful about letting them get in the way of holistically looking at the case.'

'I don't get you.'

'We all develop idiosyncrasies. In that regard, people who perform vile acts are no different from so-called normal people.'

His mobile phone bleeped: a text message. 'Who's that?' she asked.

'Mark Lynch. He says the hotel room in Rome was numbered ninety-three, not a master number.'

'Rome could be the anomaly. Although there was a fire, arguably similar to the Tower card from the Tarot, the victim shared the room with his wife. Unless he liked to bring his lovers and his wife to the same hotel room, chances are he chose the room without the influence of the killer. It has other differences too, apart from the lack of a master number.'

'Maybe the differences exist, Kate, because the wife was present.'

'The woman being pregnant could have influenced things too.'

'Anything else?'

'Whoever our killer is, it's like she's trying to escape her past. The opulence of the hotel rooms, her expensive tastes are most likely contradictory to what went before, and by before, I mean her early environment.'

'So, Kate, we have a highly intelligent, mid-thirties female with an interest in framing her victims. Someone with a tragic beginning, seeking emotional investment, coming from a modest socio-economic background, and who also happens to have an overdose of built-up anger.'

'She's also ambitious. It's unlikely she would remain stagnant. She will have progressed socially, even if that meant using manipulation.'

He checked his mobile phone. 'It's a quarter to two. We'd better get a move on if we're to get our artistic education started.'

They both stood up. Stretching his arms above his head, looking across at the Louvre, he asked, 'Have you ever been in there?'

'Yes, but we won't get to it today, if that's what you're considering. You'd need several days for a proper visit.'

'I was only asking. You can tell me all about it over dinner tonight.' Then he cupped her elbow in his hand and they mounted the stone steps together.

Amid the swell of city traffic, the stalls of paintings, souvenirs and Parisian memorabilia on the banks of the Seine, the voices of tourists and locals, another question needled her: was she the only one who saw this Paris visit as having the potential for more?

BEAUX-ARTS DE PARIS,
RUE BONAPARTE

THE COLLEGE, SITUATED opposite the Louvre in the heart of Saint-Germain-des-Prés, between the dock and the Malaquais, was steeped in history, dating from the seventeenth century, with a campus spread over two hectares. As Kate and Adam approached the front entrance, they saw hundreds of student bicycles leaning again the street railings. It was a walled enclosure, with ornate black double gates and two large stone pillars on either side. Once through the gates, they walked across the enormous cobble-locked square, with multiple archways leading from one Gothic-designed building to another.

Inspector Girardot's directions were meticulous, and they soon found themselves in a small courtyard with a stone fountain in front of a two-storey aged terracotta building.

Inside, Kate had expected a continuation of the exterior style, but it was modern. They passed a number of studios with open doors, glimpsing multiple canvases leaning against pure white walls. There was a studio with sculptures where some students sat cross-legged with sketch pads in hand. In the last room before the director's office, there was an enormous abstract canvas, vibrant with colour, in which, Kate thought, the ultramarine dripped like tears.

Adam made a knuckled fist and knocked hard on the panelled door.

'*Bonjour. Entrez, s'il vous plaît,*' called a male voice from inside.

'After you,' said Adam.

Kate turned the steel handle, pushing the large black ebony door open. '*Bonjour*, Professor Chéry. Do you speak English?'

'*Oui.*' He stood up to greet them, then gestured them both to chairs. 'Monsieur O'Connor and Dr Pearson, I assume?'

'That's right, Professor,' said Adam.

'*Julien, s'il vous plaît.*' He pulled his swivel chair closer to his desk. Julien Chéry's office was in stark contrast to the modern design outside. The furniture, Kate mused, wouldn't have been out of place in the Napoleon rooms at the Louvre. The professor was tall, dressed in a brown cord suit, with a plain shirt and jumper. One side of his white shirt collar stuck out, the other was tucked neatly away. Although he sounded friendly, his face contorted slightly on greeting them with what seemed to Kate a false smile. He was handsome, she reflected, with good bones, deep-set eyes below his heavy but somewhat tossed eyebrows. He was alert, ready for anything they might ask him.

'Julien, I understand Inspector Girardot has already briefed you on the reasons behind our visit.' Adam waited for Kate to sit, before taking his seat on the identical upholstered chair beside her.

'You are here in connection with the killing of Pierre Laurent.' Julien placed his outstretched hands on the desk, wriggling his fingers as if he was limbering up to play a musical instrument. 'You believe it may be linked to a recent murder in your country.'

'We're pretty sure it is.' Adam sat upright in the chair.

'I fail to see how I can be of help to you.'

'We're keen to talk to anyone who knew Pierre.'

'Inspector Girardot,' he opened and closed his fists, 'would have explained to you that Pierre Laurent studied at the college before I became the director.'

'Yes, but you know all the staff here.' Adam sat a little forward. 'We were hoping you would direct us to anyone who might have information.'

'Indeed.' The professor paused as if he was trying to work out whether or not he should unleash the detective on his colleagues. 'I have made some enquiries.' He looked at Kate, then at Adam. 'I've only two names for you, including Jacques Guéguen, the head of fine arts, which Inspector Girardot already mentioned to you. The other, Delphine Ager, is a former student. She studied here with Pierre, but moved to Provence late 2005.'

'Was Delphine here during the original investigation?' Kate asked.

'I believe she was, but I'm not sure of the dates. Any questions you have, I'm sure Delphine can help you.' Again that false smile.

'After the investigation, did everything return to normal at the college?' Adam locked eyes with the professor.

'As far as I understand, although there was something … I doubt it has anything to do with your investigation.'

'Tell us anyhow.' Adam gave him one of his broad smiles.

Kate didn't think Professor Chéry looked impressed. He said simply, 'Jacques can fill you in on the exact details, but after Pierre's death,' he glanced at the door as if someone might walk in, 'a number of students curtailed their studies. It wasn't many, you understand. In fact, it wasn't even noted as relevant at the time. But after Inspector Girardot contacted me, I looked into the academic year of 2005/6, examining the year's statistics and analysis.'

'And what did they tell you?' Adam's interest was aroused.

'Within the fine art faculty, there was a fifty per cent increase in dropouts, seven to be exact, two males, five females. Normally we would have three or four, but not seven. As I said, it may be nothing.'

'Did you discuss this with Jacques?' Kate kept her tone low and unthreatening.

'Yes,' he replied, and for a moment she thought this was the only answer he was going to give. Then he sat forward, speaking as if he had prepared his words in advance. 'Jacques and I are in agreement. There was a lot of distress at the time. Young people are very sensitive to events. It was – how do you say in English? – a spike, nothing more.'

With the professional formalities over with, Adam stood up. 'I assume Jacques is expecting us?'

Julien Chéry looked at his watch. 'He won't finish with his students for another half-hour. I can take you to Delphine while you're waiting. Her hours are not as intense. She is usually in Studio Nine. It isn't far.'

'*Merci*.' Kate got to her feet. 'That would be great.'

'If we have any more questions after we've talked to Delphine and Jacques, will you still be here?' Adam asked.

'But of course. For the rest of the day.'

'Good.'

'Come with me, then.'

Adam and Kate stood back as the professor took enthusiastic strides towards the door, then they followed in his wake.

BEAUX-ARTS DE PARIS, RUE BONAPARTE, STUDIO NINE

DELPHINE AGER WAS slim and petite, with short black hair tucked behind her ears. She wore jeans and a loose-fitting white T-shirt with a brown satchel across her shoulders. She had a lean face, and eyes that bounced from Julien Chéry to Adam and Kate while he spoke to her in French. Waiting to be introduced, Kate listened to the fast, low, easy conversation between them: they sounded as if they shared a mutual understanding.

'So,' said Chéry, 'I'll leave you to talk. Delphine will escort you to Jacques's room once you are done here.' Before pulling the studio door closed, he waved, saying dismissively, '*Au revoir, Adam et Kate. J'espère que vous avez un séjour agréable à Paris.*'

'What did he just say?' Adam looked at Kate.

'He says he hopes we have a pleasant stay in Paris.'

Delphine waited for her superior to leave, then removed her satchel and took out a packet of cigarettes. 'You don't mind, do you?' She was looking at Adam.

'Go right ahead,' he replied.

The room was blank, apart from a large covered canvas. 'Smoking in public buildings,' she said, lighting her cigarette. 'It is banned in Ireland, yes?'

'It is.' He coughed, caught off guard by the smoke.

'It is banned here too, but some rooms are an exception, which is why I usually work in Studio Nine. I need my fix.' She smiled, then took a deep drag, sitting against the studio wall, with her knees bent close to her chest. 'Please,' she said, 'make yourselves comfortable. It may not be as nice as Julien's office, but at least what you see is what you get.'

Kate knelt beside her on the floor, wondering what she had meant by her last remark. Awkwardly, Adam did the same.

'I believe you were at the college with Pierre Laurent?' Kate asked.

'That is correct. We were students together.' She removed a small tinfoil ashtray from her satchel.

'Can you tell us about Pierre?'

Delphine blew a waft of smoke to her right, staring at Kate. 'I can tell you what I know – that he was a prick but an amazing artist. He had talent running through his veins, and he knew it. Like his good looks, Pierre took these things and others for granted.'

'It doesn't sound like the two of you got on.' Adam looked uncomfortable on the floor, unsure where to put his large feet.

'On the contrary, even though he was a prick, we got on very well.'

'Were you lovers?' Kate had decided the direct approach would work best with Delphine.

'We had a brief fling. That was the way it was with Pierre, everything in the moment, not to be taken seriously.'

'He had a lot of female companions?'

'Kate. It is Kate?'

Kate nodded.

'This is Paris.' She wore a wide smirk.

Adam waved his hands to clear the smoke. 'We want to know about everyone associated with Pierre.'

'That is a very long list.'

'And you're one of only two people we have so far. So, your information is important.'

She nodded, solemn now. 'Ask me anything you want.'

'Among his female companions, was there anyone in particular who stood out?' Adam repositioned himself on the floor, this time leaning against the wall with his legs outstretched in front of him.

'For Pierre? No. He could have charmed them into thinking he cared, but he was self-centred. He would say whatever a woman wanted to hear.' She shrugged her shoulders. 'It was a game with him, nothing more.'

'We hear he had particular fetishes.' Kate kept eye contact with Delphine, wondering if she was as hard and uncaring as she was trying to appear.

She laughed coldly. 'He had many desires, yes. He was experimental. Le BDM was one of his favourite places.'

'Le BDM?' Kate quizzed.

'Bar du Monde, at the rue Mazarine. It was a place many of the students went for drinks, but downstairs in the basement was for the experimenters.'

'It was mentioned in the case files,' Adam told Kate, then turned back to Delphine. 'It's a sex club?'

'You could call it that.'

'Is it still there?' Adam's voice echoed around the near-empty room.

'No.'

'But you went there with Pierre?' Kate kept her tone soft.

'Yes, of course. There was a small fee to participate or to watch, but Pierre usually slipped his friends in without too much bother.'

'Can you describe the place for us, the kind of activity that went on?'

This time she blew the cigarette smoke directly into Kate's face. 'Yes.' She took another drag before she went on, 'There were usually fifty or sixty people in the club. It was small, so it was easily crowded, a regular dark dungeon … and it was full of desperate people.' Again she laughed – nervously this time, Kate thought.

'Go on.'

'Part of the downstairs was set up like a torture chamber. The leather and wooden racks were in constant demand. You didn't have to take part. As I said, you could be an onlooker. Depending on his mood, Pierre would be a participant or a spectator, but he liked bringing others there to watch. He enjoyed shocking people … *imbécile.*' Her voice had turned bitter, but then softened: 'I didn't like the sound of the bodies being lashed. The cries, they were *moche* – ugly.'

'What age were you, Delphine?' Kate's voice was gentle.

'I was nineteen. I was old enough,' she said sharply, staring at Kate's plait. 'I remember there was this fat woman at the bar all the time, dressed up like a schoolgirl. She had her hair in plaits too. She liked her bare buttocks being whipped, the harder the better. Pierre never had any interest in her. He liked his women slim.'

'Did he have a regular partner at the club?' Adam stood up, unable to take interviewing on the floor any longer.

'He often went there alone. Pierre felt more at home with people who were different.'

'Julien said you dropped out before finishing the year. Why was that?' Adam moved a step closer to her.

She stared up at him. 'My mother was unwell. I was needed back in Provence.'

'And the others?' Kate asked. 'The students who left the college after Pierre's death, do you know why they dropped out?'

'No. For the most part, they all left after me, except one.' She pressed out her cigarette butt in the tinfoil ashtray. 'She was Irish, an exchange student, I think.'

'Do you remember her name, or why she left?' Adam didn't attempt to hide his interest.

'Yes, I do. It was Sandra. I don't know her second name. She was an okay artist, but she lacked passion, and was far too meek and nervous. You cannot progress your work unless you're prepared to take risks and be adventurous.'

'Do you know why she left?' Kate repeated Adam's question.

'I heard she was homesick. Some girlfriends stayed with her in Paris for a while. One of them was very attractive. Pierre liked her.' Again, the bitter tone was in her voice.

'They had a relationship?' Kate pressed.

'I can't be sure, but meek, miserable Sandra didn't like her friend getting attention from Pierre.' She smiled. 'Pierre had given the wallflower a lot of notice before her girlfriends arrived. As I said, he liked people who were different.'

'Any idea of the girlfriend's name, the attractive one?' Adam wasn't letting go.

Again Delphine shrugged her shoulders. 'It was a long time ago. I can't be sure, but it might have been Alice.'

'And you can't remember either of their surnames?' Kate enquired.

'I'm afraid not. But you should be able to get Sandra's details from Jacques. She would have been registered at the college.'

'I don't remember seeing any statement from a Sandra in the case files. Did you see one, Kate?'

'When we arrived,' Kate ignored his question, 'you said something about this room not being as nice as Julien's office, that what you see is what you get. What did you mean by that?'

'Julien Chéry is similar to Pierre. He is an extremely talented man, but he can be different things to different people. I'm sure he didn't tell you we are lovers – or, at least, we are right now ...' Adam and Kate kept their silence. 'It is difficult to get a position here at the college. It has a history and a reputation that elevate it. Julien helped me get this placement. I have appreciation for his talent, even if, like Pierre, he has many downsides.'

SANDRA

WHEN I REACH the outskirts of the city, I pull into the car park of a large hardware store only a few kilometres from home. The girl at the cash register doesn't blink as she scans the two large bolts I intend putting on the inside of the studio door. When I get back into the car, I lock the doors again. I spent the entire time I was in the store looking over my shoulders, making sure no one was following me.

Driving home, I decide to contact Alice. Karen isn't trustworthy with information, and rightly or wrongly, Lori has already freaked me out. I need to talk to someone other than Edgar. Alice was so solid in Paris when that thing happened to

Pierre. Looking back, I know I did love him. Alice understood how I felt. Karen dismissed it as little more than an infatuation I'd grow out of, and Lori had looked as if she wanted to be the one in love with him.

None of us mentioned him once we got back to Dublin. It was like it had happened to someone else. I know why Lori wanted to avoid the subject: she had helped me forge the application papers. There was no way I could have landed a place at the Beaux-Arts de Paris otherwise. Neither of us thought we would get away with it. I think Lori felt sorry for me, not having had a university education. Lucky for me she was working in the student office at Trinity. She can be full of surprises, and that's another reason why I need to keep her out of the picture.

∞

Later I call Alice on my mobile. I'm still out of breath, having put the bolts on the studio door and hammered the windows permanently shut, using masonry nails from the garage.

'It's me, Sandra.'

'You sound out of breath.'

'I am.'

'Is something wrong?'

'Something is very wrong …' I feel better hearing myself say it '… but I can't talk over the phone.'

'Why not?'

'I can't. I need to talk to you face to face.'

'Where are you?'

'At the studio.'

'Are you alone?'

'Yes – can you come over?'

She doesn't answer for what seems like an eternity.

'Alice, are you still there?'

'I'm still here.' Another silence. 'I'm trying to work out a couple of things.'

'Why? What's there to think about? I need to talk to you. What's complicated about it?'

'Nothing, I guess.' She sounds cagey.

Maybe I've made the wrong decision. I can't trust her if she's not on my side. 'Look, if you don't want to come over, don't.'

I'm about to hang up when she says, 'Sandra, calm down. You know I'll come over. I've always been there for you.'

I let out a sigh of relief. At last I'll be able to tell someone about the madness that's been going on, but something strikes me before I hang up. 'Alice …'

'What?'

'Don't tell anyone you're coming. Make sure you're alone.'

She laughs, and I'm not sure if she's mocking me. Maybe she thinks I'm being over the top. She's always so bloody calm and composed. 'I'm serious, Alice.'

When the phone goes dead, I don't know what to think. I try to ring her back, but her mobile goes straight to voicemail. Perhaps her battery's flat. I look around the studio. It won't take her long to get here. I should have told her to tap on the studio windows. That way I'd know it was her. Damn it. She'll ring the doorbell, and I'll have to leave the studio to answer it, unsure of who is at the door. I could call out. If anyone other than

Alice answers, I won't open it. I'll tell them I'm unwell, to call
back another time. I check that I still have the knife in my bag.
The message in the diary was clear. I look at it again, reading
it for the umpteenth time: BE AFRAID. I have no doubt that
whoever wrote those words meant them.

BEAUX-ARTS DE PARIS,
RUE BONAPARTE

DELPHINE AGER EXCUSED herself before reaching Jacques Guéguen's rooms, but on the way from Studio Nine, she told Kate and Adam that Jacques lived at the college Monday to Friday, and at weekends he travelled home to his wife and children in Montrouge.

'What did you think of Delphine?' Adam asked, once she was out of earshot.

'I don't think she's as confident or as hard as she makes herself out to be.'

'Interesting about the Irish student.'

'And surprising the French police never interviewed her.'

'Perhaps Monsieur Guéguen will shed some light on that.'

'Delphine said the girl, Sandra, was meek and miserable. That's a very negative description.'

'Maybe she was jealous, Kate. I hear women can be.'

'Jealousy is common in both sexes.'

'I'll take your word for it. Shall I do the honours again?' He knuckled his fist, ready to knock on the door.

'Off you go. I'm getting used to being your sidekick.'

'Less of the sarcasm – it doesn't suit you.'

'I'll be the judge of that. Now, stop standing there like an idiot,' she teased. 'Knock on the bloody door.'

He did so.

'*Bonjour, entrez, s'il vous plaît.*'

Jacque Guéguen was close to sixty, shorter and more stooped than his superior, Julien Chéry. Kate liked him instantly. He looked comfortable in his skin, and although his rooms weren't as richly decorated as Chéry's office, they had a certain charm. He had a fire lit too, always a welcoming sign.

'Sit down.' Jacques gestured to two upholstered chairs by the hearth, pulling another over from the corner for himself. 'I understand you want to talk to me about Pierre Laurent.'

'That's right.' Adam looked relieved not to be sitting on the floor.

'A troubled young man, but a talented artist – the whole incident was terrible, such a waste.'

'According to the police report, Jacques, the police believed the murder to be a crime of passion, yet they never found anyone responsible. That's surprising, don't you think?' Adam was getting into his stride, Kate mused, putting it up to Jacques Guéguen from the beginning.

'Very little surprises me, Detective. I've learned that life isn't always simple.'

Kate smiled at him. 'Delphine Ager told us one of the students who dropped out after Pierre's death was an Irish girl.' She thought she detected a nervous twitch in his face, but couldn't be sure.

'I believe that's correct.'

'Her name was Sandra, an exchange student.' She wondered why he was being so guarded.

Getting up from his chair, he walked over to the bureau and picked up what looked like a registration book. 'I thought you might want to look at this. It has the names of all the students that year, with an asterisk beside those who didn't complete the year.'

Adam took out his notebook, ready to record the names.

'Inspector Girardot has a copy,' Jacques murmured, opening the book at the required page.

'I didn't see it in the police file,' Adam retorted.

Jacques handed it to him. 'The inspector only became aware of it this afternoon. Julien phoned him after your visit. Your interest in the students who dropped out led him to surmise that they might be important to our own investigators.'

'I see.' Adam didn't sound convinced, and neither was Kate.

'It explains why Sandra was never interviewed.' Adam was trying to find her name on the list.

'You won't find it in there,' Jacques said, tight-lipped.

'Why not?' Adam looked up.

'Because I removed it.' He sat down, suddenly seeming a lot older than his years.

'When – and why?' Adam sounded puzzled and snappy.

Kate gave him a look that said, 'Ease up.' Then she spoke: 'Jacques, you do understand that tampering with evidence is a very serious matter. Maybe you would like to go back to the beginning and explain. Every detail could be vital at this stage.' Now she understood why he had been cautious.

'The college has an impeccable record,' he sat up straight, 'but it is not without funding issues from time to time.' He still seemed uncomfortable, as if he was giving away some sworn secret.

Adam began writing in his notebook, content to let Kate lead the questions.

'It's okay, Jacques,' she said reassuringly. 'Go on.'

'Like many institutions, we have an exchange programme for students, but in certain years, like 2005, we opened up a number of paid placements for foreign applicants at the college.'

'A paid placement?'

'Yes.' He swallowed hard. 'It was one of our most lucrative years.'

Adam kept silent.

'And Sandra was one of those paying students?' Kate continued.

'Like the other successful applicants, she made a non-refundable payment of ten thousand euros at the start of the year.'

'You had a screening process, I imagine?' she asked, keeping her tone measured.

'Yes, of course, although it wasn't as meticulous as it would normally be. We assessed the student applications based on written submissions without an interview, along with scanned images of their portfolio, character references and details of education. Nothing out of the ordinary. We didn't want to make it too problematic for applicants, a simple means of entry.'

'When you say we,' Adam asked, 'who do you mean?'

'At the time, the director of the college was Victor Girard. He and I decided on the selection process.'

'If Sandra was an applicant, why is her name not in the register?' Kate probed.

'It was. At least, it was at one point.' He took the register back from Adam, pointing out a line marked through with a pen. It was impossible to make out the words underneath. To the side were two sets of initials, JG and VG, with the word *erreur*. 'It was all somewhat embarrassing.'

'Why did you strike it out?' Adam was somewhat stunned by the admission.

'It turns out Mademoiselle Ryan gave us false documentation.'

Again Kate noticed the nervous twitch in the teacher's face. 'When did you discover this?' She maintained eye contact, ignoring the muscles pulsating in his cheeks.

'It was before Pierre's death, a month before to be exact. We wrote to the Irish college in question, seeking further applications for the following year. They were interested in the programme, but said we must have made an error regarding Mademoiselle Ryan. They had no record of a Sandra Ryan with that date of birth.'

'What did you do then?' Kate asked.

'Naturally, I spoke to Mademoiselle Ryan. She was very upset. It was extremely distressing. The girl had potential. Otherwise we would never have considered her application. She spoke at length about her admiration for the college, her desire to study art, how difficult it had been for her. That she had recently received a small inheritance and had jumped in without thinking. It felt like such a wonderful opportunity. She said she had never done anything like that before.'

'So you kept her money and let her away with it?' Adam's accusation was tinged with sarcasm.

'The payment was clearly stipulated as non-refundable.'

He was on the defensive, thought Kate.

Jacques continued, in a more authoritative manner. 'I spoke to Victor. We were both unhappy with the situation, but we couldn't turn back the clock. Mademoiselle Ryan was asked to leave, which she did, and most gracefully too. We put in safeguards to ensure it wouldn't happen again. It had all been a terrible error.'

'What you're saying is, you covered up your mistake and kept quiet about it.' Adam was clearly astounded.

'Yes, we removed her details. In essence, she had not been a valid student here.'

'And when Pierre died, Sandra had already left the college?' Kate hoped her less adversarial approach would keep him onside.

'That's correct. She had left the college, but not Paris. I can't be sure, but I believe she had some time left at her accommodation. Some friends had come to join her for a brief stay. I understand she went home with them.' He looked at Kate. 'I liked

Mademoiselle Ryan. She was very gentle and unassuming. It was her love of art that led to her error of judgement. It seemed best to let the matter rest.'

'And slip under the radar?' Again Adam's tone was hostile.

'Did you meet any of her friends?' Kate asked.

'No, I don't think so.'

Kate turned to Adam. 'Sandra could be an innocent party.'

'Or she could be the missing link in the chain,' he replied, before addressing Jacques: 'You do have contact details? They didn't disappear too?'

'Of course. Now that this interest has been shown in the ex-students, we have passed all the information to Inspector Girardot. I have a copy here.' He sounded delighted to be of assistance. He pulled a brown envelope from the bureau where the register had been, and handed it to Adam. 'You will find all seven addresses and contact telephone numbers in there.'

'Can you give us a physical description of Sandra?' Kate pressed.

'About five foot six, slim build, with brown hair. At least, I think it was brown, or it could have been dark blonde.'

'Anything else?' Adam asked sharply.

'It was a very long time ago. There are so many students. It doesn't take long for their faces to fade into one another.'

The fire had practically extinguished in the grate when Adam and Kate got up to leave. 'You best put another log on, Jacques,' Adam said, sounding anything but helpful. 'There's a nasty chill in here.'

Kate pulled the door closed behind them, knowing Adam would probably have slammed it.

'Arsehole,' was the first word out of his mouth once they got outside.

'He was trying to protect the college. A stupid mistake, but a mistake.'

'I'm not feeling as kind as you, Kate. That idiot and his superior interfered with an investigation. I doubt Girardot will be jumping up and down with delight either.'

She wanted to remind him about his own error of judgement, covering up for someone he thought was innocent, and the reason behind his suspension. She decided to let it go, knowing it wouldn't help things. 'Look on the upside,' she said. 'We now have seven more leads. We need just one to be useful.'

He raised the brown envelope Jacques had given him. 'Rick Shevlin might still be alive if one of these names leads us to the killer and that idiot in there hadn't wanted to protect his precious college.'

'Can I see the names?'

He handed her the envelope.

'If you're right about that, the killer's name could be on this list.'

'And we'll be starting with Mademoiselle Ryan.'

GREY DOOR CLUB, SOUTH GREAT GEORGE'S STREET, DUBLIN

MARK LYNCH DECIDED to get two things out of the way at the same time. First, pay a visit to the Grey Door, a well-known bondage club in Dublin city. Secondly, meet up with Freddie Walsh and put some heat on O'Connor.

Although Claudia, the madam from Connections, had proved less informative than he'd hoped, she had at least told him about a couple of her girls accompanying Rick Shevlin to the club, saying, it had become a recent favourite of his. Freddie was easy to convince to tag along. He wasn't part of the unit investigating the murder, but when Lynch mentioned he needed back-up visiting a bondage club, he wasn't long in deciding to oblige.

Freddie was big and broad, with a stomach that wasn't doing his heart much good. His dark hair had started receding a while back, but in the spirit of denial, he'd let the remaining hair grow long enough for a comb-over. Lynch never understood why men did that – who were they kidding? If it ever happened to him, he would shave the whole bloody lot off. Still, he was counting on Freddie's lack of brainpower to play along with his plan. All he needed was to have him there so he could plant some words in his head, and as they made their way up South Great George's Street, there was undoubtedly vigour in Detective Freddie Walsh's step.

'Are we flashing the IDs or going undercover, Mark?'

'Don't worry about that. I've already got the clearance.'

'Sure you're a great man for the connections!'

'Funny you should say that. Our intro to the club came from a very obliging woman in a company by that name. Ten out of ten for detective work. Now, flick back that hair of yours and let's get inside.'

'What the fuck do you mean?' Walsh immediately took offence.

But Lynch was already smiling at the bouncer, saying, 'Claudia has cleared us to go inside.'

The bouncer, a Latvian, even broader than Walsh, didn't return the smile, saying, 'Don't make any trouble in there or your visit will be a short one. Clear?'

'Sure,' Lynch replied, before heading down the darkened cellar steps, Walsh behind him, the pulsating sound of the torture chamber smacking them both in the face. At the bottom, he opened the padded leather door.

'Fucking hell,' were Walsh's first words.

Lynch took it all in, the transvestite males in their wigs and corsets, one suspended from the ceiling, his wrists tied above his head, his skin red and raw from being lashed with a cat-o'-nine-tails whip. To the left, a woman wore a black bra and panties. Her arms were restrained on a wooden rack, as a leather-clad Arnold Schwarzenegger impersonator thrashed her with a whip that looked like an extension of his tattooed arm. The real reason for Walsh's expletive, though, was a young woman with bare breasts, and the hungry crowd gathered around her. She was gearing up to take a lashing, as a guy wearing a gimp mask and a black leather thong increased the tension on the ropes, opening and contorting her legs to the delight of the onlookers.

'I'll get us a couple of drinks. Grab that table, Freddie.' Lynch pointed to one in the corner, as far away as possible from the bare-breasted woman. 'Watch my back, not her boobs, will you?'

'Sure thing. Get a couple of pints. We could be here for a while.'

'We're on duty. I need to go back to the unit after this.'

'Correction. *You're* on duty. I'm helping you out, remember?'

'You're all heart, Freddie.' But Walsh was already staring at the woman being whipped.

The guy Lynch wanted to talk to wasn't due in for a quarter of an hour. He wondered if he'd be able to put up with this freak show until then, but figured it was as good a time as any to get his other mission out of the way. As he placed their drinks on the table, Walsh said, 'It's something else, isn't it?'

'Yeah, a real eye-opener.'

'Have you read *Fifty Shades*?'

'What? Me? No. I don't go in for that shit. You?'

'The wife's read it, all three books.'

'Spice up your sex life, did it?'

'There was fuck-all to begin with but, yeah, it got her horny. Never look a gift horse in the mouth and all that.'

'Too much information, Fred.' He let out a sigh. 'I've enough on my plate with this bloody investigation.'

'I'd have thought this was right up your street, high profile and all that. That Rick Shevlin fella, he was into this shit, wasn't he?'

'Yeah.'

'I hear they found ropes at the scene, and the guy's arse had been lashed with a whip.' Walsh was practically drooling.

'It's not that that's bothering me.'

'No? What is it, then?'

'I have O'Connor to deal with.'

'He's all right.'

'Do you think? He's a bit of an arsehole, if you ask me.'

Walsh took his eyes off the sideshow for the first time. 'Why do you say that?'

'Him and Dr Kate Pearson.'

'She's a looker, isn't she?'

'It seems O'Connor shares your taste in women, Freddie.'

'You mean the two of them are doing it?'

'That's what I heard, but I wouldn't be one for spreading rumours.' He took a sip from his bottle of non-alcoholic beer. 'The chief super's only gone and sent them to Paris together.'

'Fucking Paris?'

'And Rome.'

'And Rome?'

'What are you, Freddie? A feckin' parrot?'

'Keep your hair on.'

He decided not to comment on Freddie's hair remark, saying instead, 'The guy is only back from suspension, and the boss is treating him like the prodigal son.' He paused. 'He has a kid, you know.'

'Sure everyone in the unit knows that.'

'I don't think they're getting along. He didn't make contact with him for years. That doesn't sound like something a decent guy would do.'

'You're probably right. Ignoring your kid like that, Mark, that's shite, that's what that is.'

'I think the boss is playing with fire.'

'Because he doesn't know about O'Connor and your woman?'

'It doesn't look good, sending a guy who's just back from suspension on a strategic leg of an investigation.' Lynch could practically see Walsh's few brain cells ticking over.

'It's messy, all right.'

'If the papers got wind of it, they'd have a field day. I can see the headline now: "Suspended detective gets key role in Shevlin murder inquiry". They'd be talking about cutbacks, not enough trained personnel to do the job, not to mention if there was any horseplay going on, not that I know for sure there is. Only telling you what I heard, Freddie.'

'Fucking Paris? He wouldn't be able to resist, would he?'

'He's broken the rules before, covering up evidence. That says something.'

'Yeah, I hear you.'

'Fancy another pint, Freddie?' He glanced at the bar. 'The gentleman I want to talk to has just arrived.'

'Do you need a hand?'

'You're all right. I'll bring your pint down to you, but remember you're here to watch my back, not the show. I don't trust those trannies over there.'

'Fucking weirdoes.' Walsh lifted his pint, finishing it in one go, as if one of the tranny weirdoes might take it from him. Then he turned his attention back to the naked boobs, and the sound of skin being lashed.

Lynch smiled all the way to the bar. It wouldn't take Freddie Walsh long to be chatting to his journalist buddies. It didn't matter if he mentioned O'Connor and Kate Pearson: all Lynch needed was a bit of light shone on things, and sure wasn't that what *lamps* were for?

∞

Lynch figured Simon Reynolds knew he was a detective from the moment he'd stood up from where he'd been sitting with Walsh. Reynolds was renowned on the Irish fetish scene. It wasn't only the Grey Door club: it was the website, the retail outlets and the private parties. None of it caused Lynch too much concern. If people wanted to have a bit of fun, he wasn't going to make trouble when it was legal, even if it was hard to get the sound of skin being lashed out of his mind.

'Nice friendly place you have here, Simon.'

'We believe in being open-minded, Detective.' He had a bulldog face, tight red hair, a thin moustache and shoulders twice the width of his waist. He spoke with a Scottish accent that came from somewhere deep in his chest. He was well dressed, in smart black jeans, a striped linen shirt, and shoes that screamed money. Lynch couldn't be sure, but his accent wasn't street – more than likely born with a silver spoon in his mouth. 'We all have our fetishes, Detective. It's only a question of working them out.'

'A pint and another bottle of that non-alcoholic stuff.' Lynch turned to wave at Walsh.

'I'll get one of the lads to bring the pint down to your friend.'

'Decent of you, Simon. Thanks.' He took in the crowd. They didn't so much exhibit pack mentality but formed smaller groups, not only the trannies but others too, along with plenty of loners. 'What's the story with the non-participants?'

'Many start out that way. People like to look before they take the plunge. Everyone is different.'

'Claudia tells me Rick Shevlin was one of your onlookers.'

'I believe he was.'

'He never partook in the main show, then?' Lynch took a swig from his bottle of beer.

'It wouldn't have taken him long. You learn to judge these things.'

'And he brought a couple of the girls from Connections with him?'

'I've no problem, as long as they pay and don't cause trouble.'

'Were there any other lady friends?'

'There was one he was keen on. She didn't join in either, but went the whole way with her appearance, dressing mainly in leather, the way Rick liked them.'

'Was she an escort?'

'Don't think so. I heard they linked up through some dating agency.'

'She came here a few times, then?'

'That's right, but I haven't seen her for a while.'

'Since Rick snuffed it?'

'I couldn't be sure, but maybe so.'

Lynch leaned in closer. 'Did she have a name?'

'Cassie. At least, that's the name she gave.'

'Cassie what?'

'Cassie4Casanova.' He smirked.

'What?'

'It's her online tag name. You know, like the lover.'

'I don't suppose you have any pictures of her? You know, snaps on the mobile phone, that kind of thing?' He was fishing, but it never did any harm to ask.

'We don't allow cameras on the premises.' He pointed to the charter hanging over the bar, including rules of no 'frontal nudity', and safety being in the hands of 'dungeon monitors', experienced players whose decisions were final. 'But I can give you a description, if you want.'

'Let's go one step further, Simon. How about I send down one of our artists to chat with you? Together you can draw a nice picture.'

'No problem. Always willing to help the police.'

The longer he talked, the more convinced Lynch became that Simon Reynolds was from a very comfortable background – his accent sounded like money, well-educated too, a regular entrepreneur. The classy voice probably helped pull in the richer punters. Lynch decided to finish his beer with Walsh.

'How did you get on with your man?' Walsh downed the end of the second pint.

'Not bad. We might have a good lead.'

'Jaysus, that's great. Thanks for the beers. I owe you.'

'Don't worry about it. Come on, let's go.'

Before reaching the exit door, Walsh said, 'Hold on, I need to take a leak.'

'Be careful in there.'

'What do you mean?'

'There's a reason this place is still legal. No sex visible on the premises, but behind closed doors and all that … I'd say there's plenty of activity inside.'

Walsh gave him a look, a mix of caution and daring. 'Do you want to take a leak too?'

Lynch had no intention of holding his colleague's hand or anything else. 'I'm not going anywhere,' he said. 'I'll wait for you here. If you don't come out in five minutes, I'm leaving without you.'

EL PICAFLOR RESTAURANT,
9 RUE LACÉPÈDE, PARIS

EL PICAFLOR RESTAURANT was on the same street as the Hôtel Saint Christophe. From the outside, to Kate, it looked like a place you would walk straight past, and she wondered about the wisdom of leaving the choice of venue to Adam.

'Less than twenty-five euros for a three-course meal with a drink on the house,' he said. 'You wouldn't get that in Dublin.' He looked pleased with himself.

'I guess that depends on the place.' She sounded as apprehensive as she felt.

'You've become far too sceptical. There's a surprise in store for you.'

Sick with hunger, feeling overdressed in her black cocktail dress and high-heeled shoes, she wasn't in the mood for surprises. He pushed open the glass-panelled doors, and once inside, although it wasn't the Ritz, Kate was relieved it was filled with locals – always a good sign. As Adam tried to get the waiter's attention, she looked around for a spare table. There wasn't one. It was then she spotted the staircase downstairs, which was where the waiter indicated for them to go. The lower floor was a cellar with beautiful limestone walls, on which hung tiny lanterns and a scattering of framed images. Each of the round tables had a crisp white tablecloth, nicely dressed with chunky wine and water glasses, cutlery, and folded terracotta linen napkins.

'I told you I had a surprise for you.'

'It's beautiful. I would never have guessed it from the outside.'

'Don't judge a book by the cover,' he said. The waiter led them to a table at the far end. 'Or if you're not sure where to go,' he whispered, 'Google it.'

When the waiter handed them menus, one side was in French, the other in English. 'I checked this too,' he said, turning to the English version. 'Always best to look after the small details.'

'You're a regular Boy Scout,' she teased.

'You look happy.' He poured water for them both.

'Do I?'

'Yeah, and kind of different.'

'Now I'm intrigued. Why do you say that?'

'I don't know. You've looked different since we arrived here. And tonight, Kate,' he lowered his voice, 'you look hot.'

She blushed like an adolescent, remembering how long she had spent getting ready. He caught her looking down at her dress. 'It's okay to take a compliment, you know.'

'Are you psychoanalysing me, Detective?'

'I like to say it as it is.' Then, picking up the wine list, he beamed from ear to ear. 'Red or white?'

'I'm easy.'

'Now, that's dangerous talk. I'll take my cue from you, and live a little dangerously. Let's order the most expensive bottle in the house. It says here,' pointing to a Merlot, 'this one has a plum rich fragrance with a deep oak-barrelled taste.'

'What about the bargain meal of twenty-five euros? I doubt the chief superintendent's budget will stretch to sixty-five for a bottle.'

'It's my treat, Kate. It's not often I get to be in Paris with a beautiful woman.'

She tucked her hair behind her ears, something she did when she was nervous. Tread carefully, she told herself, but all the time another voice inside her head was telling her to do the very opposite.

The food, like everything else about El Picaflor, was excellent, with delivery of the courses timed to perfection. They finished off with two large cognacs, which Adam reminded her were on the house. She felt increasingly at ease as the evening progressed, and it seemed he did too. For once, he didn't talk about work. He had sent the details of the ex-students to Mark Lynch before leaving the hotel, so for now he couldn't do any more. Kate swirled the end of her cognac in the glass, the aroma giving her a sense of warmth. She was pleased that during the meal he had talked at length about his son. She had felt comfortable telling him about Charlie, too.

'Would you like another cognac?' he asked, pulling her out of her thoughts.

'No, no, I'm fine. We've an early start in the morning.'

'You can rest on the flight. Come on, we deserve to chill out.'

She looked around at the now half-filled cellar, everyone relaxed, soaking up the ambience.

'All right,' she said. 'Just the one.'

He waved to the waiter at the far end by the stairs, pointing to their empty glasses, raising his hand with two fingers, cutting through the language barrier.

When the drinks arrived, she kicked off her stilettos.

'How are you doing, Kate?' He warmed the large glass in his hand.

'What do you mean?'

'There are times, I don't know, you seem sad.'

'Do I? I don't mean to.' She forced a laugh. 'Maybe I think too much.'

'That can be hazardous, all right.' He gave her a reassuring smile.

'I didn't mean to bring the evening down …'

'No, no, you're not.'

Silence.

She was thinking that perhaps the extra cognac hadn't been such a great idea. Her head wasn't in the right place for any of this. He must have sensed the drop in the atmosphere, because he said jokingly, 'I used to be very shy, you know.'

She raised her eyebrows. 'I don't believe that.'

'It's true. I'd go as red as a tomato if I had to say a word to a girl when I was in my teens.'

'I bet you went to a single-sex school.' She was glad they had moved onto a lighter topic.

'Yeah – loaded with testosterone, it was.' Then he lowered his voice: 'The first girl I fell for, she didn't even know I cared.'

'My heart bleeds.'

'She could have been the love of my life.'

'Regret can be a terrible thing.'

'Exactly, Kate. That's why I now adopt the direct approach.'

'Nothing wrong with being direct, as long as no one gets hurt.'

'Kate, what you do, your job, I mean …'

'What about it?'

'Does it ever mess with your head?'

He's back talking work, she thought. 'Sometimes.'

'In what way?'

She let out a deep sigh. 'I don't know. I guess I look at people who are messed up, and I wish I could turn back the clock, bring them back to the beginning.'

'Some people are born evil, Kate. It's in their DNA.'

'I'm not sure about that. There are genetic influences, for sure, but it's like that experiment we were talking about earlier, the Tronick one.'

'The one with the mother's still face.'

'The mother stripped herself of emotion, and the baby reacted within seconds, but do you know what the most frightening and upsetting part is?'

'What?'

'Not so much how upset the baby got, although that was tough. It was how the baby, even at twelve months old, turned its face and body away from the mother's. It withdrew; a few minutes of apathy, and the baby's life fundamentally changed.'

'But it was all right when the mother interacted again.'

'You asked me if my job ever messed with my head.' She swallowed a large gulp of cognac, feeling the kick in her throat. 'When I think about babies, young children, when I see the aftermath of messed-up, abusive domestic situations, or wonder what would have happened to that baby in the video if the mother had held that still face for longer, and ignored the child's emotional needs on a systematic basis or, even worse, inflicted pain, emotional and/or physical, I think about the life that could have been. I also think about the aftermath, and the amount of pain that will ensue.'

'You believe that's what happened to the killer of Rick and Pierre?'

'Yes, I do.'

'It's too late for her, Kate. You do know that?'

'As I said, often there is no turning back the clock.' Again she looked around the cellar, taking in the faces of people at ease with themselves and their company. 'Adam, our killer is damaged. She could potentially be the most dangerous person either of us has encountered.'

'And you, Kate, what about your childhood?'

'What about it?'

'That thing you mentioned to me before – when you were twelve and you got separated from your friends and were attacked by that stranger.'

'I got away, didn't I? I wasn't hurt.'

'But it left its scars.'

'I know it did.' Another pause. 'Do you know the worst thing about it all?'

'Tell me.' His voice was gentle.

'I can't remember his face.'

'Is that not a good thing?'

'You said I was attacked by a stranger.' She took a deep breath. 'What if he wasn't a stranger? What if my mind played tricks on me? What if, in reality, I knew him, had always known him? He could even have been someone close to me. I could have blocked the memory out. It would explain why I can never recall his face. Yet I remember so many other details.'

'You would know.'

'No, I wouldn't. The mind is capable of a great many things. It can trick you into believing whatever it wants to, especially if it needs to protect you.'

'I wish I could turn back the clock for you, Kate.'

'I don't.' She swirled the cognac in the glass. 'The thing that happened to me, and all the other stuff along the way, has made me the person I am.'

'You mean the bad stuff can make you stronger?'

'I don't know about stronger, but it forms part of who you are, and who you will become.'

'Earlier on ...' he hesitated '... why did you get embarrassed when I complimented you?'

'I guess I'm no longer used to getting compliments about how I look.'

'It's not about your makeup or your dress, or any of that.

I thought the same thing when we met at Reception earlier, before we went to the Hôtel du Maurier.'

'What do you mean?'

'I was caught unawares. It was like I was meeting you for the first time, and somehow I knew you would be part of my life.' He laid his hand on her bare arm.

'I don't know if this is the right time.' She stared back at him.

'There's never a right time.'

'It's not just Charlie, it's me too. Things are still raw with Declan.'

'Do you still love him?' He took his hand away.

'No, it's not that, but it's taken me a while to accept things. You don't spend so long with someone, start a family together and do all the things we did without …'

'Without what?'

'Without beginning to doubt yourself, and your feelings, how one day you can be head over heels about someone and then it all changes. It gets harder to take that leap.'

'You know as well as anyone that there are never any guarantees.'

Another silence.

'Kate?'

'Yes?'

'Do you trust me?'

'Yes.'

'Then you know I would never do anything to purposely hurt you.'

'I know that.'

'I need you to take that chance, Kate. It's time.'

She didn't reply.

'I'll get the bill, shall I?' he asked.

'Why the hell not?'

∞

Once out in the night air, Adam wrapped his arm around her to walk to the hotel. It wasn't a long way, a couple of minutes at most.

'Let's not go back yet,' she said. 'The Luxembourg gardens aren't far from here.'

'I don't mind. It's up to you.'

It was late, but she didn't care. There was something about the night, the chill in the air, the narrow Parisian streets, the feeling of Adam's arm around her, a sense of the familiar and unfamiliar, histories and new beginnings all rolled into one. He was right. She needed to take that leap.

Before reaching the Boulevard Saint-Michel, he turned her to him, his hands locking around her waist. Leaning down, he kissed her, gentle at first, their first taste of each other, then more passionate, as he pulled her closer still. It felt good, being held, desired, wanted, and knowing that he wanted her as much as she wanted him. And somewhere deep in the back of her mind, she knew she would never forget their first kiss and, no matter what happened from that moment on, neither of them could ever deny it.

When his mobile phone bleeped with a text, she told him to ignore it, and for a time he did.

'Hold on,' he said eventually. 'I'll only be a second.' One arm still around her waist, he took his mobile out of his pocket.

She saw his face change. At first it showed confusion, then shock and finally anger.

'Shit,' he said, and she felt his arm slip away.

She waited, feeling the chill of the streets. There was something about the way his eyes stared at her that told her she wouldn't be feeling any more warmth or desire that evening.

'That was Mark.'

'What is it? Did he find something in the list of names?'

He looked down to the text message again, the one with a media image attached, before handing her the phone. 'Shit,' he repeated, this time with even more rage.

Kate saw the copy of the next day's front-page headline. 'I don't understand,' she said. 'What's it mean?'

'It means trouble, lots of it.'

I

MICHELE PINZINI COULD change, like the witch, charming one minute, harsh and horrible the next. I recognised a form of madness in him. His wife becoming pregnant put an end to our silly games. A baby wasn't part of the plan. I suppose he told his wife he loved her too – the selfish bastard. The wife and the baby survived the fire. People think it was good fortune, but things are rarely purely accidental, or not as far as I'm concerned. I made sure she and the baby survived. I'm not the witch. I don't harm the innocent.

He begged me when he realised what was happening, his wife unconscious on the bed, him tied up on the floor. It was too late then. I put duct tape across his mouth to shut him up. Naked, he looked like a slob as I dragged him across the room, a piece of ugly white meat. I saw the fear in his eyes. I liked that too – getting his undivided attention. I despised him then, and I know he loathed me. But I was the one in control. I would have liked to have more time, but the wife being pregnant complicated things. I thought: Kill him and be done with it.

When I flicked the lighter, he wriggled, looking up at the smoke detectors, hoping I hadn't seen them, that he was one step ahead of me, but I had already taken care of them. Staring at his wife, the woman carrying their unborn child, I thought: Too late, my friend. You didn't care about them when you were fucking me. I slit his throat with ease, the blood spurting, before my rage fully took hold. He deserved more pain. I poured alcohol from the mini-bar onto the rug and set it alight. I gave him his last kiss, like my step-father always wanted.

The hotel maid who discovered the fire, did so because I told her one of the patrons wanted her. It was a risk, but she wouldn't have recognised me. I had come prepared, in a wig and dark glasses. Melodramatic, I know, but I enjoy a dash of drama.

Either way, I was glad the child survived – a girl. I owe her a debt of gratitude. She helped me understand my lack of importance to him. Stupidly though, with my pride hurt, I tried to replace Michele too soon. That relationship didn't end well either, apart from the financial benefits. Looking back now, after Pierre, I realise going to Rome was an attempt to put loving him behind me. But life doesn't work that way. Wherever you go, your personal baggage stays with you. As I said before, I'm not looking for your sympathy. I've done my fair share of cruelty, and will do more. I got my training from the witch. She poked and pushed and mocked me to perfection.

I've waited a long time to draw the Lovers card. I've gone through my introspection, change and indecision, and now I'm ready for a fresh start. The cards tell me I deserve it. I'm entitled.

My new lover's wife won't have the same protection as Michele's. She is a naïve, stupid woman. The guileless cannot understand the depth of the dark. They cannot fathom what will come next because they have no concept of it. I don't envy them their stupidity. I revel in it.

I've played games with her for long enough. All good things must come to an end. She doesn't matter to him, not any more. She certainly doesn't matter to me. She thinks she's getting close, playing the clever little detective, but she doesn't know anything. You might think you know me too. I doubt it. I haven't told you everything, not yet.

LEONARDO DA VINCI
AIRPORT, ROME

THE MORNING FLIGHT from Charles de Gaulle airport to Rome was nothing like the one Kate and Adam had taken the previous day. They were tense, having reflected on the contents of the day's newspaper headline in Ireland. The chief super had already been in touch, and his mood was about as explosive as the engines of their plane on take-off. If the article had simply been a slur on the lack of police resources, that would have been one thing, but it fired in dirt and innuendo, not only at Adam's police record but by quoting a reliable police source close to the investigation, who placed a question mark over the relationship between the detective leading the international leg of the police inquiry and the female criminal psychologist helping to profile the killer. The article went on to say that, apart from the known lack of resources, there seemed to be more questions than answers when it came to the investigation of Rick Shevlin's death.

It wasn't going to change the task ahead of them in Rome, but it certainly concentrated their minds. Adam had moved a couple of levels down from furious to seething. Kate had phoned Declan at first light. The last thing she wanted was Charlie seeing her picture in the paper and asking why. She hadn't expected Declan to be cool with her, but he gave her the distinct impression that he believed there wasn't smoke without fire.

'What you do in your personal life,' he said, 'is no concern of mine, but you can't have it plastered all over the newspapers.'

She wanted to say she hadn't intended it to be plastered all over the bloody newspapers, that he should know Charlie was always number one with her, and that he wasn't in a position to be playing the perfect-father card, but she bit her tongue. He would protect Charlie until she got back.

The meeting with Andrea Giordano, the retired police officer from the Michele Pinzini case, was scheduled for ten o'clock at a café close to the Trevi fountain. Kate doubted that she or Adam would be flicking coins into the water any time soon. They arrived with some minutes to spare. She ordered tea, he ordered an espresso, and as the Roman sunlight glistened on the water, and the tourists thronged, everybody seemed in a better mood than either of them.

When Giordano arrived, despite the informality of the location, he looked like a secret-service agent, dressed in a dark suit, shoulders held back, with army-style tight grey hair and reflective sunglasses. His chin was distinctly Italian, with puckered lips, and when he sat down and removed his sunglasses, his eyes reminded Kate of the dark blue from a choppy, dangerous sea.

After a brief introduction, Kate was surprised to see Giordano remove a collection of photographs from his inside suit pocket.

'Don't look so shocked, Dr Pearson. I may be retired, but I still have a keen interest in this case.' His English was impeccable.

'Why is that?' Adam asked.

'You are a detective, so you understand a case getting to you, especially when it remains unsolved. When Alfredo Masciarelli in the Polizia di Stato told me Michele Pinzini's murder could be linked to an investigation in Ireland, I was intrigued.'

Kate removed her own sunglasses. 'What can you tell us about Michele's murder?'

'As you know, it was vicious. The victim was found naked and tied up, his throat slit. His wife, with their unborn child, was unconscious during the attack. The hotel room was set alight, presumably with the intent of killing everyone involved, other than the murderer.'

'You say presumably – you have another theory?'

He nodded to Kate. 'The maid who raised the alarm spoke to a woman a few moments before discovering the fire. She told the maid she was needed in a room close to the killing. We couldn't find anyone staying at the hotel who had made such a request.'

'What about a description from the maid?' Kate asked.

'Nothing concrete. The woman wore large dark glasses shielding most of her face.'

'And accent?' Adam put on his own sunglasses to cut out the sun's rays.

'She spoke only briefly, and in French. The maid again couldn't be specific.'

'And Michele Pinzini?' Adam pressed. 'What did you discover about him?'

'His profession and personal details are all in the file, but there were a number of people, mostly women, who gave information off the record.' He looked from Adam to Kate. 'As far as the finer sex was concerned, Michele had a demanding appetite.'

'He used prostitutes?' Adam finished his espresso.

'*Sì.*' Giordano rubbed his hands over his face. 'This was not unusual. What was unusual was how he was found.'

'You mean the crime scene and the method of killing?' A frown formed on Adam's forehead.

'Yes, it was a horrible death, but there were contradictions.'

'What kind of contradictions?' Kate asked.

Giordano shuffled through the photographs until he found what he was looking for. He handed Kate and Adam two close-up images of Michele Pinzini's lips. Then, sitting back in his chair, he said, 'There was ambiguity as to whether or not the killer wanted the wife and the unborn child killed, which is why I've always been suspicious of the mystery woman in the corridor. What is contradictory is that, despite the brutality of the attack, the killer left a message, one that normally denotes love or tenderness.' He pointed to Pinzini's lips. 'You can see the faded lipstick. Of course we made comparisons with the wife's brand, but it didn't match. Whoever killed Michele Pinzini kissed him before setting the room on fire. It was a minor dtail, but one that irked me.'

The significance of Giordano's last words was not lost on Kate and Adam.

'I assume you took a swab and compiled a list of properties?' Adam seemed positively energised for the first time that morning.

'Oh, yes. They would be on the file too. We couldn't get an accurate DNA profile, because of the heat in the room, but we tracked the lipstick to a major cosmetic range. At the time, the company had worldwide consolidated sales in excess of fourteen billion dollars.'

Adam leaned closer to him. 'But you got a description of the shade?'

'Yes, that is correct. It was called Carmine but the brand had an enormous distribution.'

Adam slammed the table with his fist. 'That may be the case, Andrea, but the likelihood of it being the same killer has just shot through the roof.' It was the break in the case that they had been looking for, and final confirmation that they had an international investigation on their hands.

Everyone in the café was staring at them now, so Kate lowered her voice: 'We've been told Pinzini's wife was concerned about him before the attack.'

'That is correct. He had become increasingly aggressive, drinking heavily, and appeared agitated, constantly checking who had called at the house or had been on the telephone. Their domestic situation was not a good one, which didn't help matters.'

'You said earlier, Andrea …' Kate paused, as if to clear her thoughts '… that a number of people, mostly women, refused to go on the record about their relationship with Pinzini. Were there any men?'

The Italian seemed hesitant. 'There was one. He is influential, so please do not ask me his name.'

'How did you find him?' Adam was unsure about the retired detective holding back on them, but he let it go.

'At the time of the killing, I looked for similar attacks, but I could not find anything, at least not initially. Then a friend of mine, a nurse in a private hospital, mentioned a man who had been stripped and tied up. He had suffered knife wounds, with a similar blade to the Pinzini killing.'

'A carving knife?' Kate asked.

'That is correct.'

'And you spoke to that man?' Adam kept his tone mellow, keen to get as much as he could.

'Yes, but he asked me to keep everything confidential. Because of his position, I agreed.' Giordano relaxed his shoulders. 'He said he had been with a woman, a very lovely woman. At first, everything was fine – she was very loving and sexy.' His dark blue eyes went from Adam to Kate, and back again. 'But soon she became possessive, completely obsessed with him. He had wanted to pull back, and when that happened, she threatened to tell his wife. I understand he agreed to give her a considerable amount of money.'

'Blackmail?' Kate said in surprise.

'Yes.' Giordano's lips seemed to pucker even more. 'The attack took place after that. Lucky for him, a visitor, a business colleague, called to the hotel room. The female attacker escaped through another door into an adjoining room.'

'But you got a description?' Adam could hardly believe what he was hearing.

'He refused to give one.' Giordano's face was like stone.

'Don't tell me,' Adam was even more agitated, 'you couldn't insist on a description because of his position?'

'We do some things differently here in Italy. I can tell you certain things, but not everything.'

'What else can you tell us?' Kate probed.

Again Giordano paused. Then, lowering his voice almost to a whisper, he said, 'The gentleman was experienced and experimental sexually, but apart from the possessive nature of the relationship, he said he felt he was being groomed.'

'Be specific.' Adam's tone was harsh.

'At first the man felt it was mutual exploration, but soon realised the woman sought more. Once she had identified his sexual needs and potential fetishes, she became dominant, compelling him to be more adventurous.'

'How adventurous?' Kate asked, half guessing the answer.

'Apart from the various acts of bondage, she liked using a blade.'

'Anything else?' Adam leaned forward.

'There is one thing, Detective, but I cannot be certain of it.'

'Tell us anyhow.'

'I think the woman may have been foreign. By that I mean she wasn't Italian.'

'What makes you believe that?' Kate glanced at the tourists firing coins into the fountain.

'The relationship with the gentleman began within a couple of weeks of Michele Pinzini's death. It lasted about a month, before the attack, at the end of the summer.'

'You're saying you think she was in Italy for the summer?' Adam sounded unconvinced.

'It wasn't only the timing of the affairs that brought me to that conclusion. If the woman had been Italian, living in Rome or any other part of Italy, I have no doubt the gentleman would have had her killed.'

'What makes you so sure he didn't?' Kate asked.

'When he spoke, he referred to her in the present tense, not in the past.'

∞

After Giordano had left, Adam and Kate had their first proper conversation since Adam had received the text from Lynch the previous night.

'Well, Kate, what do you think?'

'He seemed like a man who was passionate about his work. I guess his kind never retires.'

'He wasn't prepared to reveal his source.'

'It doesn't matter if his informant is connected to the Mafia, politics or both, but if it's true, we can draw some conclusions from it.'

'Such as?'

'If you combine what Andrea's mystery man said about being groomed, and what we know about Rick Shevlin's behaviour, it's likely she does groom her men, the pupil turning into the teacher.'

'I still don't get why you believe Rick Shevlin was being groomed.'

'His behaviour with the escort had inconsistencies. He was playing with both sides of the coin, wanting to receive pain and give it. People generally group sadism and masochism together as sado-masochism, but there's usually a preference one way or the other. It's seldom both. He backed off when Annabel wasn't going with the flow. She may be experienced, but she wouldn't have been able to distract him if he was used to a particular path. These things escalate over time. The more you explore a fetish, the higher the bar becomes.'

'So what is our killer looking for?'

'Control is certainly part of it, but she's also seeking affection in the only way she knows how. The idea that the killer spent the summer here is interesting. Assuming she was in Paris in the autumn of 2005, she could have stayed on in Europe then or decided to travel to Rome in the summer of 2006.'

'If she's one of the females on the list we got from Jacques, she would have set aside time for her stay in Paris. Finishing her studies early made her a free agent.'

'She would also have been younger. Her circumstances will have changed since then. For all we know, she might even be married. The lipstick on Pinzini's images undoubtedly links the killing, but with Rick and Pierre, it's probable; they simply opened the door and let her in. Unlike Andrea's mystery man, I doubt either of them became suspicious of her. They knew her prior to their deaths, and trusted her enough to let their guard down. They may still have desired her even though, in her eyes, they had fallen out of favour.'

'So?'

'If she's capable of fooling her lovers into thinking she still cares, even after she's made the decision to kill them, she's capable of fooling others, including those closest to her. So, yes, marriage is a possibility.'

'This brings us back, Kate, to her motivation, and what she actually wants.'

'We're looking at someone who has learned the art of pleasing men, whatever their sexual desires may be, but for her, emotions and sexual behaviour are inextricably linked. If she was abused as a child, difficult as it is to fathom, she may have perceived a level of affection from the abuse. When a child is starved of love, they will do everything in their power to find it, wittingly or unwittingly. It's part of the human psyche, going in tandem with wanting to be needed by others, and is for many an affirmation of their individual worth.'

'But these relationships are doomed to failure, right? She can never hold down a proper one, can she?'

'She can, if she's able to detach herself from her demons, live parallel lives. I can't shake the feeling that we're still missing a huge part of this jigsaw, but there is one other thing we've learned from Andrea.'

'What's that?'

'The killing of Pinzini happened within months of Pierre Laurent's murder. Potentially, she then formed another relationship after only weeks, perhaps even days. As I said in my report, these crimes happen because of a stressor, the result of a rise in anxiety levels. However, once she is in that mind-set, she has the ability to move on to the next victim quickly.

Her desires, despite the gap in time of the Shevlin murder, are escalating. With each new target, she will want more.'

He leaned back in his chair and let out a sigh.

'What's the matter?' she asked.

'I doubt I'll be involved with this case when we're back in Dublin.'

'You're talking about that newspaper report.'

'The force always protects itself, Kate. The chief might have given me a chance with this one, but now the heat is on, my involvement will be history. He won't risk leaving me in a key position. He'll want to sever the reason for the journalist's attention at source. It's the way we do things. Remove, keep quiet, move on, and protect the force at all costs.'

When his mobile rang, he answered it. 'Hi, Mark … I see … Thanks for letting me know.'

'What is it?'

'Mark has done a check on Sandra Ryan's details. Like her college application, her address and phone numbers are false.'

'So it's another dead end.'

'He's checking the others on the list with Girardot, but they're all French nationals. I don't have a good feeling about this. Whoever Sandra is, she's part of it, she or one of her friends.'

'You didn't tell Mark about the lipstick matching?'

'No, I didn't.'

'Why not?'

'I guess there's a part of me that still isn't thinking right today.'

She was silent, the cascading waters louder somehow, until finally she said, 'Me neither.'

'Kate …'

'Look, let's drop it for now.'

'If that's the way you want it.'

'It's not a question of what I want. It's a question of too much happening for it to be the right time.' She hadn't wanted to sound harsh, but they weren't carefree people with uncomplicated lives.

'There was a time, Kate, I would have agreed with you, but not now.'

'What do you mean?'

'It's the excuse I used for not contacting my son. It was never the right time.'

She didn't answer him, but he had sown a nagging doubt in her mind. Perhaps he was right.

SANDRA

I'VE NO IDEA how long I've been asleep, but it's dark in the studio when I wake.

Getting up from the sofa bed, I pull the tartan picnic blanket off me. I'm nervous walking over to the windows to look outside. At first, I think I see another shadow, but it's only a trick of the light. The gleam of the moon is bright, but it disappears as the trees sway back and forth. I close the curtains, before reaching down to check the radiator. The heating must be switched off. What time is it? I remember calling Alice at some point. Switching on the studio lights, I search for my mobile phone, but I can't see it anywhere.

I go to the door, listening for sounds coming from outside.

If Edgar was home, I would hear him shuffling about, but the house is silent. I turn the studio lights off again, listening a second time. Still nothing. Unlocking the door, I wonder if she has been in the house again. Maybe I could smell her perfume, or find something moved, but everything is as it should be. Even in the dark, I'm quite sure of it.

The clock in the hallway says eleven p.m. Why didn't Alice call? Perhaps she did, and I didn't hear her while I was asleep. I start touching things, the pictures on the wall, the banisters as I walk up the stairs. The carpet is soft under my bare feet. I stop midway, turning back, looking out to the drive. I can't see Edgar's car. I begin walking again, trailing my hand up the wall, connecting with the familiar, not knowing why, other than the nagging sense that I could be in terrible danger.

On the landing, a shiver passes over me, and I realise there's a cold breeze coming from our bedroom door. I have goose-bumps on my legs and arms. I hear something – are the footsteps coming from outside? At the bedroom door, I stop and listen, leaning my hands and ear against it. Hearing nothing, I turn the handle, pushing the door halfway open, peering around the room. The curtains on the windows are flapping, the sash window open. For a split second I wonder if I'm in her house at Greystones. It feels like a replica of what went before. I swallow hard, still holding the door handle, half afraid to walk in. The house creaks, jolting me. I sense she has been here, shadowing me again, trying to push me to the edge. I can't let her do that. I won't let her.

I walk quickly across the room, crashing the window down, pulling the catch into the locked position, my hands trembling uncontrollably. She opened the window, just as I opened the window in her house. She knows I was there. Then, I think about the time – eleven o'clock: the heating shouldn't have clicked off until midnight. Who switched it off? What if she's still here? It feels as if I'm not alone, and even though I'm half afraid to look behind me, and my legs are like jelly, I turn, and in the half-light of the moon, attempting to take in every part of the room, every last detail, my eyes move too quickly over the bed, but then they dart back. Her silk dressing gown is lying on my side, laid out like a person. Looking at the bedside locker, I see a tube of lipstick and pick it up without thinking, checking the shade. Carmine. Why is she doing this? But I already know the answer. She's telling me she knows what I've been up to, that she's getting closer.

I look back to the bed again, unsure what to do next. A card sticks out from under the dressing gown. It is face down, with an intricate gold fleur-de-lis pattern on the back. I pick it up, turning it quickly, needing to know what's on the other side. A face stares back at me. At first, I can't tell if it's an animal or a man. There are roman numerals, XV, at the top. The card is blurring as I read the two words at the bottom and fall to the floor. The words 'The Devil' swirl in my head as darkness takes over.

PART 3

MERVIN ROAD, RATHMINES

ADAM'S INVOLVEMENT IN the investigation had been curtailed practically the moment they landed at Dublin airport. A phone call from Chief Superintendent Gary Egan as they went through Passport Control reassigned him to desk duties, wading through a backlog of traffic fines.

Kate hadn't heard from him for a couple of days and, despite the information gained while in Paris and Rome, Mark Lynch's maverick efforts to date, the nine hundred statements taken, including re-interviewing Shevlin's ex-girlfriends and known escort companions, hours spent searching CCTV footage and the close co-operation across Europol, the investigation was no nearer to finding the killer. The sketch from Simon Reynolds, the owner of the Grey Door club, hadn't brought in any fresh leads, and Kate had wondered about its accuracy. Maybe Rick Shevlin's lady friend, like the mystery woman in Rome, had disguised herself. Either that, or Reynolds had been less specific than he might have been. Whatever the reason, the only new breakthrough came from the second round of interviews with the hotel staff and a missing room key. The security personnel had assumed the police had taken it as evidence, and vice versa, which reflected badly on Lynch. It felt like the investigation had reached another dead zone.

With Charlie asleep in bed, Kate switched on the nine o'clock evening news, filled with talk of green shoots after Ireland's six years of recession, the Pope and his new Twitter account, and the war in Syria. She flicked it off, and started reading her notes on the Shevlin case again. When the phone rang, she saw before she answered that it was Adam.

'What's up?' she asked.

'I've found something.'

'I thought you weren't on the case?'

'I'm not, at least not officially.'

'Adam …'

'Before you start giving me a lecture on following orders, listen to what I have to say.'

'Go on, then.'

'Do you remember the fake details given by Sandra Ryan on her application to that Paris college?'

'What about them?'

'I started looking at the flights out of Paris around the time she would have left.'

'That's a long trawl. We only ever had a vague idea of the dates.'

'I know, needle-in-haystack stuff, but lucky for me traffic investigations were in a lull.'

'I heard there was a large backlog.' She didn't attempt to hide her light sarcasm, curling up on the couch.

'The good news is, I found the flight – well, two, actually. I could so easily have missed the booking connections, had it not been for a lost luggage report by a Lori Smith. Her suitcase turned up in time for her second flight home to Dublin.'

'What about the first one?'

'It went from Paris to Heathrow. Then a couple of days later, the second went from Heathrow to Dublin. Direct flights weren't as common back then as they are now, or perhaps they wanted time in London. Anyhow, four passengers checked in as a group on the first flight, but only three on the second.'

'All women, I assume?'

'That right, a Lori Smith, Karen Kennedy, Alice Thompson and, finally, Sandra Connolly, who didn't take the return flight to Dublin. It was Delphine mentioning the friend's name as Alice that aroused my suspicions even more.'

'Where did Sandra go?'

'I don't know yet.'

'You've checked the flights out of London that day?'

'Yeah, but nothing so far – she could have stayed on in the UK, or left via a flight, ferry or the Eurostar for mainland Europe. The options are endless.'

'How can you be sure it's the group we're looking for? It's unusual for someone to decide to use their first name when everything else is fabricated.'

'I'm not sure, but I have enough to make me want to question Sandra Connolly. We have the location, coming out of Paris, the consistency of the dates, the number of female passengers travelling together, the probable age profile, and the final destination for at least three of them. As for using the same first name, changing your details on paperwork is one thing, but swapping your first name can be tricky, especially if you're with people who know you well, and they're used to referring to you in a particular way.'

'Okay. What else did you find out?'

'They all have clean records, so nothing interesting there. Two of them are married, Sandra being one. Her husband is Edgar Regan, a jewellery designer.'

'What does Sandra do?'

'Guess.'

'If it's the same person, she was an artist in Paris, so I assume, she still is.'

'That's right, Kate – nothing big-time, a couple of exhibitions a few years back, but not much since.'

'It doesn't necessarily mean she knew Rick Shevlin.'

'Maybe not, but it doesn't rule it out either.'

'If she didn't stay in the UK after her friends returned to Dublin, she could have travelled to Italy.'

'Which is why, Kate, I'm checking all transport links from the UK to mainland Europe between the dates her friends returned to Dublin and Michele Pinzini was killed, but it's going to take time.'

'Have you gone to Mark Lynch with this?'

'I will, but first I'm planning a visit to Sandra Regan in the morning. It's still a bit of a stretch, and before I let him know I've been digging, I want to make sure it's worth getting into trouble for.'

'He won't be impressed with your extra-curricular activities.'

'Let me take care of that.'

'How are you going to approach her?'

'I'll go in with the assumption that she's the Sandra we're looking for. She will either deny it, or if she doesn't, we'll know we're on track.'

'We?'

'I thought you'd come with me.'

'Where does she live?'

'Blackrock – I can pick you up or meet you there.'

'If you pick me up we'll make better time.'

'We'll be travelling in a squad car, Kate, compliments of Traffic.'

'I can hardly wait!'

SANDRA

THE BLACKOUTS ARE becoming more frequent now. When I look in the bathroom mirror, the dark crevices under my eyes are even worse. My skin is pale, and my lips are sagging downwards.

I've no idea who removed her things from the bedroom. I searched everywhere for them when I came to, but the dressing gown, lipstick and the Devil card were gone. Part of me wonders if I imagined it all. The doctor warned me that a withdrawal from the medication could cause problems, but I hadn't envisaged this.

I'm on my own with this battle: when you can't trust anyone, you have to trust yourself. Grabbing my makeup bag, I begin the reconstruction, bringing the deadened parts of my face to life. The extra mascara helps, and the blusher on my cheeks gives them an artificial glow. I use lip liner to define a better mouth, concealer to hide the dark pools under my eyes and, layer by layer, I turn into a brighter version of myself.

I think about taking one of the tablets, the ones designed to help me relax. I don't like admitting that I need them, but I can't go on like this. When the doorbell rings, it feels like an intrusion. I look out of the upstairs window and see a squad car parked outside. Panic sets in. For a second, I fear something awful has happened to Edgar, but then I remember breaking into that house in Greystones. She must have reported it. I've no idea what to do next. When the doorbell rings for a second time, I swallow the tablet. I need to stay calm. Somehow I walk downstairs as if I'm about to open the door to a friendly neighbour. Then, forcing a smile, I say, 'Good morning,' looking from the man to the woman, 'how can I help you?'

I don't take in everything the detective is saying, something about a murder in town, how I might be able to help them. I must have looked confused because the woman tells me I'm not to worry, there's nothing to be alarmed about. Before I know it, I've asked them inside, relieved they haven't mentioned the break-in. It could be a ploy, a way of putting me at my ease before the questions get tough. I can feel my right ear becoming hot. I cover it with my hair, trying not to bite my lip. Then they mention Pierre Laurent.

'I knew him a long time ago,' I say. 'Why do you ask?'

'Pierre Laurent was murdered.' The detective looks like he didn't spend too long shaving this morning. Maybe he has a fast growth – some people are like that. *Shut up, Sandra. This is serious.*

'Yes,' I say. 'It was tragic.'

'You knew him well?' The detective asks this with intensity – like he's digging deep. His name is O'Connor. I think he already knows the answer. He probably knows, too, that I faked the paperwork, that I'm a liar and a fraudster. Despite my best efforts, I bite hard.

'We were friends. He took me under his wing when I was homesick. He made me less so.' I sigh.

'Were you romantically involved?'

His question is like another invasion. I feel my chest going blotchy. I stall for time, telling him I don't understand the question. Then I say, 'He was a friend, a good one. Our relationship was platonic.'

'Your time in Paris, at the art college … How you got there was somewhat irregular.'

He's getting to it now. Is that what this is all about? The college would hardly press charges after all this time. Would they?

'It was a very long time ago, Detective. I'd prefer to put it behind me.'

'I'm sure you would.' His words are loaded with accusation.

'Sandra,' says the woman, 'we're not here to dig up old issues.' Her name is Kate Pearson and she's a psychologist. She's helping the police with the investigation. 'As Detective Inspector O'Connor has told you,' she says, 'we're investigating a murder from more than three weeks ago, that of Rick Shevlin.'

The name means nothing to me. 'I don't understand,' I say. 'How does this have anything to do with me?' I stare back at her.

'We think whoever killed Pierre Laurent may have killed Rick Shevlin.'

I must look shocked, because she tries to appear reassuring, saying, 'I understand this must be difficult.'

'Yes, it is,' I say. 'It's been so long.' I think again about Pierre, how talented he was. He didn't have to spend time with me. He could have been with anyone. But when we were together, it was like he saw a side of me that no one else ever did.

It's the detective who speaks next: 'Sandra, did you know Rick Shevlin?'

'No. I've never heard of him.'

He looks at me inquisitively. 'We believe he was in an extra-marital relationship before he died.'

Is he thinking I could be the other woman? I almost want to laugh with relief. I'd been worrying about the break-in, stupidly forging those papers, but this is about a man I've never met. 'I wish I could help you, Detective, but as I said, I didn't know anyone by that name.'

'Tell us a little bit about Pierre,' the woman asks. There's something soothing about her voice.

'He was a very talented artist. Some people thought he was egotistical. Perhaps he was …' I hesitate. 'He was complicated. He could change, you see. One moment he would be ultra-confident, fearless, and the next, like a scared young boy.'

'You two were obviously close.' Her words are not as threatening as the detective's.

'I guess we were. At least, I hope so.'

'Did you know anyone else involved with Pierre, one of your friends, perhaps?'

I stare at her again. 'No … well, not exactly.' I already know it's the wrong answer because of the change on her face.

'What do you mean by that, Sandra?'

'Pierre liked my friend, Alice, but I don't think anything ever happened between them.'

'But you can't be sure?'

What's she getting at? I try to remember what they've already told me. They think the same person who killed Pierre killed this Shevlin person – do they think Alice is involved? Had I been right to be suspicious of her? 'No,' I say. 'I can't be sure, not completely.'

'What about your other friends, Lori and Karen? Were they close to him?'

Lori wanted to be, I think about saying, but instead, I say, 'No.'

'Is there anything else you can tell me about Pierre?' the woman asks.

I could tell her a lot of things. I could tell her how he liked to bring people to that club, but instead I say, 'He had the most beautiful face.'

My last words seem to interest her, because she looks at the detective. 'Why do you say that?' she asks.

I think about it for a moment. 'He had perfect bone structure, but it was his eyes – they sparkled and were always full of life.' I say nothing for a minute, remembering his face again. 'I sketched him once. He reminded me of someone I knew as a child.'

'Do you still have the sketch?' Her question doesn't sound threatening.

'Yes, I think I do. I kept all my work from Paris. It would be in my studio.'

She smiles back at me, again in a reassuring way. 'You said

Pierre reminded you of someone you knew as a child. Who was that, Sandra?'

'Pierre had the same eyes as my father. They were full of love.'

'Can you get the sketch for us?' the detective interrupts.

'I can look for it, but it might take a while.'

'We can wait, but before you go searching,' he pulls out a notebook, 'can you tell us where you were when Rick Shevlin was murdered?'

This is ridiculous. I don't know anything about Rick Shevlin. 'Detective Inspector O'Connor, I don't have a hectic social life, and days drift into each other. You could talk to my husband, Edgar. He's much better on these things than I am.'

The detective stares at me suspiciously. Does he think I'm lying?

'One other thing, Sandra,' he's still holding his notebook, his pen ready to write everything down, 'we believe Rick Shevlin was seeing a woman using the tag name Cassie4Casanova. Does the name mean anything to you?'

The question comes so out of the blue I have no way to cushion my response, but I take the shocked look off my face as quickly as I can, my mind doing a quick double-take. Christ, should I tell them Edgar could be seeing a woman by that name? I still see the name repeated over and over on the computer screen. What's holding me back? It makes sense to tell them, to put an end to this mess. Then I remember the hotel key, the one I took from her house. When I reply, my words sound calmer than I feel. 'I don't know anyone by that name,' I say. 'Should I?'

His face looks stern. 'The sketch, Sandra,' he says. 'You were going to get it for us.'

'Yes, of course.' I get up to leave the room, frantically piecing the information together. If Edgar is seeing this woman, she could be the killer. I was right to be afraid. I wasn't imagining any of this, but maybe she isn't out to get me after all – maybe it's Edgar who's in danger. She could even be with him now.

Opening the door of the studio, I search for the folder, knowing I need to get rid of these two as fast as I can. I find my portfolio at the bottom of the chest of drawers. Opening it, I flick through my old work, which even now feels like it was done by someone else, a different me – an artist I no longer know.

It doesn't take long to find the sketch. Again, I urge myself to be calm. I'll contact Edgar once they're gone. I'll warn him. I'll make him believe me, whatever it takes.

Entering the room, I get the sense that they've been talking about me. 'Here,' I say, handing the sketch to the woman, 'but I'll need it back.'

'Of course,' she replies.

I turn to the detective and say, keeping my voice steady, 'Detective Inspector O'Connor?'

'Yes?'

'Where was Rick Shevlin killed?'

'Room 122, the Earlbrook Hotel.'

I

Sandra hasn't been taking her medication — very bold and particularly perilous. She has fed herself into my hands, making my position stronger. Some people have problems facing up to the truth, always looking for ways to feed their denial and their rose-tinted plan of life.

Yesterday I paid a visit to the village of my birth, the one near the woods. No one recognised me, my appearance having changed dramatically since the last time I was there.

I can't go back any more, without remembering the killing of my step-father and the witch. As I walked through the woods, I felt as if I was in a dream and that, like the witch, I had become invisible. The sounds and smells of the woodlands hadn't changed very much, Mother Nature holding on with her tenacious grip, triumphant once left in peace. It didn't take me long to find the part of the woodland I was looking for, the hidden scorned earth from thirty-two years before. I was pleased with the sharpness of my memory, and that it stood me well, even though it was dark by the time I found it.

The earth was damp with the familiar smell of moss and sap, as I lay embryonic upon the flattened earth, as if in the hollow of a hand, willing my mother to rise from the ground and take hold of me, but she was too long gone for that. Not even the photograph I clutched in my hand, of the woman I had never known, with that forlorn expression on her face, could summon her ghost.

I waited for first light, the amber sun rising between the knotted branches, me, like a sleeping princess in the castle, the witch's evil spell casting a tangled web, with everyone trapped in time. You may think I'm being silly now, as if I'm waiting for some elusive prince to cut through the thorns to me. If you think that, then you are the fool. I live a half-life. I do not sink into an eternal sleep. I roam. I feel. I touch. I bend. I seek. I lose myself and face the dark. It is loss and fear that haunt most people. I have experienced both, and have overcome the two.

If you could see me now, you would notice that I'm smiling. I'm glad Sandra has become temporarily brave, pushing out her boundaries. It will be interesting to see how far I can push her before she snaps.

I never told you how I killed my surrogate parents. I still see them in my mind's eye, their bodies lying beneath the black knight on the Death card. I chose my time well. He had mellowed, and she had become more withdrawn. They took my subservient disposition at face value, their stupidity adding to the final pleasure. I brought them to the woods on a pretext, akin to the step-father in the Grimms' fairy-tale of Hansel and Gretel, although neither was an innocent child. They had already drunk the poisoned wine. I tied them up like animals, hanging their bodies close to one another, letting them watch the other die. The first cut I made across their throats was barely deep enough to draw blood. The second was deeper than the first, and with each thrust of the carving knife, more blood escaped.

I had covered their mouths with rags to keep their silence. They screamed with their eyes. When I cut their deadened bodies down, I skinned them, trapping some of their pooling blood in a jar. The weather had been freezing for weeks so the animals were conveniently peckish. Scattering their body parts, I knew it wouldn't take long. What was left, I burned in the scorched earth of my mother, and carrying the last of their bones to a fox's den, I poured the blood from the jar over them, giving the den an unexpected party.

The witch and my step-father had been planning a trip away for some time. I doubt they envisaged the one I gave them. I had encouraged talk of a long holiday, making sure everyone knew about it so they wouldn't be missed. I filled their absence with lies. People believe what they want; most are gullible, especially if they didn't care too much to begin with. I was seventeen then, nine years after I had first contemplated killing. I had thought afterwards, when the murders were done, and the foxes had gnawed at their bones, that I would find a bitter-sweet peace. Instead, I felt fragmented. It was only when I went to Dublin that I got a sense of escape. It took me some time before I found the hidden stash of cash in the old house. Otherwise, I could never have made that trip to Paris, where my spirits changed. Then the darkness visited me again, and I learned from Pierre that their wickedness could live on in others.

Sandra has drawn the Devil card. It attracts sinister forces that overturn the order of things. The goat of lust wants to attack Heaven with its horns. I'm a believer in destiny. Another thing you now know about me. You're getting closer all the time, but there will be more twists and turns before you discover the ultimate lie.

THE BIRCHES, BLACKROCK,
COUNTY DUBLIN

KATE AND ADAM were back at the squad car when he said, 'Sandra Regan was hiding something.'

'She was nervous from the outset, for sure. But her mood kept shifting from nervousness to bravado and sometimes detachment. I assume you noticed her reaction to the tag name.'

'Something twigged in her brain, no doubt about it.'

'What are you going to do?'

'I'll move on it from the outside in. I want to have a chat with her husband, and then her friend Alice Thompson.'

'I don't need to remind you that you're no longer part of the investigation team.'

'Which is why, Kate, I'm going to have to move fast.'

'Her curiosity about the hotel was strange. I mean, there was any number of things she could have queried, yet she chose to ask about that.'

'What are you getting at?'

'It could be nothing, but something isn't right about this.'

As they drove away, Kate studied the sketch of Pierre Laurent.

'What do you hope to get from that?' he asked. 'We already know what he looked like.'

'I want to see how she perceived him, if there was any emotional attachment.'

'And?'

'It's kind of peculiar. On the one hand the sketch looks like Pierre Laurent, yet it doesn't. Pull in for a second.'

'Your wish is my command.' He turned the squad car into a side street and switched off the engine. 'Well?'

'Sandra Regan said Pierre reminded her of her father.'

'So?'

'Maybe that's why the image is confusing.'

'Let me have a look.' He took the sketch from her. 'It seems pretty abstract to me.'

'There's a lot going on here, that's for sure. She was obviously fond of him.'

'Not the emotional strain of the killer, then?'

'It wouldn't seem so, but I'd wager she's under some form of stress.'

'Killer or not, Sandra Regan knows more than she is saying.'

Kate studied the sketch again. 'It's always bothered me that Pierre Laurent's face wasn't touched.'

'Any new theories as to why?'

'There's a couple floating around in my brain.'

'Care to share them?'

'Not yet.'

'Kate, you seem bothered.'

'I am – something has always bothered me about this case.'

'What?'

'That's the thing. I can't put my finger on it. Sandra Regan didn't have a problem talking about Pierre Laurent, and it certainly seemed like Rick Shevlin's name meant nothing to her, but I'm still unsure about her, like there's something we're not seeing.'

'Maybe she's protecting someone.'

'Or maybe she's scared out of her wits.'

HARCOURT STREET STATION, SPECIAL DETECTIVE UNIT

MARK LYNCH WASN'T one bit happy that O'Connor was fishing in the investigation. He had his sources in the airport authority too, and he'd be damned if he was going to let the detective regain face with the chief super, or meddle in his investigation. He had tried to get through to him all morning, but the bloody mobile kept ringing out before going to voicemail. He didn't want to put anything out over the airwaves by contacting the squad car directly but he hadn't much choice.

'O'Connor.'

'Is that you, Mark? The signal is shocking.'

He wanted to tell him he wasn't a bloody idiot, but care was needed with other squad cars listening in.

'You're assigned to Traffic, not this investigation.' His words sounded like the order they were.

'I understand that, but I think I could be on to something. I need to talk with an Edgar Regan and an Alice Thompson before I can be sure the lead is concrete.'

'The line isn't so bad that you didn't hear what I just said. You're not part of this investigation any more and all interviews will be looked after by others. Can you hear that loud and clear?'

'Perfectly.'

'Where were you this morning?'

'I was talking to a woman called Sandra Regan. Her name came up on flight information—'

Lynch interrupted before he could finish: 'I know all about that. Get back here and fill me in on what you have.'

'I'm on my way.'

'I'm warning you, O'Connor, no detours.'

The next call Lynch made was to Kate. 'There appears to be a fresh lead on the Shevlin case, a Sandra Regan.'

'I know. I'm with Detective Inspector O'Connor now.'

'I don't take kindly, Kate, to being kept out of the loop. I'll talk to you both when you get here.'

'I'm afraid that's not possible. I've another appointment at Ocean House.'

'I'm not happy about this. I need any additional information you have.'

'I don't have any additional information, at least not yet. If I have something new, I'll be in touch.'

He was livid, and it didn't help that O'Connor was sitting in the squad car beside her, taking it all in. 'Make sure you do, Kate. You may not be an official member of the force, but you are fully aware of the guidelines that are in place. I'll be expecting you to keep to them.'

'As I said, I'll make contact if I've more to add.'

Hanging up the phone and opening his office door, Lynch roared at the first victim he could see, Detective Sergeant Martin Lennon. 'Lennon, set up a full incident-room briefing for half an hour from now. This Shevlin case is gaining some wings and we'd better all be flying in the one direction. Where's Fitzsimons?'

'He's gone for a smoke.'

'When he gets back from killing himself, I want both of you in here. I've half a dozen names that I need you to find out about.' He was about to slam his door when he caught sight of Paul Fitzsimons entering the squad room. 'Right,' he shouted. 'You two in here now.'

Both men remained standing while he began his rant. 'First off, if either of you hear wind of O'Connor meddling in my case, I want to know about it.'

They nodded.

'Second, we have six new names in the pot, four women and two male partners. O'Connor's already checked them through PULSE and they appear clean. I need you to do more digging. Find something. I want business details, family connections, where they went to school, where they were born, and every damn place they've been since.' He paused for breath. 'Lennon, make contact with Edgar Regan – he's one of the names on the list. Set up a meeting for directly after the briefing, and then I'll want to see an Alice Thompson. Arrange that too.'

'Sure, Boss,' Lennon replied.

'Fitzsimons, you work with Lennon on this. I'll use Sergeant Janet Lacy to accompany me for any house calls.'

As both men walked out of the office, Lynch roared after them, 'And remember, if O'Connor sticks his nose anywhere it shouldn't be, I want to know about it pronto.'

SANDRA

I PHONE EDGAR the moment the police squad car turns the corner. When he answers, I'm unable to talk sense, my words getting mixed up, coming out in a jumbled mess.

'Sandra, calm down.'

'The police have been here asking loads of questions.'

'Questions about what?' He lowers his voice.

'About different things, about years ago, someone I knew in Paris, about Alice and a man I've never heard of called Rick Shevlin.'

'What did you tell them?'

'Not a lot, but listen, Edgar, it doesn't matter what I told them. What matters is I think you're in danger.'

'What are you talking about? Do you mean from the police?' He sounds shocked.

I take a deep breath. 'Edgar, I followed you a few days ago, when you went to that house in Greystones. I broke into her house. I know you've been lying to me, but it doesn't matter now. None of it matters. You have to listen to me. The woman you're seeing, she isn't normal – she's been here in our home. I told you someone was moving things around. At first I thought she was playing mind games, and then I found a card with the Devil's face on it. I thought she wanted to kill me. But it isn't me. It's you she's after. I'm sorry I didn't say more of this before, but I didn't want you brushing me off, not until I had proof. You haven't believed me in the past, but I don't care about that.' I'm rocking back and forth, trying to calm myself down. My heart is thumping, and for a few seconds, no words come out, as if I'm having a panic attack. What if he doesn't believe me? What will I do then? I wait for him to say something, but all I hear is silence. Then somehow I get my voice back and yell at him, 'Edgar, do you understand what I'm saying to you? I think she killed someone, this Rick Shevlin guy. Her name is Cassie4Casanova. That's the name you know her by. She'll kill you too.' I start crying, but then I say, 'I'm so frightened.'

'I want you to listen to me.' His words come out slowly, a long pause between each one.

'I'm listening.' I try to breathe deeply and evenly.

'Don't say anything more to the police.'

'You do believe me, don't you?'

'I believe you.'

The relief feels enormous.

'Sandra, I can explain everything.'

'Look, I don't care about your reasons. I just want to make sure you're safe. We can work out all the other stuff later.'

'Sandra?'

'Yes.'

'Do you remember the house you followed me to?'

'The one in Greystones?'

'That's the one.'

Why does he sound so calm? 'What about it?'

'I want you to go there.'

'What? Now? Edgar, I can't go back there.' My voice is high-pitched, almost hysterical. None of this is making sense.

'Sandra, I need you to trust me.'

'I'm … I'm …' I want to say I'm not sure I do any more.

'Listen to me, Sandra. I'll meet you there. It will be all right. I promise you.'

I can't speak.

'Sandra, are you still there?'

I swallow hard, my hands shaking.

'Sandra!' He's shouting now, like he's the madman. Finally, I say, 'Yes, I'm here.'

'I need you to go to the house. I can't explain over the phone. Just go there. I'll meet you outside. You have to trust me.'

'But it's her house. How can you be sure she won't be there?' I bite my lips so hard that they bleed.

'She won't be. I promise you. You're completely safe. I've taken care of everything.'

OCEAN HOUSE, THE QUAYS

SINCE THE CONVERSATION with Sandra Regan earlier that morning, the investigation was in the forefront of Kate's thoughts. Mark Lynch would ensure that all four women would be interviewed, but there was something about Sandra that didn't sit easy with her. How was she connected? She didn't know Rick Shevlin, and if she didn't know the victim, she couldn't be the killer. That put those close to her in the frame – one of her girlfriends, her husband, or someone connected to them. Rick Shevlin and Michele Pinzini had had extra-marital relationships. What if Edgar Regan was having an affair? It might explain why Sandra had asked about the name of the hotel. She could have stumbled on the information by accident – information that could put the woman in danger.

It was all supposition, and she certainly hadn't spent long enough with Sandra Regan for a comprehensive assessment of her state of mind. They would have more information once the others were interviewed, but if finding Sandra turned out to be a breakthrough in the investigation, Adam would have done well, and Lynch's icy tones reflected his annoyance that he had. Opening her laptop, she looked again at her interim report, and specifically her earlier conclusions. It was as good a place as any to start.

Conclusions
- Killer: female
- Known to victims – possible previous relationships
- Psychopathic/sociopathic inferences
- Ability to detach: possible childhood or early trauma
- Interval between murders: indicative of emotional stressors prior to attack
- Killer: creative – will have link with visual-art world, photography, sculpture, painting and/or design
- Age thirty–forty
- Attractive
- Ability to deceive and gain trust
- Capable of social integration
- A planner and a dreamer; will fantasise about murders in advance
- Manipulative/charming
- Capable of delusional thinking and distortion of information
- Seeks emotional fulfilment

- Attention-seeker
- Dangerous and volatile when provoked
- Uses sexual attraction to meet victims/partners
- Has the ability to compartmentalise killings
- Early trauma: damage during development of relationship between the id, the ego and the super-ego
- Ability to adjust to preferred sexual fetish – prior sexual grooming
- Will operate solely or within a small group
- Lacks trust
- High level of hatred
- Emotionally damaged
- Violent attacks: possible pleasure/release for killer
- Creation of crime scene: reflective of visual awareness
- Takes pride in the end result
- Level of intelligence: HIGH
- Ability to avoid detection: HIGH
- Victims are chosen and are potentially groomed
- Calmness of killer during aftermath v. frenzied assault: further analysis required
- Risk of repeat killing: HIGH
- Time frame: subject to stressor/s
- Identification of stressor: unknown

Having reviewed the information a number of times, her attention kept going back to one line: *Capable of delusional thinking and distortion of information.* How delusional? How distorted? What was the level of personality disorder involved? She had treated many cases of detachment over the years, fragmented recall due to trauma, psychotic and psychopathic sufferers, but it felt like something else was driving this.

Walking around the room, she considered how, at first glance, many patients appear normal. They can hold down credible careers, give an illusion of living a normal life, but there are cracks once you start digging. They walk a tightrope: their relationships are usually fundamentally flawed, and no matter how much they achieve in life, career or other accomplishments, they cannot rid themselves of the demons that fuel their sense of worthlessness, igniting anger and a pathway to self-destruction.

Did the killer murder the victims because she craved the intimacy they could give her, even though each of the relationships was doomed to fail? With a mind capable of this level of hate and destruction, there could be no simple fix. Kate thought about another case. She had met Samantha Deering in her first year at Ocean House. Samantha had made a number of suicide attempts, and was eventually referred to her. The girl used her sexual appeal, because she desperately craved affection, hating herself afterwards, creating a vicious circle of sex, intimacy, regret, depression and then attempted suicide. She remembered having to commit the girl. It was after Samantha's mother had called, with the girl uncontrollable, that she finally had to take action.

When she had arrived at the girl's home, Samantha was in her bedroom, her eyes closed as if she was deep in sleep. When she called her by name, at first Kate thought she couldn't hear her, so she went closer, touching her on the shoulder. She would never forget the expression in the girl's eyes when she opened them. She looked lost inside her mind, breathing fast, her face contorted. She began screaming, hitting out blindly, sweat pouring from her forehead, and yelling expletives at invisible monsters in the room. She had become utterly detached from reality, her mind split, and she was visiting Hell. Samantha had been abused by one of her mother's ex-boyfriends, which only came to light when her sister told her mother about an approach he had made to her. The sister had refused him. When Samantha found out about it, it was as if she was being abused again. She blamed herself for not saying 'No', for being weaker than her sister, a part of her feeling complicit with the abuse.

If Rick Shevlin's killer walked a dangerous tightrope, the answers to why would be found in their early development. The forming of unhealthy attachments occurs for a reason. Kate opened a file on family therapy, which dealt specifically with attachment styles, examining child–parent relationships over a life cycle – how it affects the child and the forming of their adult romantic attachments. *Children exposed to constant stresses and problematic situations, exceeding their ability to cope, specifically where abuse occurs, are found within a disorganised attachment style, with deep psychological problems in adult life. Avoidance, denial and suppressed anger can all form part of their psychological makeup.* That brought Kate back to her first question: how delusional was this killer? Was a dissociative disorder involved, a means of avoiding reality, and what coping methods had she sought?

Pacing the room again, she finally realised what it was about Sandra Regan that had bothered her. It had been her facial reactions. When they had spoken about her time in Paris, and alluded to the faking of documents, the upper part of her face had been harsh, her forehead frowning, her eyes intense, yet the lower part was different: her mouth had curled downwards, her cheeks soft. It was almost as if she had two separate faces.

SANDRA

I ARRIVE IN Greystones before Edgar. I'm too fearful to park on the street and wait there alone, so I drive down to the seafront. It's sunny. There are plenty of people about, but instead of feeling safer with others around, I start thinking she could be anywhere among them.

The car is fogging up, but I daren't open a window. I've no intention of risking anything until I meet Edgar. It's then that his text comes in, saying he'll be twenty minutes late: the police had wanted to talk to him. Edgar says he's taken care of everything. But what does he mean by that? I think about how odd he has been lately. I'm not the only one who has been showing signs of pressure.

I wish I was a smoker. If I was, I would be lighting up now, and as I'm thinking this, I wonder why Alice never phoned after she didn't turn up at the studio. Before I know it, I hear my phone ring. Then, 'Hi, Sandra.'

'You never came to the house the other day.'

'I did. I couldn't get an answer.'

'Alice, I've found out the truth.'

'About what?'

'About Edgar and this other woman – I've proof he's having an affair and …' The rest of the words won't come out.

'And what?'

'The woman,' I'm stammering, 'she's dangerous.'

'What do you mean?'

'She broke into our home. She left messages for me, wrote stuff in my diary and now—' I choke up again.

'Sandra, take it easy.'

'The police have interviewed Edgar. They called to the house earlier.'

'Why? What do they want?' Her voice is agitated now.

'They wanted to know about Pierre. You remember him, don't you?'

'That was a long time ago.'

'I know it was, but now someone else has been killed, a guy called Rick Shevlin. The police think the two killings are linked. I've warned Edgar. I told him the woman he's seeing could be the killer. His life might be in danger.'

'Have you told the police all this?'

'Not yet. I wanted to talk to Edgar first. There's more to this than I can work out. He's on his way to see me now. He's told me not to worry, that he's taken care of everything, but he could be saying that to keep me from being scared.'

'Sandra,' her voice is stern, 'I want you to listen to me.'

They're the same words Edgar used earlier on. Everyone is asking me to listen to them, like I'm not capable of functioning on my own merits. Then the voice inside my head says, *You rang her, stupid, and you don't trust her. She didn't help the other day. She didn't bother phoning you to see if you were okay. For all you know she could be lying about calling over to the house. Maybe she never came.*

'Sandra, are you still there?'

The car feels suffocating. I want to hang up, but instead I say, 'Yes, I'm still here.' I open the driver's window to get air. I can hear a woman calling her dog, some teenagers passing by, chatting loudly, and music blaring from a car parked nearby. It all sounds loud and fast.

'Where are you?' she asks.

'I'm in Greystones, down by the seafront.'

'Stay there, Sandra. I can be there in fifteen minutes.'

'I can't, Alice. I've got to go. I've got to see Edgar.'

I hang up the phone, turning it off in case she tries to call back. I tell myself it's all going to be okay, as I hear the waves crashing in. I roll up the window, put my seatbelt on and drive to the street where I'm supposed to meet Edgar. As I turn the corner, I see his car parked at the top. I take the first space I can find. I see him getting out of the car, walking towards me. It's only then that I unlock the doors and step out onto the street. I pass a middle-aged man with his two terriers. He smiles as he gets closer, lifting his hand to wave at me.

'How are you? It's been a while,' he says, with a wide smile.

God, maybe I look like her. Men do that all the time, falling for similar features in a woman.

'Sorry,' I mutter. 'You must be mistaken.'

He stares at me, then says, 'Here's Edgar now,' waving at him too. 'I'd better get on.' He's practically chirping, and then, looking down at his dogs, he starts to laugh. 'These monsters are dangerous if they don't get their exercise.'

'Sandra,' Edgar says, when the man passes, 'are you all right?'

'What's going on? Why does that man think he knows me?'

'It doesn't matter.'

'But I …'

'It's okay. I told you I'd explain everything.'

He takes me by the arm, walking me in the direction of the house. I pull back. 'I can't go in there, Edgar. I told you, I can't.'

He looks at me in the sympathetic way someone might look at a foolish child.

'Sandra,' he says, 'it's all going to be okay, I promise you.'

'I don't understand.' We're in front of the house. 'I can't go in there,' I tell him again.

'Yes, you can.' His voice is more assertive as we move towards the back of the house, and he takes the key from under the plant pot, pushing me towards the back door. 'Sandra, the police are about to talk to Alice. Now get inside.'

CHRISTCHURCH, DUBLIN

STUCK IN TRAFFIC, coming from Christchurch, Kate had got a call from Mark Lynch to say they had interviewed Sandra Regan's husband, and a couple of the guys were currently talking with Alice Thompson. Both of them, in Lynch's opinion, were being particularly evasive. People knew things they weren't saying, and when that happened, the police dug their heels in.

Catching a glimpse of her face in the rear-view mirror, Kate thought again of the sketch of Pierre Laurent. Considering the traffic wasn't going anywhere fast, she phoned Lynch back. 'Mark, did you find anything of interest on Sandra Regan's father? I assume you're running background checks?'

'I am. On everyone involved, but there's nothing on him yet. Is there something particular you're fishing for?'

'I'd like to know what he looks like.'

'Why?'

'It was something Sandra Regan said about the sketch of Pierre Laurent. It could be nothing.'

'Okay. I'll see what I can do, but if you're working on any scenarios, even if they're not conclusive, I want you to run them by me.'

'If I have anything, I'll let you know.'

They spoke for a couple of minutes before she hung up. She thought about Adam. His hands were tied right now, and there wasn't a darn thing he could do about it. When the traffic lights changed to green, and only two cars got through, she made her next call to him.

'I wish you'd do something about city traffic,' she said, when he answered. 'It's a nightmare.'

'I don't plan on being here long enough to solve Dublin's road problems.'

'I guess not.'

'Did you hear any more from Mark Lynch?'

'Not a lot. Alice Thompson and Edgar Regan are being evasive. It seems neither of them had solid alibis for the night of Rick Shevlin's murder. Alice Thompson says she was at home alone, Edgar Regan says he was at home with his wife.'

'Convenient.'

'Mark's running background checks on everyone involved. I've asked him to get me an image of Sandra Regan's father. It may turn out to be nothing, but I'd like to know what he looked like.'

'I can call over later, talk things through again.'

'I'm better off working alone. I've told Mark I'll contact him first if I have anything more.'

'I'll settle for second.'

'But you're not on the case.'

'Maybe not, but rumour has it I'm a good sounding board.'

'Psychologists,' she laughed, 'are supposed to be the best listeners.'

'I'm in the wrong job, then! Remember, phone me.'

At last, the traffic began to gain pace. Charlie, she thought, wouldn't be back from football practice until after seven and, thankfully, it wasn't her week on pickup duties. She checked the time on the dashboard: five thirty-five. If she got home by six, she'd have an hour. It wasn't much, but it was something.

SANDRA

WHEN EDGAR PULLS back the curtains, the house looks different with the sun shining through the windows. I'm still terrified she'll arrive at any moment. What if this is a plan the two of them have concocted to get rid of me? I don't remember if he locked the door after we came in. As if reading my thoughts, he says, 'Sandra, there's nothing for you to worry about.'

'You keep saying that,' my voice is shaky, 'but you're not telling me anything. Why have you brought me here? What do the two of you want with me? She lives here, doesn't she? The woman you're having an affair with?'

He steps towards me. His movements seem predatory. 'You're wrong,' he says. 'I need you to take a good look around.'

'Why? I told you I've been here before. I know it was wrong to break in, but you didn't leave me much choice.'

'You didn't break in.'

'What do you mean? I've already told you I came here a couple of days ago.' I'm biting my lip again, trying to get my bearings. 'Why are you contradicting everything I'm saying?'

'You couldn't have broken in.'

'Edgar, you're not talking sense.'

He grabs my arms. 'It's you who isn't talking sense. You couldn't have broken in because this house belongs to us, you and me.'

'You're lying.' I pull away from him.

'How can you break into your own house, Sandra?'

He sounds desperate. *What game is he playing?* I stare at him as if he's mad. 'You're trying to scare me,' I say.

'Why would I lie? You were unwell, Sandra. You got very sick. The medication was supposed to help.'

'I don't believe you.'

'You got depressed again – worse than ever. What did you think the medication was for?'

'I was stressed, that's all, a little down. I was under pressure. It happens to a lot of people.' He grabs my arms again, and there's something about the way he's staring at me that tells me to run. He's messing with my mind. The two of them are in this together. He's part of her awful games. Why didn't I see this before?

'It was more than stress, Sandra.' I try to pull away from him again, only this time his grip is too tight. 'You had a complete breakdown. It had been building up for months. Ask Alice. Ask any of the others. They'll tell you.' He takes his mobile from his pocket, releasing my arms. 'Ring any one of them,' he says, holding out the phone. If I take it, he might grab me again and I'll never get away. I don't touch it. Instead I roar, 'They never said anything to me. If they had, I would have remembered.'

'You blocked it all out, Sandra. The doctor said it was part of the process. He said you would remember everything in time. It hasn't been long, not even a month. He told us not to bring up the subject unless you asked about it. There was no point upsetting you.'

He drops the arm holding out the phone, and I run to the door, but he gets in my way. 'You haven't been taking your medication,' he says, 'have you?' I see his eyes narrow. If he knows that, he knows other things too.

'You're lying!' I shriek. 'You're like her. You want to mess with my head.'

'No one's doing that, except you.'

'But things were moved around the house, her silk dressing gown and the lipstick I found in our bedroom, the notes in my diary … I don't understand. You're making this up.' My voice is hysterical.

'Why would I do that?' He fakes a sympathetic look.

'I don't know!' I yell wildly. I turn cold. 'Because you're having an affair with her – she's put you up to this, hasn't she?'

He's staring at me as if I'm crazy, then turns away, like someone defeated. I look at the open door to the hallway. I rush past him and run up the stairs. On the drawer of the bedside locker, I can see the markings on the wood where I prised it open. I pull out the drawer looking for her lipstick, Carmine, needing proof that what I remember is really true. It's then that I see the key. The one I had taken from the house, the one that should be in my bag. I grab it, put it in my pocket, not understanding how it got back into the drawer, as I hear him coming up behind me.

'Sandra, I need you to listen to me.'

Stop saying that! I scream inside my head.

He's stomping around the bedroom. Then he opens the wardrobe doors. 'Look inside,' he pleads. 'These clothes, they belonged to you.'

I don't know why he's lying, but I know I need to get out of there. I take a step back: my path to the door is clear. I run past him again, down the stairs, praying the back door isn't locked. I can hear him following me as I open the door. Rushing down the street after me, he calls, but I can't stop. I open the car as quickly as I can and, like that time at the hotel, I pull out blindly. The man and his two dogs are crossing the street. He pulls the leads to get the dogs out of the way. I blast up the road, knowing exactly where I'm going. The hotel isn't far. I see Edgar get into his car, wanting to come after me. I'll need to keep going. If I get out of here fast enough, I can lose him. I don't trust Alice or Lori any more. One of them is part of all this. I know it.

MERVIN ROAD, RATHMINES

KATE OPENED THE door to her apartment and went directly to her small office at the back, unlocked the Shevlin case file and read through all her notes again. Driving home, she had been thinking about the delusional aspects of the killer's life. Most certainly, she could convince herself of intimacy with her choice of sexual partners. She could also compartmentalise and separate the killings, submerging them within a distorted logical context. But what if her dissociative disorder was causing more than self-delusion?

Assuming the killer had experienced sustained early trauma, her brain's development in adolescence could be of primary importance, because of the potential damage and repercussions it could cause. The brain undergoes substantive changes over the early years and, depending on the severity of the abuse, can become sufficiently traumatised to split conscious thought.

Certain things began slotting into place. Kate pulled down a number of reference books covering dissociative identity disorder. She hadn't seen it in any of her patients, as it was relatively rare, but she knew it normally began as a protective piece for the sufferer, the victim behaving in a way that was at odds with other aspects of their personality. What starts as protective, when a child is unable to fight or flee, and they attempt to distance or dumb themselves, then becomes learned behaviour, the mind dividing into two sides, or more, of the person.

Despite her promise to Lynch, she phoned Adam first.

'Adam, when we were with Sandra Regan, did anything else unusual strike you about her?'

'As you said, Kate, she was detached, nervous, defensive … Why?'

'Do you remember on the flight to Paris, when we were talking about the brain's development – the id, the ego and the super-ego, and how sustained trauma can interfere with cohesive development?'

'Kind of.'

'It's because the brain goes through a massive change in the early stages. If traumatised, the temporal gyrus, which stores autobiographical memory, doesn't develop correctly and can sometimes cause a split.'

'What kind of split?'

'It's all part of a person developing a coherent sense of self.'

'Talk English, Kate.'

'Okay. A child is under a sustained level of emotional trauma. The brain is changing as they are growing older, not just psychologically but physically. The two are intertwined. When a child finds themselves under a pressure that they can't cope with, other forms of coping mechanism come into play. For example, a shy, nervous child, being bullied at school, might one day find that a different side of their personality slots into place, a more aggressive side, and they are able to take on the bully. The stronger, more assertive part of their brain defends them. At least, that's how it starts off, as a form of protection, not long-term division.'

'I'm listening.'

'Sometimes the temporal gyrus splits at a point in the brain's early development. One part of the brain doesn't like the dark, difficult memories, so it closes them off, creating two identities.'

'Are you talking schizophrenia?'

'No, no. Schizophrenia happens when a person hears voices which they can't tell are not real. This is different. There are mixed views on the development of multiple personalities, or extreme dissociative identity disorder. In every individual the clinical presentation varies, and the level of functioning can change from severely impaired to adequate and manageable. Importantly, the sufferer is capable of fooling themselves as well as others. The majority of patients with DID report early sexual and physical abuse, consistent with our killer's profile. Often, the identities are unaware of each other, as they have compartmentalised memories and knowledge to a different part of their brain, a split. Sufferers can experience time disturbance, thinking they've been asleep or even forgetful. The primary identity, which is often the one using the birth name, tends to show various established personality traits, being passive, dependent, suffering guilt or depression, with the other side of the personality assuming a more active, aggressive or hostile role. The latter of the two, the darker, more aggressive side, usually contains more complete memories, because they have the ability to face them, and can be aware of the perceived weaker strand's existence, even though the weaker side might be unaware of them.'

'Kate, I don't know. It sounds a bit far-fetched.'

'But it is possible. Multiple personalities or dissociative disorder is a way of coping. In extreme cases, one side of the brain is fully protected from the other.'

'So, there's a dominant side?'

'That can change too. Both sides operate independently. They have to, if they're to function, but the switching usually happens because of stress factors, again consistent with our killer's profile. In the earlier development of the disorder, the switching might have occurred because of the abuse, and then later, when other pressure points arose. By then it would have been a learned response mechanism, recurring over and over. The darker side was developed as the protection, so if the person is put under pressure, the learned behaviour of switching to the active aggressive and hostile side of the personality will slot into place.'

'What makes you so sure the killer could be suffering from this disorder? What did you call it? Multiple personality disorder?'

'That's right, or dissociative identity disorder. For a start, the gaps between the killings, alongside the severity of the attacks, point to intermittent stress factors, possibly initiated by depression. It is also consistent with behaviour that is the result of early trauma and damaged development. It's extreme, I know. I can't be completely sure, but when we were with Sandra Regan today, her reactions unsettled me. At times her facial expressions were contradictory. There was her nervous disposition too, biting her lip, her chest breaking out in blotches and tugging at her earlobe. Something wasn't right, and it was more than her wanting to hold something back. Just suppose for a moment that she is suffering from DID. Her subservient side might remember Pierre Laurent with affection, and it is also probable that, within that confine, she wouldn't recall the darker parts of their relationship. Even if she had known Rick Shevlin, one side of her brain could have shut him off to her.'

'She didn't look like a killer to me, Kate, but then again, the longer I'm in this job, the more I realise that doesn't count for much.'

'I'm not saying she is. I'm only saying these are possibilities that are worth looking at and, hopefully, will get us closer to the truth.'

'So what now, Kate? I assume you're going to talk to Mark.'

'I'm going to have to, but the whole thing will sound even more extreme to him than it does to you. A lot will depend on what he gets out of the background checks. We'll need fact to back up the supposition, specifically Sandra Regan's childhood circumstances, and the others' too. A number of things about her fit the profile – her age, her attractiveness. She could also have been at all three murder scenes. Then there is her interest in the arts, her frail, almost nervous, disposition. She appears intelligent and creative, yet she was vague about where she was on specific dates. You said yourself she was detached, nervous and defensive.' She paused. 'Look, Adam, I'm not saying I'm one hundred per cent certain about where to point the finger – that's not my role – and, yes, the same analysis could apply to another. What I will say is, dissociative or multiple identity disorder is a high contender for being part of the psychological make-up of the killer, and we can't ignore it.'

'Okay, I'm hearing you.'

'It would be so much easier if I was dealing with you and not Mark.'

'We'll have to work around that. If what you're saying has a chance of being correct, then our visit to the Regan household could have applied more pressure to a difficult situation. I'll have a chat with the chief super, and see if his mood has mellowed since the newspaper article. Mark might be an egotistical arsehole, but he'll want to get to the bottom of this as much as we do.'

SANDRA

I LOSE EDGAR quickly, but instead of going to the hotel as I'd planned, I pull the car into a side street. My vision has been blurring, and when I stop the car, the intermittent blackness feels heavier, like dark rainclouds hovering overhead. I feel almost devoid of any normal emotion and, with nervous exhaustion, I lie back on the head rest, closing my eyes. All the frightening faces appear again. It was like this the last time I was depressed, even though I didn't recognise it back then. Part of what Edgar had said had struck a nerve. I know I haven't been well. Everything has felt so confusing lately. I've become more withdrawn. I was the same after leaving Paris. Alice described it as maudlin.

I start thinking about Pierre again, how I had fantasised about him, imagining his kiss, our tongues entwined, him wanting to devour me. He always said I was a tease, that I flirted with him one minute, then became chillingly cold the next. All those years ago, and yet the memory is still stronger than anything I've ever felt for Edgar. *You can't seek out a dead man!*

Looking down at my hand, I see the gash where I tore it a few days ago, and for a moment, I see the flicker of the knife, opening that drawer in the house in Greystones. The more I stare at the wound, the more it distorts, the cut weeping, and what was dried blood changing form and trickling down my wrist. The wound begins to pulsate and soon my hand is covered with blood.

She had left the Devil card for me – his hands were strange too, one held up, the other downwards in the flames. My bloodied hand starts to shake violently, blurring more, turning into the blood red of the card. I open and close my eyes a few times, realising my mind is tricking me.

Reaching down, I frantically search for my iPhone in my bag. I've four bars of an internet signal. I type 'Devil card', and the image I saw on the card appears on the screen. Under it, the words read, *The Devil Card from the Tarot Deck, when found upright, means bondage, addiction and sexuality*. None of that makes any sense to me, so I scroll further down to a longer description:

At the foot of the Devil stand a naked man and a woman chained to the podium on which he sits. They seem held against their will, but the chains around their necks are loose, symbolising bondage to the Devil isn't forced. The man and woman wear tiny horns like those of the Satyr – becoming more like the Devil the longer they

stay close to him. The dark cave implies the Devil dwells in the
most inaccessible realm of your unconscious. Only crisis can break
through the walls.

Are the man and woman on the card supposed to be Edgar and
this other woman? He never mentioned the Cassie4Casanova
link on the computer. How would he explain that? He couldn't
deny it.

The phone rings, jolting me. At first I'm relieved it's Karen.
She'll know what to do. I press answer, but say nothing.

'Sandra, are you there? Can you hear me?'

'I'm here, Karen.' I sound crackly, barely audible. 'I'm very
frightened.' I start crying, the tears streaming down my face. I
don't think she can understand what I'm saying, so I try again.
'I'm scared, Karen. Edgar is making up lies. I think I'm going
mad.'

'It's okay,' she says.

'It's not okay, Karen. You don't understand. He's with
somebody else, but he's denying it.' I remember what he said
about the house in Greystones.

'I'm sure there's a perfectly reasonable explanation for all of
this.' Her voice is too calm.

I roar at her: 'There bloody well isn't. There's nothing
reasonable about any of this.' I wipe the tears away, trying to
pull myself together. 'Karen, do you know about the house in
Greystones?'

'Yes.'

'Edgar says it's our house. Is that true?' I'm full of fear for her
response.

'You and Edgar loved being by the sea.'

'Is it true?' I ask again, this time shouting.

She doesn't answer, not immediately, as if she's trying to work out what to say next.

'Don't you remember, Sandra?' Her voice is softer. 'You bought it with the money your parents gave you, after you came back from Europe. When you and Edgar moved to Blackrock, it was a weekend retreat for you both.' Her words are drifting. 'You haven't used it much lately …' She keeps talking, but I can't make out what she's saying, something about it being good to know it's there if we need it. So, it's all true. Edgar says it is, and now Karen – unless she's lying as well.

'Karen, I can't talk any more. I have to go.'

'Sandra, you don't sound well. We're all worried about you.'

I hang up the phone, like it's the enemy. The car windows are steaming up again, but this time, I daren't risk opening them. Instead, I put my phone back in my bag, taking out the diary. I flick through the pages, looking for my last entry. It doesn't take me long to find it, but stuck inside the page is a black-and-white photograph. In it, there is a large dark shadow to the right, and I can see the back of a young girl. Looking closer, I can make out her face reflected in a window. I've no idea how old the photograph is, but something about it feels familiar. The sunlight is shining on the glass, fracturing her face into obscure shades of black, grey and white. I drop the diary, before the photograph falls out of my hand like the Devil card had done and once more I'm consumed by the dark.

THE BIBLE SAYS many things about sex. A man shouldn't have sex with the daughter or granddaughter of any woman he has had sex with. But there are plenty of inconsistencies within the various versions, an error by a scribe here, a misinterpretation there, the belief that something is obvious when its absence leads others to think it's fair game. Leviticus 20 doesn't prohibit incestuous relations with a granddaughter. This is believed to be oversight, a corresponding document lost, but it's irrelevant either way. People use the Bible to make any argument they want.

Unfortunately, Edgar is now trying to take charge, navigating between his idea of the truth and so many lies. Sandra is cracking.

I feel her fear stronger than ever, her desperation: obliteration is close. The witch is following me again, watching my every move, sensing there might be another killing. It's a favourite pastime of hers, stalking me when she thinks something is about to happen. She doesn't let go easily. She still haunts the old house in Leach, even though it's boarded up, rotting from the inside out. A house has a soul, you know, with history everywhere. It doesn't take a lot to unlock the memories. The recall of a raised voice, the sound of a cane being lashed, harsh words – *You're a disgusting animal. You'll rot in Hell. The devil has a place for little whores like you.*

The witch always had things to say. She messed me up. I used to think she messed him up too. My incestuous step-father, grandfather, call him whatever you like. I dare say the witch hated sex. She probably couldn't wait for my mother to perform, the herded goat to the slaughter. I've no doubt that between my mother's death and my readiness, he travelled for his pleasures further from home.

In the end, I hated him more than I hated her. With the witch, I soon recognised the false attempts at affection, and the pleasure her withdrawal of it gave her. He was different. I sought his love, believed it to be real. Did you ever love someone so much that you were prepared to be destroyed because of it? I cannot abide weakness now. It is such a debilitating trait. I found love in his tears of guilt, and stole joy when, afterwards, he would ask for my forgiveness. I would comfort him, as a parent would a child. The lies were harder to take when his mask of deception finally became apparent to me.

I need to go back to the woods. I always gain strength from

their place of death. The Devil card has decided Sandra's fate, but there is still another to be drawn for the spread. I've asked the Reader to reveal it many times, but she can be difficult when she wants to be. She isn't meek like Sandra, but believes she has the upper hand.

I remember picking the Hangman card before I killed Rick. We had sat in the restaurant that last night, him thinking I would go back to the hotel room with him, assuming I had forgiven him for the gang rape at his precious party, and that I needed him more than he needed me. The arrogance of the ego is another debilitating characteristic. I instigated the argument, knowing which buttons to press. If you know how to pleasure someone, you know how to cause them pain. The Hangman card was perfect: I needed the wisdom from the Well of Wyrd. I took the master number as another sign in the denouncement of God and his book of biblical lies.

I shouldn't have been surprised when he booked that whore. He wouldn't have wanted to waste the bed that he planned to share with me. It had delayed things, but time wasn't of any consequence. Once the card was drawn, his fate was sealed.

My new lover has proved a disappointment too. Maybe it's all for the best. As I've told you before, I'm a believer in destiny.

HARCOURT STREET STATION,
SPECIAL DETECTIVE UNIT

MARK LYNCH WASN'T sure about Kate's theory on the mental condition of the killer, but she had proved herself in the past, and any fresh angle was a good thing. It meant broadening the background checks to anyone connected with Sandra Regan's early childhood. If Kate was right about her, and the extra pressure accelerating the risk of an adverse reaction, then he needed to adopt a more direct approach.

Both Alice Thompson and Edgar Regan had denied any knowledge of Rick Shevlin, but he had no doubt the two of them were holding something back. Kate wanted him to concentrate on Sandra, but Alice Thompson was also at the forefront of his mind. For a start, Sandra and Alice were by far the most attractive of the four women involved, and therefore more likely suspects. Working backwards, he contacted their professional colleagues, using tax records to access previous employers or associates, going all the way back to their early school days. His investigative juices began to flow when he discovered gaps in their personal records. They had disappeared from Irish records in their late teens and had both come from the same rural village, Leach, in Wicklow.

The more phone calls he made, the more he discovered. The girls had gone to the same primary and secondary schools. The local schools in Leach weren't large. With the girls being of similar age, the chance of them knowing each other from an early age was high. The then principals of the schools had retired, but they still lived locally, one in a remote location near Elliot forest, the other in the town. The first, Barry Lyons, the primary school head, would have known the girls from when they were four. He was the one living near Elliot forest and, unfortunately, didn't have a landline. If he had a mobile phone, it wouldn't have worked so close to the dense woods.

With no other option, Lynch rang the second school principal, James Gammon. He already knew from the records that Gammon had served in the police force in the earlier part of his career. Before leaving, he had gained a reputation as a troublemaker, questioning the big brass in Dublin on all sorts of murky stuff, including bad management. Still, Lynch thought, he'd probably used the discipline of the force to run that secondary school like a well-oiled machine. He hoped Gammon didn't hold grudges against the rank and file or it might prove to be an uncomfortable conversation.

He rang the number Fitzsimons had given him. 'Could I speak to James Gammon?'

'Speaking – who's asking?'

'Detective Mark Lynch, Special Detective Unit, Harcourt Street.'

'To what do I owe the pleasure?'

'We're doing background checks on a couple of people from your community. I was wondering what you can tell me about Alice Thompson and Sandra Regan. Sandra's maiden name would have been Connolly, when she attended the Sacred Heart School. They were pupils between 1994 and 1999.'

There was silence at the other end of the phone.

'Mr Gammon?'

'Yes?'

'I was wondering …'

'I heard your question the first time.' Another pause. 'I knew both girls, yes. Intelligent, hardworking, neither of them ever gave the school any bother.'

'How would you describe them individually?'

'Alice was the more outgoing of the two, much more confident than Sandra, who was a shyer girl, with a quiet demeanour …' another pause '… but she was unusual.'

'How so?'

'I always felt there was more to her than she would let others see. Funny, I still think about her at times.'

'She must have made quite an impression on you.'

'They all stay with you in one way or another. If I've any regrets about Sandra Connolly, it's that I never managed to get her to come out of her shell. I can't say I ever saw the girl smile.'

'And Alice Thompson?'

'Different again. As I said, she was more confident and outgoing, but the two of them were as thick as thieves.'

'So, they were close from the beginning?'

'Sandra depended on Alice. She was a kind of shield for her.'

'I'm not getting you.'

'Alice became the mouthpiece for the two of them. At times, Sandra was more like her shadow than a separate person.'

'Anything else odd strike you, Mr Gammon?'

Another silence. Lynch waited.

'There was something else …' Gammon sounded hesitant.

'Tell me anything that comes to mind, no matter how irrelevant you think it is.'

'After the girls left the Sacred Heart, they faced the world alone.'

'What do you mean?'

'They were both only children, and when the parents left Leach, one because of work commitments, the other for personal reasons, the girls stayed on in the village alone.'

'What were the parents like?'

'It's a small place, Detective, and, I'll be honest with you, none of them mixed well. They were odd folk, keeping themselves to themselves. The two men were okay, both quiet individuals, but there was something unsavoury about the mothers, each cold in the extreme.'

'Were there any issues with social services, Mr Gammon?'

'None that I know of.'

'That doesn't mean there wasn't a problem.'

'It was a long time ago, Detective. In the mid to late nineties, people tended to leave well enough alone. They still do, I suppose. Anyhow, it's all water under the bridge now, but I often thought it was the reason the girls struck up such a strong friendship, their common bond the oddity of their respective families.'

'I appreciate your frankness.'

'Have you spoken to Barry Lyons?'

'No, not yet.'

'You'll have your work cut out for you.'

'How's that?'

'Barry didn't take his retirement well. Teaching was his life. Afterwards, he pulled back, became withdrawn. He goes for weeks now without seeing anyone.'

'A recluse?'

'He has become a man of the woods, and once the woods have you, they say, they take your soul.'

Hanging up, Lynch thought again about his conversation with Kate. With Barry Lyons being a recluse, the mountain might have to go to Muhammad – and useful to have a psychologist tag along. He preferred working alone, but if he needed someone, he had no problem using them. He dialled Kate's number.

'Kate, something's come up.'

'What?'

'It turns out that Sandra Regan and Alice Thompson were friends practically since birth. They're both from Leach in Wicklow. I've spoken to their ex-secondary school principal, a James Gammon, and he's told me enough to make me curious.'

'Like what?'

'There was a stark contrast between the two girls, one an

introvert, the other much more confident, Sandra being the introvert. The ex-principal's description of both sets of parents was strange, especially what he said about the mothers. I want to find out more.'

'What can I do to help?'

'I need to pay a visit to Leach. It turns out the principal from the girls' national school is now something of a recluse, a guy called Barry Lyons. I thought it would be good if we spoke to him together. There's no way of contacting him other than turning up on his doorstep.'

'When do you plan on going?'

'As soon as you can, but I really think we should go early in the morning. I did a stint in a small town in the Midlands a number of years back, and I know how these tight-knit communities operate. They're slow to trust outsiders, even those in uniform. They only ever tell you the information in bits, a throwaway comment here, an observation there. As I said, James Gammon thought there was something odd about both sets of parents. If he's saying that, then it's probably true.'

'Is it only Barry Lyons you want to interview?'

'We'll start off with him, but we'll need to talk to others too. The local police officer stationed in Leach in the nineties passed away a couple of years back, but the postmistress is still alive, as is the postman. Like the school principals, they're retired, but in the absence of the local police officer, they'll know more than anyone else about the goings-on back then. A community can talk for ever about what it wants to say but when it comes to its secrets ... well, we'll need to be on our toes.'

'Okay. Pick me up at half nine.'

'Right – we'll start with the recluse. If he's a no-show, we can track the others down.'

Hanging up, he walked over to the police swipe board, added the parental links of Alice Thompson and Sandra Regan, and put a circle around the village of Leach. There was a story there, he thought, nothing surer.

SANDRA

I'M SITTING IN the foyer of the Earlbrook Hotel with no memory of how I got there. Lifting my bag up from the floor, I see the old photograph is still in the diary. I search for the key. It's there too. *You're here now — do something*.

When I stand up, I expect others to stare at me, to acknowledge my existence, but instead they pass me by, as if I don't exist, and when I take a step forward, it's as if someone other than me is moving. I press the lift button. It arrives quickly. I step in and my only company is a man and a woman. They get out on the first floor, as do I. I walk in the opposite direction, even though I know the room I'm looking for is the other way. When the corridor empties, I turn back, until I'm standing outside Room 122.

Knocking on the door, I dread someone answering. When I get no response, I knock again, harder this time – still nothing. The key feels cold in my hand as I turn it in the lock, but it won't work. Someone has changed the locks. I've no idea what to do next. I need to think clearly. If the room is empty, the key could be at Reception.

I don't want to go back downstairs, but I have no choice. Downstairs, I walk past the desk enough times to see that the key is in the wooden slot behind. I still have some cash. I could get lucky. Maybe no one has booked that room. In the Ladies, I tidy myself up, then Google the hotel number and dial it. It doesn't take long for Reception to answer. 'Yes,' the girl says, 'we do have availability,' and I hear myself reply, 'I'm right outside. I'll be there in two minutes.'

The receptionist gives me a strange look when I say I want to pay for the room in cash and, yes, I tell her, I can supply a home address and phone number. When she goes to take down a room key, I ask about Room 122. She gives me another odd look. 'Is it vacant?' I ask. 'Only I've stayed here before, and I know it's a lovely room.' She hesitates, but I sense she wants to get rid of me. I don't care. I have the key. That's all that counts.

Upstairs, I turn the key in the lock, push the door open and step inside. There is a chair at the dressing table. As I had done in the bedroom in Greystones, I wedge it between the door handle and the floor.

I know from what the detective has told me that I'm standing where Rick Shevlin was murdered. Without planning to, I open the bathroom door, seeing my reflection in the mirror. For a split second I see another face, someone with features not unlike mine. She is smiling, but it isn't a nice smile. It's mocking. I think about the man with the two dogs, how he thought he recognised me. All of my thoughts are jumbling as I remember what Karen and Edgar said about the house in Greystones, and me being unwell.

I turn, and the large bed becomes the focus of my attention. Another split image, this time of a naked man partly tied to the bed. His eyes are open, but I know he's dead. There is blood all over him. My vision blurs again, and the red blood turns black. The bed is now in a darkened room, lit by car-park lights from outside. I take a step closer to the bed, and feel his eyes following me. 'Look at me,' his eyes are saying, but instead I start to shake. I turn back to the bathroom mirror, and there's that face again, mocking. It's then I hear someone calling my name. At first I think it's her, but realise Edgar is frantically turning the door knob. I take a step back. What if everything Edgar said was true? What if I've got it all wrong? I turn back to the bed, but the body is gone, as is the face in the mirror. There is something about the way Edgar is pleading for me to open the door that makes me walk over to it. I remove the chair and unlock it, uncertain what will happen next.

'What's going on, Edgar? You know, don't you? You know everything?'

'I knew you'd come here.'

'How did you know? Rick Shevlin was killed in the room, but the key …' I hold it up. 'I found one at that house in Greystones, and the piece of paper with the room number on it.' I remember reading the address. 'It was in your handwriting. You wrote down the address of the hotel. Why did you do that?'

He puts his hands to his face, and I watch his body slowly crumple. He moves closer to me, looking like a man who is about to confess something awful.

'Edgar,' I murmur, 'what's so terrible that you had to hide it from me?'

'I wanted to protect you.'

'Protect me from what? From whom?'

'From yourself.'

'I don't understand.' I'm shaking my head again, violently now.

'You killed him, Sandra.'

I look at him as if he's mad. Then I laugh hysterically. 'You must be crazy.' I back away from him. I've stopped laughing. 'It's not true,' I say. 'It's a lie. Tell me it's a lie.'

He sits on the chair by the door, looking at his feet instead of me, the words pouring out of him, fast. 'I knew you were seeing someone else, Sandra. I found the dating link on the computer.'

'No, no!' I roar. 'That was you, not me.'

'I followed you. I saw you with him in the restaurant. I saw the two of you having that argument, and I thought, perhaps it's not too late. Maybe we can patch things up.' His face is in his hands, his shoulders shaking. I realise he's crying. 'I've never loved anyone the way I love you.' He looks up at me, as if he is begging me to understand.

I don't know what to do next, other than stare at him.

'I've never been good enough for you, Sandra. I know that. I should have tried harder to please you. Maybe then you wouldn't have wanted to be with someone else.'

I keep looking at him blankly. He continues talking, his

voice lower, barely audible: 'After you left the restaurant, I watched you follow him. Then I saw you go back to your car. You removed a large carrier-bag from the boot. At first I didn't understand why, but then I realised you were going to him. I thought about bursting into the room, but instead I walked around outside, trying to work things out. I've no idea how long it was before I found myself back at the hotel, taking the lift to this floor, standing in the shadows as I waited for you to leave.'

I look from Edgar to the bed, thinking about the image of the dead man, and again I turn to the mirror in the bathroom, to see if she's watching me, but I can see only myself.

'When you opened the door, Sandra, I called your name. At first you didn't turn. You froze like an animal caught in a snare. I know you killed him because I saw the aftermath, but there wasn't a drop of blood on you. I thought at first somebody else had done it, but then I saw the knife in your bag, and the things you used to clean the place.'

'You're lying!' I roar.

'I wish I was. You went into complete shock. I didn't know what to do. Instead of calling the police, I protected you. We took the stairs instead of the lift, not wanting to risk being seen. Thankfully, there was no one at Reception, and the next thing I remember, I was driving you home in your car. I kept thinking about you coming out of that hotel room, and how vulnerable you looked. All I could think of was getting you help, making you better. I should have paid more attention to the tell-tale signs, the forgetfulness ...' He puts his hands over his face again. 'I called Lori the following day. I needed someone to rely on, if I had any chance of pulling this off. I didn't tell her anything about the murder, but I told her how sick you were. That you were the worst I'd ever seen you. She helped me convince you to get help.'

For a few moments I say nothing, but after a while, I hear myself speak: 'What do you want to do next?'

'We need to go to the police. We can explain that you were unwell, that you've never done anything like this before. I don't know what I was thinking of that night. It was a stupid mistake. I know that now.'

'Edgar,' my voice sounds so calm, I surprise myself, 'I want to go home.'

For a moment I think he's going to refuse to take me, but he says, 'Okay, if that's what you want. I know it's a lot to take in. I understand that. We can talk to the police later. You do agree that you'll talk to them, don't you?'

'It doesn't look like I have a choice.'

I follow him out of the room, going back down in the lift, and finally out to where I parked the car.

'I'll drive,' he says. 'I can get a taxi and pick up my car later.' It's as if we're going home after an evening out.

Back at the house, I lock myself into the studio. When he leaves, I pick up my diary, looking at the old black-and-white photograph with the shadow. I finally make the call to Alice. 'It's me,' I say. 'I need to go back to the woods.'

ELLIOT FOREST, COUNTY WICKLOW

THE CLOSER KATE got to the village of Leach, the more beautiful the landscape became. Many of the houses still had thatched roofs, and as they drove past St Kevin's church, nestled among thick shrubs and trees, she tried to imagine the place thirty years earlier, when the affluent, almost cosmopolitan appearance of the small town would have been different. Lynch was right about small-town protectiveness, especially where the past was concerned. Parts of it might look like picture-postcard Ireland, but dig deep and historical scars can usually be found.

Neither she nor Lynch said much during the journey. She preferred it so, having taken the case file to read along the way.

While reviewing her notes, she remembered Lynch hadn't come back to her with an image of Sandra Regan's father.

'Any luck on that photo I asked you for?'

'That proved a bit tricky.'

'How so?'

'No one knows who Sandra Regan's father was. After her mother did a runner, the girl was raised by her grandparents.'

'When was that?'

'From birth, it would seem.'

'Did the mother ever come back?'

'It doesn't look like it. I guess being an unmarried mother thirty years ago was different from how it is today.'

'I don't doubt it but, still, it's unusual for a woman to abandon her child like that.'

He stopped the car. 'Look,' he said. 'That must be the cabin. Full marks to James Gammon for directions. It's not exactly the Ritz, is it?'

'It's certainly isolated,' she said, taking in the battered, moss-covered wooden structure surrounded by trees.

As they walked towards it, the smell of earth and moss was potent. A crowd of jackdaws scurried from one tree to the next, prompting them to look up. The sound of fallen twigs breaking underfoot exaggerated the thud of their footsteps, as a cold breeze rustled through the trees. The closer they got to the cabin, the more convinced Kate was that nobody was in. The makeshift curtains were drawn, and a large wooden bolt was clearly visible across the front door.

'There could be an entrance around the back,' Lynch said, sharing her thoughts.

The place couldn't have had more than two rooms, although it was longer than it was wide. Kate waited at the side of the cabin, while Lynch went to the back.

'Find anything?' she called, after a few minutes, but she didn't get an answer. 'Damn him,' she muttered under her breath. The place was unsettling, and the longer she stood alone, the more she felt as if something or someone in the forest was watching her. She went around to the back and saw that the door was ajar. 'Mark, are you in there?'

'Come in. It's empty.'

She stood at the doorway, trying to work out which of the two rooms his voice had come from. 'This is breaking and entering, Mark. You can't be in there without a warrant.'

'I heard something crashing down inside. I thought I'd better check it out.'

'Liar.' She stepped inside. The interior of the cabin was little more than a hovel, with wood chippings on the floor, a dirty sleeping bag below a small indoor wooden frame. She put her hand over the ashes in the grate. They were still hot. 'Mark,' she called into the other room, one that looked to be used as a kitchen, with a gas cylinder beside a two-ringed hob. There were basic utensils and tin cans on a square wooden table, with only one chair, facing the back door. 'He hasn't gone far,' she said. 'The ashes are still hot.'

'Some place, isn't it?' He smiled, walking back towards her. The smile disappeared when they heard the sound of rushed footsteps coming their way.

'What the hell?' were the first words out of the old man's mouth. A rifle hung on his shoulder.

'The door was open,' Lynch ventured.

'That doesn't mean you're invited inside.' Kate heard a mix of anger and fear in his voice.

'Barry Lyons?' Mark took a step closer, holding out his hand, but the old man walked past him, slamming the rifle onto the wooden table in the kitchen.

'Who's doing the asking?' he bellowed.

They followed Lyons into the makeshift kitchen.

'I'm Detective Mark Lynch, and this is Dr Kate Pearson.'

'What do you want with me?'

'We need to talk to you about two of your ex-pupils,' Lynch continued.

The old man let out a sigh. 'Which two?'

'Alice Thompson and Sandra Regan – you would have known Sandra by her maiden name of Connolly.'

Kate thought she detected sadness in the old man's eyes. He remembered them, all right.

'That was a long time ago.' He pulled out the one chair at the table, sat down and folded his arms.

'Maybe so,' Lynch replied, 'but it's important that you tell us what you know of them.'

'I know an awful lot. I'm an old man, and I've acquired a great deal of knowledge over the years ... but wisdom is far greater than knowledge. It took me a while to learn that.' His eyes were fixed on Lynch.

'Barry ... is it okay to call you Barry?' Kate ventured.

'That's my name, isn't it?'

'Barry, you knew both girls from the age of four, is that right?'

'That's correct, and I taught them for two years running, between the ages of six and seven.'

'You've a very good memory.' She smiled. 'Can you tell us if they were happy girls?' She walked over to the table, squatting on the wood chippings, in the absence of any other seating.

'The two of them were close, I can tell you that.' He pointed to the window opposite, looking out to the forest. 'They were always playing out there, more at home in the woods than anywhere else.'

'Were they intelligent? Were they talkative?'

'They were extremely intelligent, Sandra particularly so. Mathematically, they were each beyond their years. That's always a good indicator of IQ. Sandra was the quieter of the two.' He sighed. 'Sometimes I wondered if she was taking the information in at all, but she always did well in the end-of-term tests. I guess being quiet doesn't mean you're not listening.'

'What about the girls' parents?' Kate watched for his reaction. This time his eyes looked angry.

'I didn't teach the parents, only the children.' His tone was notably hostile too.

Kate let it go. 'What you said about them being more at home in the woods than anywhere else, did you think they were running away from something, or someone?'

For the first time, he unfolded his arms, tapping the table with the fingers of his right hand. 'Sandra's mother – or, rather, her grandmother – was a cold fish. Her harshness came from somewhere rotten.' He emphasised the last word. 'I doubt the child was ever hugged or praised, or received a kind word from that woman. Alice's mother was a drinker. Her parents led a somewhat bohemian lifestyle. Most folks around here put them down as eccentric, but it was borderline abandonment, if you ask me. The girls learned to fend for themselves. Although they were different, they were equally desperate. I guess desperation and fear can make the strangest partnerships.'

'Did you report either set of parents to Social Services?' Lynch asked flatly.

Barry Lyons gave him another sharp look. 'A lot has changed in this country in thirty years. When those two girls were children, an alcoholic mother was tolerated, and an unloving one was far too common. They were fed, dressed and sent to school. They got on with their education. That was enough for folk not to meddle. As I said, I had a lot of knowledge, but not so much wisdom ...' He trailed off.

Kate wasn't sure how her next question would go down, but decided to forge ahead. 'Did you ever think that either of the girls had been abused?'

Instead of the hostile look he had given Lynch, sadness was again etched across his face. 'Yes,' he replied, breathing deeply. 'I've thought about that over the years, and not only in relation to those two girls. Back then, we only ever saw what we wanted to see. As I said, it was a different time.' His voice rose. 'Some people think it was a time of innocence,' he spat on the floor, 'but it wasn't. Ignorance, selective or otherwise, was the mantra of the day.'

'You said they were always in the woods.' Kate needed him to stay on-side. 'How did you know that?'

'Even before I retired, I found the woods a place of solace. I would be out walking, and at varying times I'd come across the girls. They would be up to some childhood mischief or other. Later, before they moved to secondary school, I saw them less, but that didn't mean they weren't there.'

'Did they hang out anywhere in particular?'

'They had a few favourite spots. I would often catch the two of them smoking, or lighting fires to stay out late at night.' His voice lowered again, as he looked out towards the forest. 'There was something almost bewitching about them.'

'How do you mean?' Lynch asked, leaning against the back door.

'Although they were physically different, you could tell they had a certain quality that would attract others, especially men. The last time I saw them together in the woods was a month before they moved to secondary.'

'That last day,' Kate asked, 'what were they doing?'

He didn't answer immediately, looking away from the forest to the floor where Kate sat. 'As far as I remember, they were messing around with cards, not your regular kind but those Tarot cards, the cards of the devil. I had seen them with them before, but there was something different that afternoon.'

'What?' Lynch pushed.

'It was the concentration on their young faces, their enthusiastic glances to each other, almost as if they believed the cards had answers. I remember ...' he scratched his head '... they had this large red cloth laid out on a flat boulder. There was a fire crackling to their side, as they each took a turn picking a card from the deck and turning it upwards. They looked at one another almost as if there was no need for words.'

'Did you approach them?' Kate asked, keeping her tone gentle.

'No, but I kept watching. Something stopped me going over. I can't be sure what, but I do know that at one point one of them looked at me. Maybe she heard something, but either way, they stood up, gathering the cards. Then they picked up the red cloth, each of them holding a side. The wind bellied the cloth as they ran. It was like …'

'Like what?' Kate asked.

'Both of them were so slight,' he whispered. 'The further they moved away from me, their bodies got more lost among the trees, the red cloth looking as if it was flying magically within the green of the forest, as if somehow I'd been put under a spell.'

LEACH, COUNTY WICKLOW

'THAT GUY WAS a right crackpot, wasn't he?' Lynch turned the key in the ignition.

Kate waited while he reversed the car, the tyres getting stuck in the mud, before accelerating forward. Then she said, 'He's cut himself off from reality, Mark, but Barry Lyons didn't spend his adult life working with children not to recognise a strong bond, and the Tarot cards are another concrete link. Whatever partnership was struck up between Alice and Sandra, it was strong, and friendships formed during this critical stage in development are unlike those formed in later life.'

'The Tarot cards are a link, but so far, Kate, everything we have is circumstantial.'

'The background story fits – potential abuse, two young girls allowed to roam the forest alone, questionable family structures, each of them in Paris at the time of Pierre Laurent's murder, no definitive knowledge of their whereabouts when Michele Pinzini was killed, and what we got from Barry Lyons about the Tarot means both girls at least experimented with darker themes. People turn to the occult and the Tarot when other forms of belief fail them.'

'You're talking conventional religion?'

'You saw St Kevin's Church on the drive to Barry Lyons's place. It had almost a fairy-tale setting, but in the past, like many similar structures, it was a formidable force in community life. It doesn't sound to me like the community did very much for either Sandra or Alice.'

'Let's call to Billy Meagher, the retired postman, next. His house is closest. We should be there in five minutes.'

Kate opened her holdall and pulled out the case file, flicking through her notes.

'What are you looking for?' he asked.

'It's something Sandra said about Pierre Laurent's face. She said it reminded her of her father's, that he had the same eyes, full of love.'

'So?'

'We already know Sandra Connolly never knew her father.'

'She could have been talking about the grandfather, the surrogate replacement.'

'Or she could have imagined someone else to be her father, a fantasy figure, an image she clung to when there was little else.'

As they pulled into the centre of town, Lynch's phone rang. 'Hold on a second, Kate. I need to take this. It's the chief super.'

Kate listened to his side of the conversation.

'Hi, Boss, what's up? … Yeah, we're making progress. We've spoken to the ex-principal of the national school. He's confirmed what we got from James Gammon about questionable family set-ups and the two girls being close. It seems they practically reared themselves. We've also established a link with the Tarot cards. Dr Pearson thinks it's important … I don't think that's necessary, Boss. I've plenty on the team who can take care of that.'

Kate watched Lynch's expression change from upbeat to defensive, then to annoyance. Whatever the chief super was suggesting, it wasn't something he favoured.

'Well?' she asked, when he finished the call.

He took a deep breath, locking the steering wheel with unnecessary force. 'He's bringing O'Connor back in.'

'How come?' Kate kept her voice deadpan.

'The chief super wants him to take over the enquiries into Alice Thompson's parents and Sandra Regan's grandparents. He also wants him to find Sandra's natural mother. He's of the mind that O'Connor is very good at finding missing needles in haystacks. He's officially back on the team, but with instructions to keep a low profile.'

Lynch stepped out of the car and slammed the door. Kate decided to let it go, but wondered for the first time, if, perhaps, Mark Lynch might have been the one to leak the story to the press.

I

GOOD OLD EDGAR wants to tell the police. He thinks it's the best way forward. He wants poor, stupid, pathetic Sandra to get help, to become the woman he fell in love with. If he wasn't so blind, some might think him loyal. People with tunnel vision are ill-equipped to understand their own reality, let alone someone else's. I can't let him go to the police. It would ruin everything.

I don't despise him, but life is transient, in the same way that photographic images fade over time, becoming fugitives of what went before.

The silence of the studio is soothing, with him off on his little errand. He says he's doing all this for the best, but do you think that if the police hadn't ruffled him, he would have kept quiet? I dare say he would. People always do things for a reason. He's looking for a way to ease the terrible burden he's carrying. I don't care any more. Alice brushed me off earlier when I mentioned going back to the woods. I will phone her again, knowing I can make her listen. It's time for us to talk straight to one another. There will be no more hiding behind lies.

LEACH, COUNTY WICKLOW

BILLY MEAGHER'S HOUSE was in the centre of town. The street sloped down towards a row of shops, a grocer's, a newsagent's, a hair salon, and one of half a dozen local pubs. Each house was pebble-dashed to the front and painted a different colour. The ex-postman's house was a watery shade of blue. Lynch had phoned ahead, so that by the time they arrived, the kettle was boiled and a plate of assorted biscuits lay on the kitchen table. From Lynch's face, he wasn't in the mood for tea after his conversation with the chief super.

'You'll both have a cuppa, then?' Billy asked, more as a statement than a question.

Kate figured she would have to supply the goodwill for both

of them. Lynch took his cue from her: despite his bad mood, he knew he'd get nothing out of Billy Meagher if the ritual of tea-sharing was declined.

'Are you retired long?' Kate asked.

'A couple of years – I got out when the going was good. The country's going downhill, there's nothing surer.'

'You live alone, then?'

'I do, Miss. It suits me well. Only me and Rocky here.' He leaned down to pat a collie's head. 'Rocky's nearly as old as myself, if you count his time in dog years. Great company, though – I'd be lost without him.'

Lynch put down his tea. 'Billy, we're hoping you can tell us about the Thompson and Connolly families, especially Alice and Sandra.'

'Yeah, I knew them. What do you want to know?'

'Anything you can tell us.'

'They lived here, they left, and most people were glad to see them go.'

'Why?' Lynch gulped some tea.

'Some folk are queer. None of them were friendly, like. It's a tight community, this.'

'Can you be more specific?' The edge in Lynch's voice revealed his tetchiness.

'What Mark is getting at, Billy,' Kate added, 'is that you must have seen your fair share of odd stuff over the years. I'd say you're a very observant man.'

Lynch stood up from the table.

Billy ignored him, focusing his attention on Kate. 'I am, yes, for sure. You wouldn't believe the half of it. There was a family here once, a mother and her son, a queer pair they were. They lived on the outskirts, so it was damn awkward delivering their mail. They had a bloody awful dog too, never shut up barking.' He patted Rocky again. 'The son, he must have been in his thirties, he took to playing with himself at the upstairs window. I never paid it any mind. I mean, you see all kinds of stuff. But then some of the schoolgirls took to taking a shortcut that way so I had to have words.'

'What did you say?' Kate asked, unsure where this was going.

'I told him to pull the bloody curtains. The mother was no better. She used to go around half naked. At least, she did when I was delivering the post. I had a set routine, you see,' he said, biting into a custard cream. 'The auld one was eventually put in a home. The son wasn't long following her. There was something odd going on there for sure, mark my words.'

'And the Thompsons and the Connollys – would you say there was something queer going on there too?' Kate drank her tea, like this was the most normal conversation in the world.

'Hard to say, but old Mrs Connolly was probably the worst of the bunch.' He seemed to be enjoying himself, dragging out the information, being the centre of attention.

'The daughter, Sandra's natural mother, what became of her?'

'I can't say I know,' his face darkened, 'not for sure.'

'Why? I heard she left after the baby was born.'

'That's the spin they put on it. I was always suspicious. She wasn't a bad sort, that youngster. All I know is, the girl was the size of a house with that child of hers. No one asked any awkward questions. The next thing, old Mrs Connolly had the baby, and the mother had gone off to England.' He helped himself to another custard cream. 'As I said, I had my doubts. I mean, the girl never came back, not once – it's hard to credit.'

Lynch sat down again. 'Did you suspect foul play?'

'I didn't say that. All I'm saying is, it was odd, nothing more.' Billy Meagher was on the defensive now.

'Don't worry, Billy,' Kate said gently. 'We can check out what happened to the mother from our end.'

He nodded, seeming somewhat relieved.

'I hear Sandra and Alice were close,' she continued.

'Ah, yeah, they were for sure.'

'And Sandra was the quieter of the two?'

'Aye, she was quiet, in her own way.'

'In her own way?'

'She could be a bit of a flirt, that one. The two of them could be. They'd roll them school skirts up until there wasn't much left to the imagination, if you get what I'm saying.'

'Did you think all was right at home, with the parents and the grandparents?' Kate gave him a reassuring look.

'I only know what I've told you, about that old cow Connolly. Maryann Thompson, she was a drinker, but …' He swirled the dregs of his tea in the cup.

Sensing he was holding something back, Kate said, 'Billy, everything you tell us is confidential. We're not even sure if there is any direct connection to our investigation, but if you know something, or think you do, it's probably best that you tell us now.'

'Aye, maybe you're right.' He looked from Kate to Lynch, then back to Kate. 'It's a long time back, but I saw him up to no good.'

'Who?' Kate maintained eye contact.

'It was when both girls were in their teens that I saw the two of them together.'

'Who are we talking about?' Lynch pulled his chair in closer.

'Young Sandra Connolly and Alice's father, Sam Thompson,' he blurted, as if surprised they weren't keeping up with the conversation.

'What did you see?' Kate kept her tone level.

'I couldn't be sure, at least not at first. The light can be tricky in the forest, especially late evening.' Once more, he looked from Kate to Mark and back to Kate. 'It was the school uniform I recognised, that red tartan skirt. I thought, for feck sake, it's not right, school kids carrying on like that.' Indignation was written on his face. 'I was going to pull the two of them off each other, but then I realised it was Sam who was doing the loving.'

'So,' Lynch said, 'you did nothing?'

'A man has to think about these things, but in the end, I decided to let it be.'

'Do you know if it happened again?' Kate asked softly.

'I don't know, but it wasn't long afterwards that Sam and Maryann moved to Dublin, and Alice stayed here to finish her schooling. A right pair of hippies, they were. They rolled their own cigarettes, you know. I saw both of them out of their heads more than once. They did their fair share of tripping, that's for sure.'

'Did you ever hear what happened to them?'

'Aye. Maryann passed away not long after she left here. The drink killed her liver before any of the other stuff.' He sat back in the chair, pointing to the window. 'She's buried up there with her parents in the cemetery.'

'And Sam?' she asked.

'For all I know he's still in Dublin. He was here for the funeral. The whole village turned out. It's the way we do it down here.'

'It seems Sandra's grandparents made a quick exit too – do you know anything about them?' Lynch looked distinctly suspicious of Billy Meagher.

'There weren't too many questions asked after that pair left, but I daresay you'll be talking to our ex-postmistress, Lily Bright. She'll fill you in on what's what.'

'You sound like you already know what she's going to say,' Lynch remarked.

'Maybe it's nothing, but I remember … there was something very peculiar about their mail. Lily jabbered on about it for months, and you'll find that normally she's a woman of few words.'

MEAGHER'S PUB, LEACH,
COUNTY WICKLOW

'THAT WAS TESTING,' Lynch said to Kate, once they were outside Billy Meagher's house.

'You knew it wasn't going to be easy.' Kate hesitated, then added, 'You're going to have to talk to O'Connor. He's the one digging for information on the parents. We'll have to let him know that Billy Meagher considered Sandra's mother's disappearance suspicious. If he thought something wasn't right, he wouldn't be the only one.'

He looked up the street. 'All right, Kate, but I'm in need of something proper to eat. Let's see if we can grab some food in that pub.' He pointed to Meagher's. 'Do you think there's a connection to our ex-postman, village inbreeding?'

'I don't know, but what Billy Meagher said about Sandra and Alice Thompson's father is certainly painting an interesting picture.'

'What's your take on it?'

'Sandra engaging in sexual activity at a young age and, apparently, doing so willingly with an older man tells us a lot about her mental and emotional state back then.'

'Meaning what?'

'She isn't the same girl described to us by Barry Lyons. On the one hand we have an image of someone who isn't as talkative as her peers, shy, intelligent, probably letting Alice be the forceful one. Yet on the other, as a teenager, she openly had sex with her friend's father. It doesn't add up. If she was promiscuous from an early age, assuming Alice never found out about it, Sandra had the ability to deceive the one person she was close to.'

'Could she be our killer, Kate?'

'I know people can put up a façade to fool others. If Sandra Regan is the person we're looking for, and we find proof of severe abuse in her early years, she would have become socially dysfunctional, her moral compass different from that of others, and primed to set out on a devastating path.'

Lynch held the pub door open for her. 'Keep talking, Kate, but quietly. We don't want to frighten the locals.'

Once they were seated, Kate took up where she had left off. 'Early promiscuity, especially in close-knit communities, and in someone of Sandra's intelligence, tells us there were other factors influencing her behaviour, outside the obvious lack of parental care. If she was abused, we can draw inferences based on what we now believe.'

'Go on.'

'I've been reviewing the profile again, and a certain pattern is occurring.'

'Hold on. Let me order something to eat, so it's out of the way. What do you want?'

'I don't mind – tea and a toasted sandwich.'

'More bloody tea. Right, I'll be back in a second.'

Kate looked around at the half-dozen people scattered throughout the room, all engrossed in conversation. She checked her phone. Charlie would be home with Sophie, their child-minder, by now. With Lynch at the bar, she rang the apartment.

'Hi. Sophie, it's Kate. Is everything okay? … That's great … Can I have a quick word with him?' She heard the clatter of the phone going down, Sophie telling Charlie to hurry up in the bathroom as his mum was on the phone.

'Hi, Charlie, how are you doing, my clever clogs? I hear you got an A for your Dolphin project!'

'And a book token, Mum, for five euro!'

'Wow, that's brilliant! We can go shopping on Saturday, if you like.'

'Cool. Can I bring Simon? He got an A as well.'

'If it's okay with his parents, absolutely.'

'Mum, I gotta go. Sophie's making pancakes, and they smell yummy.'

'Keep me some. I won't be late.'

'Bye, Mum, love you.'

'Love you too.' She hung up, placed the phone on the table, and waited for Lynch to return from the bar.

Sitting down, he said, 'You were telling me, Kate, about a pattern.'

'Yes, of course. Sorry, I got lost in my thoughts there for a minute.' She pulled out the case file from her bag. 'I've been thinking about our killer's behaviour, specifically how she's forging her relationships with men. She has a need to move from one person to the next, each relationship offering her whatever she believes she's looking for, then essentially failing her. I think her view of men isn't far removed from the parameters of her potential dissociative disorder.'

'You mean this multiple personality idea.'

'That's right. Initially, she's looking for emotional feedback, her sexuality and attractiveness drawing her targets in, and at first this works well. It's important for her to be in a relationship, to believe somebody loves her, but because her view of men is warped, it's also inevitable that she'll look for a reason ultimately to hate them, to seek revenge for whatever trapped her in this emotional cauldron, creating two extremes within the one person, love and hate.'

'I'll leave the psychoanalysis bit to you, Kate, but we still need a concrete link.'

'We'll find it. Something tells me Sandra Regan has learned the art of keeping secrets. At face value, she appears normal, but we know too much about her to believe that now. Assuming the abuse in her case went beyond neglect, it's not unusual for abuse sufferers to seek affection in any number of ways, including the pattern I've described. As I said, young girls don't have sex with their friend's father unless something isn't right. It would certainly have tested the friendship, especially if Alice ever found out about it.'

'I found Alice nearly as evasive as Edgar Regan.'

'That's the thing about secrets. They have a complicated path, and you're not always sure who is keeping what from whom.'

When her mobile rang, Kate saw straight away it was Adam, and so too did Lynch. 'You'll want to take that,' he said coldly.

'Hi,' she said. 'I'm in Leach with Mark.'

'Great,' Adam replied. 'I intended phoning him after you.'

'You want to speak to him? Hold on a second.'

He took the phone from her. 'Are the usual communication channels causing you a difficulty, O'Connor?'

'Do you want to hear what I have to say or not?'

'I'm listening.'

'The last record of Thomas and Cynthia Connolly, Sandra's grandparents, that I can find is from 1999. An application for a medical card of all things – Thomas Connolly was a general handyman, but his income was low. He put Cynthia and Sandra down as dependants. His card wasn't approved, but I've checked everything else, including driver licence renewals, utilities, bank details and the electoral register. It's like the trail went cold some time around the autumn of that year. Sandra Connolly changed the billing name on the family home in early 2000 and, as far as I can tell, she is now the legal owner of their house. She probably took care of everything else as well.'

'And there's no record of them arriving across the water, or anywhere else?'

'Not that I can find.'

'I assume you're thinking what I'm thinking, O'Connor?'

'Essentially Thomas and Cynthia Connolly are missing persons, but with the absence of a missing persons report, it looks like their disappearance went unnoticed.'

'I have another potential missing person for you.'

'Who?'

'Sandra Connolly's natural mother.' Lynch turned to Kate. 'Did Barry Lyons or Billy Meagher mention Sandra's mother's name?'

'No, I don't think so,' she replied.

'O'Connor, did you find anything on the natural mother during your searches?'

'Not a lot, but I do have a name from the births, marriages and deaths register.'

'What is it?'

'Ellen Connolly – her name is also on Sandra Connolly's birth certificate, as the birth mother. The father is down as unknown.'

'Dig some more on Ellen Connolly. Rumour has it she went to the UK. Ring me back as soon as you have anything. If she joins the missing persons list, we have a bigger shitbag on our hands. Also, I might need you to talk to Alice Thompson. We've got information that could test the friendship between her and Sandra Regan, and if we have to use it, we will.'

'I thought I was to take a back seat.'

'It's your lucky day, O'Connor. I've decided to promote you temporarily, but don't go off on any tangents. You have my number if you need any more instructions.'

'I haven't told you the most interesting thing about Sandra Connolly.'

'And what's that?' Lynch wasn't enjoying the power play.

'Sandra isn't her full name – at least, it wasn't the name on the birth certificate.'

'Spit it out, O'Connor. I don't have time for this.'

'Her full name is Cassandra.'

Mark Lynch went quiet.

'What is it?' Kate asked, seeing the look on his face.

'He says Sandra's full name is Cassandra.'

'The tag name – Cassie is short for Cassandra, Cassie4Casanova. It's the link – why didn't any of us think of it before?'

'I don't know, and I don't particularly care.' Kate sensed heightened determination driving him now. 'O'Connor, pull in Alice Thompson and press whatever buttons you need to but get her talking. It turns out her friend had sex with Alice's daddy when she was a teenager, not exactly something a good friend should do.'

'Are you sure about that?'

'As far as Alice Thompson is concerned, we are.'

'What about Edgar and Sandra Regan?'

'We'll hold off on them for now, O'Connor. When we bring them in, I want to be able to hit them hard.'

'You're taking a risk waiting. I'd discuss that with Kate if I were you.'

'Well, you're not me. Get talking to the Thompson woman and let me know as soon as you have anything.' Hanging up, he handed the phone to Kate. 'I guess you got the gist of that?'

'Thomas, Cynthia and Ellen Connolly are all unaccounted for?'

'Exactly.' He stared ahead of him.

'There's one other thing we can be certain of, Mark.'

'What's that?'

'If Sandra is connected to her grandparents' disappearance, we can at least assume she isn't responsible for the disappearance of her mother.'

'As you said yourself, Kate, secrets have their own complicated path, and you're not always sure who's keeping them from you.'

'You'll be questioning Sandra and Edgar, I assume.'

'Not yet. We've a link with the name, but not a hell of a lot else.' He stood up. 'Come on. Let's get this conversation with Lily Bright out of the way.'

'I guess we won't be eating these,' Kate said, as the barman placed the toasted sandwiches on the table.

'I don't know about you, but I've lost my appetite.'

I

I'VE SET UP the studio for another self-portrait before Edgar comes back. I know I won't be returning here. There's no need for Sandra any more — my lesser self. I've always known of her existence, even though she has been unaware of mine. She has made limited attempts at keeping a diary, but half pictures are never any good. The reason I've seen more than her is because I'm prepared to face the dark. Cowards are best taken out of their misery.

Remember the road through the woods that can't be seen, hidden by time past, disguised? I still see it, every evil twist and turn of it. It's etched onto my wall of memory, which is why *I'm* the keeper, not her.

It's time to phone Alice.

'Alice,' I say, fretful, like Sandra might be, 'I need you to do something for me.'

'What?'

I'm not surprised she doesn't sound like her usual cool self. 'I need you to pick another card.'

'Sandra, we're not children now. This is nonsense.' Her words drift into anger.

'Humour me,' I reply, trying not to sound patronising. 'Remember how we used to take turns?'

'You know the police have been asking questions?'

'Don't worry about them. Pick the card.'

'Sandra …'

'Don't have me ask you again. Even if you don't want to play the game, I still do.'

'Thirteen from the top,' she says, then lets out an exasperated sigh. 'Sandra, you must know you need help.'

'Edgar is going to give me all the help I require.'

'Good. That's good.'

'Oh, and, Alice …'

'Yes?'

'I meant what I said earlier, I am going back to the woods.'

'I told you, that's futile.'

'You never understood, Alice, did you?'

'I understood it was a game.'

'It was more than a game.'

I hang up the phone, spreading the Tarot cards out like a fan on the floor, picking the one that's thirteen from the top. I'm satisfied with the result. It's the Death card again. The one I picked when the witch and her huntsman died. Some might find the black skeleton ominous, surrounded by the dead and dying. They fail to understand the importance of the sickle he carries in his hand, emblazoned with the white flower from the crashing towers of the moon, the sun rising behind. It's the ending of a cycle. The spread makes sense now. We're back to the beginning, ready to renew.

Despite our friendship, I know my betrayal has forged an invisible wedge between Alice and me. She never guessed. But then again, how could she know I wanted her father for myself? She has always been far too possessive of me, criticising all my relationships. That day in the woods, when I took him for myself, I returned later to the spot where we had made love. I stood in the high grasses, my shadow covering the ground on which he entered me, hard and wanting. His whimpering afterwards I took as a good sign.

Shadows are tricky things, you know. When you paint, you want to capture them, but depending on how long you're standing there, the shadows move. If you catch them in a photograph, you trap them in that space. They're forced to be still. I took the self-portrait of my shadow hovering above the high grasses using a Polaroid camera. Once it was solidified in time and space, the slut of a girl, with her red tartan skirt pulled up high, was left behind. I could move on.

I can hear Edgar returning. Everything is perfect now. This time the shadows will be multiplied. I have every mirror we possess in the studio, facing different directions, my reflection repeated in each one. The lights are angled well, creating a tapestry of form. Before he arrives, I hold the camera, smiling beneath the lens, facing the largest mirror, seeing myself looking at me, capturing the many multiples of self.

'Sandra, are you okay?' I hear Edgar's stifling words from the hallway.

'I won't be long, darling,' I reply, clicking the button, before glancing at the Death card, strategically positioned on the floor, completing the perfect picture.

RATHIN ROAD, LEACH,
COUNTY WICKLOW

LILY BRIGHT WAS a fit and healthy woman, despite her advanced years. She had the kind of pep in her step, thought Kate, which had probably defined her throughout her adult life. Less than five feet tall, slight of frame, with permed white-grey hair, and a dress code that would have fitted well on a sixties cover of *Woman's Way*, the ex-postmistress was the quintessential respectable spinster about town. To the front of her house, an old bicycle was parked, with a small wicker basket for groceries, and a note stuck to the letterbox, saying, 'No junk mail'.

'No tea for us,' Lynch jumped in, as Lily went to fill the kettle.

'Very well.' She ushered them to seats at the kitchen table, which was covered with a polka-dot tablecloth in cream and luminous yellow. 'I hear you want to talk to me about the Connolly family.' Her voice was croaky, but clear.

'News travels fast around here,' Lynch replied, his words light-hearted and mildly condescending, almost as if Lily Bright's eighty years warranted positive discrimination.

She picked up on it immediately. 'There's no need to patronise me. I've been using the telephone for more years than you've been on this earth.'

'I wasn't—'

'No need to apologise, just get on with asking your questions. I have a busy afternoon ahead of me.'

'Very well, Lily. Why don't you start by telling us what was unusual about the Connollys' mail? I hear it caused you some bother.'

'A nuisance it was, the two of them going off like that, and that insolent granddaughter of theirs wasn't much help. I mean, at their age, you'd have imagined they'd look after things properly, paid the postal redirection fee, and I wouldn't have been left to pick up the pieces.'

'How did you pick up the pieces?' Kate asked.

'Well, I knew they weren't in the town any more, and her ladyship, their granddaughter, said they wouldn't be back. I mean, it wasn't right that she was receiving their mail, and I told her that, yet she point-blank refused to sort it out.'

'What happened then?' Lynch adopted a no-nonsense tone.

'The mail eventually stopped. I assume whoever was sending

it got the information about their new details, even though they were never shared with me.'

Kate could see the woman took this as an affront to her position as postmistress of the town. 'Lily, you described Sandra Connolly as insolent. That seems at odds with the character description we've received from others.'

'Well,' Lily puckered her lips, 'that might be because you've only talked to men.'

'We've spoken to Billy Meagher and Barry Lyons,' Kate told her.

'Barry?' Lily's smile looked far too satisfied for Kate not to ask why.

'You don't trust Barry's assessment, then?'

'Let's just say the two of them were friendly. I'm not one for spreading rumours, but I do believe in calling a spade a spade.'

I

THE FOREST FLOOR has seen it all, fury and attack, secrets and lies, sex, birth and death. Edgar thinks I'm bringing him to the woods because I need time to think. He isn't totally wrong. He still believes he's saving me, but he has no idea how many people I've killed, or that he will be next. I contemplate the serious look on his face as our car speeds along the road, him trying to make good time, not realising each forward movement takes us closer to the end game. It will be dark by the time we reach the old house. He has insisted on taking firewood, and heavy blankets to keep us warm, a quaint touch but it caused me to wonder.

I've always been fascinated by fire, even before I knew the

witch had burned Ellen. Flames are fierce and free, their rich colour tempting and dangerous. Have you ever heard the roar of a wild fire? The crackle, spit and power are intoxicating. I smile across at Edgar. He takes it as a reassuring sign.

I've decided I won't tell him the why. He fell in love with two women, the vulnerable and soft Sandra, and the alluring, tempting Cassie. His pathetic desire to bring Sandra back is the most despicable betrayal of all.

The woods are not far now. Soon, I will be home.

ELLIOT FOREST, COUNTY WICKLOW

AFTER TALKING WITH Lily Bright, Mark and Kate had no choice but to head back to Barry Lyons's place. They had no guarantees he would be there. The late-afternoon sun blinded them, as Mark negotiated the narrow country roads.

'I didn't take Barry Lyons for a paedophile, Kate. I mean that's what Lily Bright alluded to, wasn't it?'

'Me neither, but if Barry Lyons had a sexual relationship with Sandra, it's all part of her behaviour pattern. The sex was a tool at her disposal, one she quickly learned worked well with men.'

'I've sent a surveillance team to the Regans' house, by the way.'

'When did you do that?'

'While I was waiting for you outside Lily Bright's – what did you go back in to ask her?'

'I wanted her opinion on Cynthia Connolly.'

'And?'

'Lily also knew Cynthia's mother – like mother, like daughter, was how she described them, both hard and miserable. Cynthia's mother died when she was five. She was brought up by her father. Some believed their relationship wasn't healthy.'

'Incest, you mean?'

'That's not all. She was pregnant when she married Thomas Connolly – another symptom of abuse, and not unusual for it to be handed down from one generation to the next.'

'So Ellen, Sandra's mother, was potentially the result of inbreeding.'

'Who can say for sure? But Lily said there was always something not right about Ellen. The description she used was "soft in the head".'

'It could explain her disappearance?'

'This case, Mark, is rife with cruelty, one act of badness loaded onto the back of another.'

He slowed the car as they neared the cabin.

'Hold on a second,' Kate said. 'I want to check something before we go inside.'

'What?'

'I want to review the sketch of Pierre Laurent's face again. Something's still bothering me about it.'

She focused on the eyes in the abstract image of Pierre.

'What is it?' Lynch asked, turning off the engine.

'I wasn't sure, at least not at first.'

Both of them looked up, seeing Barry Lyons step out of the cabin, his hands on his forehead blocking the sun from his eyes.

'Mark?' she said, looking back at the sketch.

'What?'

'Look at the eyes. They belong to Barry Lyons.'

'Right. Let's get some answers.'

∞

The look on the retired teacher's face was of resignation rather than surprise.

'We've a few more questions for you, Barry,' Lynch said, loud and accusing.

'Best come inside, so.'

All three of them walked into the tumbledown cabin. If anything, Kate thought, it looked even more dismal with the sun shooting in from outside.

They remained standing while Barry took the seat he had occupied a couple of hours earlier.

'I don't think you've been completely honest with us, Barry,' Lynch continued, in the same tone he had used outside.

'How's that?'

'We understand you were a lot closer to Sandra Connolly than you led us to believe.'

'I never said I didn't care for the girl.'

Lynch took a step forward, hovering over him. 'There's caring, and then there's abuse. You wouldn't be the first teacher caught with your trousers down.'

Kate could hardly believe the speed by which the old man

jumped up and grabbed Lynch by the throat. The detective responded by pinning him against the wall.

'Look, let's all settle down, shall we?' Kate shouted. 'This isn't going to get us anywhere.' The hatred in both men's eyes was palpable.

Lynch reluctantly stood back, while Barry Lyons recomposed himself.

'Barry,' Kate said, 'we have a number of questions for you.'

'Ask me anything you want,' he replied, sitting down again and cupping his face in his hands.

'We believe Sandra Connolly has a direct link to our investigation. We also believe the two of you had a relationship.'

'I never touched her. She wanted me to, but I never did.'

Kate watched as Barry Lyons's face crumpled and tears formed in his eyes. He was hurting, she thought, and badly. 'Tell us exactly what happened,' she said.

He clenched his fists, his body and voice tensing more as he spoke. 'She used to visit me some afternoons after school. It was a little irregular, I admit, but I felt sorry for her. I had the feeling she didn't have anyone else. She would bring some artwork, keen to hear my observations on it.' He looked away from Kate, staring ahead of him. 'We had art lessons in the school, but not at the level Sandra had reached.' He drew a deep breath. 'She came to my house late one night ...' He swallowed hard. 'I could tell she was upset, so I didn't mention the hour. I went into the kitchen to make some cocoa. I told her to sit by the fire and get some warmth back into her.'

'And what happened then?' Lynch butted in, clearly fearful that Lyons might clam up.

Lyons was silent.

Kate tried again: 'Listen, Barry, we know Sandra was promiscuous from a young age. If you didn't do anything wrong, you've nothing to fear.'

He stared at her. 'I wasn't totally innocent either.' His head dropped into his hands.

Kate gave him a few seconds to recover, and this time, so did Lynch.

Splaying his fingers on the table, he said, 'I think she knew I was in love with her, long before I knew it myself. Call it the foolishness of a middle-aged man, but there was something about her I was drawn to.'

'Barry, you said you went into the kitchen to make cocoa. What happened then?' Kate knew she needed to push him.

'When I came back, there was only the light of the fire. She had stripped to her underwear. Her breasts were already showing signs of development ...' Again he swallowed hard. 'She was so beautiful, not a child, but not yet a woman, a body metamorphosing in the most thrilling way.' He looked from Kate to Lynch, then back to Kate. 'As I said, I think she knew I loved her long before I did. It took all my strength to resist, with her standing like some mythical vision by the fire and the flames dancing off the wall.'

'So what stopped you?' Kate asked.

'She was still a child, and undoubtedly a child who had seen her fair share of hurt. When I looked into her eyes, I realised I was being tested, one part of her wanting me to take her, the other part hoping I wouldn't.'

'So you passed the test?' Kate replied.

'Yes.' He nodded. Then, standing up, he said, 'You see, all I could think of was the girl I had come to know, the one who was obsessed with Grimms' fairy tales, her wanting me to read them over and over in school. That night I told her she was beautiful, which wasn't a lie.' He exhaled. 'I gave her a blanket to wrap around herself, knowing if I forced her to get dressed there and then, it would have heightened her shame. I needed to be careful. She was so fragile ...'

'And then what?' Kate was relieved that Lynch had decided to leave the questioning to her.

'She told me about her mother – or, at least, what she had fantasised about her.'

'What did she tell you?'

'She said her grandfather had abused her mother, and that after she was born, her grandmother ...'

'Go on,' Kate pressed.

'I doubt any of this is true, you understand, but ...'

'What about her grandmother?'

'Sandra believed her grandmother killed her mother, or at least left her to die, before burning her in the woods.'

Kate kept her voice low: 'It may be truer than you think, Barry.'

'She said that when she used to run through the woods she hoped one day she would find her.'

As if remembering something else, he began to pull stuff from the corner of the cabin. 'I have some of her artwork here. Do you want to see it?'

Without either of them answering, he pulled two empty sacks from the top of a tea chest. Reaching in, he took out a scrap album and opened it on the small table. When he started talking, it was as if he was remembering a prized student.

'You see here how advanced she was, capable of working in abstract from a very young age. It was all about perspective with her.' Kate looked down at the sketches and paintings, varying collages made up of cubes, while Lyons grew increasingly animated. 'Cubism,' he continued, 'isn't about cubes. It's about creating a greater reflection of reality. Sandra used different perspectives to elevate the work from a flattened vision.' He flicked through the pages. 'Look how her work developed. Her use of shadow is extraordinary. We used to watch old black-and-white movies together. She became obsessed with how the light created the shadows across the screen. What some people saw as a negative, with the early black-and-white movie pictures, inadequate to re-create real life, she was fascinated by.'

'It's all making sense.' Kate looked at Lynch.

'What is?'

'Don't you see? Look at her artwork, the breaking up of the world into segments, fragments, creating an obscured reality. Look at her use of shadow, the splitting of self, and the self-portraits.' Kate turned back and forth through the scrapbook. 'She's experimenting with light and the use of the dark. As her work advanced, the shadows in the self-portraits became increasingly dominant.'

'I still don't get you.'

'She has control of the re-creation, a world she is comfortable within. The portraits would have become progressively more important to her, especially as she couldn't control reality. The artwork was becoming an expression of her identity …'

'How is this connected to the killing?' He still sounded unsure.

'It's what she does after she kills. She creates the scenes so she can be photographed in them. That's why the reflection in the mirror is so important. It's like …' Kate began pacing around the cabin, both men staring at her '… she is using the images as markers. It's her way of proving she exists.'

'Why would she do that?' Lynch sounded more confused than ever.

'She's never sure when the other identity is going to take over. The darker, more aggressive and daring side would have known of the existence of her other self. When the weaker personality was put under pressure, it allowed the darker one to take over and become dominant. Creating self-portraits was her proof of existence.'

'I always wondered why she could change,' Barry Lyons said, 'from being mostly shy to more forceful, almost demanding my attention. I put it down to her insecurity, nothing more. I should have realised. Maybe if I had …'

'It would have been impossible for you to know, at least not fully.' Kate touched his arm. 'If it's any consolation, I think she did love you – at least, one side of her personality certainly did.'

'How do you know?' he asked.

'Sandra did a sketch of someone who looked very like you, especially the eyes. It illustrated she cared, and certainly enough not to harm anything that reminded her of you.'

'We'll need to visit her old home.' Lynch was clearly itching to move on. 'I can get the address from O'Connor.'

'This time you'll need a search warrant,' Kate responded, 'if you want me to be part of it.'

HARCOURT STREET STATION, SPECIAL DETECTIVE UNIT

THERE WAS NO denying Adam O'Connor's adrenalin rush at being back in the centre of the investigation. He had no idea what to expect with Alice Thompson, but one thing on which he was in complete agreement with Lynch was that he would get answers. He chose Interview Room 9B, the smallest and darkest room in the unit. It faced west, with only one small window, and was constantly in need of artificial light.

He knew Sergeant Janet Lacy had been part of the first interview with Alice Thompson, and was keen to hear what she had to say. Initially he was surprised by her hostility: she described the woman as up herself, and a pain in the rear end. He liked Janet's passion, even if it sounded over the top.

'Janet, you'll be joining me for the interview with Alice Thompson.'

'You know she's already here, don't you? She won't like being kept waiting.'

'There's nothing like pre-interview nerves to add energy. Give her another ten minutes, then bring her down.'

He wanted Alice Thompson on edge, and for her to believe he knew more than he did. If he could chisel out even the smallest crack, he'd know he was on the right track, keeping the relationship between Sandra and Alice's father in reserve. He had made more enquiries about the father, Sam Thompson. He was still alive and kicking, and had remarried a woman the same age as his daughter, with two kids in tow. He wondered if Alice felt a sense of abandonment. Without meaning to, he thought of his son. The last conversation he'd had with him was difficult, as was the previous one, and the one before that.

Janet Lacy opened the interview-room door. 'Are you ready?'

'I am.'

'Detective Inspector O'Connor will speak to you now.'

Some women are hard to forget, and as Alice Thompson walked through the doorway of 9B, Adam knew he was face to face with one of them. She was tall and slender with perfect proportions, blonde hair scooped up at the back, a long side fringe half covering her beautiful face. She moved with grace and poise, wore black high heels, a dark pencil skirt and a powder pink blouse, loosely hugging her curves. What looked like an expensive handbag hung on her shoulder. Her skin was pale, but she wore vibrant red lipstick and had magnificent blue eyes. If she was aware of him staring, she gave no hint of it. Women like her, he thought, took male admiration as a given.

'Alice, I know Detective Lynch has already spoken to you.'

She stared back at him without a word.

'Since then, a lot of fresh information has come to light.'

Still nothing. He was going to have to change tactics.

'Your father has recently remarried, I understand.'

The first glimmer of something: a momentary balking of the eyes. 'I don't see what that has to do with anything.'

'Don't you?' Adam raised his eyebrows in surprise. Let her wait a few seconds. 'You and Sandra Regan are very close?'

'We're friends, if that's what you mean.'

'From childhood?'

'Look, Detective, you and I already know that. Why don't you get to the point and save us both time and energy?'

'Very well. We'll move through this quickly. Tell me what you know about the Pierre Laurent murder.'

'Not a lot. It was a long time ago.'

'Did you sleep with him?'

Another flinch. 'No, I did not.' She sounded indignant.

'You were in Paris when he was killed.'

'So were a great many other people.'

'Including Sandra?'

'Yes,' she eased her shoulders, 'including Sandra.' Her voice hinted at concern for the first time.

'You're worried about her, aren't you?'

Another silence.

'And her husband Edgar – are you concerned about him too?'

'He's Sandra's husband, not mine.' A tinge of anger in her voice.

'I imagine you two know a lot about each other, what with Sandra being a lifelong friend?'

She gave him another stone-wall look – time to pull off the gloves.

'Alice, can I be honest with you?'

'That's what we're here for, isn't it?'

'Sandra is under suspicion for the murder of Rick Shevlin.'

'Don't be ridiculous.'

Now, he thought, she looks rattled. 'And other killings. There is every reason to believe those closest to her, including you and Edgar, were well aware of this.'

'I don't know what you're talking about. Sandra has been under a lot of pressure lately. She suffers from depression, forgetfulness, but she isn't capable of what you're saying. Edgar was worried about her, as was I.'

'When was the last time you spoke to him?'

'I'm not sure – a few days ago.'

'Was Sandra aware of your conversations behind her back? Not exactly the actions of a friend.'

'Maybe not, but I can't help it if he sought my advice.'

'Has he looked for it before? Does he see you as some kind of confidante?'

'This is ridiculous.'

'We have already spoken to Edgar.' He was referring to the earlier interview, but there was no harm in her thinking they had talked more recently. 'He spoke very highly of you.' It was a gamble, but worth a try.

She looked away, as if gathering her thoughts. 'It's …
difficult.' She sounded defeated now.

'I realise that, Alice.' What was she hiding? He needed to
keep this vague until he got onto concrete ground.

'I care for Sandra very much,' she continued.

'I'm sure you do.'

'I wouldn't have chosen Edgar for her. I knew the marriage
would eventually have difficulties.'

'Why don't you tell me your side of the story?'

She stared uncomfortably at Janet Lacy, who was leaning
against the wall.

Adam gestured at Janet with his eyes that she should move
further back, out of sight. He lowered his voice: 'Look, Alice,
you can speak in confidence here. You're not under arrest, being
cautioned or anything else at this point. We're simply looking
for the truth. You want that too, don't you?'

She relaxed her shoulders, and he thought how easy it would
be to believe anything she had to say. He needed to be careful.

'He was unhappy about the lack of pleasure he was giving her.'

'Sexual pleasure?'

'Yes – they've had problems since early in the marriage.'

'What kind of problems?'

'Initially, Edgar thought everything was fine – she was
adventurous, seductive. He said he became totally obsessed with
her …'

'And then?'

'He started to worry about it being a one-way indulgence.
Everything revolved around his enjoyment. It preyed on his
mind. I think he felt less of a man because of it.'

'It's kind of unusual, him speaking to you about it?'

'He had his reasons.'

He didn't push the point, not yet, wanting to hear more about the Regans' marital problems. 'You were saying about their difficulties …'

'The first time he told me he was drunk. As I said, I think his male ego was compromised. I told him to give it time, but he became increasingly dependent on me for advice.'

'Go on.'

'I thought things had settled, but then Sandra's behaviour became unpredictable, angry outbursts, bouts of forgetfulness, shutting him out. He told me he'd tried being gentle with her, constantly reassuring her of how much he loved her. I thought it would be okay. As I said, I wouldn't have chosen him as her partner, but I didn't doubt he cared for her. Otherwise I wouldn't have given him the time of day.'

'And then what?'

'He began contacting me again, phoning daily, telling me he thought she was having an affair.'

'And was she?'

She stared at him blankly. 'I can't be sure. She might have been. I spoke to her about it, but she laughed it off.'

'Did she ever speak to you about the Tarot cards?' This time her flinch was filled with fear. Was she wondering how much more she should tell him? If he was to get anywhere, he had to move quickly. 'You're familiar with them? Perhaps you messed around with them at some point?'

'It was just a silly game.'

'What kind of game?'

'The kind little girls play, imagining their future.'

'What were the rules? There were rules, I assume.'

'Yes – we would take turns picking a card for the other. Whatever card you picked meant something. Sandra had a book on them. We would look up their meanings.'

'Did they ever land you in trouble?'

'Sometimes.' Again a blank look. 'I thought Sandra had forgotten all about them, but then …'

'Then what?'

'It doesn't matter. They don't count for anything.'

'Let me be the judge of that.'

Another silence.

He got up and walked over to her side of the table. 'You do know Sandra and your father were lovers?'

'You're lying!' she spat, instantly angry.

'Why would I lie?'

'I don't believe you.' Again the seething rage, far too much for her not to have had her doubts.

He held back for a minute. She would either recompose herself or come clean. He hoped it would be the latter.

'I should hate her, shouldn't I?' Her words were reflective now, no longer angry. 'I did for a long time … I thought I despised her. It put a divide between us, one that has never gone away, but eventually I came around.'

'Why do you think that was?'

'We share a common bond.'

'What's that?'

Another damned silence.

'Do you believe Sandra was abused as a child?'

'Yes.' Tears formed in her eyes. 'We both were.' Her composure crumbled. 'It was the two of us against the world.'

He could see even Janet Lacy was softening.

'Keep talking, Alice. If you still care for Sandra, anything you tell us will help.'

'As children, we thought we could live in the woods for ever, have a silly life of fantasy, wild with the wind, nothing would ever stop us. It was ridiculous, of course, but looking back, despite everything, there was still something wonderful about it, believing we could create our own future, that we were mythical creatures of the forest. I can still see the two of us running through the woods, the light from above splintering through the branches. When I think back, do you know what I hear?'

'No, Alice, I'm afraid I don't.'

'I hear the sound of laughter, the kind only children can make. It was everywhere, blocking out the darkness.'

'Alice?'

'Yes?'

'When was the last time you spoke to Sandra?'

'Today.'

'Did she say anything important? Think hard.'

The tears were back in her eyes, and for the first time, Adam saw the unhappy young girl she might have been. He didn't want to press her, but he needed answers. 'Alice, your last conversation with Sandra, what did she say?'

'She wanted me to pick another card.'

'Like you did as children?'

'Yes, but she's asked me at other times too – I would humour her, hoping she would get better.'

'What card did you pick?'

'The Death card – it means a new beginning, all the negativity and those creating it will be no more, and you can move on with the energy of the sun.'

'Did she say anything else?'

'That she needed to go back to the woods.'

Alice Thompson looked far removed from the cool, confident beauty who had entered Interview Room 9B, but there was one question he still had unanswered.

'Alice, you said Edgar had his reasons for confiding in you. Can you tell me what they were?'

'He didn't find my sexuality threatening.'

'Why not?'

'He saw what many others didn't.'

'Which is?'

'I desire women, not men. In a way, he saw me as an ally. I think it led Sandra to believe we were close for other reasons. Lately, she has doubted my loyalty.'

'Why did you help him?'

'Because I knew he loved her, and I loved her more than anyone else ever could. I have done since we ran through the forest together as children.'

I

WHEN WE REACH the house, Edgar's enthusiasm is draining my spirits. He thinks my bringing him here for the first time is positive.

I check the knives in the kitchen drawer as he lights the fire, the flames catching fast with the dryness of the wood.

'Come and sit by the fire,' he says.

'I will – give me a moment.'

'Will I put our stuff upstairs?' he asks – stupid lapdog.

'No, don't worry about that. There's plenty of time to have a look around.'

He doesn't know how much I hate this house, how the memories linger in my mind, my grandfather holding me down, pretending love, with more cruelty than the witch. At least she paraded her evil.

I don't want Edgar finding the cellar too soon, so I watch his every move from the other room, keeping the kitchen door ajar. The house is small, and has certainly suffered the wrath of abandonment: the windowpanes are crumbling, the wallpaper in the front room is torn, the old carpets and curtains reek of dirt and dust, and every part of the place creaks against the sharp crackle of the fire.

Edgar knows he's still walking a tightrope, taking it one step at a time. I wonder should I give him my body one last time, for old times' sake. I could strip naked and take him now, the way the flames are consuming the branches. He wouldn't refuse — why would he?

As I walk into the sitting room, he turns, the fire magnificent behind him. Before he speaks, I pull him towards me, pressing my mouth against his, our tongues tasting each other, my hand caressing the back of his head. I feel his arousal. My voice sounds husky, as I tell him how much I need him. He sinks into me. I lick my lips, putting my finger to his mouth, asking him to close his eyes.

Naked, I tell him he can open his eyes again. He looks at my arms, seeing the cuts of the knife. 'You've been harming yourself again,' he says, his voice pitiful, full of shame for both of us.

'It doesn't matter,' I say. 'Nothing matters now.'

He lets me strip him, transfixed, afraid to break the spell, and still the fire crackles, loud and wild. We embrace again, his fingers travelling down my body, scratching, needing me desperately. I put his hand between my legs. He's nearly mine. Kneeling in front of the fire, grinning playfully, I run my fingers through my hair. I hear him gasp, before he lays me beneath him. I arch my back, holding him at arm's length. 'Oh, God,' I say, 'you're inside me.' My words thrill him, his face contorting, his body like a large hungry bear, beyond stopping, as he comes far too quickly.

He'll sleep now. That will give me the time I need. I put more wood on the fire, taking the blade from the kitchen, watching the flames glisten with its reflection, the edge sharp, cutting myself again, the blood trickling down on his face.

ELLIOT FOREST, COUNTY WICKLOW

KATE HAD MADE a couple of attempts to get in touch with Sophie and Charlie, but she hadn't been able to get an answer. At six o'clock, she dialled the apartment again. She could have insisted on Lynch getting her back to Dublin in a separate car, but with the prospect of the search warrant coming through at any moment, coupled with the news from Adam that Sandra had planned a trip to the woods, she hoped she wouldn't regret her decision to stay.

This time, thankfully, Sophie answered: 'Sorry, Kate, we popped out to the shops to get more ingredients for pancakes. The traffic was awful. Are you nearly home?'

'No, unfortunately not – I'm stuck in Wicklow. I was hoping

you could either wait on at the apartment, or take Charlie with you to stay over. I know it's a lot to ask, but if it isn't possible, I can be there in half an hour.' Kate felt crap asking her the favour, but she hoped Sophie would swing with it – she didn't ask often.

'Hmm, yeah …' She sounded a little hesitant. 'That should be okay. I can stay on for a while. If it gets really late, Charlie can stay with me. I'll put him on to you, will I?'

'Hi, Mum, are you on your way?'

'No, honey, I'm stuck in work. Sophie says she can stay on for a bit. If it gets late, you can sleep over in her place.'

'But we got stuff to make more pancakes.' He sounded disappointed.

'I know, honey. I'll be there as soon as I can.'

'No, you won't. You're always saying things like that. I hate you.' She heard him drop the phone and then, a couple of seconds later, his bedroom door slammed.

'Charlie,' she called down the phone.

The next voice she heard was Sophie's: 'Hi, Kate – don't worry, he's upset, that's all. He's probably overtired. He'll be okay in a while.'

'But …'

'Look, don't worry. It can't be helped.'

'Tell him I love him, and I'll be there soon.'

'I will. Listen, I best go into him.'

'Yes, of course. We can talk later.'

She hung up. Mark Lynch walked towards her. 'Everything okay?' he asked.

'Fine,' she replied, even though she felt like the worst mother in the world.

'We should have the warrant in the next fifteen minutes. O'Connor's on his way down. The recon team have been at the Regan house for the last four hours. There hasn't been a sighting of either of them.'

'How far away from the woods is Sandra's old home?' she asked, shivering now the sun had gone down.

'No more than ten minutes. In the dark, it could take us longer. There's back-up on standby from Dublin, depending on what we find. I'll need you to hang back if this thing starts to unravel.'

'I didn't stay on to sit in the car.'

'Look, calm down. The truth is, Kate, if Sandra Regan and her husband are down here, they could be anywhere in these woods.'

'People always return to the familiar. She may not have happy memories of that house but it would be her starting point. We're all creatures of habit, and killers are no different from the rest of us.'

∞

Driving through the village, the back road to the house was no more than five minutes away, but far enough to be isolated. Soon the secondary road gave way to a dirt track, coming to a stop at a rusted gate.

When Lynch opened the gate, even in the dark, under an archway of blackthorn bushes, he could see the impression of recent tyre marks on the overgrown pathway. Kate rolled down the window. 'Well?'

'They're here, all right.' He looked at the three squad cars stopped behind them. Going to the car furthest from the gate, he said to the driver, 'You stay here while we check it out. If O'Connor comes, tell him to hang back with you. The other two cars can follow me.'

Getting back in, he turned to Kate. 'We'll drive on another bit.'

The cars rumbled their way slowly up the path, the only light guiding them that of the moon. Halfway up, the road took another twist. Mark stopped the car, got out and instructed everyone, except Kate, to walk the rest of the way.

'You stay here until we give you the all-clear. Lock the doors and don't attempt to open them for anyone except me.'

'Okay,' she replied, and watched the half-dozen detectives set off along the narrow path.

She checked her phone – seven o'clock: an hour since she had spoken to Charlie. Unless there was a miracle, there was no way she'd be back to Dublin in time to put him to bed. She leaned back, suddenly exhausted as she stared at the full moon. In the distance, she could see the woodlands. The tips of the trees were engulfed in a fast-falling fog, reminding her of a mystical landscape.

She jumped out of her skin when she heard tapping on the glass.

'Bloody hell, Adam,' she said, opening the door. 'You gave me a fright.'

'I thought I'd join you for a bit of moon-gazing. Where's the Lone Ranger?'

'You mean Mark?'

'Yeah.'

'He's up at the house. I'm to stay put here until he gives the all-clear.'

'Looks like we're about to get it,' he said, pointing at the torchlight approaching the car. When Lynch was level with him, he asked, 'What's the situation up there?'

'They were here, all right. There was a fire lit in the grate and the car is still there, but no sign of either of them.'

'So they've gone for a night excursion?' Adam lit his own flashlight.

'Wherever they are, they travelled by foot. I'm going to call in more back-up and spread the search as far out as we can. In the meantime, I've left three of the guys at the house. I want Kate to take a look upstairs. There's a shitload of art stuff and photographs in the rear bedroom. Maybe she'll be able to make sense of it.'

'Will I go with her?'

'Yeah, walk her to the house, but let the guys take over. She'll need to be booted and gloved as a precaution. After that, I'll want you back in the village – see if you can get some of the locals to give us guidance on the terrain. Any help we can get will increase our chances of finding them sooner.'

'A bit of a risk using locals?'

'We'll only use them to get a bearing on possible tracks. If necessary, we'll keep it to one local with two armed officers. Our killer may be crazy, but she hasn't yet used firearms.'

'Still?'

'O'Connor, I don't need to remind you, I'm the one in charge.'

'Grand so.' Opening the car door, Adam said to Kate, 'It seems I'm your guide.'

It didn't take them long to reach the house. Although similar to a farmhouse in design, it was taller and narrower, looking more like a townhouse than something you'd see in the countryside. The chipped windowpanes were painted a murky grey, against what had once been bright, whitewashed walls. Two detectives were positioned at the front of the house. One stood beside Edgar Regan's car, the other at the front door. Kate assumed the third detective was stationed at the rear.

'Are you okay?' Adam asked, handing her the protective gloves and booties.

'Yes, I'm fine. You go on.'

'The guys here will make sure no one gets in.'

'Stop worrying. It's an empty house.'

'Okay, but don't take any chances.'

Once inside, Kate tried to familiarise herself with the surroundings. Thankfully, the guys had turned on all the lights. Despite her bravado, she wouldn't have fancied going through the place with a torch. She could see the burning embers in the grate, two sleeping bags and blankets on the floor. An opened door led to the kitchen.

Lynch had wanted her to look in one of the bedrooms, so she climbed the stairs. It was impossible to walk through the house and not imagine Sandra Connolly and her grandparents living in it. If walls could talk, she thought, as she stepped onto the landing. The house had not been lived in for some time, and was completely at odds with the opulent surroundings the killer had chosen for her victims.

There were three doors off the landing. One led to a small bathroom, in which the sink and bath were full of mildew. There was a large bedroom at the front, but Lynch had mentioned the one at the rear.

With her gloved hand, she opened the door, immediately seeing the artwork spread out on the bed, but it was the photographs pinned to the walls that drew her attention. All in black-and-white, the multiple images of Sandra Connolly stared back at her, one after another, reproduced in mirrors, windows or other reflective objects. The use of shadow was extraordinary, and her facial expressions, although varied, were distant and unhinged. Kate stepped into the room, and realised the photographs were reflected against a large mirror on the side wall and a smaller one angled in the corner. Over and over, the images were multiplied.

One set of photographs in particular caught Kate's attention. They were Polaroid snapshots, depicting a young girl. In one, the girl looked into a window of this house, the sun splintering her reflection, and in another, her body threw a large shadow across flattened ground.

Kate walked over to the bed, finding dozens of paintings on canvas. Some were similar to those she had seen in Barry Lyons's place, segmented, cubed and projecting the subject matter from different perspectives. Others showed almost childlike fantasy images, a red cloak flying through a darkened wood, two young children holding hands, with what looked like breadcrumbs beneath their feet. 'Grimms' fairy tales,' she muttered. Hadn't Barry Lyons mention Sandra's obsession with them? The more paintings Kate studied, the more aware she became that the artist was developing her talent, but also drifting further into black fantasy. There were depictions of the devil, with 'XV' stamped on his forehead, and at the bottom of each a Bible, seeping blood over a baby's face. There were sketches too, again depicting Tarot images; others showed contorted faces without eyes, all layered with numbers, varying sizes and contrary angles, and each with the constant use of shadow. The biblical references, the Tarot, the fairy tales, the contorted faces all pointed to an alternative world, an alternative self, a dark, shadowy escape from reality, but every one mapped out, numbered, re-created, controlled and endlessly duplicated.

I

I STARE AT Edgar's dead body, his facial skin sinking into his bones. He is already taking on the appearance of the black skeleton of the Death card. It was tricky engraving the number thirteen, in roman numerals, on his forehead, but I'm glad I did it. Soon the sun will rise and I can start afresh.

As I apply Carmine to my lips, ready to kiss Edgar for the last time, I hear the intruders above me, moving through the house like a pack of hungry wolves. I hold my breath, as I did in this cellar when I was a child. I've become accustomed to the low ceiling over the years, but the witch and her huntsman didn't like it, unwilling to crawl and bend.

It isn't long before the silence returns. Should I remain hidden, or should I take their visitation as a sign that I should flee? It's then I hear movement outside, their voices low, muttering secrets.

When the talking stops, I creep to the cellar door, barely opening it, the rug beneath the kitchen table sliding back. I'm surprised to see a woman standing at the fireplace. She doesn't stay long. I hear her walking up the stairs, opening the doors to each of the rooms. I check that I still have the knife. Pulling myself up, I wipe Edgar's blood off it, crawling across the floor out of sight of prying eyes.

I see her go into my bedroom, the meddling bitch. Just like the witch, she thinks she can intrude, pry, plunder and take what's mine. As I climb the stairs, away from the windows, the light of the bare bulb behind me, I see my shadow creep beside me, and I smile.

KATE

LOOKING AT THE photographs and paintings, Kate was getting a real sense of Cassandra Connolly, and the madness that engulfed her. Was she capable of killing her grandparents? Most certainly. Was she at risk of killing again? There was no doubt that she was. Things had advanced too far for any hope of a normal life for her. Maybe if she had received help earlier, if someone, anyone, had intervened, stuck their neck out and taken her away from an environment that was warping and maiming her, she might have had a chance.

Kate walked back to the smaller photographs on the wall and lifted the one of the young girl partially reflected in the window. Was it Sandra, Cassie or both? The answer didn't matter now.

What mattered was that back then the girl had been scared. She had needed to make sense of her world. She had desperately sought answers by experimenting with fantasy, using numbers to gain a level of control, and later her sexuality to grasp the faintest glimpse of emotional connection. It had led her to forge a way out of the terror: she had split her mind to protect herself, creating an alternative self, one who could walk in the dark without fear, a self who had become her damnation.

Not for the first time in her career, Kate lamented the harm humans do to one another. How evil within families can breed a fresh incarnation in a vicious self-fulfilling prophecy, with the innocents suffering the most. She pinned the photograph back to the wall in the exact place the killer had left it. Her work was done. With any luck they would find Edgar and Sandra soon, and another sordid case would be over. She could go back to Charlie, tuck him up in bed, and use the leftover ingredients to make pancakes for their breakfast.

Turning, she saw what looked like a diary on the bed. Lifting it, she felt the knife glide across her throat and the warm breath of another close behind her. 'Put it down,' the woman said, and a droplet of blood slid down her neck, touching her breast, as gentle as a moth.

ELLIOT FOREST, COUNTY WICKLOW

THEY HAD MANAGED to get a number of volunteers from the village, mainly because of Barry Lyons's involvement. As the ex-school principal, he still wielded power, and the vast majority of the search party was made up of ex-pupils of his school. With the back-up arriving from Dublin, each local was teamed with two detectives, with the strict instruction to act only as guides: no heroics were required.

Mark Lynch's mood had deteriorated, the difficult terrain starting to bother him.

'Maybe we should leave this until daylight,' Adam suggested.

'We could have a dead body by then, O'Connor. I'm not taking the risk.'

'Barry knows the woods better than anyone. He's divided the area into six key blocks.'

'Good,' Lynch replied, looking into the woodlands. 'By the way,' he turned back to O'Connor, 'there's a car bringing Alice Thompson down.'

'What for?'

'She and Sandra lived in the woods as kids. If Sandra has a number of places to go, Alice will know them.'

Adam heard a car pull up near the gate. 'Perhaps this is her now.'

When she stepped out of the car, and Adam saw her bright blonde hair blowing wild and free against the backdrop of the woods, she looked even more beautiful than she had done earlier. She nodded to him.

He joined her. 'Listen,' he said, 'you think you know your friend, but she isn't the little girl you grew up with, not any more.'

'I know her better than anyone else does.'

'Maybe so, but you need to remember she's a killer.'

Again, her response was silence, but her face told him she understood that she was in unknown territory.

'Right, O'Connor,' Lynch yelled over the night breeze. 'Get whatever information you can from Alice, and then let's move.'

I

'TELL ME WHY I shouldn't kill you,' I ask the bitch, as I hold the knife tight to her throat.

'Maybe there has been enough killing, Sandra.'

'Sandra's dead,' I hiss in her ear. 'Do you hear me? She's dead. I killed her.'

I look across my old room, seeing the two of us reflected in the mirror on the far wall. 'Interesting pose, don't you think?'

'What?' she asks.

'The shadow on the wall of the two of us entwined, but I'm the larger shadow, more powerful.'

'What shall I call you?' she asks.

I laugh at her. 'Why? Are you looking to be my friend?'

'I'm Kate.'

'Lovely name,' I say. 'There once was a man called Frederick. He had a wife called Kate! He said, "I'm going to work in the fields. When I come back, I shall be hungry…"'

'Grimms' fairy tales?' she replies.

'Very good – that buys you a few more seconds.'

'You never said what I should call you.'

'Cassie.'

'Your work is extraordinary, Cassie.'

'Complimenting the lunatic, are you?'

'I'm speaking the truth.'

'Ah, yes, Kate, the precious truth.' I rub the knife up her neck, causing more blood to trickle down. 'One false move, and you'll be a dead Kate. That has a nice ring to it, don't you think?'

I can see torchlights outside. 'We'll need to go down below,' I say. 'No funny stuff until I work out what to do with you.'

When she turns, and I see her face, I say, 'You're that shrink?'

'Yes, that's me.' She's nervous.

'Good, you're not stupid, then. Now, do exactly as I tell you, or I'll ruin your pretty face.'

'Where are we going?'

'We're taking a trip to the basement. It will require crawling.'

She does as I say, but I keep close to her. She has made things complicated, but I've been tested before. 'Keep making your way out onto the landing and down the stairs,' I tell her. 'I'm right behind you.'

'Okay,' she answers, barely above the sound of a mouse.

'I've only ever killed one woman,' I say. 'She was a witch – a nosy, prying, sadistic bitch – but I can make an exception for you.'

ELLIOT FOREST, COUNTY WICKLOW

WITH EACH OF the search teams coming up empty, Adam couldn't help but think that Mark Lynch had gone about this the wrong way. The empty house had turned their attention outwards, to the surrounding terrain, but what if Kate was right, and Sandra Regan had needed to stay close to home, the very place she had suffered most? Nor was he happy leaving Kate there, armed guards or not.

'Listen,' he said, turning to Barry Lyons, 'I think we should head back to the house.'

'That's up to you.'

They soon reached the rusted gate at the end of the pathway. Adam saw the team with Alice Thompson coming towards them, ready to search the far side of the woods. He flashed his torch in their direction, signalling for them to come over. 'Alice,' he said, his voice low, when she was within hearing distance, 'I'm going up to the house. I want you to come with me.' Then, to Barry Lyons, 'You stay here with Fitzsimons. I'll be taking the other two detectives with me.'

He had a bad feeling, even though he couldn't pinpoint exactly why. Approaching the house, he looked around for Kate, and the bad feeling got worse: he could see no sign of her.

'Where's Dr Pearson?' he asked the detective stationed by Regan's car.

'She's still inside.'

'What? She's been there nearly an hour.'

The detective stared back at him blankly. 'We were told to stay out here.'

'I don't like this.' Adam knew he needed to think fast. Kate wouldn't have stayed in there that long, not unless something was wrong.

Addressing the same detective, he said, 'Get the other two guys. There's no bloody signal here with the woods. We'll have to recheck the house without back-up.'

'But Lynch said—'

'Fuck Lynch – I'm calling the shots now.'

'What are you going to do?' Alice asked, so matter-of-factly that she spooked him.

'We need to work out what's going on inside.'

'You won't see them if they're in the cellar.' Again, she delivered it deadpan.

'What cellar?'

'Under the house. They stopped putting coal in it years ago. Sandra and I used to hide in it.'

He wanted to ask, why the fuck didn't you say so before? But he knew if anyone was going to suffer his wrath, it would have to be Lynch for missing the bloody cellar in the first place.

'Okay, listen to me, Alice. If they're in the cellar, I'm assuming there's only one way in.'

'Yes. Through the kitchen. There's a flap under the table.'

'I'll need you to come with me. She is closer to you than anyone else. It's a risk, but it might be the only way of getting your friend, and mine, out of there alive. Are you okay with that?'

'I'm okay.'

KATE

RIGOR MORTIS HAD already set in on Edgar Regan's body. The only hope Kate had lay in the knowledge that, for whatever reason, Cassie hadn't killed her straight away. It was a split-second realisation, feeling the knife against her throat and knowing it could all end within moments. No goodbyes to Charlie, no time to reflect, no prospect of ever doing the most mundane or extraordinary things again.

As she crawled down the stairs, across the floor and into the dark cellar, she told herself that she was still alive. Cassie had said she'd only ever killed one woman, a witch. Kate had to assume she was talking about her grandmother, but no matter how cruel her grandmother had been to her, the likely abuse of her grandfather would have solidified her hate to the extreme. However Kate looked at it, if Sandra or Cassie wanted her dead, she would be. Somewhere in her moral compass, she wasn't going to kill without reason, and Kate had no intention of supplying one.

Although it hadn't taken Kate's eyes long to accustom to the dark, it was difficult to make out Cassie's expression. The more time passed, Kate also knew, the greater the risk of Cassie turning aggressive, especially with pressure from outside. She needed to distract her.

'Why did you kill Edgar?' she finally asked. It was a risk starting there, but she had to start somewhere.

Cassie didn't reply straight away, so Kate kept her eyes on her dark shape. Eventually, she said, 'He loved Sandra more than he loved me.'

'Love is important to you?'

'I'm not a monster.'

'I didn't say you were. You've suffered. I can see that.'

'You think you can work me out?' she sneered.

'I saw the pain in your paintings and sketches. None of this is your fault.'

'Too late.' She spat the words with venom.

'You know Sandra will come back. You can't kill her.'

'This time is different. This time she was pushed too far.'

'How can you be sure? She could come back at any moment.'

'Shut the fuck up.'

'If it wasn't for Sandra, you wouldn't exist. You owe her your life.'

'I owe her nothing,' she hissed, through gritted teeth. 'I took the fucking pain for the precious, pathetic coward. I lived the hellhole, not her.'

'You remember it all, don't you?'

'You learn to compartmentalise things.' She laughed hysterically. 'It's a good coping mechanism, but you know all about that, Doctor. You've dealt with this shit before.'

'I've never met anyone like you.'

'Lucky you.' Again she spat the words, but this time they were loaded with sarcasm.

'I'm lucky, yes.'

'Tell me, Kate, what was your mother like? Did she dress you prettily, put ribbons in your hair, tell you how great you were?'

'She didn't do any of that.'

'Really? I'm intrigued. Tell me about her, now we're getting along so well.'

'She was a bit like Sandra.'

'In what way?'

'She was frightened most of her life.'

'Of what?'

'Of never being good enough, thinking others were better than her, of settling for less than she should have.'

'And what about with you, Kate? Was she a good mother?'

'She did her best.'

'Was that good enough for you?'

'Not always, but things changed.'

'How?'

'I learned that sometimes people become who they are because of the cruelty of others.'

'I think about her all the time – my mother. You'd think she'd have come back for me, wouldn't you?'

'She couldn't.'

'You mean because she died?' The rage fired up again. 'The witch died, but she wouldn't leave me in peace, crawling in and out of my life.'

'The witch stays with you because you let her.'

Kate pulled back, seeing the shadow jump in the dark, as Cassie put the knife back to her throat. 'You want to be a dead woman?'

Both of them heard the overhead noises at the same time. 'Not a word from you, bitch, or you're dead.'

When the trapdoor opened, it was a female voice they heard, a voice Kate didn't recognise.

'Sandra, is that you? Are you down there?'

'Sandra isn't here right now.' Again the sarcasm. 'Stay away from here, Alice. I warn you, I'll kill this woman if you don't.'

'Is Edgar with you?'

'You don't need to worry about him – not any more.'

'I've been to the forest.' There was excitement in her voice. 'Even in the dark, I found our old rock. Do you remember how we used to set it up like an altar, with the cards, putting the red cloth on top? The place is still there. I thought I'd never find it, but the moon guided me.' She gave what Kate thought was a sob. 'If you let me, I can take you there. We can go there together. We can send all the evil spirits away. You'd like that, wouldn't you, Cassandra?'

'You know I would.'

Alice knew enough to switch from Sandra to Cassandra, Kate thought. If anyone was going to get them out of there alive, it would be her.

'You're tired, baby,' Alice pleaded. 'You know you are. I can hold you tight, like we used to when we were scared. My arms are still strong. I can wrap them around you. Please, Cassandra, can I come down?'

'You became so harsh, Alice.' The words were delivered with hurt.

If the stress levels reduce, thought Kate, Sandra may come back.

'I know I did, baby. But it was only pretence.' Another sob from Alice. 'It was a way of not being wounded.'

'I didn't hurt you.'

'You did. I saw you with him.'

'You saw us?' Another lowering and softening of her tone. 'You knew about your father and—'

'I know you didn't mean to hurt me. Listen, I'm coming down.'

'You can't. The cards didn't predict it.'

'They did. They said there would be a new beginning. You want a new beginning, don't you?'

'The room is getting darker, Alice. I don't understand … I'm scared. I don't know what's happening any more.'

'You don't have to be scared. I'm here.'

Kate couldn't believe what was happening, but she knew when to stay completely still. With the light shafting down from above, she felt the release of the grip around her neck before the knife dropped out of Cassie's hand.

Adam wasn't long in following Alice into the cellar, but it was Kate who reached over and picked up the knife.

'Is this our new beginning?' she heard Cassandra ask Alice.

'Yes, baby. Everything will be all right now.'

LEACH, COUNTY WICKLOW

BY THE TIME Kate and Adam reached the centre of Leach, the whole village, including Billy Meagher and Lily Bright, was assembled, all trying to come to terms with the two dozen squad cars with blue lights flashing that had invaded them during the night.

Kate stepped away from the crowd to phone Sophie, happy to hear that Charlie was sound asleep in bed, oblivious to it all. She didn't feel much like talking to anyone, not even Adam as he approached her. Instead of greeting him, she put her head down and turned away.

'What's wrong, Kate?'

'It's all such a bloody waste, how people get messed up. Did you hear them down there?' Her voice cracked.

'What – Alice and Sandra?'

'They sounded like two desperate little girls.'

'I heard them.'

'Why do we have to fuck with each other?'

'Look, Kate, you're in shock. It can't have been easy down there.'

'She wasn't a monster.'

'I know she wasn't. Alice said something to me earlier about the two of them.'

'What did she say?' She lifted her head and turned to look at him.

'When she thinks back to them being in the woods, what she hears is the sound of laughter, the kind only children can make.'

'I guess they found some happiness in the madness,' she wiped the tears from her eyes, 'but there is no "happy ever after" ending for Cassie or Sandra. Fairy tales are stories we tell our children. Real life isn't always like that. The longer I do this job, the more I realise the potential for evil exists inside us all. Sometimes it wins. Mess a person up from the beginning, and there is no going back, no easy fix. The legacy debt has taken its toll. It has made her who she is no matter which mask she wears, and the harrowing part is, Adam, she knows that more than any of us. There is no get-out clause, not for her.'

'This has really gotten to you, Kate. I've never seen you this upset.'

'Don't worry about me.'

'The thing is, Kate, I do.'

She didn't answer him.

'What's the prognosis for Sandra now?' he asked, sensing she wanted to change the subject.

'A life filled with one kind of therapy or another. Her other identity will come back and forth intermittently as the stress levels change. She might fool some people along the way, including the odd therapist, but there's no going back for her. The wrongs can never be undone. It's like you and your son, Adam. You can never get those memories back, the ones that for whatever reason never had a chance to be created, any more than Sandra can live a different life.'

'That's a bit harsh.'

'Life is harsh.' She drew in a deep breath. 'Look, I'm not picking on you. God knows, I've made any number of mistakes myself.'

They took a step back as the squad car with Sandra Regan and Alice Thompson inside it sped past and away from the village, Kate staring long and hard after it.

'Adam, do you know what I see when I look at them, particularly Sandra?'

'What?'

'I don't see the darkness, or her multiples of self, I see a baby born with an innate instinct to survive, and the potential for so many wonderful things taken from her.'

'Which is why, Kate, we have to grab whatever good we can out of this messy, bloody life.'

'Maybe you're right. Certainly, Charlie is a huge part of mine, and back there, when that knife was at my throat, the thought of never seeing him again filled me with utter fear, for me and for him.' She looked away. 'I've avoided some hard truths for far too long.'

'Are you talking about that old memory from when you were a kid?'

'It is part of it. So many unanswered questions.' She let out a sarcastic laugh before turning to look at him. 'I'm no different to everybody else. Old habits take a long time to change. Pushing things to the side from a young age, it sets you on a path of avoiding the difficult bits of life.'

'People can change, maybe not Sandra, but you can. Some things are worth going for – risks and all.'

'Is that what you feel about your son?'

'In a way, but it's also what I feel about you.'

'I'm still nervous after Declan. It's like I don't trust my judgement any more.'

He stepped closer, turning his body sideways to block out the array of squad cars and onlookers, placing his hand around her waist, 'I asked you in Paris to take a leap of faith. I should have ignored those bloody newspaper headlines.'

'No, you did the right thing. We both did. The time wasn't right.'

'Maybe so, but I'm not letting you slip away from me a second time. Like it or not, Kate, I care for you, and nothing you can say will change that.'

Mark Lynch walked towards them, shouting, 'Kate, I'm heading back now.'

'That's okay, Mark.' Adam waved. 'Kate is coming with me.'

Together, they walked to his car. He held the passenger door open for her. 'Are you ready, Kate?'

'As ready as I'll ever be.'

ACKNOWLEDGEMENTS

A SPARK FOR a story can come from anywhere. For *The Doll's House*, it was a casual conversation about hypnosis, for *Red Ribbons*, being a parent, and the fear of the bad man in society. Ideas get fused within our life experiences and the impetus for a good story is an idea that doesn't want to go away until you get around to writing it. I think *Last Kiss* is such a story.

On a cold January morning in 1984, Ann Lovett, aged fifteen, having started labour, took a detour to a local graveyard instead of returning to school. She laboured alone for hours in the rain. Ann and her baby died that day. *Last Kiss* is not the story of Ann Lovett, or of her son. Nonetheless, the story stayed with me. The question arose in my mind: What would happen if a baby survived the death of their mother and, in the context of this fictional story, was reared by someone evil? In writing *Last Kiss*, the theme of nature versus nurture, good versus evil, fascinated me. I hope you agree it was a story worth telling.

I owe a huge debt to everyone directly involved with the creation of this novel, starting with my agent, Ger Nichol, of The Book Bureau, the team at Hachette Books Ireland, especially Ciara Doorley, Editorial Director, and Hazel Orme, copy editor. My research has been a fascinating journey, and I have a lot of people to thank: Dave Grogan, for his wonderful psychological insights, Joanne Richardson, ex-coroner from Colorado, for her advice on tache noir, members of An Garda Síochána, who shared their knowledge, but especially Detective Tom Doyle. Also, the immensely talented painter, Angela Hackett, whom I had the pleasure to meet at the Tyrone Guthrie Centre, the brilliant photographic artist, Matthew Gammon of Yew Tree Studio, and finally, the ever-supportive and cracking journalist and crime writer, Niamh O'Connor.

Finally, I want to thank my husband, Robert, my children, Jennifer, Lorraine and Graham, and my granddaughter and grandson, Caitríona and Carrig, to whom this book is dedicated.

I would also like to thank you, my friends, family, colleagues, and readers, and anyone who has helped me directly or indirectly along the way who is not mentioned individually here. I feel privileged to have been gifted with so many wonderful people in my life, and I hope you enjoy this story.

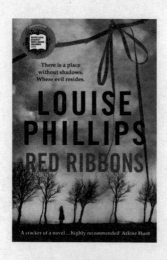

RED RIBBONS
There is a place without shadows. Where evil resides …

A missing schoolgirl is found buried in the Dublin mountains, hands clasped together in prayer, two red ribbons in her hair. Twenty-four hours later, a second schoolgirl is found in a shallow grave – her body identically arranged. The hunt for the killer is on. The police call in profiler Dr Kate Pearson to get inside the mind of the murderer before he strikes again. But there's one vital connection to be made – Ellie Brady, a mother institutionalised fifteen years earlier for the murder of her daughter Amy. What connects the death of Amy Brady to the murdered schoolgirls? As Kate Pearson begins to unravel the truth, danger is closer than she knows …

Shortlisted for the Ireland AM Crime Fiction
Book of the Year Award (BGE Irish Book Awards 2012)

Also available as an ebook

The past is waiting . . .

'A gripping, suspenseful story'
Irish Independent

LOUISE
PHILLIPS
THE DOLL'S HOUSE

THE DOLL'S HOUSE

Winner of the Ireland AM Crime Fiction
Book of the Year Award (BGE Irish Book Awards 2013)

The past is waiting . . .

Thirty-five years ago Adrian Hamilton drowned. At the time his death was deemed a tragic accident but the exact circumstances remain a mystery.

His daughter Clodagh now visits a hypnotherapist in an attempt to come to terms with her past, and her father's death. As disturbing childhood memories are unleashed, memories of another tragedy begin to come to light.

Meanwhile criminal psychologist Dr Kate Pearson is called to assist in a murder investigation after a body is found in a Dublin canal. And when Kate digs beneath the surface of the killing, she discovers a sinister connection to the Hamilton family.

Time is running out for Clodagh and Kate.

And the killer has already chosen his next victim . . .

Also available as an ebook

READING is so much more than the act of moving from page to page. It's the exploration of new worlds; the pursuit of adventure; the forging of friendships; the breaking of hearts; and the chance to begin to live through a new story each time the first sentence is devoured.

We at Hachette Ireland are very passionate about what we read, and what we publish. And we'd love to hear what you think about our books.

If you'd like to let us know, or to find out more about us and our titles, please visit www.hachette.ie or our Facebook page www.facebook.com/hachetteireland, or follow us on Twitter @HachetteIre.